The Gospel Truth

By

Helen Stubbs

PROLOGUE

The fact that we only hurt one person turned out to be a blessing in disguise. We hadn't intended to harm anyone and had planned to blow up the market under the cover of darkness without endangering lives. We were angry young men, furious that as immigrants we were always treated differently, only allowed to live in the poorest areas of the city, often with cousins, grandmas, nephews, and nieces, sometimes up to a dozen living in small terraces houses. We were always passed over for jobs and promotions. It was my cousin Nish who decided that we should make our mark and show that we too belonged in this new country.

Our forefathers were an enslaved minority who were subject to many harsh decrees. This is how we felt we were being treated in today's world.

We believed that our ancestors would have wanted us to take action, and this was the reason why we should rebel.

Nish told me earlier that evening that the market would be empty at night. Except it wasn't as one old lady who had worked the market for years was for some unknown reason been at the back of her stall. It seemed to me that it was her purpose in life, to save me, and to her, I am eternally grateful.

She once told me that there are three sides to every story; your truth, their truth, and the actual truth. There is the other truth though, the gospel truth. The truth is I miss Nish.

TABLE OF CONTENTS

PART 1 PRESENT DAY

EXTRACT FROM DIARY – AUTHOR UNKNOWN – 23RD DECEMBER 2024

I didn't know that through all of this, I would be involved. I certainly didn't sign up for it, not in the first place anyway. North London is supposed quiet, isn't it? Originally thought it was an enclave for ex-Labour MPs and retired MEPs. Also, according to my sister and her husband it, is where the chatty class live in nearby Islington, and she should know because she and her husband live there just around the corner from Sainsbury and close enough to Angel Tube. She religiously reads the Daily Mail which I once quipped was the Fascist Times. Rather Ironic on my part if you think about it.

If I knew what was going to happen, how it would turn out would I have been drawn in? Probably?

CHAPTER 1

THE HOUSE ON THE CRESCENT

If you were to wander off the Caledonian Road and walk a stone's throw away from Kings Cross, and Station tucked behind the Fried Chicken shops and other gourmet takeaways that seem to have invaded the High Streets of England's towns, and if you could ignore the lure of the outlets that promise passers-by cheap mobile sim-cards then you would perhaps quite by chance find yourself in a picturesque semi-circular street that looks like it is straight out of the Victorian era. A place called Keystone Crescent.

Its inner and outer circles, with a formidable curve, consist of twenty-four houses, and they were constructed to house early Victorian workers. It has been named England's smallest Crescent and has the smallest radius of any crescent in Europe.

In the mid-1840s Robert James Stuckey who was the son of a Shoreditch bricklayer built what was then named Caledonia (later Caledonian) Crescent. The old name is still visible on a sign at the north end of the street. It took its name as did Caledonian Road and Caledonia Street from the nearby Caledonian Asylum for Scottish children. Maybe there had always been bad Karma in the surrounding district. In 1917 the enclave was renamed from Caledonian to Keystone Crescent.

The houses of the outer circle are comprised of four floors including a basement. Originally there were two rooms on each floor and a common toilet and washhouse in the backyard. Those on the inner circle are comprised of three floors, and because of the tight radius of the crescent have slightly more cramped rooms and a smaller back garden.

On the hottest day of the year so far, a Saturday in May, an unremarkable man would soon be arriving there. No one would recall seeing him even though he limped badly walking with the long support cane in one gnarled hand, along with a battered old suitcase in the other. He had no real reason for being there, but by a most unusual coincidence, he had rather surprisingly received a telephone phone call earlier that day that might change his life and would almost certainly give him a chance of redemption for his sins.

If you could have plucked out of the air the very essence of a ghost, then this man was the epitome of a Cadaver. He appeared to be surrounded by a grey cloud, a mere whisp of a man; one who had recently returned from abroad but without the addition of a tan. Even by his own standards, it had not been a long journey. In a different lifetime, he had travelled much further. On this occasion though his train from somewhere in Europe terminated at St Pancras International Station. On arrival he found that he had a short time to pass before his meeting, so coffee seemed to be the order of the day just to keep him occupied for a while.

After securing a beverage he found a dirty, cluttered, round metal table with pools of cold liquid on it. Perching on a metal chair head bowed he placed the worn, battered suitcase down between his feet. He did not want the warm comforting feeling of its security taken away from him. His long walking stick was placed firmly between his feet and the table leg forming a barrier of sorts.

Ten minutes later he pulled out a pocket watch, examined it, drained the rest of his coffee and muttered a swift prayer. Painfully and slowly, he headed for the main exit only to be greeted by a cacophony of traffic noise that London like many other cities makes. For a moment he was bewildered and unsure of the direction he should take. Feet rooted to the spot he tried to recall the directions that he had been given, and eventually hurried off towards Keystone Crescent as fast as possible considering that he had a gammy leg. Past the flower seller by the church, stumbling occasionally through a feeble attempt at the speed he appeared to anyone passing him by an emancipated figure dressed despite the heat and hour of the day in a long, tatty opera cloak with a blood-red motheaten silk lining. His eyes darted rapidly and nervously around searching frantically before it was too late for him to stop anything, before a change of mind he blundered on passing the Drapers Arms where a constant stream of noise discharged from the many people gathered there in the late spring warmth.

Retreating into himself like a snail returns to its shell as a natural safeguard against strangers, and never making eye contact with the merry band of drinkers spilling out onto the pavement he pressed on hoping there was no CCTV outside the public house that he passed. Had there been it would have shown a gaunt figure pulling and tugging an opera cloak being wrapped around a wraith like a security blanket.

Having finally dodged the catcalls of the near-do-wells and skirted past the youngsters gathering in small groups a little out of general view to smoke their dope, he turned into Keystone Crescent. Barely noticing his surroundings, he was unaware that dwellings in a crescent-like this rarely sold for less than seven figures. Had he the time he would have wondered how the person he was visiting could have afforded such an expensive residence.

For the most, the houses surrounding him were well kept, the preserve of the yuppie type who had probably bought them for a song during the last property crash and were spending their many non-sleeping hours at work just riding the wave until the next big property boom and then cashing in and moving on.

Arriving at number twenty he painfully started to navigate the five uneven stone steps before him by grasping onto the iron railings with one hand whilst tucking his suitcase under his arm and using his stick to aid his ascent noting that the front garden was paved and barren, where nothing grew, and no birds ever came to sing their sweet melodious song. It was almost as if they instinctively knew that something here was wrong. Something very wrong indeed.

The original house was once converted into two two-bedroom freehold flats in the nineties but now had been resorted back to being a rather shabby, dilapidated-looking establishment with peeling paintwork on the front door. No longer a wonderful Victorian iron or brass doorknocker graced but a rather tawdry unitarian metal letterbox was the only means of knocking to gain entry. Unexpectedly though the door was already slightly ajar.

Gingerly pushing it open with two fingers of a claw-like, disfigured blue and purple-veined hand the man slid through the small gap that he had created with an air of caution. Now breathing heavily, and utterly out of breath from his previous ministrations on the steps he tiptoed into a dark claustrophobic hall. There was a distinct smell of mildew, and just at the very edge of his sense something else that he could not quite place, an elusive, distant memory that he knew, but from where and what was it?

Inside he shivered and pulled his cloak even tighter as though it would protect him from evil. He did not like this place one iota. What with the mildew and the elusive smell he wondered what he was letting himself in for. Maybe this was not for him at all. He thought back to what things were like then, things that made him do atrocious things himself, how he wanted payback, how he wanted to seek redemption. He wondered if the therapist was any good. Was he the man that he said he was? Could he look him in the eye and put an end to it all?

He was sure that the damned elusive smell was going progressively stronger. It was almost as though someone had opened a door. Looking around he saw that the doors leading off were all firmly shut.

CHAPTER 2

THE CHOICES WE MAKE

In front of him were four doors, and in the middle of the hall a twisting, rickety, wrought iron spiral staircase. Having to choose one of the doors would surely seal his fate. This time the power to select one was his, so he pushed open the nearest one as it was the brightest and painted in pillar-box red. Inside was a minuscule, cramped kitchen overflowing with dirty crockery on every available surface and rubbish spilling out of the waste bin. The cupboards and units were mismatched and hung unceremoniously in odd angles whose juxtaposition jangled his nerves. Again, that elusive smell seemed to permutate through its very walls.

The next door led to an uninspiring dining room, with four MFD chairs and a scarred table. The moth-eaten curtains were drawn, possibly to keep the heat out. A small portable T.V. sat on a shelf in the corner. Again, signs of neglect abounded, with browning peeling wallpaper, and layers of dust everywhere. The oddest thing that he spotted was a small alcove holding a stuffed Crow, a silver goblet, and an empty plinth with a single spotlight shining down on it. Fumbling, he reached for the light switch but to no avail, the room remained dark apart from the single piercing spotlight. Wondering what on earth could be missing from the alcove, he flipped the light switch off and closed the door as quietly as he could.

The third door, immediately to the left of the kitchen was inexplicably locked, and no amount of tugging would open it. The memory of the smell was painfully so much stronger here. Shrugging, he reminded himself that was not here to play detective just yet. So that just left the fourth door. Taking a deep breath and holding it as though he were an underwater swimmer, he nudged it cautiously.

The first thing that he noticed was that the whole room was rammed from floor to ceiling with books. Secondly, the air in there was stale. Slowly he began to tiptoe around the room as quietly as possible without bumping into any furniture. He must remember the rules, the golden one being Do Not Make a Sound. The books he thought deserved a closer inspection. As a child, he had so few possessions, but books were his first love. Bizarrely these were sorted in subject matter order which was incredible given the chaos in the other rooms.

The first section was on criminology. Working his way around he found that the house dweller had an eclectic taste including a complete first edition of the Encyclopaedia Britannica from 1768. Then there were whole sections on Karl Marx, America in the nineteen thirties and several on the human Psyche.

Eventually after taking what he thought was everything in he spied even more books in a corner. Their subject was Psychology, including those by Freud who was a non-practising Jew born in the Czech Republic, but who studied Medicine in Vienna. Some books were on Hypnosis Techniques. Suddenly he spotted side by side two books that made him instantly recoil. One on the Holocaust, and one on the NZP (Dutch Pro-Nazi Police Force during WW2). Having an inbred hatred of the books and confined spaces he quickly scanned the room to see if there were any windows to be opened as there was not a breath of fresh air inside. Not even a gentle breeze that in his old age had come to appreciate. After today how many more breezes would fan gently across his face?

He was feeling so tired and weary, nervous too due to his inane fear of rooms like the one he was in. He liked open spaces that were like his own place in Chelsea. He thought longingly of his artwork collection at home which consisted of many pictures of flowers, and abstract butterflies. He wished he were back there but knew he could not leave. The very room he stood in brought to mind a painting that he was once offered the chance to buy; a dark, yet beautiful painting of Christ on the cross, with Mary Magdalene weeping at his side by

Gebhardt Fugel a renowned German Artist. It wasn't the brushwork, nor was it the million or so Euro price tag which made him turn it down; It was to him the darkness of its soul with a gargantuan cloud hanging over everything like a dark shadow which had evoked too many bad memories.

Suddenly feeling weak and giddy. His legs starting to buckle. He examined with distaste the two available fading tatty armchairs which once had pink swirling patterns and tassels. Putting his suitcase and stick down on the threadbare carpet He chose the one nearest to the door out of habit and watched detachedly as motes of dust arose from the chair's cushions when he gingerly sat down on the edge of it. Of course, the dust motes had by then mixed with the detritus from his cloak that he inherited and had not been worn for many years.

He closed his eyes and started to gather his thoughts when its train was rudely interrupted by a loud thumping noise on a small, overfilled table which he had failed to notice before in the gloom. His eyes flew open, and he found himself staring into the peculiar blue ones of a fair-haired man. These eyes gave him a feeling that there was nothing behind them, and he wondered if there was going to be empathy to be had that day. Gripping the arms of the chair he almost fainted such was the other man's likeness to someone he once knew and hated. He had felt shaken to the core and felt sick to the stomach.

'My apologies to you,' the fair-haired had begun abruptly almost as though he hadn't meant it. 'Nina my secretary should have been here to let you in, but it appears that she has taken the day off with a migraine again'.

The old man was confused, surely the younger man must have come from the locked room. He hadn't come from upstairs, or he would indisputably have heard the stairs creak. He had walked in with an unsteady gait. An artificial leg perhaps, but if so, why so much silence upon his arrival?

Sitting on the far side of the table, and apparently having the advantage the younger man began a speech.

'Firstly', he began, 'everything you tell me today will be kept strictly confidential between the two of us, but I expect this to be a two-way street, and any exercise that I give to you must be carried out. Furthermore, no one must know about what we say or do, even what I may ask you to do at home. Do not discuss with anyone as every encounter, every person I speak with is different from anyone else. I hope you understand this and then hopefully I will be able to help you.

The old man nodded vigorously at this and grunted his consent then he held his breath in as much as his lungs would allow him to in anticipation of what might happen next.

'Tell me firstly me firstly why you are here?', asked the fair-haired man a little too eagerly.

The old man's head dropped to his chest. Sighing deeply, he screwed up his eyes as if to remember.

'Where do I begin' 'How do I start', he enquired. His facial muscles tightened up so that his countenance became more wizened, shrunken, and of grey pallor as though he had not seen sunlight for many decades. The only remarkable feature about him was his nose, which was large and shaped like a grip hook sprouting a few grey hairs coming out of its nostril.

'Why not the beginning', said the slightly younger man gently.

'It is too painful', whispered the first. 'After all, it was nineteen-forty-two, and I was only six years old therefore perhaps I choose to forget'.

'Maybe you are too old to remember then', intoned the fair-haired man, 'but after all I am your therapist, and you can tell me about anything in the strictest confidence' he continued. 'Think of me as you would a priest, unburden yourself. If you want to, tell me as if it were a story, that is what my old English teacher used to say.

The man sitting opposite him grimaced slightly. He desperately wanted to ask the therapist where he learned English as it obviously was not his native language and it was too precise, too exact. For now, he kept his own counsel. It was in his nature to give nothing away. He rubbed his rheumy

'I am not so old, or too forgetful, it is just that some things are best left in the past. That is all I am saying for now suffice to say it was horrible, so very horrible and a nightmarish experience.'

Had he been a practising Catholic the therapist would have crossed himself. Instead, he considered what he should say next so leaning forward he patted the old man on his knee. Jerking back sharply as though he hated to be touched the old man opened his mouth and began to speak in hushed tones. Like a chess match, the words passed between them. Thus began the slow verbal dance between the two men. Both spoke in careful, precise English, sizing each other up, not breaking eye contact. Neither of them wanted to give too much away, each treading carefully through a minefield of words trying to not set off an explosion. The first wanted to unburden himself, but could he trust the man sitting across from him who sat ramrod straight listening intently and obviously eager to learn of the other's past?

The elderly one mumbled a few words to himself.

'You need to know it was the other boys, it wasn't me, although they were in the same place by chance or coincidence, I do not know. They were all older, much older than me, and they would beat me up all the time.

'What were their names?' asked the therapist. 'Sometimes it is useful to speak out loudly the names of those who have wronged us and that way we are beginning to be confronting our demons'.

The older man shrank further back into his chair and curled himself up like a foetus, although, unlike an un-born who does not know fear yet, his fists were clenched tightly.

'I am not going to say', he stammered. 'I cannot bring myself speak their names now'.

Leaning forward the therapist tried hard to hear more clearly what the old man sitting in front of him was now mumbling incoherently. He strained to catch what was being said and managed to catch the words Mutter, Torah, and the Hebrew word for the number five. The therapist now began to realise that there might be a storm brewing that he wanted no part of and yet wanted to listen to with a kind of morbid fascination.

He already knew that the Torah was a compilation of the first five books of the Hebrew Bible. It is also a synonym for the whole twenty-four chapters or the totality of Jewish teaching. He desperately wanted to un-hear what was being said, but at the same time was enraptured. Who knows what rabbit hole it may lead him down? In the room, there was silence apart from an old wall clock ticking away marking the passing minutes and seconds loudly like a metronome in between words.

Silently the therapist just sat there with his fingers interlaced. He desperately wanted to know what knowledge the old man had of the Torah which he himself had already heard about from generations long gone. This could be what he had been searching for. His reason d'etre. He hesitated for a while not wanting to spook the old man. He knew that he had to tread carefully and drew himself even further upright in his armchair.

The old man who came to seek solace, redemption, even forgiveness was now sitting up straight too so that they both looked like two different sides of a coin with eyes locked on each other. One of them was fair of hair with blue eyes, the other brown-eyed but with little hair and with a look of almost anticipation.

The therapist thought to himself that the old man should get on with it but wanted to disguise the fact that his curiosity had been piqued. He knew how to interrogate just by silence alone. One strange thing he noticed was to catch the old man surreptitiously glancing at a watch on his skinny wrist. This seemed rather an odd gesture seeing as the large clock on the wall.

Finally, the Therapist inquired, 'Waiting for something? You seem to be very interested in your watch. Good make isn't. Swiss I believe?', he asked with a tiny hint of curiosity.

Without waiting for a response, he ploughed on perhaps risking losing the other's interest which is something he most definitely could not have afforded to happen.

'You can take as long as you want to, or I can see you later' he rushed on. 'Tomorrow perhaps?', he added trying not to sound too eager.

'Im yittzeh hashem ', (God willing) was the response.

Odd reply thought the therapist. This man was proving more difficult than he first thought. He was led to believe that he had no understanding of Hebrew and given his background where could he have possibly learnt an intimate knowledge of the Torah plus advanced Hebrew phrases that had been spoken a little too easily? Maybe he had the wrong idea about the man, maybe just maybe it was the wrong one who was sitting opposite him. Sighing he wished he could have had a cigarette, but he had imposed a no-smoking ban in his treatment room, as it distracted people from opening to him. Now was crunch time, and one way or another he was determined to get something out of this session, or he was not the Interrogator that he thought he was. His grandfather would not have been proud of him.

CHAPTER 3

HELL ON EARTH

The therapist was extremely annoyed by now and rapidly losing his patience with the old man. This session was not going the way he wanted it to. Deciding that he would change tack and trying to make things a little easier, to put the old man's mind at rest, and to get him to focus he asked coaxingly, 'It seems that have reached an impasse. You have skated over the subjects of the following things, the Torah, your mother, and the other boys. Perhaps you would like to tell me a little more about your mother? Was she fair or dark-haired, short or tall, brown eyes or blue? Do you remember her at all?' Falling silent now he held his breath in anticipation. To get a response at this stage would be the pinnacle of his career.

A fly unaware of the tension in the room buzzed lazily around looking for somewhere to land or possibly to seek a way out. It kept on darting around aimlessly with no intended direction. Maybe it had picked up the mood and it needed to escape from the room's confines. Frustrated by its monotonous droning, and with alarming accuracy for one who was apparently so old and frail, with a force that belied his age the old man reached out and swiftly swatted it with his hand. The fly, dizzy and disoriented attempted to crawl off the arm of the armchair where it had fallen. With another swipe, it dropped to the floor. For good measure, the old man stamped on it.

Watching with horror at the old man's treatment with the fly the therapist was astounded at the speed at which the poor fly was killed. Considering a fly has a good, but a near 360-degree visual range he was actually very impressed by the accuracy of its demise and had not heard about anything like that for a very long time. This was the clue that he was looking for. He had in his presence the very man that he needed.

'Wow that was quick, but may I ask you two things? Number one why kill it, and number two where did you learn to kill something so small so accurately?' Asked the therapist who was more than a little alarmed at the speed and accuracy of the old man. He had already started to recalibrate things in his mind and planned his next move like a Grand Master of Chess.

'The answer my friend to the why is because it was beginning to annoy me with its persistent buzzing, secondly where I lived as a young boy I had plenty of time to practice the art, and in answer to your earlier questions about my mother I don't want to remember her, and I hope she rots in hell!'.

'Why Hell?' asked the fair-haired man. 'What did she ever do to you to make you say that? Did she abandon you?'

'Let me ask you something,' replied the old man with a blunt tone to his voice, 'have you ever been to Hades and back, because I have several times. I have seen as far as perdition and beyond. I have seen things that no one should ever see.' Gathering momentum in his speech, finally unleashing his feelings, spitting the next words out with un-disguised venom the old man shouted, 'Yes, she did abandon me. At first, I thought it was my fault, but then I realised it was beyond my control. Worse was to befall me because whilst I was in hell, whilst I was being beaten up, tortured, and raped by the boys, and when I thought I could fall no further, I learnt from these same boys that my dear mother was a slut, a prostitute, a whore, and she did it for her own gratification. She had physically and mentally abandoned me.'

The therapist looked visually shocked by this outburst and wondered who exactly the person was who sat opposite him. He could see that the actions of the mother had had a profound effect on his patient and that the session was not taking the direction that it should have. The French connection who had originally set it up had obviously not envisaged that this would happen, and they have their grasp on reality a little, becoming too big for their boots. They obviously sent the wrong person; this is not what he expected, he must have words with them later.

'Do you mind,' he began, 'I think we may use a different method. Remember what I told you earlier about any exercise that I may ask you to do? But firstly, why don't you take off your cloak? You must be extraordinarily hot in it.'

Instead of taking it off the old man wrapped the clock closer around himself as though it would offer some form of protection. He nodded hesitantly then looked at his watch for one last time. Why on earth would he do that? Was he expecting something to happen, or maybe he was anticipating something?

'If you would like to follow me downstairs,' suggested the therapist.

The old man had begun to wonder if this was part of the plan. Maybe the therapist had known all along who he was and then the tables would be turned. Killing the fly had not been one of his better ideas, nor was the follow-up comment that he made. He was so wound up at this stage that he would have admitted to anything, even murder.

He had not realised that the house held a subterranean room. He certainly did not recall a door when he was doing his initial search. Maybe it was a set of stairs leading down in the room whose door he could not open earlier? Slowly, hesitantly he reluctantly started to leaver himself up from the armchair. Ant a thing to buy a few seconds. It was not the perfect setting that he wanted. On the other hand, if they went below ground level, there was less chance of being heard.

He knew that somehow, he had to look the therapist in the eye, and wanted him to share one-millionth of the fear that he had felt.

'Before we go,' began the old man, 'let me tell you about May Nineteen- Eight-Five.

Suddenly and unexpectedly the whole house shook violently, and the old man's expression changed to one of relief. The therapist remained seated and outwardly calm, but his knuckles whitened as he grasped the arms of his chair. Not sure what to do he sat silently waiting in anticipation of what might happen next.

Islington Fire Station is located at Upper Street in Islington, and there is also one at Holloway it didn't take long for a cacophony of engine sirens to cut through the commonplace murmur of London traffic. Shortly following this there was a further mix of two-tone sirens signalling that the police and Ambulance Services were out in force with the distinct diploic noise of at least eight ambulances. A few minutes after that there was the loud rotor noise of the Police Helicopter blades.

The old man continued his early struggle out of the armchair. When had managed to do so with great difficulty and lots of creaking bones he knelt on the stained, worn carpet, bowed his head and began reciting the Slach Lanu', the everyday Jewish Prayer for forgiveness.

'My God', cried the therapist. 'What the hell has been done, you have released purgatory onto all of us.' He cast his eyes upwards praying to one deity or the other but did not notice until he lowered his eyes from the havens that he could feel cold metal against his temple. The old man held a gun to his head. The old man must have been play-acting when he knelt as now, he was upright and had drawn a weapon from underneath his cloak.

The therapist fleetingly wondered if he could knock the gun from the old man's hand. The old devil must have had it concealed in his tatty old opera cloak. He was preparing himself to act when there was a sudden sound from the room next door. He felt a sudden whoosh of air then a blow to his head, and a sigh from the old man who tumbled over. Felling dazed he glanced around. To his horror, he still had a gun pointing at his head only this time Nina his erstwhile secretary was aiming the barrel at his head.

A cold sweat broke out on his brow. What was the woman going to do? He had not pegged her as a woman who knew her way around firearms. Maybe he had been too quick to employ her, but he needed someone who was trustworthy, someone who could keep secrets, someone who would stay out of the locked room. She must have found the key and the stone steps leading downstairs that were secreted behind the bookcase. If she found her way to the underground room that would mean she had seen its contents. He was in even more danger now.

CHAPTER 4

PARIS – GARE DU NORDE 12 O'CLOCK LUNCHTIME (CET)

Cole Porter penned the illustrious lyrics 'I Love Paris in the Springtime'. These words resonated so much on a sunny, equable day in May when thousands had flocked to the city to walk hand in hand with their loved ones along the river Seine or to venture as far as they could up the Eiffel Tower just because. There are many reasons why people visit Paris. Some may like to take a cheeky peek at Les Pigalle's sex shops, although the area has been cleaned up since the city put itself forward for the 2012 Olympics. One might even take in a show at the famous Moulin Rouge.

Having had your fill of the famous sights of Paris and having taken the vernacular railway up from Montmartre and marvelled at one of the city's most unique and beautiful monuments, the Basilica of the Sacred Heart of Paris, or Sacré-Cœur, the jewel that towers 213 metres above sea level, you can honestly say that you have 'done' Paris.

One question remains though, how on earth do you get home? You could take a flight from Paris's main airport Charles De Gaulle a mere fifteen miles Northwest of the centre of Paris, maybe Orly the city's second airport which surprisingly is even closer being a mere eight miles from the heart of Paris. Until that was the advent of Eurostar in 1994. Servicing over 700,000 passengers every day (for a total of 190 million a year) Gare du Nord is the busiest railway station in Europe and the busiest in the world apart from the one at Shinjuku in Tokyo, Japan.

On this day you would find standing in an irregular line like racehorses under starter orders at the Grand National, impatiently waiting for the signal so that they could surge forward and be one of the first on the train, stood a line of nervous, anxious, and maybe a handful of indifferent humans of varying nationalities plus one or two dogs. Looking at the line it gives out the impression that they were impenitently stomping their hooves in anticipation of starters orders so they could run towards the late-running Eurostar Paris to London train.

You have your first-class travellers who wished that they had instead, asked their wives, chauffeurs, children or in-laws to whisk them off to Charles-De-Gaul to catch a plane or meet them in the UK instead of standing waiting with the general populace. Then there were the grannies and granddads with their offspring's children who were in Paris for the first time. Standing by themselves are the solo travellers like the lady with what seems like a hundred shopping bags from Gallery Lafayette or the woman in a bright red coat and dark hair neatly swept up in a chignon. Then you have a handful of unlikely-looking weary travellers who seem to appear that they don't want to be in Paris and that they would rather be somewhere else. Making a lot of noise were a few revellers from a party who were still in their evening clothes as they had been kicked out of their hotel and whose parents were rich enough to pay for last-minute changes to their first-class train tickets. This last group looked like the 'Made in Chelsea' type with names like Rupert or Clementine.

In the Gare du Nord when you queue to get on Eurostar it's not as fabulous or as posh as St Pancras International because once you have passed through security there is no going back. There is a coffee shop, and few duty-free shops, an expensive chocolate shop, a newsagent, and a food outlet then that's it. As you head down to the train – which good heavens was running at least seven minutes late, you have to walk over an open structure wooden bridge to get to the platform. For those who haven't travelled much, it is quite entertaining as you catch a glimpse of the train waiting on the platform below straining like an untamed beast on a leash.

Lingering in the coffee shop and immune to the excited mix of French and English outbursts of chatter repeated rapidly over the new super gold speaker-tanned address system a certain Professor John Houlihan sits with head hanging down gripping the small round metal table in front of him hoping against hope that he can make it to his seat on the very last coach of the Eurostar e300 which so his wife told him, though god knows why, has two power cars and eighteen coaches. On the next table, a stunning dark-haired woman in a very expensive red coat is seated by herself trying to ignore him and the obnoxious alcohol fumes which surround him like a dank London smog. He struggles to ask her in English, and then in French if she is joining the train, but she just shrugs her shoulders expansively in a very gallic sort of way and turns away to avoid his lecherous stare whilst sneaking a swift peek at her expensive wristwatch.

Gripping the edge of the table even harder now the professor decides that it's time to make a move. The race toward the train has already started. People surging forward conveniently forget that they have a seat reserved for them. It’s human nature like standing up when a plane has landed and waiting for the plane to be attached to a bridge before the seatbelt signs go off. Everyone does it, doesn’t they?

Having spent a week’s sabbatical purportedly at the Sorbonne which is so very different to the ancient Oxford University with its self-governing collages, where he holds a Professorship. He wishes that he were staying in France a little longer eating good food and drinking good wine. He hadn’t wanted to come at first, but under pressure from a colleague who was an expert on the French Napoleonic Empire, he decided with a gentle nudge from his domineering wife that it may give him the space and opportunity to do exactly what he needed to do.

Glancing around he no longer can see the dark-haired woman, so mentally shaking himself he heads down to the platform. Feeling like he is wading through a very sticky thick treacle he vaguely hears a French train guard telling him to hurry up. With a throbbing head he manages to heave himself and his rucksack onto the train. Climbing over numerous children and a mountain of suitcases, rucksacks and feet he successfully squeezes himself into his window seat next to a woman who must hold the world record for the greatest number of carrier bags. Mean spiritually he thinks that his super-rich stay-at-home wife could have paid for a first-class ticket for him as he is starting to regret the window seat sitting next to the Imelda Marcos of shopping bags. After all his wife has plenty of money thanks to her father. Finally, seven minutes late Eurostar pulls out of the station. Not everyone on board wanted it to reach London.

CHAPTER 5

THE INCIDENT

Afterwards when everything had been cleared away, when lives were saved, or when people died, when devastation was all around the Government referred to it as an 'Incident 'as if it was a minor thing to be shrugged off. It was thus called because although it was serious it came immediately on the heels of the one that occurred at a synagogue. The consensus was not to let the public's imagination run riot. If they did then conspiracy theories would become the normal thing. Heaven knows what the press would make of it. Questions would undoubtedly be raised in the House of Commons shout National Security, but the PM already clinging to his position would want it downplayed as much as possible. Of course, it was a tragedy the like that had not been seen since the 7th of July 2005. Of course, this one was just as horrific, and for the first time in his reign, the King sent out personal messages to the families of those involved. Yet it was still referred to as The Incident.

Reaching into his rucksack for a bottle of water and a paracetamol John tries to shield its illicit contents from prying eyes. Glancing swiftly around to see if anyone is watching him, he hastily swallows his sixth painkiller of the day and hopes to God that his headache will recede from little men running around with hammers in his skull to just a dull ache. Just as he is closing his wary bloodshot eyes hoping against hope that he can fall asleep for a couple of hours and forget about all the terrible things he has done and the consequences he's going to face when he gets back to England the woman with all the bags sitting next to him pulls out her mobile phone and starts jabbering away.

'Of course, I'm travelling first class you know', she says in a faux posh accent. 'Personally, I prefer Harrods, but George was insistent that I came to Paris for shopping. It's been a whirlwind of posh shops for the last couple of days, and I found the most darling little boutique hidden away where the owner only spoke French you know.' Oblivious to her surroundings and John's heartfelt sighs next to her she ploughed on barely pausing for breath telling her friend what a wonderful time she had had, and it was a pity that she couldn't bring George with her, but he was so awfully busy with something hush-hush at work.

Trying to tune out but admitting defeat he finally gives up, muttering an excuse he pushes his way past her to the buffet car. Leaning sluggishly on the already sticky counter he asked for his eighth coffee of the day. Wearily opening his eyes, they are immediately drawn to the woman standing just two people away from him wearing a bright red, expensive coat that is so out of place considering the balmy May weather. He recognises her from the Paris station café waiting room and tries to catch her eye but to no avail, so he resorts to studying her shoes instead. Having bought his rucksack along with him as he wouldn't leave it near the chatty woman who had a conspicuous amount of shopping bags, he wondered if the female with the red coat had any luggage at all. He can't remember seeing her with any at the terminal, but he was probably too hungover to notice.

Chancing his luck, he leans across the old man next to him with a polite French 'Pardon 'and tries to engage in conversation with the woman. Deciding that he's not going to give up on her, and as there are approximately two hours left of a two-hour sixteen-minute journey which is going to be utterly boring, the woman concedes defeat and smiles politely at him. John thinks that this may be his best chance to engage in conversation with her which could be potentially dangerous at this stage, especially with a beautiful woman. He turns on his most charming smile, grimacing slightly in the vain hope that he won't be sick. Trying to force his mouth open to speak he finds that his tongue is so thick and furry, and his throat so dry that he can't get any words out. Smiling she tilts her head and leans across towards him amused by his ineptitude to speak, holds one beautifully manicured hand out complete with a high-end One Hundred and seventy-one Thousand pounds worth of Patek Philippe Aquanaut Rose Gold Watch. Taking this as a sign he huskily asks her in English if she is travelling further than London. Shaking her hand, he attempts to bring her hand to his lips to kiss it she hastily snatches it back. Of course, he by now is sufficiently intrigued and feels like he is duty-bound to offer her further information about himself.

'John', he offers by way of introduction.

'Laura', she replies in a clipped accent that even as a Professor of Languages he finds difficult to characterize.

Stuck for words, and not wanting the embryonic conversation to falter he blurts out, 'I'm a professor of languages returning to Oxford University, and you are?'

Bored, she thinks to herself but doesn't say it.

'Influencer and YouTube guru if you have that in dusty old Oxford where no doubt you keep your rusty old Riley Car or should that be bicycle', she answers taking a dig at him. She has nothing in common at all with this dusty, drunk fuddy-duddy.

'Ok then', he just about manages to say whilst trying to keep at bay the rising nausea; 'you've got me on Influencer. I know what YouTube is many of my students surprisingly watch it although admittedly mainly of cats doing stunts, I haven't a clue about the influencer bit so for an old fogey please elucidate, before you do so you must know that my car is a nineteen-sixty-two two tome yellow and grey classic Ford Anglia, not a Riley that I own', omitting to the fact that his tight-arsed wife controlled all of the money and wouldn't by him a new car.

'Basically', she replied, 'I am a person who has built my reputation for my knowledge and expertise on a specific topic. Mine just happens to be a high-end fashion.

"Ah I see', he replies,' hence the very expensive watch I take it?' he answers. Again, the Gaelic shrug of her shoulders is worthy of any Frenchwoman, although she speaks impeccable English.

'So why Eurostar?', he asks.' Why not take a plane? ', he inquired.

'Simple', is her reply making him feel like such a dumb idiot for asking her. 'It's safer by Train, no? Plus, I hate all of that wasted time and energy at an airport when I'd rather be doing something else. If God wanted me to fly, he would have given me wings?'

He wonders if she's flirting with him, and decides that she is, but he can't flirt back as he is under strict orders. She still is an enigma to him, so he decides to press her further for more information.

'And where do you reside Ms influencer?', he queries trying hard not to appear too interested but hoping against hope that it's somewhere north of the M25. If she lives close to Oxford, and she can blag a hugely expensive watch, she may be good for a bit of crowdfunding, especially for his causes.

A small pause then, 'Oh here and there, but for now I must return to my seat in first class'.

Of course, you must, he thinks bowing slightly in her direction. Maybe he should chance his arm and follow her. Not flirting, of course, he needs to find out more about her though. Maybe he will swing by first class casually a little later, but for now, he reluctantly returns to his seat next to Double-B as he has nicknamed the woman who is occupying the seat next to him: Banshee and Bags.

Returning to her first-class seat and trying hard to ignore the lawyer-type man in the seat opposite to hers who is trying hard to catch her eye Laura sinks down into the luxury of her extra legroom spot. Diving into her oversized handbag she pulls out and opens a copy of the day's "La Monde" and starts reading. She has no desire to enter a conversation with Monsieur Lawyer. One semi-drunken man accosting her in the buffet car was quite enough. Knowing that she could have had beverage brought to her seat in 1st class, she had taken it upon herself to explore a little and get the lay of the land so to speak. She doesn't want her competitors to get the better of her. The lawyer type who is a KC glances rapidly away from her, eyes shifting to the speeding countryside outside, and sighing as though to prove his boredom and his lack of interest in her, although her high heels do give her a certain cachet.

He looks down at his own feet admiring his own closed lacing highly polished shoes made for him by Foster and Sons of Jermyn Street and gives a louder sigh-cum-snort this time along with a little harrumph sound like the noise that an impatient nag would make. He hoped against hope that she wasn't a former client that he had seen at his chambers. Delightful little filly though she is.

Having had an enormous lunch at 'Bistrot Instinct' and now suffering from heartburn the lawyer is keen to get back to his rooms for a little dalliance with his new Pupil. That aside he must catch up with his Clerk, as he has one or two other non-related work issues to catch up with too. Worryingly perhaps for the first time in his life, he wool gathers about what he is going to do when he gets home, the feeling worsening due to the whole bottle or was it two of 74 Chateauneuf Du Pap that he imbibed. Fishing out his latest model iPhone which is in a solid gold case embellished with his initials (a gift from another of one of his grateful pupils) he attempts with clumsy fingers to dial his chamber's telephone number.

The response is brief." Le numero qui vouz avez compose nest pas disponible." (The number you have dialled is unavailable.) He glares at the phone in disbelief, as if it is whoever recorded the standard message is personally responsible for him not being connected, slams down his phone on the table that separates him from Laura grumpily like a child who is denied a biscuit, and with a great show un-crosses his legs muttering under his breath something about damned frogs, after which he closes his eyes.

Underneath her lashes, Laura watches him wondering what the matter is with the damn idiot who Is acting like a spoilt brat. After all her phone worked perfectly well in the confines of the toilet a few minutes ago when she needed to make a private 'phone call away from prying eyes and ears. For a moment she thinks of telling him that her call was successful in connecting, but thinks then again why? It was a confidential call, and the layer type is obviously a sexist boor. She doesn't want the whole world to know of her personal habits. Especially not a lawyer. The lawyer type obviously wanted to get in touch with someone as a matter of urgency, and she briefly wondered who. As an influencer and blogger,

she likes to keep her eyes and ears open as you never know what you might learn. Take the elderly couple with the two grandkids who were creating havoc in the station coffee bar earlier. They could be incredibly useful in her line of work. Maybe she should swing past them in second class, but then again ugh she may bump into the awful Mr. Houlihan, and she most definitely doesn't want that.

In the First-Class carriage behind Laura's, the revellers from a party held on the Left bank last night are for the most gently snoring, sleeping off the booze and cocaine that they consumed yesterday. All that is except for one small mousey-looking girl who is desperately trying to get in touch with her elderly Grandmother to inform her that she will be a little late home. Luckily her on-off boyfriend Frank paid for her new First-Class ticket, or rather his father did. Sadly, she only has an older model flip phone as her grandma thought that a newer model was a waste of money so there is little chance of getting through to England.

She starts to snake her hand around into Frank's jacket pocket only to be met with a vice-like grip on her wrist, and a voice hissing at her to leave his damn jacket alone as there are things inside its pockets that are not for public viewing. Trying to wrangle her wrist free she lets out a sharp yelp as he nips at her arm just above the tattoo of their entwined initials.

'Don't say a word', he snarls at her through booze and smoke-soured breath. 'When we get home, you know where to deliver the goods like a good little girl'.

Biting her lip, and nodding she turns her head away to hide the tears. Looking at her own dishevelled reflection in the window she wonders how it came to this but then has a spark of an idea of how she can get out of it and free herself from Frank's influence if she only can do one thing. The problem is that one thing could potentially lead to another problem, but then again nothing ventured.

Lifting her head up she looks at his face and for a moment she is utterly terrified as he has never looked at her with such loathing and hatred before now, His eyes are steely, his mouth set in a grim line. It is about time she confessed all to Grandma who would surely help her second eldest grandchild.

In a Second-class carriage, quite near the back of the train the two children dubbed the terrible twins by other travellers are acting like a pair of overzealous puppies bickering and playfighting. They had never been to Paris before. Their elderly grandparents just shrug their shoulders. Let the little ones enjoy the freedom they imply. After all, they loved going through Eurotunnel on the outbound journey. On their return journey after a whistle-stop tour of the Eiffel Tower, Sacre Coeur, and the partially re-built Notre Dame it appeared that the twins were by now officially bored and getting on other people's nerves by whispering about the train breaking down in the middle of the tunnel or the possibility of it being blown up by terrorists.

Glenn their grandfather is surreptitiously listening to the England V Jamacia Cricket match which is being held at Lords. Not a million miles from where they are right now, he muses. With eyes closed, and earbuds rammed in he cannot hear his grandson Joe whispering that he can smell smoke. A gentle tugging on his favourite sports Jacket by Julia his granddaughter and twin to Joe brings him to his senses. He opens his eyes, but all around him is blackness. Quickly pulling out his earbuds, all he can hear is gut-wrenching screaming. This is wrong, so very wrong. The whole train has taken on the appearance of the seventh Circle of Hell Violence, with men and women pushing and kicking each other trying to escape. But where oh where is his wife, Claire? He was sure she was sitting next to him a moment ago. Maybe she had slipped off to the toilet whilst listening to the radio. He had to find her, but with all the mayhem around him could not see how, especially with two tearful frightened children clinging to him.

First things first he thinks to himself, get the children to safety then yourself. Looking around some brave souls have already started to form a chain of sorts, so all he can do is hope that the grandkids can be passed along to freedom.

CHAPTER 6

SYNSOPSYS OF POLICE INTERVIEW NOTES

On the morning after the Eurostar incident, no one dared to call it a bomb yet, items had already been collected from the remains of the ill-fated train by CSI (Crime Scene Investigators) and had been forwarded to Golders Green Police Station under the direct orders of the Deputy Commissioner of the Metropolitan Police as they might be pertinent to ongoing inquiries. The chain of evidence has not been broken and there are strict procedures that must be adhered to, but when word comes directly from the Home Secretary then everybody jumps to attention.

DI White one two Detective Inspectors at Golder Green Nick currently has two Sargent under his direct command, and one of them is on long-term sick leave. The first thing he did was to double-check personally that the exhibits had been logged in the way that he approved. He wanted no tampering with them now that they were under his care.

Before any interaction with any of the survivors DI White had tasked his sergeant to take notes as the process was not at this stage formal, but DI White did not want his boss to question him about what had been said at the interviews do he needed an aid memoir. DI White had sat in the CCTV control room watching as the interviewees waited in the police station's reception area before being called forward. He wanted to read their body language before he started chatting with them.

The interviews proceeded as follows:

IW – Good Morning sir, you don't mind if I call you John, do you he enquired knowing full well that the man's first name appeared as Sean on his passport and that he had dropped the Irish connotations of O' Houlihan for the everyday moniker of plain John Houlihan.

JH – No not at all, but can I ask why I have been summoned to Golders Green Police Station instead of one near to where I live in Oxford? It's a tad inconvenient as I was supposed to be lecturing today. I do hope that you are at least going to reimburse me for my train fare.

(SB glances at IW with raised eyebrows and a 'can you believe this Guy' look.)

IW – I'm afraid not sir or we would be held to account by the taxpayer. We would be doing it for all and sundry. Now if it was jury duty for instance, then naturally you would be reimbursed, but sadly it doesn't work that way so think of it as your contribution to helping the police and the Taxpayer.

JH Well if you put it like that ...

SB (Interjecting) - We needed to chat informally with all the able passengers who were travelling on Eurostar yesterday. This is happening at Police Stations across London as there were many survivors like yourself who we need a quick word with. I can assure you that you haven't been singled out. I do understand and sympathise with you regarding the traumatic experience that you went through yesterday. However, could you tell us what you remember from when you arrived at the train station, please?

JH – Well I was late turning up, but lucky for me the train was running late.

(SB knows from other witnesses that John was at the café in the Gare de Nord for a long time before the train departed drinking copious cups of coffee, smelling of alcohol, and behaving like a letch towards a woman in a red coat. However, SB let it slide for now)

IW – Why was it lucky for you John?

JH – I admit that I was hungover and I nearly missed the bloody thing.

SB – (Trying to suppress a wry smile) Carry on.

JH – I had a very quick coffee as I was thirsty. Then I got on the train, sat down in my seat next to the window, and after a while, I got up and went to the buffet car in search of another coffee. After that, I went back to my seat to catch some ZZs and then nothing. I woke up to thick smoke and people screaming so I tried to help open the doors and the rest of course you know.

IW – So you didn't speak to anyone in the buffet car prior to the incident?

JH – Not that I recall.

IW (Consulting notes) – So you didn't speak to Miss Laura Merchant?

JH – Sorry yes, I forgot that I was very briefly in the Buffet Car for about five minutes as I had a thumping headache and needed caffeine and she was ahead of me in the queue. I thought I recognised her coat from earlier on, so we had a very brief exchange of words.

JH – God no, not really. It's just that it was such a beautiful coat, and I thought that she would have been quite hot in it given the weather.

SB- May I ask what you talked to Ms Marchant about then, please? Was it in fact about the coat and the heat then?

JH- Vaguely - Oh no, just the usual sort of chitchat like where we were from, what were our professions etc. She struck me as a professional lady that's all, one who had something sensible to say instead of the inane chatter that you tend to get from some women.

IW – And what are they, Sir?

JH – I'm a professor at Oxford, and Ms Marchant is an influencer, though I still don't know what that really is.

SB – Did you talk about anything else during your little chat, like where she was from for instance?

JH – Not really. To be frank she was a bit abrupt and cut the cut the conversation off by saying she was going back to her seat.

SB – Then you followed her?

JH – Most definitely not. I'm a happily married man thank you. I would never follow a strange woman.

SB – Just to let you know we will be interviewing Ms Marchant as well, so I do hope for both your sakes that your stories tally.

JH – They will. I hope that is all then.

IW – It is for now sir, apart from one thing. Is it true your original name is Mr Sean O' Houlihan and are you an Irish National with loyalties to Sinn Fein?

JH – Not anymore. I go by the moniker of John Houlihan and have done since the 1990s as I didn't want to be associated with the IRA bombings in London. So, if that satisfies your curiosity, I take it we are done.

IW – For the time being yes it will be and thank you for coming in. Let me give you my card in case you remember anything else. I have written a number for a Red Cross Counsellor on the back should you need someone to talk to about the stress of the incident.

When JH had left IW whispers sotto voice to SB – Well he was more than avaricious about his bloody train fare than giving the poor sods who were killed or injured a single thought. Also, it seemed to me that it was just a tad too inconvenient for him to turn up here.

JH dumps the card in a trashcan on the way out.

Synopsis of notes taken between Detective Inspector White and Major Glenn Cooper (Retired) with Detective Sargent Beacker also present.

Observing Major Cooper whilst he waited to be asked in it was noted that he had an upright military-like bearing, and did not twitch or break out in a sweat. However, his neck seemed to get redder by the passing seconds. IW thought that maybe his collar and shirt were too tight, or that the man had something to hide knowing that he was being recorded by CCTV.

SB – Please take a seat Sir, and may I offer you a Tea, Coffee, or a glass of water. It's not too cold for you here, is it?

IW glowers at this.

GC shakes his head in a 'no' gesture.

IW – I have a few questions about the explosion that took place yesterday if you don't mind Major. Try and recall what happened.

GC– Of course anything I Can do to help. Terrible, wasn't it?

SB- What were you doing at the time of the incident?

GC– Listening to the Cricket England V Jamaica at Lords on my little radio, with my headphones on. I don't hear a bloody thing when I have got them in my ears.

SB (Interrupting) – Yes, good Match – England won. Did you board the train early by any chance?

GC – Yes, we did board the train as soon as it was ready. We were eager to get the grandchildren seated. They had rather a tiring time in Paris, and we hoped that they would fall asleep.

IW –So how were they? We have reason to believe that they were causing a bit of a ruckus with other passengers and were talking about explosions just before the incident.

GC – Yes little blighters were running up and down all the time in the café at the station which is why we boarded early. Other people obviously don't take too well to the high jinks of kids of their age. I was concentrating on the match and didn't hear them say anything about a bomb. I mean if they did, they were joking. You know how kids of today watch too much drivel on the television.

SB – Quite so sir. So, as you were too busy listening to the cricket, I take it you didn't see them wander off in the direction of the first-class portion of the train, in the direction of the toilet maybe?

GC - Err no, I don't think they would do anything like that. They are good children really.

IW – Were you travelling with anyone else?

GC – Yes, my wife Claire, but she disappeared.

IW – I'm sorry to say that for now, we have found no record of her whereabouts. Did she end up at St Thomas's, or any other hospital with the injured or deceased?

GC – No she didn't

SB – Then where is she, sir?

GC – Missing I presume.

IW - Did you report her missing? Sorry let me rephrase that, did you look for her at all the major London Hospitals at all, or did you inquire about the drop-in centre that the Red Cross had set up at the Bloomsbury Hotel?

GC – Believe me, the old girl can look after herself. She's probably at Judith's, her best friend who lives close to Greenwich Park.

SB – Have you telephoned Judith to find out?

GC – What a silly question, Judith does not have a telephone. I would have thought that given your detective skills, you would have known that.

SB – I'm sorry to say we didn't sir. Will you be visiting Judith any time soon to see if Claire is staying with her?

GC- Maybe this afternoon. It's quite a way from North to South London. I'm not sure I have the energy to do it today.

IW – I think that will be it for now. If you hear anything from your wife, please let us know.

SB – If you need any counselling, I can let you have a number.

GC – Bloody counselling. No, thank you. One of those namby pamby things that kids today always seem to use as an excuse. Not for me. Made of sterner stuff than my generation. (Stomps out of interview room)

Synopsis of notes taken between Detective Inspector White and Mrs Mary Pickles with Detective Sargent Beacker also present.

IW observed Mary Pickles. She sat in reception and pulled a half-finished sleeve of a jumper out of her copious bag. The knitting wool was the most hideous shade of green. This was the last thing that DI White expected her to do. She did not strike him as the yarn artist type. Maybe she was using it to steady her nerves or to hide the fact that her hands might be shaking. Her feet were also taping away as well possibly to the rhythm of the knitting needles.

IW – Good morning, Madam, I just wanted to know what you were doing just before the indecent Yesterday.

SB – If you could start from when you joined the train, please.

MP – (Who loved more than a good natter and salacious gossip if it wasn't about her or her husband). *I made my way to the train. I was just inside the carriage behind the first-class portion. I settled myself down and plonked my shopping around me. I mean you never know if there are any light-fingered people around, do you? I had just managed to get comfortable. The seats in the second class are rock hard on one's derrière aren't they? Then an obnoxious man stinking of booze and carrying a tatty old rucksack rudely climbed over my legs and laddered my tights. I think at some point he left his seat, probably to vomit. At least he had the manners to say, 'Excuse me'.*

IW – And after that what happened.

MP – Well, I was reading this month's copy of Vogue, sitting there minding my own business. By the way, I object to you questioning me. I am the wife of Judge Pickles you know.

IW – Yes Madam, we know that you are the wife of Judge Pickles.

MP – He knows the Lord Chancellor very well, I often take tea with his wife, and I don't need any rumours reaching her ears. You must have read some rubbish about my husband in the newspapers.

IW – I don't pay attention to the tabloids, and we are very discreet.

SB – Did you bump into anyone you knew on the train?

MP – No, as I say I was reading.

IW – So you didn't go to the toilets in the first-class portion of then?

MP – Maybe I strayed into First Class by mistake. I don't really remember.

IW – Did you notice anyone when you 'strayed' into the first-class vestibule?

MP – Really if I did stray it, was an honest mistake. I can't recall if saw anyone. Knowing me I was in a bit of a hurry to reach the loo she added girlishly.

IW – Did the man return from the buffet? I mean the one next to you with the rucksack.

MP – Eventually. He was probably away from his seat for about twenty minutes, then he made a big show of stowing his rucksack between his feet as if it had precious cargo in it. He caught the edge of one of my bags, the one with the haute couture dress inside. Silly man. He just shrugged it off as if it were a joke, and promptly fell asleep.

SB - What about when the explosion happened? Tell us a little about that.

MP- My dear it was ghastly. Smoke and debris are everywhere. One minute I was happily reading, the next I was being manhandled by two rough-looking types, but they did manage to get me to the nice fireman who probably saved my life.

IW– You showed great fortitude then. I take it that you are feeling fine now though.

MP waving her hand dismissively – Yes fine thank you.

SB – Out of interest did you spot anyone wearing a red coat?

MP – Now why would anyone be wearing a coat on a day like yesterday?

SB – So you didn't see anyone.

MP – For goodness' sake no. Now have you finished harassing me, I am a very busy woman.

IW – We are done for now madam, and you are free to leave to attend to your important business.

Synopsis of notes taken between Detective Inspector White and Gordon Moss KC Detective Sargent Becker

IW thought it was intrusive to watch GM on the CCTV covertly especially as the man was a KC so he would check back later. He did not want the man to have any cause for complaint, so he did not keep him waiting like the rest.

IW – I'm sorry to inconvenience you, Sir. I will say that I realise this must be tiresome for you. Nothing is being recorded, and you are not under caution and are free to leave at any time. (Little did GM realise that SB had an eidetic memory and wrote notes later)

GM – Not good enough, I should have been in my Chambers about an hour ago, and you haul me in here like a common criminal.

IW – I am so sorry but it's important that we get some sort of timeline. Tell me about your time prior to boarding the train yesterday please sir?

GM – Had a damn good lunch, got on the train, which was seven whole minutes late, and then I fell asleep. I hope this isn't going to take up too much of *my time. I am a very busy man you know. Also, I have left my Porsche parked outside. I mean I do live close, but this is the rougher end of North London.*

IW – It will be fine sir, like most places we have CCTV everywhere. (Bloody Wanker he thought and on reviewing the CCTV later noted that GM arrived in a Black Cab*). I won't keep you much longer, just*

one last thing sir, Prior to the incident did you attempt to make a phone call?

GM – I tried to call my wife.

SB – Did you manage to get through to her?

GM – Of course I bloody well did. I have the latest model iPhone you know. No trouble whatsoever in contacting the old girl.

IW – So you were on the phone what a couple of minutes.

GM – Something like that

IW – You're quite sure you didn't call anyone else.

GM – No, and you will have a damn hard time getting permission to see my 'phone records given what I do for a living. Now I'm going. If you need you need anything else you can contact any of my colleagues who will act as my lawyer if I need one, but I must say you are on thin ice. Good morning to you.

(Later on, IW also noticed from the CCTV that Moss didn't catch a cab home, but was picked up in a Range Rover with the distinctive number plate LRR1 – now what was Mr Moss KC doing with the renowned TV Lawyer Richard Roberts?

Synopsis of notes taken between Detective Inspector White and Miss Susan Proctor with Detective Sargent Beacker also present.

IW Watched the CCTV when Susan Proctor arrived at the station. She looked like she had been crying and was nervously wringing her hands whilst she kept her head bowed. She was shaking from head to toe. Was it through nerves, or did she have anything to hide? He would have to tread very carefully with her as she looked like a poor wounded animal sitting there.

IW – Thank you for coming in Miss Proctor

SP – Please call me Susan

SB – Tell me Susan where were you prior to joining the train, and what coach did you sit in?

SP - (Rather vaguely) *I was at a party on the Left Bank with the others. Stupidly we had been chucked out of our hotel earlier for being too rowdy. I guess you'll be interviewing my other friends, the group I was with.*

IW – Someone will be interviewing all of them. As for you, what happened?

SP – We managed to get tickets in First Class. Dear God, I wished we had caught a flight home instead. For goodness' sake (head in hands now sobbing quietly) We could have all been killed.

SB – I know it's hard Susan, but we have a witness that said you had an argument whilst on the train.

SP - (in a whisper) Yes, I did

SB – Who did you argue with?

SP – With the Honourable Frank Dwyer my boyfriend. It was over nothing. I probably reacted with anger to something he said.

SB – Do you have any memory at all about what was said between the two of you to spark a row?

SP – No I don't. No not at all. I can hardly recall the journey as I was so tired and just wanted to sleep.

IW – Does Frank usually lose his temper?

SP -It was my fault. I started the row.

SB – Did either of you leave your seat at all to go to the loo perhaps?

SP – No we stayed put.

IW – No further information you would like to share with us then.

SP – Why should there be?

IW – Susan do you know where is Frank now?

SP – No He kind of disappeared. One minute he was there, the next he wasn't.

IW – And you weren't concerned at all about this.

SP – No I'm used to him disappearing for no reason, and I don't question why. Why should I tell you guys anything? You've got it in for Frank you lot have.

IW -Please Miss there is no need to be offensive, we just need to speak to Frank. If you are certain that you have no idea where he is then you may leave.

Synopsis of notes taken between Detective Inspector White and MS Laura Marchant with Police Detective Sargent Beacker also present.

Laura Marchant turned up at the station bang on time. She gave out an air of a woman who knew her rights, and that she was not a person to be messed with, so she was shown straight into the interview room.

IW – Good Morning Ms Marchant

LM – I'm not sure why you are interviewing me am I being interviewed under caution? If so, I want my lawyer Richard Roberts Present.

IW – No you are not under caution yet. We just needed an informal chat about yesterday's incident.

LM – OK then. I boarded the train. It was two-thirds full. After about Ten minutes I went to get a coffee from the buffet and bumped into a professor of languages from Oxford. I then returned to my First-Class seat where I read Le Monde. I noticed a lawyer type trying to make a phone call. He was initially studying me intently.

SB- After that what did you do? Did you leave your seat again for instance? LM - As I was not feeling too good and as my feet hurt, I nixed the idea to wander up and down. I was going to look for information for my Blog.

IW – Had you done a lot of walking before joining the train then Ms Marchant?

LM – I was wearing Louboutin shoes. Beautiful things but deadly.

IW – Did you go to the toilets at the end of your carriage, and if you did, did you see anyone?

LM – Most definitely not. Also, if I had gone, I would remember if I had seen someone.

SB – Can ask why you would have remembered?

LM – I love to people-watch, and as an influencer and blogger, I love the human interaction between people.

IW –I don't suppose you left your car at Ebbsfleet, a 1983 plate Pink Mini Cooper?

LM – No I have an Aqua Blue Aston Martin Valhalla, it's in my garage at my house, can I ask why?

IW – A person with dark hair, dressed in a red coat like the one that you were seen wearing yesterday was captured on CCTV acting suspiciously in the Ebbsfleet Car Park.

LM – No I've never seen a car like that.

IW One other thing (Pushing a photo towards LM) – I am showing Ms Marchant exhibit D22. Do you recognise this?

LM – Yes that's my Patek Phillipe watch, where did you find it?

SB – It was found in what remained of the toilet portion of First-Class, along with exhibit D24, a mobile phone which I presume is yours.

LM – No Not mine, it must be someone else's. I have mine on me if you want to check.

IW – No that's fine. It's so badly damaged but we can get our Tech. Team onto it. Who knows what they will find.

LM (Keeping a Poker Face) – Is that all then?

SB – *Yes, we have done for now.*

IW (Interrupting) – We may need to interview you again under caution.

LM – In that case, I will bring my Lawyer I'm sure you have heard of his reputation. It's Richard Rosenberg.

(DI White is now cursing under his breath. Richard Rosenberg is known as one of the country's leading Criminal Lawyers who gets more coverage in the press than the Princess of Wales). His services were engaged by one-half of a well-known TV Duo when they got divorced)

After concluding the interviews DI White's thoughts were that his sergeant would recall exactly what was said and by whom and give him a summary so that he could take things forward, but surmised that at least one of them was lying, but who and why?

CHAPTER 7

POST-INTERVIEWS

After the interviews a team of Detectives gathered, waiting for the outcome of the interviews so that they could be given their orders about what to do to help this investigation As DI White a taciturn man walked in the room was no preamble from him. He hated wasting time and got straight to the point. No preamble from him. It was a waste of time, especially after the lies and half-lies that heard from a bunch of liars whom he did not trust to tell the truth.

He had listened to six versions of the truth. Some were to expand, and get things off their chests whilst some held things in. At this stage. He did not know who was lying. He had never found that 'Copper's Instinct', so he knew he had to rely on his team to do all of the work for him. When the case was solved, he would get all the accolades, and finally a promotion.

'Right then team Supernatant Pitts wants results ASAP, and as she is breathing down my neck and needs something to release to the press PDQ.

Find out if Prof. Houlihan has any links to the IRA or Sinn Féin, Major Cooper -why wasn't he more concerned about his missing wife, and where is she? Mary Pickles – Was she trying to avoid her husband's scandal, or was she in Paris for something else? Gordan Moss KC – Find out from the phone provider who he was trying to phone, plus anything else you can find out about him even though there was a thinly veiled threat of legal action.

Susan Proctor – Who's party did she attend on the Left Bank if indeed that's where she was, and again not concerned about her missing boyfriend. See who he hangs out with and the same goes for Miss Proctor. Finally, Laura Marchant who the hell is she?

I know that a few of you will wonder why we have taken some interviews here. Counter Terrorism is doing its bit, but this has come from the top, and I do mean the very top. Counter Terrorism is conducting its own investigation, and we will share everything we find with them. No details have been released to the press yet so no letting the press office here, your mother or your dog know about a signet ring that was found at the epicentre of the blast. As it has mostly disintegrated, we can only work out the initials G and M. There Could be one missing, could be a C, not a G. Judging by what's left of it, it possibly belonged to a man.

It may or may not have come to your attention seeing as it was splashed all over the news yesterday - Counter Terrorism is heavily involved in a big explosion that took place at a synagogue at Bevis Marks in the City last night where many people were injured. They are currently seeking out a Jihadist's Cell and trying to see if there is a link between the two explosions. They are working in conjunction with the City Police over this so a bit of cooperation would not go amiss.'

Pausing to look around his team Whites eyes landed on DS Beaker.

'Sargent – A quick word in my office as you will be digging up any bodies that Laura Marchant may have buried.

Knocking cautiously on White's office door DS Beacker paused for a minute, wondering what they were letting themselves in for.

'Come in Sargent', barked DI White. 'Have a seat. I thought we should have an informal chat, so why don't we use first names in the confines of my office OK'.

Yes Sir -err I mean Bob', stammered his Sargent.

'So, Laura Marchant what do we know about her? Blogger and Influencer. Not a proper bloody job, is it?

'Well sir, my wife watches her on YouTube and Tick Tock, but on her lowly salary as a Temp, she has been known to moan about the fact that she can't afford any of the clothes or any of the items that Laura parades about in. They are all high-end goods though'.

'Right then Rosie, what are your other thoughts? I hear you like a bit of canteen banter and gossip', asked White.

Trying to hide her surprise that the Inspector knew all about her Rosie continued, 'My Initial thought is that she's a high-end hooker and is using Tick-Tock etc. as a cover-up, but I've already spoken to Vice, and she's not on their radar. I have already been looking into her social pre-interview, and it's pretty much what we already know, nothing that raises a flag so far.'

OK', said Inspector White. 'Keep digging but keep it quiet. I have a bad feeling about her. Incidentally, have you personally watched any of her Tick-Tock things?'

Chuckling to herself Rosie shook her head. Using a mixture of her native tongue and English she laughed showing a row of pearly white teeth. 'Me oh no, what would an honest Jamaican woman like me want with de make-up and dressing up tutorials? Now, my wife is a different kettle of fish man. She likes all that frippery stuff.

By now Inspector White was trying to hide a smile behind his hand, coupled with a few loud nasal snorts. Whites' usual MO was jumping from subject to subject from subject to catch his subordinates out.

'Just out of interest why did you keep your maiden name when you got married?' He inquired.

With screwed-up brows and wondering why he should change the subject to her marriage Rosie replied, 'Well Rosedale Blessed

Beacker-Cohen was a bit of a mouthful, and before you ask, yes Nineveh is from Israel, and I met her by swiping right. Best way to find the partner you know.

Now blushing fiercely Inspector White could only wave his hand dismissively. Truth be told he knew what swiping left and right meant, after all had not just spent most of his time off swiping Right on gentleman n of a certain age including one that he interviewed earlier, and that unnerved him a great deal.

Once Rosie had left, DI White unearthed a burner 'phone concealed in a floor panel which no one apart from himself knew about. He had by chance found it one day. He had noticed when sitting at his desk. Only because he was so anal about things being precise that he noted changes in the carpet pattern. This upset his sense of order. The zigzags of the carpet pattern did not seem to conform to the pattern in one spot. Either it was a poorly made floor covering with a mistake in the manufacture of it or it was something else.

Crouching down he ran his hands over the carpet and found that one of the zigzags had been stitched with a slightly different thread. Using a penknife, he cut away the piece of carpet that was annoying him.

Underneath the station's original floorboards were revealed. One of the boards had a knot in its wood. Running his index finger along the wood he managed to find a small groove. With some tugging and pulling. He levered out a section of the floorboard to reveal a hole, a hiding place.

Now that he had discovered the hole, he purchased a burner 'phone that he could use for his illicit activities. He could hide it away from prying eyes if necessary.

Having interviewed a broad spectrum of suspects during his career he knew the importance of swapping out the sim card every time he used it. Changing the sim after his sergeant's departure and crushing the old one in the palm of his hand to be flushed down the toilet at a later stage he dialled the one number that was stored in the 'phone.

A female voice answered, and after a brief exchange of words, he changed the sim again and hid the 'phone in the floor hollow. No one needed to know who he had contacted, but the conversation that he had with the unknown female confirmed that so far everything was going to plan. He would do as much as he could to help her.

With a jerk, he almost dropped the phone. He was sure that a shadow was lurking behind the door of his office which was constructed of opaque glass.

Outside someone watched what he was doing. Though they could not make out the conversation from the whispered call they suspected that Whit was up to something. Time to have a dig around once everyone had left for the night. They would also track White's digital footprint as well.

CHAPTER 8

TWO DAYS POST-EUROSTAR – RULES RESTAURANT CONVENT GARDEN

It was pouring rain when she exited the tube station. After an interminable wait for the lift to take her up to street level, and having stood against wet steaming bodies, all crammed together like a giant game of sardines with what seemed like a hundred umbrella spokes and tips poking into her legs, ribs, and even at one point her thighs she was not in the best of moods.

Having started out from her home in Holland Park which she had bought through one of the many shell companies that she had connections with, and having already walked to Holland Park Tube, caught the circle line to Holborn, then changed to the Piccadilly Line whilst keeping an eye out all the time she was not really in the right headspace for this. In addition, the driving rain and gusts of wind did not alleviate her current frame of mind.

Getting ready earlier and after changing her outfit three times until she was sure that she would make a good impression on him she had to give herself a pep talk about what she was going to face She needed to come up with reasons why she did what she did. Deciding that shoes were a girl's best friend like Carrie from Sex in the City, she slipped on a pair of her favourite Jimmy Choo's, decided that yes, they did complete the outfit, a very expensive dress with slightly less expensive shoes. She hoped that she gave out the impression that she was a girl who was going out for a good time.

Catching her heel slightly on the edge of the kerb just outside the tube station, and righting herself quickly, she took a deep breath, glanced around and walked reluctantly to face up to one of her worst nightmares. A serious number of umbrellas and heads bowed against the torrential rain ensured that no one was interested in her, and no one glanced in her direction. There was no poor unfortunate soul begging for money by the cash point only waves of people trying to get home or get to the Lamb and Flag which was the nearest pub to down a swift pint.

Why they had to meet at a place of his choice she did not know. It had to be busy wherever they met so that no one would notice them. He had chosen one of the places that was to mind the last bastion of misogyny, and that made her inwardly cringe. He was a stickler for rules and made her come to meet him in a place that he knew she hated as if he was punishing her already.

She had already had her fill of meetings, especially it seemed mostly with obnoxious little men of late. Already having to tell the half-truth once, and lied maybe just a little bit, she wished that she was going for a night out with her good friend Suzie. When they went out together, she wouldn't be wearing her 'pulling' dress, nor the shoes with a four-inch spiked heel. It would have been Jeans, a T-shirt and trainers, no makeup, and no wig. She knew that she could let her hair down with her friend; something she needed to do very soon. All she seemed to do was work and damned hard at it too.

Tugging on the hem of her short dress she thought that maybe it hadn't been the best of choice to wear with her long gym-toned legs. This part of the aftermath of a job was what she hated least about her work. Kowtowing to another fucking man was not on her agenda. Taking a deep breath, she ignored the doorman who was too busy looking at her legs she viciously pulled the restaurant door open. At seven in the evening despite the foul weather the room was dominated mainly by men most of them anxious to have a very good reason for not going home to their wives; probably citing a business meeting or some other bullshit. Shaking the droplets of water from her umbrella and handing it to a passing waiter she rapidly scanned the room, eyes alighting on H. She didn't know his real name, and anyway, she was paid way too much to care.

Beckoning her over to him like she was an errant schoolgirl she grudgingly noticed that ever the gentleman he stood up and then kissed her lightly on her cheek leaving a tiny mark on one bronze-blushed cheek. On this occasion, this was her professional visage. Trying not to recoil from his slimy, rubbery lips, she touched him lightly on the shoulder by way of acknowledgement, luckily a passing waiter caught her eye. Giving him a warm smile she was rewarded with a glass of Champagne. At least the dress has some positives she thought.

Ever chivalrous H pulled out her chair and then sat himself back down. Handing her a menu she held it between two fingers as though it were a ticking time bomb about to explode. With growing distaste, she started to skim its content whilst keeping a wary eye on the door. With purple contact lenses and a blond Marilyn Monroe-styled wig, she glanced once more at the menu although she knew its contents off by heart. Putting the menu on the very edge of the table to annoy H who hated untidiness she folded her hands neatly and precisely in her lap.

The object of the exercise was not to be spotted by standing out. Knowing that she must fit in to be one of the boys she selected the Steak and Kidney Pudding. By nature, she was normally vegetarian, but needs must. Even before her dish had been served, and after declining wine she opened her mouth and asked,

'Well, Gov watchya wanna know?'

Not sure if the accent was pure Southeast London, or another of her persona, H leaned forward towards her so that their noses were most touching.

'I want to know', he said through clenched teeth, 'what the hell was that clusterfuck forty-eight hours ago?'

Eyes cast down she mumbled something about it wasn't all her fault. She had left tiny devices in the toilets, and it wasn't enough for sixty per cent of Eurostar to be blown to kingdom come. He held up one hand to stop her tirade.

'Well,', he began, 'if it wasn't you whoever is responsible caused three deaths, sixteen life-changing injuries, numerous missing persons, not to mention two hundred officers from the Met, sixteen ambulances, nine fire engines, and what's left of the bomb disposal unit, and me on the carpet Infront of the PM'.

'I'm guessing then', she said slowly 'you want to either sack me or to find out who the hell's behind it'.

'Much as I would dearly love to do the former, my dear, for now, I want you to do the latter by any means possible. Now get the fuck out of here and get me some answers', retorted H.

'Slight problem', She replied, biting her bottom lip, 'I am currently the Met's number one suspect for it, so if you want answers call the sodding dogs off'.

'No can do', retorted H mockingly. 'There are protocols to follow don't you know. I suggest you are a redhead with glasses and a limp next time, so you won't get noticed. Playing the harlot doesn't quite suit you. For instance, just look at the dress that you are wearing now.

Flipping her middle finger at him she stood up as if to make her escape.

'FYI, sir its Balenciaga. Not that you would know or pronounce the label name properly. Also, the company owe me a new watch, as mine is being held in evidence at Golders Green Police station neatly bagged and tagged.

Stalking out of Rules with most of the male clientele and a few of the female ones as well watching her she disappeared into Maidens Lane where the exit from Rules was located. She didn't give a stuff that he didn't like her dress, or that he had intimated that she looked like a whore. All she needed now was to call in a few favours, and then nail down bastards who had taken out Eurostar. Already she had a good idea who it probably was unless her spidery senses were twitching in the wrong direction. Someone was gunning for her, and it didn't take much brainpower to work out who and why.

H, who had been left fuming in her wake nodded imperceptibly to a woman with short steel grey hair who was sitting by herself in a booth apparently scrolling through her phone and intermittently sipping from a glass of sparkling water. Sliding sideways, and without acknowledging him she slipped silently out of her seat, and without casting a glance at the waiters or in H's direction strode purposefully out into the night.

Expecting to be followed, would the silly man never learn, the blonde woman with purple eyes turned swiftly into Southampton Row and disappeared amongst the throng of office workers and tourists. The grey-haired woman who she had first clocked in Rules was good but not as good as she was. Slowing her pace marginally the hairs on the back of her neck started to tingle. The trouble with H was that he was so old-school and always used the same operatives to follow her as though he almost didn't trust her. It would be surprising if they ever managed to keep up with her though. She had learnt her trade from the best many years ago. Dodging and weaving were in her very nature.

She could hear and almost feel the hum of the traffic around Leicester Square, but also the unmistakable sound of someone with a slight limp trailing behind her. Pausing briefly by exit 4 of Leicester Square tube located on Cranbourne Street and turning on one very high heel she finds herself confronted by a small, thin middle-aged Asian with a lit cigarette dangling from the corner of his mouth.

'Bloody Hell Dinesh Patel, you didn't half give me a fright. I mean really an Asian man and a blonde woman in a short dress meeting at the entrance to the Tube?'. Then, with her face breaking into a huge grin she pulled him in for a hug. 'Christ it must be sixteen or more years, how the hell did you find me?'

'Pure luck like Leicester City winning the FA Cup in 2021', he replied with a huge smirk taking the cigarette out of his mouth and stamping it out on the ground. He was a fervent Leicester City supporter.

Letting her go he spun her round. 'Bleddy Hell, you look good L', he said with a laugh using her shortened name like had always done.

'But blonde. I mean really. I thought we had this discussion about this when I took you to Fenella's hairdresser where we agreed that it wasn't your colour. You only went in to get your fringe trimmed and after two minutes in there you had already the stylist to change your hair colour'.

'Times have changed old friend', 'she retorted, 'and so have I. I'm an Influencer and Blogger now. Also, as I recall I was the last time we met was in Two Thousand and Eight. It was the final time I saw Muriel then suddenly I was whisked away to the children's home. How is she by the way?', she carried on.

'Muriel passed away last August, you know,' said Dinesh with a huge sigh. 'At the Bingo it was, she had just called the house on the link game with a prize of eight thousand pounds then dropped down dead of a heart attack. She only wanted her bleddy ashes scattering there didn't she, so yours truly had to climb over the car park barrier and do the deed in the dead of night. Did you ever realise how heavy a box containing someone's ashes weighs? Four to five per cent of their body weight, and she was one hefty woman I'll tell you.'

A mutual silence descended whilst an old friend was fondly remembered.

'So, what brings you here? 'She asked. God, it was so good to see Dinesh after all this time. Still swearing like a trooper, but then she and Muriel did teach him English and Muriel used to swear like a navvy all the time. Muriel had been a market trader many years ago selling knicker elastic and lace – knock-offs from the factory where their Gail used to work.

'Had a Grocery Store innit near to the Post Office, but bleddy Morrisons and Amazon, bastards. Closed two months ago now so me and the Mrs. are visiting family. Came down to see my niece pass out at Hendon, joined the Met now innit', he said without pausing to draw breath. Muriel obviously had had a much stronger influence on his swearing.

'Wow the Met', said she replied with little enthusiasm. 'Whereabouts is her first posting?' she asked, although she already knew what the answer would be.

'Golders Green Nick'. I mean really sending a nice Hindu girl to a Jewish enclave. Sometimes I don't know what twat it was that they put in charge of the Met.

Knowing that it was Mark Rowley had been appointed Commissioner in July 2022 she wasn't going to let Dinesh know that nugget of information. Ignorance is bliss and all that. Besides she had bigger things to worry about like Dinesh's niece being posted to Golders Green.

Glancing at the time on her mobile to swerve any more questions as she no longer had her watch she frowned slightly. She had her suspicions, and much as she loved Dinesh, she still had to be extra cautious around him. It wasn't just swearing Muriel had taught Dinesh, it was another trade as well. She was sure it wasn't a coincidence that he was there. What troubled her was that she had smelt his brand of cigarette from half a mile away. Now that was a schoolboy error for sure unless he wanted her to know he was following her. She thought she had smelt it in the lift at the Tube but given the amount of people who pass through its doors each day, it could have been anyone. This brand was imported from India, so what the hell was he up to?

'Got to dash kiddo', she said to Dinesh. 'Much as I love your company, I need my beauty sleep and my P J's even more.'

'Maybe I can walk you home?', queried Dinesh. 'Where do you live now? I can't see a young lady walking home by herself at this time of night can I'?

Snorting she answered, 'Not too far, end of the Northern Line at Elephant and Castle'. Five minutes' walk from there honestly. I'll be as safe as houses, promise'.

Conceding defeat Dinesh gave her a mock salute and then disappeared into the fading light. Climbing up the few steps that she had started to go down to convince Dinesh that she was getting the Tube to Elephant and Castle the woman, came back up and did a quick scan around to see that the coast was clear then stuck her hand out to hail a cab. Leaning through the wound-down passenger window of the cab and using her normal accent, slightly posh with just a hint of the East Midlands about it, she politely asked the driver to take her to her house in Holland Park. The last thing, she thought grimly was getting entangled with Dinesh or his niece. She'd worry about that another day. Firstly, she had to get herself off the hook with the Police.

CHAPTER 9

DINESH ON LEAVING LEICESTER SQUARE

Dinesh had disappeared into the fading light. It had started to drizzle now instead of the intense downpour earlier. This was the one thing that he loathed about England; it was always raining even in May. He had stood and watched the woman climb back up the steps and walk a little towards Charring Cross station before retracing her steps and hailing a cab. This had piqued his interest. He wasn't the only one to lie about where they had come from, or where they were going. He paused, slapping his forehead with the palm of his hand. He should have asked her what she was doing in town on a wet and rainy night. He would get into big trouble for forgetting to ask a simple question.

After Muriel had died, he admitted to himself he was at a loss as to what to do. True enough he had opened a grocery store, and struggled along, but then the Covid pandemic of 2020 had hit his business hard. One evening when he was closing, he was approached by a stranger who was clothed from head to toe in black and had a black ski mask over his face. Fearing that he was about to be robbed or shot or both Dinesh stood behind the counter with both hands resting palms up to show the stranger that he would comply.

'You don't know me,' said the stranger. I did you a big favour many years ago. I want you to do one for me in return.

The stranger offered him a chance to earn a vast amount of money, more than he had ever had in his life. All he had to do was to keep an eye on a certain woman in London and report back to him as to what she got up to. Using his niece's passing out parade at Hendon as an excuse Dinesh convinced his wife that they should take an extended visit to the big smoke. He lied to her that he had sold the shop for far more than it was worth and that from now on money was no object. She could now visit Harrods with her sister if she wanted to, something they had never been able to afford to do before.

Without needing to be asked twice his wife had booked one-way tickets from Leicester to London; opportunities like this never happened to her. Counting her blessings that deep down Dinesh was really a good husband she never thought to question him. It wasn't her culture's way of life for a woman to question her husband especially when it came to financial matters.

Once the pair had settled in an Airbnb between Hendon and London's Westend it wasn't very long before his wife and her sister Pushpa were spending his money. He didn't bear them any grudges though as he now had the freedom to find and track his target. After the encounter with her at Leicester Square he didn't believe for one minute that she had turned out to be a blogger and influencer, but he was going to find out what the hell she was up to as he had a report to give his benefactor that very night. A thing he was not looking forward to.

When he had engaged with his target and had seen her flag down a cab, he realised that it was too busy to follow her on a rickshaw bike whose owners you see plying their trade. He lost sight of her because of the cinema-goers, and hungry masses seeming to be seeking sustenance along with hundreds of tourists all got in the way until he felt like he was being engulfed by a Tsunami. There were two things that he had to do now. One was to meet his benefactor, the other his niece. Fortunately for him, they lived in the same part of London. He supposed it should be his niece first though. She had cited her religious beliefs and sex for not wanting to be accommodated with her fellow Met Officers. Instead, she had managed to rent (with some of Dinesh's newly found wealth), a tiny little one-bedroomed flat in Southgate above a Chinese Restaurant. He hoped that she wouldn't turn her back on her culture and take up eating Chinese Cuisine.

Rattling along the Piccadilly line in an almost empty tube train he kept his eyes down. Some folks didn't want to engage with people like him anymore. Had he been an actor you could say that he had already been type-cast. Maybe thirty or so years ago he would have been all right but now he was usually perceived as a Religious Fanatic about to blow up the underground. People were less suspicious back then. Now many considered him a terrorist even though he made a point of not carrying a homemade bomb around with him.

Exiting Southgate Tube Station, he almost immediately came across the Chinese eatery on the corner. Running up the outside stairs he knocked softly on his niece's door. It was almost as if she had expected him and slid the safety chain back and unlocked both door locks. Given that she was now an officer of the law she really didn't need to worry, especially as she had a baseball bat with a metal core hidden inside. Dinesh never knew which family member she would go and chat to later so for now he tried to keep his swearing under check.

'Uncle D', she said in delight. I didn't know you would be calling so late. Would you like a cup of chia?

Glancing over her shoulder into the small kitchen that was stacked with dirty dishes and empty Pizza boxes he shook his head.

'Not now my dear niece, though bless Allah for asking me. I was just wondering about your work situation. You start soon, yes?'

Nodding in agreement she ushered him to the small living room which housed an armchair, a beanbag, and a small TV which appeared to be on the blink. Nodding towards the armchair she gestured him to sit down.

'Three days, well two and a half. I'm on an early shift on my first day. I must say I'm intrigued as to why I was posted to this neck of the woods, but hey beggars can't be choosers can they? Now what can I do for my favourite Uncle eh?'

Glancing around and through the very walls might grow ears he leant forward.

'I want you to let me know if a certain Laura Marchant ever crosses your path in work, what she is there for, and what she says'.

Frowning she knotted her hands behind her head, which she always did when she was stressed.

'Wow you don't want much from me do you Uncle, I mean I haven't even started the job yet, and as the probationer, and given the fact that the Met is renowned for being institutionally racist, not least to say sexist I guess the closest I would get to an actual criminal is er never. I'll probably be making tea for the next six months. Anyway, why the interest in this woman, and why should I cross paths with her? What is it that she has supposedly done?'

'Let's just say that I need to keep someone sweet for the time being, and you may or may not come across that person at work. If I told you who it was that I was working for I would be giving away confidence, and you know me I am I man of honour and morals.' He replied sternly.

Snorting and trying to choke back her amusement she passed her hand in front of her face and nodded silently.

'If that's all,' she said, ushering him out, 'I need my beauty sleep.'

Now it was Dinesh's turn to smile. He knew when he was being given the brush-off.

'Just take care little one, take care', he murmured heading out of the front door and leaving his niece alone and wondering what she had just let herself in for.

It was true that he was concerned for Tahira, and what could happen to her. Having no children of his own he had always looked on her as the daughter that he never had. Unlike her lazy, fat mother Pushpa who was his wife's sister Tahria had turned out to be thin, athletic and beautiful. Dinesh knew that she would make a good police officer as she was very inelegant too. He hated getting her involved but what could he do about it?

On leaving Tahira's flat Dinesh with a heavy heart made his way to his next meeting. It wouldn't do to keep that person waiting. Finding himself before a block of council maisonettes he took the stairs two a time up inside the red brick-enclosed tower-like stairs. Stepping carefully along the walkway between dwellings that were littered with discarded needles and other detritus he finally located the correct door which was the most hideous shade of purple. Something or someone had fouled themselves by the doorstep which meant that the most disgusting smell wafted through the air combined with the sickly-sweet smell that you associate with cannabis.

Holding his breath and pulling out a clean white handkerchief which he covered his nose and mouth he mentally braced himself for what was to come. As he was about to knock on the door – no doorbells here, they'd nick anything on this estate given half the chance, a man wearing a cashmere coat came out and brushed past him. Each to his own, thought Dinesh catching sight of the briefcase the man was carrying which was embellished with the initials RR.

The stranger who had offered him vast amounts of cash a few weeks ago stood in the doorway.

'Well,' they said, 'you had better come in'.

Dinesh followed the stranger into a small lounge heated by a one-bar electric fire even though it had stopped raining and was very humid. Glancing around he saw no signs of wealth, which was surprising given all the money that had passed between them.

'I couldn't get anything out of her, not a bleddy thing. All I can say was that she pretended to catch a tube, then changed her mind and caught a cab. Tourists and the like trying to get home were milling around so I couldn't exactly follow her, could I? However, I can offer one thing though.' Breaking off he looked down at his own rain-spotted expensive Gucci shoes.

'You couldn't follow her but?' inquired his benefactor.

'My niece sir, she starts in a few days' time at Golders Green Nick. I've asked her to keep an eye out for Ms Marchant. I mean it was fortuitous that she got her first posting there. Wasn't that a stroke of luck.'

'Wasn't it just', his benefactor agreed nodding their head.' I will obviously try to get her on my team, but you must remember I usually have more experienced officers, and all are DCs. I'm sure your niece is a very bright young lady though'.

'Top of the class at Hendon I say top of the class, you will be very lucky indeed', said Dinesh rubbing his hands together in anticipation of even more money.

Looking at the ornate Omalu clock on the mantlepiece which seemed oddly out of place amongst the cheap furnishings, Dinesh swore under his breath. He was going to be very late back to the Airbnb. Edging towards the door, he paused, bowed his head at his benefactor, and said,

'If that's all I'll be going back to my wife now. She will be worried about me.'

Nodding their head in dismissal his benefactor turned away. Little did Dinesh know that they hated anyone from Asia. Their hatred of an inferior race was ingrained in them, but they needed the small Indian for one thing and one thing only. After that, well who knew?

CHAPTER 10

GOLDERS GREEN POLICE STATION DAY 5 POST EUROSTAR

It was a few minutes before seven in the morning. The investigating team who had been hastily pulled together for the independent investigation into the explosion were for the most sitting and staring morosely into cups of lukewarm coffee with one exception. DC Martin Sweet was hammering away at his computer keyboard. This did not endear him to the rest of the team. Little did they know he was trying unsuccessfully to access files that he shouldn't have. Most of the team had crossed paths with each other before, or they knew someone who knew someone on the team.

They gossiped amongst themselves at Refs and decided that he was White's inside man, sent to spy on them. Why would a yokel from Lincolnshire transfer to the Met? There wasn't any sheep rustling happening in Islington as far they knew, and Lincolnshire was not that far from the DI's original county of birth. The other thing was that he arrived after the Eurostar incident which set the gossipmongers clacking.

At seven am on the dot DI White swept into the room looking a little worse for wear. With a day's worth of stubble forming on his chin, he did not give out the impression of a good, strong leader. It was undoubtedly true that this case was taking its toll on him. He had been called in to do this investigation in an unexpected manner. One minute he was happily whiling away the hours until his retirement, the next he was facing Chief Superintendent (call me Suzie) Pitts in her south-facing office that had an enviable view across North London; one that he aspired to but would never achieve in this life.

He was told, not even politely requested gather a small team to investigate the explosion of Eurostar. Although Counter Terrorism were 'dealing with it' she wanted an independent review. Five people who had popped on the Police radar, and the Super wanted a team of White's choice pulled together. The only proviso was that he included a certain DC Sweet on his team as Sweet hadn't been a Detective for long, and she thought that it might help him gain valuable experience.

Having polished off a bottle of Whiskey, after finally tying up things at the nick, and then having yet another clandestine meeting with the Indian Man he was not much further along in finding out about Laura Marchant the woman whom Dinesh had 'accidentally' bumped into three days ago. He had a reason for wanting to know all about her, but for now, he wanted to keep that reason to himself. It wasn't just about the bomb on Eurostar, there was another more urgent reason to keep tabs on her. He suspected, but could not prove that she worked for MI5, and that made her connection to the bombing very interesting. It also made DI White very worried.

He had enough money from taking backhanders off various criminals, lawyers, and politicians to buy Dinesh's loyalty and services. To date only thing that White knew so far about Laura Marchant was that she lived in Holland Park, and was not, as she stated in her interview with him, an influencer, and blogger. Feeling a bit pissed off with Dinesh for not delivering anything, plus being very hung over from last night's booze he was not in the best of moods that morning.

'Update he snapped', with almost a snarl.

A few of the team present were aware of how abrupt White was though not many of them had worked closely with him before. The sergeant was newly promoted, and DC Jenny Blore was the only one and she stuck around because she had a soft spot for the D.I. The investigating team had been thrown together hastily. Chief Superintendent Pitts had let White choose his own team. She really wanted to know if the rumours about him were true. A few of the Officers including Suzie were bemused by the eclectic mix that White had selected.

'I was going to start with Sargent Becker, but she doesn't seem to be here. Does anyone know why she's late?', asked White, obviously trying to keep his patience in check.

'Suspicious death Sir', Martin Sweet replied. Like his name, he pretended to be sweet. The rest of the team thought they could see right through him and had already decided that he liked to suck up to the Senior Officers. From the back of the room, someone started to make sucking noises.

Short of breath and panting, Sargent Beacker burst into the room. White frowned at her throwing a tell me about it later look in her direction.

Sweet shot his hand up first. 'Update on Gordon Moss Sir. He joined ZJP on 1st November last year after leaving Willis and Hyde. Was head of chambers there, but numerous members of staff have said off the record he has a penchant for more junior lawyers both male and female, but none of them would go on record. Typical Lawyer stuff.

We have however had word back from his phone provider. He was attempting to reach Fenix Harper one of the pupils at his chamber whom he appears to be particularly close to. Speculation amongst the clerks that work there is that they are seeing each other, but this is not confirmed yet and the call failed as there was no apparent signal at the time.

He likes hanging out at the Ivy with his wife and sister, has a big house on Windmill Hill, has no debts, and has a huge bank balance and ego to match. The trip to Paris was ostensibly for good food and wine.

He does however', he added quickly, by now knowing that White hated time wasters, 'have or rather had a signet ring with his initials on it, and he presumes it was lost during the aftermath of the explosion.

Not acknowledging Sweet, White's eyes landed on Jenny Blore. One of the more experienced members of his team, he had known Jenny for many years and knew her answer would be succinct. Just by glancing in her direction, he knew she would respond immediately.

'Major Cooper, Sir', she began confidently.

'He was a Major in the now defunct Derbyshire Yeomanry Regiment and had an older brother Jack who rose to the rank of Colonel in the same Regiment which pissed Glenn off big time as he never quite made it to the upper echelons. Married to Claire ne Mortimer of Dorking Surrey, four children, and eight grandchildren, the youngest two being taken to Paris by them for a break.

Pausing to read her notes with glasses perched on the bridge of her nose she continued.

'Two things strike me as odd sir, Jack Cooper is still alive although he's 96, but he used to be based at Bletchley Park during the war, and two, the Major father-in-law was also at Bletchley at the same time. I did some digging around and seems that within Bletchley there may have been something else going on, but when I asked more about that through my army contact (Jenny herself was ex-army) he decided to keep schtzum and clammed up immediately. However, the Major did have a signet ring with the initials GM, not his though he inherited it from his father-in-law who had been coincidentally in the same regiment as the Major himself and the Major's brother. The initials on it stood for General Mortimer'.

Furthermore, and this is maybe of some significance is that the Major's wife Claire who is still missing has dementia and may have already hidden the ring prior to their departure for Paris. As he was being run ragged by the Twins, he can't recall putting it on.

'What else did you find about the wife Claire?', quizzed White.

'Ah, an interesting woman. She mainly spent her time at the W.I and she ran a Guide Troop in the village where they live. Apparently, she was an all-round do-gooder until the dementia started about five years ago.

'Excellent Jenny', said White, nodding approvingly. 'I knew I could rely on you to get deep answers. Keep trying to find out more about the family, and anything on the in-laws as well.'

'Right next', he went on, 'you the new DC Jane Hodges isn't. I know this is your first briefing with CID, so the idea is to keep it short and sweet. (Titters all around apart from DC Sweet).

Hesitantly Jane cast her eyes down at her notes. God, she hated her new boss already and felt like she was back at school being hauled in front of the Head Teacher. She fervently wished that she was back in uniform with DI Andy Fletcher. He was always thorough, though a little pedantic at times. As his work was thorough and methodical, he often got a good result. He had taken Jane under his wing when she had exchanged one career as a trainee Lawyer for another in the police Force three years ago.

Fletcher has been a Farther figure towards her especially as her own father died of a brain tumour when Jane was just nine. He'd worked in logistics all of his life, and she still missed him, even his odd, meticulous ways. She realised that she had become quite dependent on Andy Fletcher. Now Fletcher was getting a new Officer to replace her on his team. To her chagrin, he was quite looking forward to it, and in retrospect was in a hurry for her to move on.

'Err Mary Pickles', she stammered. 'She did go shopping mainly to avoid the Judge Pickles scandal. She spent the morning in Gallery Lafayette shopping, and the early afternoon called in at a café called Le Chat Noir. Then was spotted by a witness going into the Moulin

Rouge. In my book that's very strange as I phoned their box office and the first show doesn't start till 7 pm so I'm wondering what that's all about. The other odd thing is that she sent something to Paris today via DPD. According to the courier we questioned it was a brown envelope. That's all I could find out for now.

'Hmm interesting', said White scratching the day-old stubble on his chin. 'Try and find out a bit more about her journey back. For instance, what time did check back in at the Gare du Nord'.

'Yes Sir', said Janet, relieved that she had delivered her report with only one tiny stammer realising that her checks were flushed. What DI White didn't know was that Susan Proctor one of the people who had been called in for an interview was her estranged younger stepsister.

She knew that Granny was still in touch with her errant sibling though, even if both girls had made different life choices. They shared a mother but had different Fathers which would explain their totally different personalities. Perhaps she should get in touch with Granny. She thought that she might be able to glean some information on Susan that she could bring to the next meeting and then Whit wouldn't think she was a completely useless DC.

'Valentine', said White, snapping his head read in the direction of DC Ian Valentine the oldest and laziest person on the team, 'if you can keep awake for five minutes I and the rest of the team would appreciate it,' he continued sardonically.

'Yes, right Ms Procter', he began laconically, trying to stifle a yawn. 'Ms Proctor was staying at The George Cinque Hotel Paris, with the Hon Frank and Co., but according to the Concierge, they were asked to leave due to their disruptive behaviour. They did indeed party on the left bank, and drinks and drugs were imbibed. I find an interesting fact too; our dear Ms Proctor was not as innocent as she looked. She has been stopped and searched twice at Heathrow, nothing found, but according to the drugs Squad she keeps dropping off small parcels on the Cater Estate in Greenwich.'

'Find out more', pressed White, now turning his full attention to Rosie, who was getting more, and more fidgety.

'Sir, the suspicious death was the Hon. Frank Dwyer. Found in a known crack house in Edmonton. First off, they thought it was an O.D., but there was an attempt to carve a letter or something on his chest. Forensics are scratching their heads as they are trying to figure out what it represents, at present there was no DNA recovered from the body.

DI Mould of the Murder Squad is taking the and obviously complete transparency from them at lead', she said trailing off.

'Then onto Ms Marchant. I could find nothing about her earlier than four years ago. Nothing on social media, no passport, driving licence, or bank account. Suddenly burst on the scene blogging, now a renowned influencer.'

'Right, well I'm sure DI Mould will do a great job', said White', witheringly. 'Now have all got things to get on with. Rosie, keep digging and see what else you can find. There must be more out there unless she was bloody MI5, or 6', and Sweet, he said in a resigned tone, you know what you've got to do, get up close and personal with our Mr Moss.'

And I bloody well hope you don't find that I've swiped right he thought to himself. Then again Sweet was apparently a useless bugger which is why he assigned G. Moss for him to investigate.

DC Jock Mackintosh was the last to give his report. A small, red-haired, bearded, bespectacled man of thirty he had seen it all before. Feeling DI White's eyes boring into him he responded as well as one of Pavlov's dogs who had been subjected to classical-conditioning. Small and rodent-like in his appearance he could lurk in the shadows without being noticed.

'Mr John Houlihan. Lives in Oxford. His wife is the money in the partnership. She comes from a very wealthy family. He has a bit of a chequered history. He got into a bit of trouble when he was a student. Since then, he's apparently been on the straight-narrow. He made a trip to Paris to see what it was like at the Sorbonne as I believe his wife wants to relocate to France for some reason. After that, I can find anything else at present, but you know me I'll keep on at it for a wee while.'

White seemed to be ok with this summary from Jock as he didn't say anything in response.

The DI glanced around the room casting a beady eye on all his team.

'I forgot to mention, "he said in a lowered tone, I know that we have already gelled as a team, but there is a new PC starting at the station today. A Miss Tahira Sharma. If you bump into her in the canteen or otherwise, please give her a warm welcome. She's a very ambitious young lady, very ambitious indeed, so much so that I have appointed her as exhibits officer for now as she requested that she should sink her teeth into something juicy right from the off.

Leaving a puzzled team, he slipped out of the station. Next stop HMP Belmarsh. Meanwhile, the new PC lingered outside the briefing room. She had a lot to tell her uncle when she next saw him.

Extract from Diary – Author Unknown 5 Days Post Eurostar

ONE OF US IS LYING

PART 2 - PAYBACK

CHAPTER N DAY OF RECKONING

EXTRACT FROM THE DIARY - AUTHOR UNKNOWN.

'Of course, I was up to my neck in it from the start, by accident or design I don't know. Maybe it's because I wanted to be involved.'

CHAPTER 1

3TD MAY 1985 M1 LEICESTER FOREST EAST SERVICE STATION NORTHBOUND

At 5 a.m. precisely on Friday 3rd May 1985 five white Transit Vans all bearing an '83 plate pulled up in the Leicester Forest East M1 Services Northbound car park at regular five-minute intervals. The vans were not new so they didn't attract any untoward attention and they were not too old, so equally they didn't attract any untoward attention. Merely five regular white vans. It was precisely 5:20 a.m. when the last one pulled up and reversed into its parking space. It was way too early for any bleary-eyed traveller to notice them. If some clever clogs had spotted them, they may have remarked on five vans being in the same place, and what a coincidence it was. Only it wasn't.

The vehicles were all parked equidistance from each other, five spaces apart and each one lined up ready for a quick getaway. No one got in, no one got out. The occupants had not arrived there to eat at the recently rebranded Welcome Break, nor had they all unanimously decided to pull up within regular five-minute intervals between vans to use the other facilities there. The five drivers were all simply following orders.

Not that any of them cared one iota about the vans that they were driving. All had been procured from a certain Neil's Autos which was situated under the arches at London Bridge Railway Station. Luckily the owner Neil lived in Bermondsey, so he didn't have far to walk to work, nor to return from work. As there were no pubs between work and home Neil's wife Sarah always knew that he would be home on time.

On a bitterly cold day in January when the new year had only started a week ago and with frequent frosts and snowfalls already, just as Neil was about to call it quits for the day because all he had achieved was to flog an ancient Morris Minor to an old biddy and spent the rest of his time giving an old Mini a respray and as he had pulled closed the heavy doors to his garage and was fishing out an ancient padlock out of his pocket, a pugilist looking man walked into the arrow pathway between the arches. His request was very simple. He wanted Neil to procure five White '83 plate Ford Transit vans garage They had to be two years old, and all of them white.

Neil knew exactly where he could lay his hands on that brand, year, and type of van as he had connections with some very dodgy people. He told the muscle-bound visitor that he could lay his hands on four white and one blue van. He was however gently perused to find another white one instead of the blue one.

The vans were obtained firstly by Neil who handed them over in exchange for a large wedge of cash. As the customer wanted the purchases to be strictly off the books, an agreement Neil was not averse to as he enjoyed a bit of dodgy dealing, he was quite happy to tell the buyer that the new style V5 logbooks were lost somewhere in the system when the DVLA closed the new upgrade system to logbooks in 1983.

Neil's euphoria at having so much cash was however short-lived. He was found dead in a lock-up somewhere north of the River over Enfield Way. The cash that he got for the vans had disappeared. It would be a few months until his body, with a single shotgun around through the roof of his mouth was discovered, and only because the local hairdresser had complained to the council about the bad smell coming from the garages at the back of her salon.

When the police found a decomposing corpse complete with face and brains shattered by a bullet the conclusion was that it was suicide even though a gun was nowhere to be found His heavily pregnant widow did not agree with the coroner's verdict and campaigned tirelessly to get the authorities to change their minds.

She had pleaded with them that he had everything to live for, what with the new baby coming, but the Police had convinced her that the responsibility of a new mouth to feed was too much for her husband and had pushed him over the cliff so to speak.

There was of course an investigation into Neil's financial affairs, but the cash for the five vans sold without V5s had disappeared into thin air. They were never entered on the books. Neil's wife and the son he never got to meet also called Neil in honour of his dead dad never accepted that Neil senior had committed suicide, and when Neil junior fell in with a bad crowd sixteen years later all of his friends were baying for the blood of the investigating Dibble, and when he was twenty Neil junior was on the dole, and a fully paid- up member of the National Front; he and his Nazi cohorts vowed revenge as they considered it a police pig bastard cover-up.

As the five White Vans pulled in one by one five miles away a blue Mercedes Benz was hidden from view but its driver could still observe everything that was happening. This was the prelude to the main event. Through field glasses the Mercs driver saw the five vans were all parked up all facing out, all paused waiting to leave. This is where the main act would start, and all the driver of the Mercedes had to do was make one telephone call. Whilst he watched, the vans departed one by one at five-minute intervals timed by a very expensive Swiss watch. The Mercedes driver felt satisfaction like he hadn't felt since August 1961 when the Antifascist Scutzwall was constructed of barbed wire and concrete in Berlin. He loved to have a finger in every pie.

The nearest public 'phone box was a five-minute walk away. The car's driver being by nature an organised person had five and ten pence pieces already in his jacket pocket which was tweed with a silk lining.

He was supposed to blend in like a countryman if by chance anyone spotted him.

An organised person had five and ten pence pieces ready in his jacket pocket. His boss insisted on him having spare change before he left London. Nothing was to be left to chance, nothing at all.

No one had spotted his Blue Mercedes that had pulled up, reversed in, and was blocking what appeared to be a disused farm track. Its driver rammed the automatic gear shift into the park, got out, and locked the car's doors. Breathing heavily the man left the car and started to jog to the little red box. By the time he got there, he was sweating profusely which annoyed him greatly as it would be the devil's own job to get the stains out of the oxters of his checked shirt. Pulling open the 'phone door he almost recoiled at the smell of urine in it, so holding a handkerchief over his nose quickly dialled a number as timing was of the essence. A voice answered barking out 'Hendrix'.

'To się stało' (It is done), the Mercedes driver said briefly. Distastefully he wiped the receiver with his handkerchief as he did not want to leave any prints, and gently put it. It is back in its cradle.

Now that the first act of the mission was complete, he could return to London. He knew that he should walk casually not rush back to his car, get in, and drive off keeping just under the speed limit. He didn't want to attract any attention, so his steps were measured and precise. He could see his car parked on the curve of the road, in front of the farm track. So far everything was going to plan. Rounding a right-hand curve in the road he stopped in his tracks. Inching up behind his car was something enormous. What the fuck he thought to himself. A dirty great tractor towered over his precious piece of metal like a giant getting ready to devour it. The driver of the Mercedes was well prepared for the unexpected so pulled his Walther PPX pistol from out of the waistband of his trousers. There was no need to attach the silencer which he had secreted in his inner -jacket pocket. For god's sake, he was in the middle of some godforsaken county in an insignificant country. As he approached all he could see was the outline of a ruddy-looking face in high up in the tractor's cabin.

The Tractor driver, a farmer, opened his mouth to expel an expletive. Instead, a bullet was sent from the PPX. It shattered the tractor's windscreen into a million tiny shards, powered on and its 380 ACP bullet lodged itself in the frontal lobe of the farmer's brain. The frontal lobe of the brain contains the motor cortex and controls Thinking, Planning, Organising, Problem-solving, Short-term memory, and Movement. So basically, the farmer would become like one of his crops, a floppy-limbed useless cabbage. His brother, who ran the farm with him would care for him along a road from which there was no return.

The Mercedes driver put his gun back into the waistband of his trousers, got in the car and drove away without a backward glance. All he had to do now was to go home and wait to hear from his police contact about the fate of five different, apparently unconnected van drivers and their passengers. He cracked open a window and felt a cool breeze that ruffled his hair; it felt good, it felt clean after the recent shooting. Cleaner and more satisfied than he had done in a very long time.

CHAPTER 2

THE GEOLOGIST

At seven am on a Friday morning in early May a certain Dr Steven Lawson sighed and stretched out his lean thin frame. His legs being ridiculously long poked out from under his desk along with his size eleven feet which stuck out either side. Sighing, he tried to concentrate on the curriculum that he needed to present to his boss for next year's intake of students. The Faculty Dean had personally insisted that it was handed to him before the end of the current term which was only a few weeks away. Steven Lawson was feeling happy about the upcoming holiday away from the noisy, disgusting students. More so he would be away from the awful Dean. Bloody man thought Steven. Anyone would begin to believe he couldn't be trusted to do his own work.

As usual, Steven had not slept well which was a regular occurrence around this time of year, and he yearned for a caffeine fix. It was way too early to get a hot, lifesaving beverage at this time of day. The damn tea-trolley woman wouldn't be around for a couple of hours yet, and by that time he would be lecturing Engineering Students in Geology. Thinking once, then twice about the drinks machine he rapidly discarded the idea as its 'drinks' were disgusting, foul-tasting stuff, and he did have his standards when it came to coffee after so many years of drinking crap.

An idiotic idea of the Science Faculty Dean was to integrate some of the first-year Mechanical Engineering Students with the Geology course. Steven couldn't complain as he knew that he had to toe the line to earn his meagre stipend and to keep his job. He was proud of the title bestowed on him 'Dr'. It was not just pure luck that he had got the position here. It was all to do with contacts. After a couple more semesters with spotty men (and a few women), he would find a post doing real fieldwork the likes of which he had been trained to many years ago. He had already put feelers out and there was already one possibility. Once he had secured a new job could then try and seek out one of Jo's relatives to let them know how well he was doing. Unfortunately, Jo had died in South America in nineteen-seventy-nine.

The work for now was campus-based but soon the little dears could be let loose with some outdoor work, and when that happened then God helped them (and him). He always considered the engineering students to be Neanderthals. Most of those he would be lecturing to today were big, smelly and hairy, and in his opinion was that they were all dragging their knuckles on the ground. He laughed briefly reflecting that none of the engineering students would ever measure up physically to his ideal specimen of what a man should be.

Trying to balance out practical and theoretical work so that he wasn't going to do too much actual lecturing his train of thought was interrupted by the persistent ringing of the telephone on his desk. He almost didn't answer it, but he would be in even more trouble if he didn't. The night switchboard operator was obviously still on shift. Daft cow, now give him the little blonde who worked the day shift. Picking up the receiver he bawled 'Yes!', rather loudly into it.

'Apologies Dr Lawson ', said the night operator, 'I have just taken a call from a Mr Smith, he urgently wants to meet you at the James Watt gate, sir'. Not known for her discretion, Dr Lawson wanted to keep the conversion brief. 'Mr Smith' was the name of the Gentleman who was giving him a job opportunity away from this hell hole. He had spotted the job as an on-site position for a geologist in the job section of Friday's Leicester Mercury.

It was quite by chance that he had seen it. He had picked up the newspaper that one of his pupils had been reading instead of listening to his Lecture. Glad now that an errant student was not paying attention to his Lecture, he scooped up the journal before anyone else could nab it.

There it was in black and white, so he had dashed off an application that very evening to the PO. Box number that was advertised.

By Monday he had got a reply by return post intimating that he was just right for the job and could expect a call from Mr Smith shortly.

Now this was it! This opportunity could be his golden goose, and the Dean could as the student vernacular said, 'suck it up'.

'Please tell Mr Smith I'll be out immediately, and Mary, don't tell anyone about this', he said imperiously.

Before Mary Goodbody could think of a tart reply to Lawson had slammed the 'phone down and was heading rapidly down the stairs taking them two at a time. Heaven knows what Mr Smith was thinking. The James Watt gate was on the main road and was a busy entrance. It was named after the preserved James Watt & Co. Beam Engine that marked the entry to the university.

Looking out for a prestigious car Dr Lawson was unimpressed by a white van which seemed to be the only vehicle in sight parked up by the James Watt Gate, its engine idling. Just as he was about to tap on the driver-side window the back door of the van opened, and a masked figure grabbed him roughly by the arms and bundled him in the back. Tying Steven's hands and feet and gagging him the back doors were slammed to and locked. Steven could offer little resistance to this as although he was tall, he was useless in a fight or tussle, having very little leg or arm muscle. Banging on the back door with his bound fists and trying to shout for help through the gag. Kicking was not an option as his feet were bound tightly.

If this were a student prank, he was determined that the perpetrators would suffer. Sinking down with a sigh he closed his eyes and hoped that the ordeal would soon be over. No longer banging and thumping he was resigned to the fact that it was one or more student's idea of fun, but then how could they possibly know about his meeting with Mr Smith? Perhaps it was a test of endurance on his part of the unknown Mr Smith. He wasn't going to spoil it now. If it was Smith's idea to test his metal, then so be it.

The driver of the first white van that had departed from the Service Station drove at a steady Sixty-Eight Miles Per Hour until he reached Junction 23 of the M1 Motorway where he had exited on the slip road and took the third exit towards Loughborough then carried on driving towards the town's university. He had been handsomely paid to abduct a man from the James Watt Gate, take him to a predetermined destination, make sure that a package was disposed of and then he could do what he wanted with the captured man. The only proviso was that he drove the designated route first so that he knew how long it would take. Timing was of the essence.

With the snatched doctor now keeping quiet the van drove off just under the speed through Loughborough on the A6, destination Mountsorrel which boasted a granite quarry that was of Special Scientific Interest. What was even better for the van driver was the thirty-six acres of private land surrounding it with no access for the public.

Given that it was still early there was not much traffic on the way to the locality. The only thing that had spotted the white van as it puttered along was a large black crow with an iridescent shine to its feathers who took an instant dislike to the moving object. It swooped down and flapped its wings in front of the van's windshield. Severing a little and cursing under his breath the van driver who wasn't normally superstitious hoped that this was all that was going to befall him on his mission.

The entire journey took eleven minutes and then the van came to a sudden halt crunching on gravel and spraying it everywhere. In the back, using his bound long legs to try and reach the catch on the back door but having to do it by guesswork because of his blindfold, Dr Lawson felt like he was performing an unnatural balancing act as he had to lay flat on his back, legs bound reaching upwards towards where he thought the latch of the door was. The effort it took along with the fact that he was trussed up like a Christmas Turkey made Dr Lawson's breathing b sharp and ragged as he was rapidly trying to suck in air through the gag. When the van had stopped abruptly the man fell back and his head sharply on the side of it.

This shouldn't be happening to him. He should be lecturing undergrads about the earth's crust. Maybe this was Smith's way of testing his metal, but it was a stupid test. After all, he had already been offered a tentative position via a letter from Smith's secretary, hadn't he? He had no reason to suspect Smith. The man was obviously a true gentleman preferring a handwritten letter to a phone call. After all, he was only after employing Lawson for his knowledge, wasn't he?

Doubt began creeping into Dr Lawson's mind. He tried to recall what was said in the letter, and he was damned sure it was something like 'you have the exact knowledge that I am looking for'. Surely that was enough affirmation. Shaken out of his reverie after having been bounced over rough ground, Dr Lawson felt a little bit cheerier. Maybe, at last, he was going to meet the elusive Mr Smith. He told himself to hold in check his thoughts on being bundled unceremoniously into the back of a van. After all, he was about to meet his potential employer.

Getting out of the driver's side and walking around to the back of the van the driver opened the back doors, and grunting pulled out his cargo, then using one hand slammed the van's back doors shut and locked them. He didn't want any chance of seeing the contents of the van - a sawn-off shotgun. He then untied Dr Lawson's hands and feet, then with a swift glance around to see if there were any bystanders the van driver grabbed the Doctor under one arm, and marched him halfway up the quarry, via a steep path, that had been used occasionally and illicitly by lovers and dog walkers.

After telling the doctor he would give him what far if he tried to escape Lawson's captor undid the blindfold that was over the man's eyes. The warnings he had given were the only words he spoke, and the rest of the task was given by hand gestures. Dr Lawson was forced to the ground then he had to dig out a hollow. He was then handed a sackcloth parcel which he had to place in the dugout hollow and cover with the dirt and scrub that lay around.

Doctor Lawson was confused. On being handed the parcel he was sure that he had felt something similar a very long time ago, but it couldn't be, could it? As the object was wrapped in sackcloth, he couldn't confirm his suspicions, but he was sure he remembered the shape, size, and weight of it. What worried him was that he knew blasting would be carried out there later that day and wondered why he had to place the object in such a place. It was also emitting heat and a small pulse-like sensation. As part of his knowledge of granite stone which was the type quarried at Mountsorrel and the extraction thereof, he knew that very soon that it would be either buried under a tonne of rock or would be blown to smithereens.

Thinking that his ordeal would soon be over Lawson was more than a little relieved when he was pulled up from the ground. However, his relief was short-lived when the van driver re-tied the blindfold and started to push him further up the quarry's incline where the well-worn path petered out. Finally, they came to a halt. By Lawson's reckoning, they were near to the very top of the quarry. By now he was sweating profusely with the combined effort of the digging, and then the walk to the top. Gasping for air and struggling to breathe he felt a sharp prod in his back.

Without warning he felt himself toppling over what he assumed was at the very edge at the top of the quarry judging by how far they had walked uphill. As he was blindfolded, he could see nothing but felt a slight warm breeze rustling his hair. Beginning to panic he realised that there was nothing between and thin air. Like a drowning man he scrabbled around for whatever he could grab hold of to break his fall, but on finding nothing, and knowing the imminent danger that hard granite could do on impact he wet himself.

Juddering and bouncing from a great height his broken body came to rest at an awkward angle in a lower area that was due for blasting that day. The scheduled blast did not kill him but the impact of his landing on hard granite did. His neck broken, his arms and legs at odd angles with the blast that afternoon shattering his skull and limbs then exploded granite raining down on top of his body.

Later that morning back at the university twenty-five engineering students gave an almighty cheer when the Faculty Dean entered the lecture theatre just after 9.30 am. They were informed that Doctor Lawson had to take sick leave and that their lecture would be rescheduled. It never was. Had the students found the site where Dr Lawson's remains lay under the pile of granite, they would have spotted in red lettering or possibly blood the words REMEMBER POLAND.

After disposing of the Doctor, the van driver carefully edged his way back down the slope. Jumping cheerily into the driver's seat he started the van. No one appeached him it was too early for the workforce to be out. The only thing that spied him was the obnoxious crow that had divebombed his van earlier. It seemed to be following him around like a harbinger of doom. With a wave of relief and a sigh, he re-joined the A6.

Arriving on the outskirts of the village of Quorn the crow appeared again apparently from nowhere and divebombed his van once more causing him to swerve violently which resulted in him using all his strength to tug at the steering wheel.

An articulated lorry driver, carrying a heavy load had been despatched earlier that day to take goods to Leicester and was heading in the opposite direction. Whistling cheerily, the driver saw a flash of white and then felt something go underneath the wheels of his vehicle. Slamming on the brakes, he climbed out of his cabin.

Five Hundred meters down the road, in a ditch, turned through one hundred and eighty degrees was a white van on its side. Hoping that no one had seen the accident and presuming that the driver wouldn't have survived such a crash the lorry driver had no compunction in getting back into the cab of his lorry. No damage was done to his lorry, no one had seen anything, so with a sigh of relief he continued his journey.

A paperboy late for his rounds that morning spotted the upturned van and cycled hell for leather to the nearest phone box to call the emergency services. A local policeman who had been with the Police Force for just two weeks and an Inspector sent over from Leicester both came to the same conclusion. It was an accident; the road was notorious for incidents on that stretch. Whatever had crushed the van, and its occupant was huge, the road was narrow, and the van driver was obviously distracted. The Inspector surmised that it was something big, possibly a tractor. After all, this was rural Leicestershire so there were plenty of them around. Also being rural Leicestershire there were no witnesses and although cities and towns had some CCTV this village did not. The police records at the time recorded it as an unfortunate accident.

CHAPTER 3

THE MARINE BIOLOGIST

Nottingham University Campus is close enough to Highfield Park for a person to have an early morning dalliance. Peter Higham had slipped away at an unusually early hour from his wife and family at his home in nearby shady Woolton, a sub-district of Nottingham. He had not slept much before. He eagerly anticipated what he was about to indulge in the next day. Trying to hide it from his wife was difficult especially as she had been extremely amorous in bed, so he concocted a headache as an excuse.

It threw his wife off the scent as she knew that had suffered debilitating headaches caused by something that had happened in his past. She never asked, she was just grateful that she had finally caught a man.

Despite having been married for twelve years Peter conceded that the life he had nearly four decades ago was more exciting. Being a young man back then he had at the time as many female companions as he wanted could be procured. He still had wet dreams about one buxom, more mature lady with dark tumbling hair. Rozanne had been gentle with him at first. The harder he worked at his tasks the rougher she treated him. This didn't put him off in the slightest. He had discovered his inner animal through her.

He had met Ruby Cunningham by chance in Slab Square where he had taken an extended lunch break there to eat his egg and cress sandwiches which his wife had dutifully made for him. Ruby was different, exotic, and young. The complete opposite of his miserable fat wife. What Ruby saw in him he did not know. Rather on the short rotund side himself with thick horn-rimmed glasses, he was no Errol Flynn.

He was meeting the delicious Ruby before lectures began. He couldn't think of anything more boring than imparting his knowledge to a charmless bunch of undergrads about Marine Biology. Ironically most of them were more qualified than he was, many of them having obtained a good 'A' level qualification in the subject, or at least in one of the natural sciences.

Ruby was collecting her new Mini today. Of course, he had been only happy to help her out by giving her five hundred pounds towards it. She had squealed with delight when he had agreed to cough up the cash.

She had been so excited and danced around him like a puppy being taken out on a walk the evening that he had eagerly handed over the money. What she didn't know was that he was handing over part of his family's holiday fund. Repeating incessantly time after time in a gleeful voice she shouted, 'It's Pink you know, it's Pink'. Her enthusiasm was catching, and he hoped today they could arrange a little jaunt out in it that evening. Who knew where that would lead him? Hopefully to a little B&B that he knew in Matlock Bath.

Out on the road that passed by Highfield Park he waited a little anxiously. It was early May, and he could smell summer coming. Although he didn't get on with his wife anymore, it was days like these that he was glad that she had at least blessed him with two little ones, who would be begging him for an ice cream from the van that always stopped at the main entrance to Wollaton Hall near to his home.

Inhaling the smell coming from the Bluebells scattered like a carpet under the trees he felt good about life. The Bluebells reminded him of the Edelweiss that spread like a thick coating of icing sugar by Lake Zurich which he had seen once from a boat. He remembered the lake with its glittering water and the little chalets nestling in the hillside. They were simpler days.

Sighing, he glanced at his watch. It was an expensive Swiss precision one that he had to have sent over to him at an enormous cost. His wife berated him about it, but he had just shrugged his shoulders nonchalantly.

Thinking that he may have missed the Pink Mini he stepped forward towards the edge of the kerb. As he did so a white van almost knocked him flying. The driver of the van pulled up sharply, got out and gestured towards the back doors. Thinking that there was a first aid kit in the back, as he was damn sure he had sprained his ankle and hoping that the driver had a first-aid kit he was surprised to feel a meaty hand on his back, guiding him roughly towards the back of the van. What he didn't notice was a Crow in the treetop above beadily watching them both.

Putting up a struggle and yelling for help the other meaty hang clamped itself firmly around his mouth. He was damned if he was giving in without a fight. Things like that didn't happen in Nottingham in broad daylight, did it? Kicking out he managed to catch his captor on the shin. Cursing at him, the van driver took the rope he was holding in one hand and tied Higham's hands behind his back.

Bundling him into the back of the van face down on the floor he was then blindfolded and gagged, with ropes binding his hands and feet. There was nothing more that he could do apart from lying there trying hard to breathe. The floor of the van smelt of diesel. God, he hoped he wasn't going to be sick he thought to himself. He would surely choke with this gag in his mouth.

Inside the van, all sorts of thoughts swam through the man's head. Maybe his wife had twigged about what was happening between him and Ruby or had discovered the missing five hundred pounds and was getting her revenge in some sort of warped sort of way, but surely even she wouldn't do that. Then he had the fleeting thought that it could be one of Ruby's family, seeing as she was from a different culture, and they would not approve. Breathing heavily, he squirmed around on the uncomfortable floor.

Earlier that day, after leaving the enclave of vans at the service station, the second van driver made his way North up the M1 until he reached junction 26 where he picked up the route for Nottingham. Dawdling a little, as he had to get there by a certain time, he waved graciously at cars honking their horns as they overtook him. Eyes on his rearview mirror, he spotted a Police Car about 200 meters away also in the slow lane. So he sped up a little; not enough to draw attention to himself though. He was just an ordinary man, on his way to work, with an ordinary sawn-off shotgun hidden under the front passenger seat. Once he had secured his target in the back of his van, he proceeded to his designated destination which was Ratcliffe on Soar approximately ten miles away.

Encountering very little traffic and with only the Marine Biologist specialist as silent company he pulled up in a lay-by and felt underneath the front passenger for a parcel wrapped in sackcloth that needed to be delivered. Juggling it in his hands, as it had started to radiate a gentle yet persistent heat he walked around to the back doors of the van. Grunting and panting it took him some physical efforts and pushing and shoving to get the Marine Biologist out of the van even though he had tucked the parcel underneath his armpit where it still radiated a strange heat.

As they were in the middle of nowhere and given that the next stage of the operation was tricky, he untied the man's hands and feet. By now Higham was extremely pissed off and tried to make a run for it. He wasn't fit at all nor in the prime of youth. He managed to get twenty yards away before he was felled swiftly and efficiently at the knees by the van driver who in another life was a rugby player. Without being able to see a thing, as he was still blindfolded Higham was grabbed roughly by the hands of the van driver until he was upright, then frogmarched a few hundred yards.

Peter's sense of smell was very, very keen, which had saved him many years ago from an almost certain death. He hadn't passed any exams in science, but he did know all about river, stream, and pond life. He could detect a whiff the of distinctive odour of Otter spraint (poo), which must have meant they were close to an Otter's Holt. He couldn't for the life of him think as to why he had to be captured and brought to the water's edge where one could usually find this evasive, shy, creature.

Gasping suddenly, his blindfold was torn from his eyes, and all he could see was bright sunlight. He was indeed at the edge of a very fast-flowing stream His sense of smell had not let him down. Grunting and shoving again, he was pushed downwards and then pressed so close to the stream's bank that he feared he might fall in. He was handed a package by the van driver who was extremely pleased to pass it on; a little like the childhood party game of passing the parcel, only the time he was the one who didn't want to unwrap any layers.

Pointing to the Otters Holt, which was a hole in the bank of the stream the van driver grunted. Presuming that the van driver wanted the parcel to be placed at this spot and holding it carefully so as not to drop it in the stream, Higham gently pushed it into the Holt. Although he was under a lot of duress, he felt sorry for the poor otters who would find something that now blocked their natural habitat. Sighing heavily, he was about to elbow his way from the edge when he felt a sharp jab to his kidneys.

Physically he was in poor shape. Because of the way he was dangling over the stream, he felt the top part of his torso sliding. Glancing up he realised that the scenario was all wrong. A flapping sound caught his attention. It was a nasty big crow staring directly at him with its beady eyes, of this, he was sure. But then it was just a bird, wasn't it?

Now Peter was not a superstitious man. He always walked under ladders and wasn't too bothered about a black cat crossing his path;

Friday the thirteenth didn't worry him particularly either. But this big black thing was to him a harbinger of doom, an omen of some sort.

The gathering momentum with the combination of his body and the slippery stream bank began to take its toll. His body slid gracelessly into the stream. Screaming loudly his mouth filled quickly with water. Flaying around he managed to grab hold of the side of the bank. Thinking he would be able to hoist himself up he gave a might heave. One thing was against him being successful in his attempt to save himself, and that was his size. His portly figure wedged itself between the bank and a large stone.

Struggling to breathe, sweating and cursing he was relieved to find what he thought was a foothold. Footholds are fine if they are dry. This one wasn't as it was submerged in water and was covered in green, slippery slime. The slime was his undoing, and with the feeling that the earth was shifting from under his foot, he crashed into another large bolder, banged his head, and fell back into the stream landing on his back, and looking very much like a stranded whale with water lapping over his face.

From the bank, the van driver watched in satisfaction. What he wasn't counting on though was the most bizarre thing happening. He spotted about twenty or so otters crossing a dimly lit path. The animal encounter went south after a jogger out for an early morning run ran across the path causing the fish-eaters to go crazy. Instead of following the jogger they turned on the van driver who up until now was watching the spectacle and started to bite and attack him on the ankles.

Pushing the van driver down they leapt on him and proceeded to bite the prone man on the legs and buttocks, with one having the audacity to nip his finger. He was bitten maybe twenty-six times in a frenzied attack that lasted for ten seconds. The cantankerous creatures then ceased the assault and jumped off the stream's bank into the fast-flowing water.

The jogger, although a little bemused by seeing a bunch of otters did not want to break stride and carried on as though nothing had happened. He did not see two separate reports in the Nottingham Evening Post one about a man who had seemingly been attacked by an unidentified wild creature, nor the report on a Lecturer of Marine Biology lecturer from Nottingham University dying in a drowning accident after apparently slipping and hurting his head on a rock whilst searching for pond-life; why he had decided to go to the stream when he should have been at the University that morning was never established.

Before the residents of the Holt returned, and before the Police had discovered the two bodies, water swirled rapidly around the Holt and into it. All that was left was a piece of sacking that made a nice cosy nest for the otters. The contents of the package, secured now in a goatskin tube, sailed merrily down the stream.

What the Police had failed to mention in any of their reports or press rereleases was the fact that they didn't think that it was pertinent to the case, the words carved out just above the waterline of the stream in what appeared to be red paint were two words - they read REMEMBER POLAND. They assumed it was local yobs.

CHAPTER 4

THE SWIMMING INSTRUCTOR

It was a glorious May evening. Neil who was a Swimming Instructor at the cities' swimming baths was bored, so very bored. This wasn't what he signed up for when he took the job. He thought that there would be an endless line of bikini-clad beauties clamouring for swimming lessons with him. Instead of a bevvy of beauties, he had an endless line of school kids, queueing up to get the fifty pence crash course for the under fourteen. He swore blind that considering the height of some the boys, and girls come to that were well over the age of fourteen and had joined the course so that they could swim for less.

Possibly it was his bad acne that had put the ladies off, but he made up for it in the looks department by having collar-length blonde hair, and piercing baby-blue eyes.

His duties due to the fact that the city's council leisure services were vastly underfunded also included cleaning out the changing rooms. He began to hate the chewing gum he kept finding in the boys' changing room, and unmentionable items in the girls changing room. The trouble was, despite his swimming prowess, this shitty little job was all he could get.

As most of the kids who came to his lessons were from the nearby council estate he had to his disappointment not come across any fancy underwear yet. Hope springs eternal he thought. One day, just one day he might meet someone like the lovely Rozanne, who despite her circumstances always managed to wear the most perfect silk underwear and stockings.

Sighing wistfully, he was jerked back into the present by a man easily in his twenties posing a question to him.

'Excuse me, Sir, please', asked the man in pidgin English. 'You give me swimming lessons, no?'

'Not here' the swimming instructor whispered looking shiftily around. Maybe he could make a bob or two out of this odd-speaking man. Deciding that he fancied a bit of danger and fed up with his current duties, he murmured out of the corner of his mouth, 'Do you know the Red Lion on Carrington Street? Meet me there at 8 p.m. tonight and we can reach a mutual agreement.

Not waiting for a response, he carried on sweeping out the male changing room, whistling tunelessly. Possibly this was the goose that would lay the golden egg. Now his work did not seem that boring at all. A foreigner without a good grasp of the English language could scam a lot of money from him, and a couple of free beers off him if he played his cards right.

At eight precisely the swimming instructor strolled into the Red Lion on Carrington Street. The bar was jam-packed that evening. After scanning the room, he spotted the stranger from earlier on propping up the bar. Looking like he had been drinking a while the swimming instructor casually sidled through the crowd. On reaching the bar, which took a bit of effort on his part, and noticing that the stranger was brandishing a ten-pound note trying to catch the busy barman's eye, he gave him a hearty clap on the back.

'Mines a Pint of Double Diamond', he said to the stranger cheerfully as though they were old mates.

Once they had their drinks, the Swimming Instructor whispered into the stranger's ear,

'Over here mate, let's see if we can find a quiet corner to talk.'

Holding his Pint carefully in one hand, he guided the stranger to a table that had fortuitously been vacated in a dark corner right next to the fireplace that was set back in an inglenook.

He noticed that the stranger had followed him with an unsteady gait. Good, the man was already three sheets to the wind. Placing his Pint of Guinness precariously on the edge of the copper-topped table the stranger sank down with a sigh. Looking quizzically at the swimming instructor he slumped forward almost knocking his drink off the table.

'So', began the swimming Instructor, 'where do you hail from then, I haven't seen you around these parts.'

'Please Sir, I am coming from the Market Harborough if you know it Sir', answered the stranger politely.

Puffing his chest out with some pride and pleased that the stranger knew his place in life, the swimming instructor scratched his chin as though in deep thought when really his mind was racing through all sorts of possibilities.

As though reading his thoughts, the stranger then posed a question which took the swimming instructor by surprise and completely blindsided the swimming instructor. With so much eagerness in the stranger's voice, how could he possibly refuse a request? It was an odd one though the stranger wanted to learn to swim in Foxton Locks.

'Please Mr Sir, I am good friends with Lock Keeper at Foxton Locks. If I ask then he will ensure gates are left unlocked, and we can go there to learn to swim. I pay you one hundred of the English Pounds Sir'.

Again, the scratching of the skin. The swimming instructor knew that Foxton Locks was a series of five descending locks. It was fraught with danger for a beginner, and yet one hundred Pounds was a lot of money.

'Two things', he said in a faux serious voice. 'One yes, we can go to Foxton Locks, but it will have to be early in the morning and two how the hell will you get to Foxton Locks?'

'Well Mr Sir, I travel to Foxton Locks on my Bicycle. It is three little miles from where I am living. I can do seven of the clocks if you allow me to go home now, and if you teach me the swimming tomorrow, I pay you another fifty pounds.'

Never for one to look a gift horse in the mouth, and thinking what he could do with the money, he extended his hand to the stranger.

'We have a deal. I'll see you at seven, there is a layby nearby. I'll wait in my car until I see your bike,' replied the Swimming Instructor a little shakily. He had never had that sort of money in his life.

The swimming instructor eagerly drove to Foxton Locks and parked up early the next morning. He waited in the layby as instructed near the locks in anticipation of spotting the stranger's bike. It was well after seven by now, and he'd almost given up hope when he spied a white van coming towards him. His hopes were dashed. What if the Van followed him and the stranger to Foxton Locks, or worse got there before him?

The third van driver drove North up the M1 until he reached Junction 23. His orders also told him to exit at this junction and take the A6 South. Before leaving London, he had tested the parcel that he would take with him in a fish tank the night before to see how long it took to decompose. He hadn't got the time to check on it the next day, he had a journey up the M1 to early the next day.

If he had checked the tank, he would have found the parcel bobbing around at the top of it trying to untangle itself from the sackcloth it was wrapped in. He would also have seen his tropical fish floating dead at the top of the tank. But he didn't do any of those things. He just assumed that it wasn't heavy enough to sink when he found it early the next morning. Rolling up his short sleeve he plunged his hand into the tank to get the parcel out of the with one hand whilst drinking a cup of tea with the other. Shaking off the water he rewrapped it in its sackcloth.

After leaving the A6 the van driver took the A459 to Market Harborough, and then a few minor roads to Foxton Locks which consisted of ten Locks which had been backbreakingly carved by hand through the Leicestershire countryside.

Just before seven after waiting over the brow of a hill, the van driver watched as a car pulled in close to the Locks. He drove towards the lay-by and pulled up behind the swimming instructor's car. Then he got out of his van and tapped sharply on the car window. Opening the car door, and swinging his legs to the ground, the swimming instructor was taken by surprise with a blow to his Solar Plexus. Winded, and uncertain as to what was happening to him, he was unceremoniously bound and gagged then roughly thrown roughly into the back of the white van.

The van driver headed towards the locks. One problem that he had to navigate which hopefully shouldn't provide too much of an inconvenience was that the entrance to the Locks was always padlocked overnight to stop misuse of the water. Lady Luck was on his side. No one was around so he got out and opened the back door of the van. He then took a pair of bolt cutters and a parcel wrapped in sackcloth which he held gingerly as he already knew what damage it could do to his fingers.

Leaving the van parked behind the deserted Lock-Keepers cottage he pushed the swimming instructor slowly along in the small of his back he told the swimming instructor that if he tried to escape, he would shoot him in the head. His instructions were to improvise as much as he could and to keep communication to a minimum, so being a sadistic bastard, he thought he might as well engage in a bit of sport.

The van driver repeated his last words again, took his eyes off the swimming instructor for a second or two, took out his bolt cutters again and snapped open the padlocks on the fifth lock. For a fleeting moment, the swimming instructor thought about escaping. A swift glance at the van driver stopped him in his tracks. The man had a parcel under his arm which may have been a gun.

Pushing the Swimming Instructor down on the dew-soaked grass the van driver rolled the swimming instructor onto his stomach as close to the edge of the canal as he could. Handing the unfortunate and sobbing man an object wrapped in sackcloth he guided the man's hands towards the water where the object dropped in with a satisfying plop.

Congratulating himself on a job well done, the van driver started manhandling the lock until it started to fill up. The swimming instructor lying on his stomach could only hope and pray that he would survive. He had no idea what was about to befall him.

A boat hook that the sadistic van driver had found abandoned nearby was his weapon of choice, and he cleaved the poor swimming instructor's skull with it, causing an awful, bloody mess. He then hoisted the body with the skull caved in, a few feet into the air, and dumped him over the side of the canal.

Feeling a sudden change in the air, a whiff of petrol maybe, the van driver turned around quickly, but too late, his own white van was bearing down on him and hit him with force. The van driver fell without ceremony into the filled lock.

The lockkeeper was on an unexpected holiday in the peak district with his wife and children at the time. An unknown person had posted two hundred pounds in used fivers through his letter box. Maybe it was the lovely O'Malley family whom he had shown the locks the other week. They all took a keen interest in the working of the locks, especially the father who asked all sorts of questions on the mechanics and whether was it possible to open a lock oneself without any help.

The lockkeeper was exonerated from both unfortunate incidents. The assumption that the Police made was that the first body had fallen into the lock after trying to open the lock gate. The second was apparently trying to rescue the first with a boat hook but had stumbled on it, and had also fallen into the lock. It was also assumed that the van driver had left the handbrake off, and the van had rolled forward.

As for the swimming instructor's car that had been found abandoned in a layby; well, it was an old wreck of a Ford Cortina that had no insurance and no MOT so the owner could not be traced. There was something strange about the whole situation though. No matter how much scrubbing and overpainting there remains to this day on the wall of lock five, emblazoned in Red Paint orb Blood the words REMEMBER POLAND.

Nottingham City Council were pissed off that their swimming Instructor-cum cleaner had upped sticks and left without a word. They only used to pay him at just below minimum wage, and it would cost them dearly to find a replacement.

A week later a nice Asian gentleman who spoke perfect English showed up at the swimming pool enquiring about a job. He has many commendations for his swimming and was happy to clean the changing rooms as well.

CHAPTER 5

THE CHEMIST

Chris Paulson hated doing a double shift. He usually got home in the early hours of the morning, had a few hours of skip, and then managed to see the kids before they skipped off to school. All apart from Johnny who was placed in a wooden playpen and given saucepans and a wooden spoon with the new baby coming soon, he needed all the sleep he could get. Five kids with another on the way plus two adults in a two up two down with an outside toilet. After the war, he didn't get married for a long time. Not that he'd gone off woman, there just wasn't the one. So here he was at fifty-six married to Rachel who already had a baby by someone else when he married her, worrying about how they would be able to feed all of them.

This shift was going to be a bitch though and would completely throw his body clock out of kilter. He had been persuaded by the new guy who hailed from Hong Kong to cover his shift for today. There had been some talk about a Chinese holiday that the new twerp couldn't miss out on as he was purportedly very religious.

The position that he and the new guy held was that of Chief Mixers. Chris had earned his name The Chemist by always boasting about his degree in Chemistry, and that he was too grand for the job of a mere mixer. Several people had plucked up the courage over the eighteen years he had been at the factory, but Chris had always managed to deflect having to answer directly by always muttering something vaguely about abroad.

The fourth van that had rendezvoused at Leicester Forest East also as per instructions drove North up the M1, exited at junction 25, then took the A52 to Derby, from whence it took the A6005, its destination the British Celanese Factory. During the 2nd World War, the Company amongst other things manufactured fabrics for clothing, webbing, and parachutes. Also, one of the main things being used in the mix was acetone, which was an ideal substitute for glass, of which a lot was smashed due to bombing during the war. It still uses Acetone now.

The name of British Celanese had long gone, the company being taken over several times over the decades. All the van driver cared about was getting to a designated place at a designated time. What the van driver also didn't know was that the Spontoon site that he was heading towards was constructed of over 30 million bricks, and the original site covered 121 hectares. This was almost as big as the three Auschwitz camps which if you added up camps 1, 2, and were about 150 hectares. Not relevant to the job, was it?

The security guard at Spondon's British Celanese site had already been bribed heavily. He was moving to Hong Kong soon. His old pal from the Royal Navy Reserve was the now governor of Hong Kong and Edward Youde would probably welcome him with open arms and would agree that what was doing was just a minor blip in an otherwise unblemished career. He might even get himself a job at Government House running the security there.

The arm of the security gate was lifted without any hesitation by the security guard to let a single white van through. The last shift had gone home, the am shift had cloaked on, but the Chemist was still at his position. The new man, whose shift he had swapped with hadn't turned up for work yet, and Chris couldn't leave his Vats unattended.

This drop-off was probably one of the most difficult of the operation. The fourth van driver had to take his get into the mixing room. He had to get the Chemist to take the parcel and place it into the VAT which contained the acetone mix.

Tiptoeing in, the van driver had a quick look around and was relieved that no one was there apart from the one Chemist. The Van driver had already donned all-black clothing and a ski mask. He looked a terrifying sight to the Chemist as he was pointing a sawn-off shotgun in his direction which resulted in the Chemist throwing his hands up in abject horror.

Gingerly passing the parcel and feeling foolish as if he were in a children's party game, he gestured towards the open Vat. Taking the parcel the Chemist grimaced. Although he was wearing protective gear to ward off any misspelt acetone, he thought that his hands were going to burn. The parcel was hot.

Nodding towards the Vat, the van driver stepped back a few paces as though he knew something would happen. He really wanted to flee the room and retreat to the safety of his van. The Chemist, knowing that the slightest change to the contents of the Vat could have disastrous consequences was loath to put the parcel in it. He was caught between a rock and a hard place; risk getting his hands burnt off by this innocuous sackcloth-wrapped parcel or risk a hazardous incident.

He wanted to preserve his hands. He had dealt with difficult situations before, so he tossed the parcel into the Vat, and quickly ran to the door where the van driver now crouched with his hands over his head and face. Doing the same, they both waited with bated breath. At first, nothing seemed to happen, and then slowly like a red mist stealthily rolling in at floor level, a low-level layer of smoke started to creep slowly towards them.

The van driver had had enough. He wasn't paid danger money, so he tried to yank the door of the mixing room open, but it wouldn't budge. The Chemist on seeing this put one arm across his face so as not to breathe in more fumes. The red mist was spreading its tendrils through the mixing room now snaking around every corner. Standing up the Chemist slammed a shoulder into the door, but it remained closed.

Neither man could reach the alarm button which was located on the wall next to the door. There was no escape. Both men tried to hammer on the bottom of the door with their feet. What they didn't realise is that gradually their limbs were becoming paralysed. Neither had the energy or the capacity to make an impact on the door.

The Company's Chief Operating Officer just happened to pay a visit that day. As a senior manager, he didn't need to request access to the mixing room. His company accountant had told him that he had to start cutting costs or else the company would go under. One of the first things he had done to counter this was to change to a cheaper supplier of acetone; one that was produced in Hong Kong.

The COO's first call was to the mixing room so that he could see for himself how things were working out. The only trouble was he couldn't open the door. Two bodies lay slumped on the other side, both dead. Thinking that one of his Chief Mixers had deliberately locked the door, and being as he was important, he hit the other emergency button which was located on the outside of the mixing room next to the door like its twin inside.

Three men came charging towards the COO. He stood there as cool as a cucumber timing how long they took to respond. Frustratingly they took too long. The first responder smashed a glass box next to the alarm and took out a key which he waved in front of the COO's nose as if to wordlessly say that the COO was a prize prick. Smoothly inserting the key in the lock, he smirked as he turned it, but nothing happened. Wiggling it around a bit he tried again. Now feeling like a prize prick, he nodded to the man next to him who had grabbed a pickaxe on his way to the emergency.

Hacking at the door and glass, which were both incredibly strong due to the fact that it was a safety door. By now the COO was getting angrier and angrier. He ran his fingers under the collar of his pristine white shirt which his wife had lovingly ironed for him that morning. Beads of sweat were gripping down his now furrowed brow, and his beetled brows were drawn close together, so his face started to the look of a wet catapultier.

His breathing became laboured. Something was triggering an asthma attack. Sneaking under the door, and first tickling, then irritating everyone's throat, a fine red mist started to rise around them. Thinking he was going to have a heart attack at any moment, the

COO pointed weakly to a 'phone that was on the wall furthest from him.

Nodding briefly the third member of the rescue team grabbed the CCO under one arm, dragged him towards the 'phone and then dialled 999. Clearing the area around him and shouting for everyone to get outside he dragged the COO to the car park. As the alarm had been triggered, hundreds of people ran our walked nonchalantly out of he is building like a line of ants at a picnic. Most of them seemed to be gathering around where he had parked his new Bentley. Gulping in the fresh air, and still feeling slightly sick he elbowed his way through the crowd parted like the Red Sea. A white van had smashed into his pride and joy, leaving it almost destroyed. He now was physically sick. This was a sight; some may say a treat to see the COO vomit over his highly polished black Loakes shoes.

As the fire brigade started to arrive the crowd moved so they could watch their arrival. After a brief discussion with the company's first responder, the sub-officer barked out orders to the crews. Two of the crew members were then suited in Hazchem suits and given breathing apparatus. After giving them both a tally (a way of keeping a tab on who went in and out) he patted them on the back and sent them inside.

Ten minutes later they both came out, each carrying a man on their backs. They both lay the bodies on the ground. The older crew member shook his head at the sub-officer, and the younger crew member was bravely trying to hold back his tears.

When the fire crews had finished, and when the bodies found in the mixing room had been taken to the morgue from whence, they would eventually go autopsied all that was left was the sad task of informing Chris's wife as to what had happened. The other body had not been identified. On clearing the mixing room an eagle-eyed fireman had spotted a sawn-off shotgun, which unsurprisingly yielded no fingerprints.

No one saw the parcel that the van driver had been carrying, that the chemist had put into the Vat, whose chemical reaction caused the catastrophe to fall from the edge of the Vat and into roll the drain at the end of the mixing room. This was the drain that got sluiced down every day after each shift had finished.

What the Chairman of the company did find though when visiting the factory late that afternoon to boost the morale of the workers was an unexpected sight. In red blood, or maybe paint on the side of the Vat were two words – REMEMBER POLAND.

CHAPTER 6

THE MATHEMATICIAN

Fredrick Najdowski hated the new Headmaster. The man was too keen on making his mark with the school Governors. Fredrick despised the way his boss fawned over the Chair of the school governors who to Fredrick's disgust drove a a bright Yellow BMW. This begged the question in Fredrick man was it possible that the Chairman had been receiving back-handers to be appointed?

The new school governor wanted the staff to come up with new teaching incentives. He held the view that the school was stuck in the nineteen-fifties. The place had been built nineteen-fifty-six and its teaching methods had not changed much since then. What stuck in Fredrick's craw was that both headmaster and governor seemed to be working hand in glove. Change was happening, he didn't like it, did not want it, he had seen enough, and had been through enough upheavals to last him a lifetime. One of the new incentives was the Mathletes every week. To prepare for them, and as head of maths, Fredrick found to his dismay that he was starting work earlier and earlier.

The 5th van driver exited the M1 at junction 23, and took the New Ashby Road, then turned right onto the Old Ashby Road. Heading towards the school where Fredrick taught, he spotted road signs indicating that road works were in place ½ mile away. Leicestershire County Council had decided in their infinite wisdom that the Old Ashby Road was in much need of repair after the preceding winter storms.

Deciding that he would chance it and knowing that there was a big bonus for completing the job, the van driver drove through a red temporary traffic light with the assumption that no one would be coming the other way. Bruce Champion, an experienced HGV driver decided that as he had plenty of time before his load had to be delivered would drive down Old Ashby Road and pay a visit to his sister who lived at number 76. As the temporary traffic lights were green, he swung his arctic through them, and across into the other lane.

Heading towards him was a white transit van, which swerved violently to the left, ploughed through a hedgerow, and came to its final resting place a few hundred yards into Garendon Parkland. The Lorry driver shrugged his shoulders, decided he would not call in on his sister, and carried on heading for the M1. He decided not to report the incident to the authorities as technically he was breaking the terms of his work contract.

Looking out of his bedroom window, having claimed the best and biggest one from his nan, whom he had lived with since his mum had died, Andrew Bruce, a pupil at the local Junior school saw what had happened. As the van had bounced across the fields out of control, he had seen the back door fly open. Thinking he might find some 'spoils' in the back of it, he called out to his nan that he was off to see his friend Gary who lived on the street behind him. His back garden fence happened to be Gary's back garden fence as well, which was convenient for what he had in mind.

Standing on tiptoe, he whistled twice. The boys had been old muckers ever since they started Junior School nearly four years ago. They were the bane of their poor teacher's life and were always up to shenanigans. They had both promised solemnly to behave at the end-of-year disco in a few weeks' time, but that was a few weeks, and like many eleven-year-olds, they lived in the here and now.

Meeting up outside Mrs. Bruce's front gate they dashed across the road to the fields opposite. Legally this was De Lisle land owned by one of the local gentries, but most of the kids, and some of the adults off the council estate where Andrew and Gary resided had illicitly tramped through the corn fields leaving a well-worn path. Following this took them onto Garenden Park, also privately owned land, where the folly known as the Temple of Venus was located. ⍰

By now both boys were a little wary and circled around the upturned van. They weren't afraid of dead or mutilated bodies as they had read enough of Gary's older brother's horror comics to know what a headless corpse looked like. They were less sceptical about the tales of the temple being haunted by one Ambrose Phillips who had the temple erected during the mid-thirties of the eighteenth century. They might have been two worldly-wise boys always ready with plenty of backchat at school, but this was on a different level.

To their astonishment, no one was in either the driver or passenger seat. Running gleefully around to the back where they knew the back doors were open, they saw teetering on the edge of the open door poised to tumble out at any moment an object wrapped in sackcloth. A gift from the Gods surely?

Reaching up to grab it and stuffing it up his tatty jumper Gary decided that he and Andy could have some fun with it at the end-of-term disco in a few weeks' time. What better way than to frighten teachers and pupils than with a sawn-off shotgun?

Deciding that there may be more inside he gave Andy a leg up to climb inside. Andy briefly scanned the inside of the van homing in like a homing Pidgeon to something that had tumbled over. Whistling to Gary to indicate that he needed a hand getting out of the van, he took one last look around, gripped Gary by the hand, and jumped out onto the ground.

What he did see but didn't tell Gary was another item also wrapped up in sackcloth. He knew that he and Gary had a friend's code, but this was one little secret he would keep to himself and collect under the cover of darkness.

Giggling all the way home they parted at Andy's front date, with Gary now carrying their cache under his arm. His mum and dad were permanently pissed and wouldn't notice anything out of the ordinary. In fact, they noticed truly little these days. The only concern to Gary was his older brother Mark who was nearly 16. Still, he could stash it in the outhouse at the back of the coal bunker for now.

That evening Andy waited impatiently for his Nan to leave for her regular weekly bingo. As it was getting on for midsummer it didn't get dark until late. His nan's bingo finished at 10.00 p.m., then it was coat on and a swift Guinness at the social club, and then the last bus back to the estate, a brief walk, and a soak her feet if her bunions were giving her gyp.

He calculated that he had about an hour. Maybe a bit longer if Nan bumped into Mrs Nosey Barker who lived at No. 48 by the jitty, and whose house his nan would have to pass on the way back from the bus; she did like to natter the old bag, but it would work in his favour tonight. Pulling on an old well-worn khaki jumper – a cast off from Gary's Brother's army cadet phase, and after considering blackening his face with boot polish, then deciding no, how would he explain it he sneaked out of the front door. Holding his breath, he ran swiftly across the open field where the moon was lighting his path. He didn't want to take a torch on the off chance he would be spotted by a nosey neighbour. When he got within striking distance of the temple of Venus, he thought for a moment that he was in the wrong place, or it had been an hallucination.

He knew he was in the right spot when he spotted a wrapper for PK chewing gum on the ground. This was the brand that Gary favoured and had ferociously been chewing it that morning. What he also spotted, but failed to connect the dots was the end of a still glowing cigarette butt, which was flashing like a warning beacon. Alongside, it was the second sackcloth-wrapped parcel also glowing and pulsating.

Gingerly picking it up and stuffing it into one of his Nan's shopping bags which he had liberated for the job he swiftly glanced around. With a sudden feeling of doom, even greater than when Mr Beighton who taught the top set at school was about to give you the cane, he spotted the words painted in fresh red or maybe in blood. REMEMBER POLAND.

Not caring to hang around he stumbled blindly back the way he came, stuffed the parcel under his bed, and jumped in still dressed in the old combat jumper. The next day when his nan went to wake him, she thought with a sigh that the poor lad had been playing soldiers and had fallen asleep fully clothed. Little did she know.

Earlier that day, before the two boys had managed to get across the fields, and whilst Andy was whistling for then waiting for Gary to meet him, unbeknown to them, on his way to school to make an early start was Fredrick Najdowski who decided to take a detour via the temple of Venus. He was accompanied by his springer spaniel Torrid who he sometimes sneaked into school.

Torrid was in full tracking mode with both tail and ears up and nose to the ground. With an excited yelp, he suddenly shot off and started barking furiously. Huffing and puffing behind due to his 20 fags a day habit, Fredrick followed, and to his surprise found Torrid sniffing around an upside-down white Transit Van, with an unconscious man draped over the steering wheel. Looking back Fredrick saw tyre tracks in the dust where the van had skidded.

Leaning his head through at an awkward angle, he called out to the unconscious man who was struggling to come around.

'Daft Bugger', intoned Fredrick. 'Now if he's local, he'd know that those traffic lights haven't worked in weeks.'

Slinging a meaty arm around him and hoisting the now groaning man out of the window, a sudden movement caught Fredrick's eye. A piece of paper fluttered to the ground. Curious as to what it said he held the man under one armpit and read aloud what the paper said. Two words Fredrick Najdowski. Almost dropping the man back into the van, he staggered back.

Deciding that he wanted to find out more he managed to tug open the driver's door and pulled the van driver fully out, and with Torrid now yapping excitedly at his heels, dragged the semi-conscious man back to his Morris Traveller Estate.

Opening his car's back door, he unceremoniously shoved the van driver in the boot then opened the passenger door for Torrid to jump in. Gunning his car towards home and making it back in record time pushing all thoughts of school and Matheletes to the back of his mind, he pulled up some 15 minutes later outside a well-kept double-fronted bungalow.

Firstly, he let an excited Torrid out then he yanked the van driver out of the boot of the Traveller. Forgetting to wipe his feet, and the paws of Torrid, he called out, 'Muriel we have a visitor'.

Seconds later a small, homely woman who was barely four feet eleven inches compared to Fredricks Six feet two, and with round spectacles perched on the end of her nose appeared. She had long yellow hair and was of an interminable age. Showing an excited Torrid into the kitchen she peered up at the man that her husband had dragged in.

'Bleddy Hell', she shouted. 'You should be at your sodding job by now. What the bleddy hell are you doing back home?

Dropping the unconscious man in a heap on the floor, Fredrick shoved the piece of paper with his name on it under her nose. Standing on tiptoe she reached up to snatch it out of his hand.

'Double hell teeth', she said sinking down onto a plump overstuffed sofa. 'What the actual...'. Trailing off she looked at the man on the floor. 'You don't suppose', she continued almost in a whisper, 'that they've found out about you. I mean had he a gun or anything?

'Crashed his van running some lights he did', replied. Fredrick. 'I don't think there was a gun. If it was there then it disappeared. All that I could find was this scrap of very disturbing paper. I take it you won't be going to the Bingo tonight then as you'll be this little problem out?'

'Consider it done', chortled Muriel. I'll get D.P. to help me out, though technically he ain't passed his driving test yet, as they say, is a minor detail'.

Patting her hand with one huge paw he hauled the van driver to his feet.

'Coal bunker for you lad until tonight', he whispered into the man's ear.

Extract from the Leicester Mercury 4th May 1985

"A man was found wandering around Bradgate Park early this morning. The man who was naked and who had a broken arm, a sprained ankle, and mild hypothermia has been taken to Leicester Royal Infirmary where police hope to question him later.

The man was in no state to give out any information but kept on babbling the words 'Remember Poland' repeatedly.

The man was found by an early dog walker who wishes to remain anonymous.

Below is a sketch of the person who was found. If anyone has any information about him, then please call Leicestershire Police on ...."

PART 3 – REMEMBER POLAND

EXTRACT FROM THE DIARY - AUTHOR UNKNOWN.

Of course, I found the man wandering around Bradgate part. He didn't have any clothes on. I didn't expect to find him there. I was just killing time. I hated my job so much that I didn't want to do anything today.

I remember that it was a wet and foggy day. I decided to call in at the tea rooms in Newtown Linford, a charming Leicestershire village. After that, I decided that a roam in Bradgate Park was just the ticket, so I drove over there in the car that was provided to me by my job. I would have to explain all the mud on it later, but that was another problem.

As I walked along the path trying to spot the deer that roamed there I literally stumbled across a naked man. He was shivering due to the cold. His eyes were pleading with me to help him, his teeth were chattering making it impossible for him to speak. I took one disgusted look at him, decided that it was too much trouble to notify anyone, and legged it back to my car leaving the poor sod moaning and groaning. Someone would stumble on him surely.

CHAPTER 1

לפני הלכידה (BEFORE CAPTURE)

My name is Hamadej which means Love of God. I was born in 1936 in Gdansk which was officially annexed by Germany on the 1st of September 1939. By 1941 only six hundred Jews were still living there. Most of the Jewish community had already left apart from the elderly, or infirm. Many of the remaining people were herded into a ghetto.

My parents were Jewish or so I thought. Neither of them was elderly nor infirm. We remained there because my mother was stubborn and would not leave in 1939 for Palestine like many of our compatriots who fled Poland on an organised emigration. We had however not been herded into a ghetto yet. My mother kept herself to herself, and we rarely ventured outside.

At five years old I was allowed to start at the local school; that was until I got called names by the other children both in school and on the way home. They would pounce on me at any time and beat me up calling me a 'Dirty Little Jew'. My education was short-lived as overnight Jewish children were not allowed in school.

My Father was weak-willed and always agreed with my mother. By 1942 he was long gone. As a banker, he was one of the first to be taken by the Germans in 1939. I'll always remember the knock on the door of our flat above the bank. In the beginning, my mother told me later that it was because he was on a list that had been compiled by the secret police started in 1937.

As it turned out they took him away. I still don't know where to. Later I found that he was not on a list. He had something that they wanted.

Aside from his Banking business he also had a secret, or rather held a secret. In one gloomy corner of our flat was an old carved Ark covered in a chenille tablecloth. This would be his and my undoing.

As a child, I was curious about but was never allowed to open or play with the ark. I had seen my father open it once or twice and take out an object wrapped in goatskin. I would kneel quietly on an old wooden chair that had one crooked arm watching him to see what he was doing. My Father's activities with the ark were always under the cover of darkness when my mother was asleep in our only bedroom. I had a small settee in the main room-cum-kitchen. My father was always very secretive about what the Ark contained. Every time he opened the ark my father chanted biblical verses in Hebrew.

At the time I was unaware of their significance. I was also unaware (as we were not allowed to practice our religion in our own home lest we were caught) that what was contained inside the goatskin should have been bought out every Saturday and Tuesday.

My Father never knew that I watched out of a sleep-filled somewhat weary eye, nor that I membered what he chanted. Before the Ark doors were closed my father would always chant other words, again I would never forget them. Once my mother came in and almost caught my father in the closing of the ark. My father forgot the final words. The next day I noticed that one of his fingers had been burnt badly.

When the Secret Police finally banged on our door before kicking it down and forcing their way inside their eyes were immediately drawn to the corner where the ark was kept. How they knew it was there I did not know at the time, but later found out it was my mother's doing. Both the Ark and my father disappeared from our lives. When he had gone my dear mother just shrugged her shoulders and told me to be a brave boy and carry on as though nothing had happened.

Life did carry on if you can call it that. There was no food, no school, no fuel for the fire. In the winter of 1941, my mother burnt what was left of our merge furnishings to provide fuel for heat, all except for one chair with a crooked arm which I begged her not to throw away as it was a last memory of my father. By now we were living in one room. No second room for dear mother. She sold her bed and blankets for as much as she could get, which wasn't very much as there was no money around either.

By the February of 1942, I still was not allowed to go out by myself. That is until one morning, Thursday 13th February to be precise. For some reason, my mother was humming to herself and dancing a little around our living room. She pushed a few Zloty coins into my hands and told me to go out and find whatever food I could lay my hands on. It was the day after Tu BiShvat which is a minor Jewish holiday, occurring on the 15th day of the Hebrew month of Shevat. It is also called "The New Year of the Trees".

Feeling relaxed for the first time in months, skipping around the corner, and intent on getting to the shops which were about half a kilometre away – not too far for a six-year-old. Boy, I was so glad to get out, and away from my mother's bad moods. I unconsciously started chanting the words that I had heard my father say when he opened the Ark. Forgetting our hardships for a few seconds and forgetting my mother too I failed to notice her standing in the doorway to the Bank where my father had previously worked - the one below our flat. She seemed to be searching for something in the middle distance, but I was too preoccupied.

Happy to be out, and that I had a few coins to buy food I carried on chanting verses to myself. I was too busy to notice if there was anyone else around. As a normal 6-year-old boy who had had up to now led a sheltered life I did not spot an old couple walking hurriedly in the other direction supporting each other as they moved because they had crumbled bones and swollen misshapen feet and hands. Nor did I see a 'spotter' on the corner of the street opposite. Had I paid any attention to my surroundings I would have noticed the armbands that the old couple wore which were white with a blue Star of David depicted on them indicating that the couple were Jewish.

Mrs Kawsaski the shopkeeper of the shop that I entered was a bitter twisted old crow. She looked me up and down like I was an animal in the zoo or a circus freak. Snagging a head of a day-old cabbage, I proffered her a few coins which she viewed as though they were directly from the devil himself. Muttering 'Kurwa' (whore) she took far too many coins from me, but I was not bothered. The stupid old bag was always using words that a six-year-old shouldn't hear.

Shrugging my shoulders and walking out of the shop I tried to work out why she had said that to my face. I hoped that my mother would be pleased with what I had procured and hoped that she may make a thin watery soup out of it for our lunch. Now chanting the final verse that I had heard my father chant I started to trudge home. Walking around the corner I spotted my mother in the doorway of the Bank. She was chatting away to a stranger in a long black coat who was leaning on the bonnet of a car.

I had never seen a car before, let alone a lovely, shiny black one like this. Eagerly running towards it so that I could catch a glimpse of it before it disappeared, I was too naive and had been sheltered at home for far too long to recognise that this was the car of the enemy and that my mother was chatting away to an SS officer. Strangely she was pointing a hand in my direction. Thinking that she had procured me a ride in the car was rudely brought down to earth when two men grabbed me from behind and tossed me roughly into the back of an open lorry which I had not noticed before because I was so taken with seeing an actual car.

Landing with a thump, and momentarily dazed I managed to look up expecting my mother to follow, but of course, she didn't. All I could see around me was a sea of bowed heads, eyes downcast studiously avoiding me, or maybe they were too shocked to notice me. I had been thrown amongst a pile of sad suitcases and battered bags alongside a few pots and pans. What I did manage to see from my obscure angle was that almost everyone on that lorry, young or old had a white armband with a blue star on it. My mother had studiously avoided the orders to sew such a badge on our sleeves as she kept telling me that we were not of the Jewish persuasion.

Not daring to get up or move, hardly daring to breathe in case someone heard my heart beating loudly, and after having several more bags tossed on top of me, I lay there silently as my mother had always decreed. We must stay silent; we cannot be spotted.

The open lorry, after making several more stops until there was no room left in it finally juddered to a stop in what appeared to be a goods yard where there were many train- tracks converging. Being a skinny, undernourished four-feet-nothing six-year-old I wondered how on earth I would be expected to jump out of the back. If I couldn't get out would be shot on the spot? With a shout of 'Bewegung', (out), the downtrodden folk began to climb out, then stood there silently as if they already knew their fate.

A chill wind blew, and swirls of dust made this the most surreal thing I had ever witnessed so far. Many of the people gathering in a ragged line hadn't had time to collect coats or hats to protect themselves against the elements. One or two of the older ones began to shiver and shake.

When snowflakes began to fall, gently at first, then coming faster and thicker I decided that perhaps I should make a move. A German soldier stood by the lorry eyeing up the occupants as they got off as if he were eyeing up cattle at a market. A man of about eighty or so helped his wife down. These were the two that I had seen earlier when I went out to the shops. I managed to shuffle myself out from under what was left of the various suitcases and move to the edge of the lorry where I dangled my stick-thin legs over the end so that it looked like two twigs were hanging there waiting to be snapped off.

The guards just stood there watching, not doing anything, standing stock still to attention with ramrod straight backs, rifles by their sides. Brooding, glaring, waiting. Amongst the gathered line of people standing in what was the coldest of winters one brave soul, a man of about thirty decided to break cover. He was shot on the spot, his crimson blood spreading to form an unseemly bright red patch across the snow.

He had left behind his wife and children. Maybe he had realised that it was easier to be shot in the back by a single shot than to face what was coming. Little did he know arriving at our destination he would have been told he would have to take a shower first then would have been led to a camouflaged gas chamber with fake showerheads and trapped inside where large doors would be sealed. Then, an orderly, who wore a mask, would open a vent on the roof of the gas chamber and pour Zyklon B pellets down the shaft. He would then close the vent to seal the gas chamber.

The Zyklon B pellets turned immediately into a deadly gas. In a panic and gasping for air, prisoners would push, shove, and climb over each other to reach the door. But there was no way out. In five to twenty minutes, depending on the weather, all inside would be dead from suffocation.

Seeing the escapee being shot made me jump out of the lorry hurting my ankle as I hit the now frozen ground, and for a moment I looked like a newborn deer slipping and sliding around, arms flaying. It didn't surprise me that I did so, neither did the fact that my compatriots were rounded up at the end of a Jewish Holiday when everyone was a little more relaxed and celebrating that they were still alive. Ours was not the only lorry converging at the railway lines. Lorries from across the whole of Poland were arriving one by one. Straggling lines of downtrodden people, mainly Jews were also being escorted to the station. These were the people who lived in the Ghettos of nearby towns.

Having arrived at the railway station we were brutally bundled into waiting cattle trucks which were fitted out with wooden shelves/bunks to pack in as many people as possible, some 50 — 70 people in one truck. The standard means of transport was a 10-metre long (32 ft 9+3⁄4) freight car.

CHAPTER 2

המחנה (THE CAMP)

The doors to the freight train were slammed, locked from the outside by putting an iron bar across them, and the train started slowly to pull out of the sidings. A microsome of all humanity with its sweat and piss and shit was enclosed inside a wooden coffin. Little did we know that we would not have food or water on our journey even when the transports had to wait days on railroad spurs for other trains to pass.

Our incarceration was an inhuman nightmare. Because we were travelling in livestock trucks there were hardly any sanitary provisions. Just one hole in the floor for toiletry purposes. This was monstrously hideous, exposing children, women and men to perform their private bodily functions openly. The stench was terrible. We were treated like animals. There was one circular cast iron stove in the middle, which did not supply anywhere near the required degree of warmth. Remember we were travelling at the height of winter.

There was no supply of water either for drinking or washing. Now and then the train would stop, and so during those stops watched by guards, those who managed to pack kettles or pots would be allowed to gather snow into these containers, start up a fire, suspend these containers on hastily prepared stands to boil the resultant melting snow, which would then be used for drinking or for washing needs.

The elderly and frail were dying right there in front of me, a sight no one should have ever seen. This was the death of my childhood. I couldn't tell night from day. The old man who had helped his wife off the lorry succumbed to his death as the nights were freezing, and he had not taken any sips of the rancid water that was passed around from time to time. As the water came from melted snow who knew what it contained even though it was boiled first? The old man's wife sat hunched up after her husband's death and started muttering deliriously to herself. No one offered her any words of comfort as they were too wrapped up in their own misery and suffering.

The rumours started spreading after a while. We were going to be employed as slave labour in the production of munitions, synthetic rubber and other products considered essential to Germany's efforts in World War II.

Eventually, the train stopped, and one girl of about thirteen or so peered through a crack in the door of the stopped cattle car and read the name Auschwitz. She spelt it out for her blind mother who said, 'I don't know where it is, I've never heard of the place.' And then suddenly a clatter of the doors opening, and when the doors opened, I mean there was just like all of hell being let loose. 'Out, out, out, out!' was shouted to us. We were shocked, we didn't know what was going on.

I spied piles of rotting bodies, barking dogs, SS officers shouting in German, and smelt thick grey ash clogging the air. An official scrambled into our freight car. He cast his eyes disdainfully at all of us in one fell swoop, and singled out the old and the blind, the women and the children. He didn't spot me though as I was hiding beneath the old man who had died. The Official who had entered our car had quickly ascertained that they would be no good for work, and he (but we did not at that point) knew that they would be heading for the gas chambers straight away. The dead bodies from the carriage were now being tossed onto the ever-growing pile outside.

Once all the dead bodies had been removed the women and children and the frail and elderly were ordered to line up and were marched away. The old woman whose husband had died in the cattle truck, the one whose body I was hiding underneath refused to walk and fell to the ground wailing for her dead husband. There was a brief conversation between two of the guards, and then one of them pulled out a pistol from his waistband and shot her in the head, then flung her amongst the mounting piles of rotting corpses.

Meanwhile, the men and stronger male children were forced to line up, and two of the guards prowled up and down their line trying to ascertain if any of them had a trade in manufacturing. A few stepped forward, and this same exercise was repeated asking for Taylors or Cobblers. This time quite a few stepped forward, although I am certain that amongst the males left, there couldn't possibly be that number amongst us who had such a trade.

Those who had no trade were laughingly told that they would be on gardening duty, which really meant that they had the job of sifting through the remains from the gas chambers where they would cut off the women's hair and remove all metal dental work and jewellery. Then they burned the corpses in pits, on pyres, or in the crematorium furnaces. As if this were not horrific enough, the bones that did not burn completely were ground to powder with pestles and then dumped, along with the ashes in nearby ponds, strewn in the fields as fertiliser, or used as landfill on uneven ground and in marshes.

By now I was shaking from head to toe. I realised that I couldn't stay in the cattle truck, that is unless the train was turned around and sent elsewhere to pick up more unfortunate people. The only problem with this is that I would be found sooner or later, or I would die of hunger or thirst. There was only one solution and that was to give myself up although I may face death If I did so. I was damned if I did and damned if I didn't. Hoping that I looked older than my six years I poked my head out of the cattle truck door. Although I had led a sheltered existence, I was already Wiley. You had to be if you had a mother like mine.

It took a few seconds before I was noticed by one of the guards. Feigning sleepiness I stretched and yawned a little as though I had only just woken up from slumber. With a triumphant shout, the guard called out to his fellow guard. Jumping down from the train I landed on sheer ice, and slipped on my backside so that I ended up sprawled across the asphalt underneath. The guards watched me with growing amusement, until a larger man with a stripe on his shoulder and a big bushy moustache called across at them. Pulling themselves together sharply they matched swiftly over to me and pulled me up underneath both armpits and held me there swinging in the bitterly cold wind and snow.

The large guard swaggered over. Still being held under the arms he asked me in my native language what my name was. I replied with as much force as I could muster with the name of a boy who had lived in the flat next door to me, but who had died from a cycling accident a few years ago, and who was a couple of years older than me. In my few years on this earth that was the first time that I had ever lied, and I prayed that it would be the last. As far as I knew the boy whose name I stole was not a known Jew, nor did he come from a Jewish family so maybe I would be treated slightly better. Little did I know that they had already singled me out on purpose and knew exactly who I was.

As I had been snatched from the streets swiftly and suddenly, I didn't have any paperwork with me. I wasn't particularly bothered about this and had already decided to stick to a half-truth – that I was on the way to the shops for my mother and she had sent me out without any papers. Casting an eye over me the big guard ordered the other two to let go of me. At this point, I never considered running off as I knew they would shoot me as soon as my back was turned.

After a hurried conversation between the three of them, I was led away by the guard who had first spotted me. Not knowing my fate, I trailed along beside him through the ever-increasing snow that was falling. Normally I would take delight in watching it fall, but it was mixed with a grey obnoxious-smelling ash. From the train, I was taken into a washroom of sorts where I was stripped and then hosed down with freezing cold water by a rotund man with half-moon glassed and no hair. He was dressed in ragged pyjama-like clothes, and these were covered with a large rubber apron. Reeling from the shock of the cold water I was further stripped of my dignity by having my hair shaved off. The tattooing of my left forearm with my registration number would be another day.

Once again, I followed the same guard who had been lounging outside smoking a crafty a fag whilst I was being hosed down and I was led to a wooden barracks of a single story. The barracks which were originally used as stables had no windows, but instead a row of skylights on either side at the top. The guard who was escorting me pushed me in through an ill-fitting door which opened by removing a big piece of wood. Once shut the wood would not be removed until the barracks occupants were either escorted to work at 4.30 am in the summer or 5.30 am in the winter.

The interior was divided into eighteen stalls intended originally for fifty-two horses. The two stalls nearest the door were obviously reserved for the prisoner's bodily needs., and containers of excrement stood on the two stalls at the far end. Three-tier wooden bunks intended for fifteen people to sleep in were installed in the other stalls. Pointing to one of the bunks where five boys lay on a straw mattress, I shuddered at what I saw.

The bunks were about three meters wide. If prisoners wanted to turn, the whole row had to turn over with them. The three deck hutches were originally intended to hold 15 prisoners, with a total population of about 400. The number of prisoners in each barrack varied according to the size and number of arriving transports. This was going to be my home for the next three years. During the entire course of my journey to the jaws of Hades, I hadn't really given my mother any consideration. Now I hope that she rotted in Hell.

CHAPTER 3

החמישה (THE FIVE)

Several corpse-like figures lay on the floor, and two or three occupied each tier of bunks. Probably nine men of varying ages, each in a pair of striped pyjamas, each shaven head covered with a cap, each one not interested in a small boy. I had never felt so alone in my entire life. My heart ached, and I longed for my apartment with the small bathroom even though we didn't have any heat the place that I was in now was much colder. The chill that swept through my body though had nothing to do with the extreme temperature of the place. It was a chill within me, a chill of abject fear.

However, I realised with a start that five pairs of eyes did watch me as I entered the stalls. These eyes belonged to five boys of varying ages, from about sixteen years of age down to twelve. They may have been older, but I couldn't really tell as they looked more nourished than the other inmates, and had rosier cheeks whereas cheeks belonging to the others were grey. More to the point the five boys had shown interest in me an undernourished six-year-old. Maybe in my ignorance, I thought that we could strike up some form of friendship. The Germans may have taken away our families and stripped us of our dignity, but surely, they had not taken away our sense of comradery.

The SS guard gave the biggest of the boys a small nod and exited swiftly, locking the door behind him. The biggest boy jumped down from his top bunk, which was obviously much prized, and stood with his hand on his hips. Tall and thin with long legs he wanted me to feel imposed by him, maybe a little frightened of him. The other four boy's gazes flicked backwards and forwards sizing me up. Standing my ground, I tipped my head back and looked up to the eldest one, my eyes not wavering. My immediate instinct was to hide, but unlike home, there was no corner or nook to hide in. It wasn't his size, although he towered at least a foot over me, it was his menacing glare that truly terrified me, and I felt like a lamb being led to slaughter under his scrutiny,

'I 'm Stefan', he said in a growl. 'I run this bunk space, and what I say goes, and let me tell you there are no dirty Jews allowed around in here, because if you are a Yid, I'll let the guards know, and you'll be getting an early shower. We keep ourselves away from the other dupeks (Arseholes) and never mingle with them, so my word is the law.'

I hadn't a clue what he was talking about. I had already been subjected to having been hosed down with icy water and had my head shaved. What I found out later was that if anyone was being sent to the gas chamber, they were told that they were getting an early 'shower'.

Without having to say another word he nodded briefly at two more of the boys. One was short and on the rotund side, with thick horn-rimmed glass. The other had terrible acne but made up in the looks department with blonde hair that had just started to grow again, and blue eyes. Circling around me in the confined space like a pack of hyenas had my pulse quickening. Stephan then ordered that I should be examined for anything suspicious. After a moment's hesitation, the boy with acne swiftly pulled down the bottom of my pyjamas.

Gasping they both took a step back. As the son of a Jew, and according to my father's religion I had been circumcised not long after I was born. This was patently obvious to the three boys, and now Stefan was barging his way between them.

'Well, well', he muttered, 'and what do we have here? I told you before what would happen to dirty Jews'.

Giving him my false name, I swiftly needed a way out of this.

'My Father wasn't Jewish, but my mother was', I said with as much conviction as I could. 'Her name was Rozanne'.

With this face broke into a huge grin. I wondered what I had wrongly said. Had I spoken out of turn, or was the older boy just too thick to take things in? It didn't matter if your father were Jewish, but to be classed as a Jewish person your mother had to be as it's been since biblical times. I may have hanged myself on the spot, but there was no way that I was going to let them know that my father was Jewish, nor that he had been taken by the Germans, and had his Ark confiscated.

'Well, if you are Rozanne's boy like you say you are, then you must know that she is the new camp companion here, and all of us here can go visit her for special attention when we've worked hard which is often. Let's just say that the dark-haired temptress can be very free with her favours, and we hope that you are too. We could do with some fresh blood, and we do like to share everything here, even Fryderyke there although he's usually interested in Maths', he said jerking his head into a giant-sized youth who lay lounging in the middle of the bunk.

My mind was in a whirl. Surely, they couldn't be talking about my mother. The last time I saw her was when she was pointing me out to a German Officer. Yet didn't the shopkeeper whom I'd bought a cabbage off call her something nasty? Also, if it was her the boys were joking about what on earth was, she was doing at a concentration camp? I must find a way of seeing her, I must. I needed an explanation as to why she gave me up. Why would Stefan lie about her unless I really didn't know her at all?

'Well Rozanne's son, let's see what you're made of ', said Stefan. 'Fryderyke, why don't you go first and take your mind off bloody numbers before you drive us all crazy'.

'Cezar should have first go,' replied Frederick. 'After all, he is rather good with his hands isn't he, I'll bet our newcomer would really love that, especially if he takes after his mother. Why only the other day I hear he had his finger up her arse hole.'

'Should have been a different hole,' guffawed Stefan laughing. 'In that case, Cezar if you would do the honours, please', he said with a mock bow.

At that, I pissed myself which made the boys grimace and pull faces in disgust.

'Other end's dry,' said Stefan fondling himself.

With that, Cesar got up and for a few seconds, I couldn't see him. Then I felt hot rancid breath on my neck and felt the most terrible stabbing pain erupt in my nether regions.

I don't know how many times I was raped that day. I must have passed out at some point and fallen asleep up in pain. It was pitch black, and I was awoken by a whisper in my ear. I thought I would have to go through it all again, but instead, to my relief it was Fryderyke proffering me a metal cup of water.

'Sleep now', he said gruffly. With that, I nodded off again until I was awoken from my shallow slumber by a loud banging and clanging outside. The doors were flung open, and it still seemed like night-time as it was dark. Wincing in pain I propped myself up one skinny elbow. Two SS officers stood silently in our stall. I prayed to God that Stefan hadn't regressed on his promise after yesterday's ordeal. Steeling myself from the worst, shut my eyes and began to breathe shallowly.

The five boys who had taken part in my ordeal were ordered to get up. They then fell in between the two SS Officers and marched away. I stupidly hoped that they were going to be punished for what they had done to me, but then how could the SS men know what had happened?

I had nearly missed the gong at 5.30 am whereby prisoners got up at its sound and had to carefully tidy their living quarters. Next, they were supposed to attempt to wash and relieve themselves before drinking their "coffee" or "tea". Apparently, that's what the banging and clanging was outside. I hopped out of bed and performed my ablutions as best I could. As I was there under a false name, and being of small stature I hid in a corner and silently watched the proceedings.

At the sound of a second gong, the men around me ran outside to the roll-call square, where they lined up in rows of ten by block. The prisoners were counted during the roll call. Once about a month after I had been tattooed with my prisoner number, whilst taking part in roll call if the numbers didn't add we had to stand outside in the cold and ice not moving until the Germans were satisfied the numbers tallied. The same happened in the evening at 7.30 pm. The bitter nights standing out there meant that colds, flu, and pneumonia were prevalent amongst the prisoners., not to mention typhoid.

It wasn't until a few days later that I began to understand where the five in my bunk were, and why they always missed roll call. They were working elsewhere on the camp, and as they were always escorted out and back by two SS officers, they were excused from roll call, plus they also managed to blag extra tea, coffee, and sometimes fags. The only trouble was I was no further along about finding my mother, nor what the five in my bunk got up to during the day. They inexpiably never talked about it.

I use the term 'my bunk 'loosely here. I was made to sleep on the stone floor every night. I managed to gather a few stray pieces of loose straw every day to rest my head on, but the five boys took great delight in kicking my 'pillow' away every night. If they did not have the time or energy then the SS Officers would fling me to the ground and scrabble around on my hands and knees until I had collected every bit of straw, then they would march me out to dispose of the straw. Often the wind would howl, and great gusts would disperse all the straw. This meant that sometimes I had to sleep on the bare floor. To make matters worse the five boys would remove my striped pyjama garments and make me sleep naked in sub-zero temperatures.

After a few months, the abuse and assaults on my body stopped. This was probably because I never gave the five boys any satisfaction by crying in front of them. The only time I cried was when they were out of the stalls and working God knows where.

They then n decided that I must be fair game for kicking and beating instead. By now I had been tattooed on my left arm with my identification number. I thought that this would make me one of them, but it didn't. You could tell if the five had had a good or bad day by the number of beatings that I had. It became a normal part of my life, and I relished the time that they were away. The worst day of the week was Sunday. They would knock me around all through the day as there was little else to amuse them.

I still hadn't found where my mother was or what the boys did all day. They often came back late taunting me about my mother's charms and what she had let them do. I tried to glean bits of information about them and my mother as some nights they would come back full of excited chatter. Apart from Stefan, Frederyke and Cezar, I learnt that the other two were Nelek and Petroniusz. I would never forget them or forgive them for what they had done to me. I would hunt them down and kill them no matter what precautions they took to disguise their identities. They could change their name, they could change their looks, but I would never forgive or forget what they had done to me.

The days turned into weeks then into months then into years. A normal boy of my age would have growth spurts, but I didn't have many. My fine hair started to fall out and I walked with a stoop like an old man. My face was skeletal, and my body was shrunken and malnourished.

Then wonder of wonders it must have been late in 1944 or early 1945 as by now I had lost track of the days the rumours started not just in our stall but in the whole block. People who usually were quiet, people who usually kept themselves to themselves in as much as just acknowledging one another when they were taking a piss began now to mummer amongst themselves. As soon as any German Officer walked in inmates would clamp their mouths together; there was a sudden shift in the air, the force fields that the Germans gave off had moved ever so slightly like there was a gradual chink appearing in the timeline.

Eventually, the murmurs rose to a crescendo, so much so that it gave me a headache. The five in my bunk were keeping themselves to themselves. Because of our ages were mostly left alone to do our own thing, and then, it suddenly dawned on me, the five of them never joined in with any conversation. I began to wonder why, and though waves of noise and rumours made my head spin I did get the general gist of what was going on.

I decided to start a rumour of my own. I mean who wouldn't believe an innocent young boy? It was a rumour that took shape out of an existing rumour. The first rumour that I had heard from the adults was that Josef Mengele was, and always had been at Auschwitz II, and that he conducted terrible experiments. He had seen the opportunity to conduct genetic research on human subjects. His experiments focused primarily on twins, with no regard for the health or safety of the victims that he chose.

When I was going about my ablutions one morning, and when the five had been escorted out, as usual, the talk all around me had begun again. I happened to find myself next to an old man. He must have felt sorry for me as he turned away from me so I had a shred of dignity left. He must have seen that my body by now was bruised and battered. When I'd finished, I nodded towards my shared bunk and whispered out of the corner of my mouth,

'You know that Nelek and Petroniusz are fraternal twins. Where do you think they go all day? As for the others, they have physical defects like being too short or too fat, and Mengele is starting to take an interest in physical characteristics as well.'

The rumour swelled and took on a life of their own. I innocently sat in the corner of the stall all day honing my skill of catching flies and then working out how to swat them as they were always fast little buggers. The Five were not happy that talk had switched to them, so they started their own counter rumour which immediately caught my attention. I began to wonder that given my previous life, there was any truth in the rumours. Each day, because of their specialist t knowledge they were called into Mengele's office every day to work on, decipher the contents of, and confirm the provenance of an item they called The Ark.

CHAPTER 4

הארון (The Ark)

I had started to believe again that maybe there was a God After all, and that all paths would lead me to him. Maybe, just maybe it was 'The Ark'. The one that had been the downfall of my father, the one that had taken him away from me. The only trouble was I had to see it and touch it to see if it felt right. It was no good if I could not do either of these two, the only trouble was how.

I knew that the Five went out every day and that for some reason which after all this time I had not fathomed was that all of them set off early each day and returned late. Somehow, I had to get them to convince Mengele that I knew all about The Ark. Then it struck me that I did know about the Ark if it was the one that my father used. I wished now I had come clean about my heritage, but then again maybe not. If I had told the complete truth I may well be dead by now. Thinking about how my father got his hands burnt when he did not complete the ritual with the Ark made me think that maybe if I carried it out, I might not get burned. This could be my one chance to get The Ark back. I suddenly had a compulsion to retrieve it, and I knew how.

Firstly, I had to check to see if any of the Five had burn marks on them. I was too obsessed and full of self-pity to notice that they touched my body often, but I never bothered to check their hands. For the next few days, I paid particular attention to them, and to my relief saw that they all had burns of some sort on their hands. This was a good sign, surely an omen from God. The next thing I needed was a miracle.

When the Five came back noisily I pretended to be asleep, which seemed to be my default setting. This time I started muttering the verses that my father used to whenever he got the Ark out every Shabbat. I knew its contents word for word, and no one could deny that they were the true words. Gradually the Five would quieten down a bit when they returned, until eventually, things came to a head.

After repeating the Torah every Monday and Thursday (the day when ancient markets were held in Israel, I also recited words on a Saturday. As far as the five were concerned I could have been reciting any old tripe, but I knew that 1) This would be blasphemous, and 2) although they all denied it one of them may be Jewish and would know the Torah inside out.

On the third week of my mutterings, Stefan jumped off the top bunk and squatted down on the concrete floor next to me. Shaking me by both shoulders he shouted at me 'Oy Jewish scum, come on tell us the truth. We know that your bitch of a mother isn't Jewish. If she was, she would cover her hair when in the presence of men other than her husband or close family members.'

This was my only chance. Taking a deep breath, I uttered the following words,

'She is not a practising Jew, but my father is or rather was, my name is Hamadej. Furthermore, I know the secrets of the Ark that you are working on. It belonged to my father who sacrificed his own life for it. It contains the Torah. Not just any Torah though, it is the one that God dictated to Moses and has been passed down through the generations to my family.

There was a collective gasp from the Five. Bemused they looked towards Stefan who was their de facto leader. For once Stefan could not find his voice. Instead, he held out his blistered hands to me and said,

'If this is true, then you can heal my hands, if not then it is certain death for you, as I will take you to the Gas Chamber myself right now'.

This was a pivotal moment, and I was briefly reminded of Pontius Piolet who wanted Jesus to perform Miracles to prove that he was the Son of God. For the first time in many years, I uttered a Jewish prayer that God would help and guide me. Closing my eyes and taking his blistered hands in my own much smaller ones I clasped them in mine and guided them toward my heart. I felt a heat rise from them, and with an 'ouch' Stefan dropped them rapidly and then held them out in front of him in wonder.

His blisters were healed, so there were such things as miracles. Spent I collapsed on the floor and fell into a deep sleep. I felt like I had just run a Marathon. Waking the next morning Stefan and the rest of the Five were staring at me in awe. When the two usual SS Guards came in to escort them away, Stefan pretended that he was sick, a great risk on his part. After a brief exchange with one of the SS Guards, I was beckoned over. Telling me that if I stepped out of line I would be shot, we were led outside. I hadn't really had the chance to breathe fresh air if that's what you could call it with all the smoke and ash bellowing out of huge chimneys. The only time I had been outside was during roll call.

Walking behind the two strong blonde SS Officers we were marched from the Killing Centre to the main camp and taken to an office marked with Mengele's name. One of the officers beat a brief tattoo on the door, went in, and then shut it firmly behind him. I along with the remaining four boys stood squirming under the eye of the remaining SS officer. After hearing raised voices my hopes began to recede, and doubt began to creep in. Had I done the right thing, or had I just sealed my own fate with my own foolish actions?

The door to Mengele's office was flung open. The four other boys surged forward. Shyly I hung back with my eyes downcast until I was pushed in the back by the SS Officer who was watching my every move. Almost falling I caught sight of my father's beloved Ark on a shelf, unwrapped from its usual cloth just sitting there on a shelf above Mengele's head. It seemed to have taken on a drabness and was not shiny which was not surprising as it was in the office of the Devil's own sperm.

That wasn't the only thing in the room that had caught my attention. Sitting right next to Josef Mengele at his desk was my mother, the Whore.

Seeing me, although I am not sure she recognised me after nearly three years she didn't even hesitate, nor look in my direction. True I had a shaved head, and I walked with a pronounced limp after being kicked many times by the Five. The rumours were true then, she was Mengele's whore.

She could have saved me from three years of incarceration. She could have saved me from my near misses to the Gas Chamber, she could have spared me the indignity of being raped and tortured by the Five. But she hadn't done any of those things. She was a woman of loose morals. As she stood up, I noticed something else. She was obviously Pregnant.

To say I was blindsided was an understatement. As for my mother well, she didn't miss a beat. Instead, she clasped Mengele's arm with one hand and lovingly cradled her stomach with the other. Mengele did nothing to brush her off and did nothing to stop her from protecting her unborn offspring. That was the final nail in the coffin, and there and then I vowed to myself that she was no longer my mother.

Although I wanted nothing more to do with her, any half-sibling of mine would also be stan's offspring whether it be Mengele's or one of the Five. All the boys in my bunk had told me in detail how they had enjoyed my mother's 'company' many times. It could be that one of them was the father. I had no way of knowing which of them it was, but again I would hunt them down and make them pay. I didn't realise that it would be forty years until I found them, forty years before I got my revenge.

Mengele was tapping his fingers on the edge of his desk. She gestured towards the Ark, and barked,

'I believe that you know what the content of this Ark is, and from whence it came. What you may not know that is contains a precious artefact that the best minds in the Third Reich have tried to translate but to no avail. But now I have you and these four plus your dear sick friend to help me out', he said sweeping his hand in the four boys' general direction.

'They are wunderkind, and despite their ages have joined me here covertly to uncover things I need to know about various artefacts. Now tell me what you know about this Ark.'

I was conscious that all eyes were on me, and this worried me greatly. What if the Five had done any damage to the Ark's contents? Stammering slightly, and aware that my mother was now waiting for me to fail, I began to tell the history and purpose of the Ark.

'Inside the Ark is the Torah scroll, the one true scroll, the truth. From seeing my father take it out I knew that it was wrapped and decorated ornately, with silk coverings. When it is read, a yad is used. This is a pointing device used to follow the text so that the holy words are not damaged. When we say Torah, we are speaking of the five books of Moses'.

I continued to tell him what it meant, and what the cover over it was, saying that it should have curtains, but this was a later addition to our tradition, and that the Torah themselves should be wrapped and bound. What I failed to tell him, and I hoped that my mother was stupid enough even though she was a Jew was to fail to remember what my father always said, that the Ark should always face Jerusalem.

Holding a finger up, Mengele interjected, 'If these are indeed the true Torah from Moses as I was led to believe, then they should be written on parchment. Not only that but something is bothering me. Where would the silk that they are wrapped in have come from?

At this Cezar hesitantly stepped forward. I had never seen him so cowed or meek as now.

'If you please, Sir,' he said addressing Mengele, 'silk dates to the 30th century BC. If somehow, we can prove a connection between this and the Scroll wrappings, then this could be further proof that you are looking for.

I finally got what Mengele was aiming for, by owning the true Torah, he could undermine the whole of Judaism. And so, I came up with yet another plan, to translate the Torah for him, but not completely, and not the whole content, and may God forgive me. Muttering the words that my father had I picked up the Ark, which seemed suddenly to gleam in my presence. Opening it up I peered inside, and as I had hoped, the one scroll which contained the five of the laws Torah was there. Thus began my work with the Five. They didn't respect me anymore, but they didn't bother me. Occasionally When they had a spare bit of dry 'bread', they would throw it in my direction, and no longer laugh and jeer as I scrabbled around to retrieve it. This situation lasted for a few weeks if not less, because a big change was about to come.

Until then I trotted behind the Five when the SS Officers came to collect us to march us to Mengele's office. The man himself had mentioned more than one artefact as he had used the plural artefacts. Perhaps I had misunderstood him, but he only seemed to have the Ark with the Torah inside. Maybe once I had finished my translation, he would set some other tasks to do. It was a known fact that the Germans had stolen precious works of art. The systematic dispossession of Jewish people and the transfer of their homes, businesses, artworks, financial assets, musical instruments, books, and even home furnishings to the Reich were an integral component of the Holocaust In every country controlled by Nazis, Jews were stripped of their assets through a wide array of mechanisms and Nazi looting organisations.

When I set eyes on the Torah, the first time since I had seen it since my father was taken away, I could have wept. Someone, not understanding how important it was Judaism had sliced it into five portions, each one containing a book of the Torah. They either disregarded its importance, or they wanted to undermine our religion completely. My guess was that it was Mengele himself that had done it. This made me more determined not to tell him what the words exactly meant.

I translated but fabricated a half-lie about the Torah's contents. I was the only person who they trusted to translate it. They could trust to translate it. There were perhaps many scholarly people being held in Auschwitz who could have done a true translation, but I had connections to the true Torah. It had taken me a while, but whilst I was doing the translation I began to realise why things had happened, and things slowly slotted into place. Firstly, they took my father and the Ark. Then they would have asked him to translate its contents, but because of his commitment to his faith, he would have refused knowing that he would most certainly face death.

Then my mother had somehow (I still had to figure out this part) let it be known that I could translate from Hebrew and as I had often stayed awake listening to my father. Also, I had the correct linage. You could trace my family back to Moses himself. My mother also did other favours for the Germans and had become the camp harlot. So, this was why I had been taken, beaten, raped, tortured by the Five. It was so that I would willingly translate the Torah.

It was also why I was never taken to the gas chambers although Stefan used this as a metaphorical stick to beat me with, to make sure I towed the line. The Five must have been faithful to the Nazi cause, which is why when they did something well, they were rewarded with favours from my mother. Up until now, I could never imagine my own mother having sex, but often one of the five would let slip what they had done to her, and I felt disgusted and sick by it.

The only question remaining was had my mother sold my sole to protect me, or to protect herself? I remembered how she had acted in the days leading up to my incarceration. She was happy, and giddy, and had a few coins to buy food. She let me out to shop even though she had kept me indoors for months. Was she also whoring to save herself or me? The truth was I never found out. It was always too hard to accept different versions of the truth, especially as one was through the eyes of an innocent six-year-old boy.

CHAPTER 5

שחרור (LIBERATION)

First came the rumours, then the Death March. The Soviets broke through the German defences and began to approach Krakow. As the Red Army marched closer the SS decided that it was time to evacuate. I knew this because on a bitterly cold day, the 17th of January 1945, most of the prisoners were forced into long columns. They had heard whisperings about walking towards German-held territory. Little did they know that they would either die on the way or if they fell would be shot and left at the wayside. If they survived the march they would end up after a long and arduous journey in another prison camp.

Only those in 'good health' (if you didn't count malnutrition and disease) could participate. There were probably nine thousand or so prisoners who remained, mostly those who were in poor health but I and the Five hid in the hope that we could escape. Of course, there was no food, fuel or water. Some of the prisoners scavenged among what was left of the possessions that the SS had left. When I found out that this was being done it sent me into a panic. What if someone had already taken the Ark, what if Mengele had decided it was too precious, or another prisoner chanced on it? There was nothing for it, I would have to find it myself.

After the Death march was completed on 21st January, when the evening had cast lazy shadows, and when night had crept around me, and the Five were asleep and snoring, I crept out of my hiding place. Although I loathed the Five when the Death March started, we had agreed that there was safety in numbers, and so we hid behind an outbuilding that had originally stored precious food for the Germans. We knew this place had been cleared out, both by the SS and the Prisoners scavenging for food. The only problem was that it was quite a distance away from the main camp and more importantly Mengele's office.

As I learnt the art of staying quiet while sharing a bunk with the Five just after midnight with bated breath I crept out of our hiding place. I had no means of light, but I for some unfathomable reason an instinct as to the direction of Mengele's office. Usually, I was escorted by SS officers, but this time I was alone. Drawing in my breath, which pained my chest, I silently and swiftly moved through the night grateful that there wasn't a full moon. I paused every time I heard a sound. Hoping against hope that I wouldn't be caught, or that the Germans had returned. With a concentrated effort, I got to the Ark's resting place where I had last seen it a few days ago.

I had bad memories of Mengele's office. Not because he had beaten or tortured me physically, but the mental scars would always be there, and I always when in his presence felt like I was playing a game of Cat and Mouse, and that he was waiting to pounce should I step out of line. The worst memory of all was seeing my mother for the last time, belly swollen, encased in the finest fur coat, and dripping with jewellery. There was no doubt who the father of her bastard was, as she clung to Mengele's every word, but never did she cast an eye in my direction.

In Mengele's office there appeared to be a soft humming sound that was not of human origin. As all the light fittings had been stripped, and telephones disconnected and torn out it couldn't possibly be coming from one of these. Glancing up the shelf where it usually reposed, I breathed a small sigh of relief. It was still there. Even under its clothes, I could see it glowing in the dark.

Reciting the prayers that I had heard my father use a lifetime ago I reached up and stretched my skeletal-like arms up and gingerly lifted it from the shelf. After all this it seemed to me that I was the one designated to rescue it, but where to go to now. I could not return to where the Five were hiding as they most certainly had been working hand in glove with Mengele. I could not risk hiding elsewhere, as someone else might be hiding there too. I had to protect it at all costs.

Then I had a sudden inspirational thought. Scrabbling through what was left of the objects in the office I spied an old leather suitcase. I had no idea who it belonged to yet, so I opened it and carefully slipped the Ark inside, and then I ran. I had no idea where I was going but I told myself that as I had saved something of God's then surely, he would guide me.

Walking all night and into the next morning I finally reached the iron gates of Auschwitz's death camp and uttering a prayer for those who had died here in the gas chambers, by disease, by starvation I realised that life would never be the same again.

Meanwhile, back at the camp, a group of Russian Army Scouts stumbled into Birkenau on the 27th of January 1945. This was only five days after I left. Had I remained I would not have had the chance to retrieve the Ark. What the shocked Russian soldiers did find though was piles of ash that used to be human remains, and people living in stables in the worst possible conditions covered with excrement, weak and emancipated. A week after I left Auschwitz, I was weaker and hungrier than I had ever been before. I had stumbled along muttering incoherently to myself when I literally fell into the arms of my saviour.

Auschwitz was in Southern Poland, and I had almost reached Czechoslovakia which had already been liberated by the Russian Army. Had I known that I may have continued walking, possibly not. I was wary of everyone and as soon as I caught a glimpse of anyone, I would dive into the nearest ditch always trying to keep the suitcase containing the Ark dry. On this day when I was about to give up, I spied in the distance a column of soldiers marching in my direction. I had no idea where they were from, but I did not intend to take any chances. Jumping into the nearest ditch I landed on something soft that made a loud 'whoof' quickly followed by a language that I did not understand, but the voice sounded so annoyed and almost rude.

A callused hand clamped around my mouth. I was kicked out, but then I felt one knee digging into my crotch. The voice then whispered, "Sshhh" just as the column of soldiers went marching by. My luck had changed, and I had a strange feeling that things were going to be all right.

Groping around I found the handle of the suitcase. If I hadn't been a top of a giant bear (or so I thought) I would have laughed out loud. The giant bear-man released his hand from my mouth. Gulping for air I found myself eye to eye with a sun-weathered man who had the largest emerald-green eyes I had ever seen with a face covered with a bushy beard, I gulped and waited to see what he would do. To me, he was the image of a picture of our saviour who I recall was on an Icon that my father kept stashed away out of sight from my mother. The only trouble was could he indeed be my redeemer, or could he turn out to be my nemesis? Trying to fight my way into standing or at least a sitting position I kept on falling back as I was so very weak, so I just lay there on top of the bear-man and waited to see what would happen next.

CHAPTER 6

מזל (LUCK)

'Polski?', inquired a deep rumbling voice.

Blinking as though he were a vision I shrugged. I was not going to let on who I was or what was in the suitcase. I don't think he was German, or he wouldn't have stopped me from crying out. He spoke a little more Polish to me then and taking my shrug as assent he suggested we untangle ourselves. I could not believe my luck. I had landed on someone who spoke my native language.

Climbing easily up out of the ditch as though he had done it a thousand times he stood silently waiting After a few beats he nodded towards the suitcase. Realising that the only way I was going to get out was with a helping hand from the giant I silently handed him the suitcase and waited to be hauled out. After years of imprisonment, I hardly weighed anything, and he pulled me up with one meaty paw.

To give the man his due he didn't ask about nor attempt to open or snatch the case. I wasn't sure who my saviour was but realised that he was wearing a mismatched uniform of Germany, Poland, and another country which I did not recognise. He gave no sign of being shocked nor was he troubled that I wore the pyjama-type clothes that I had been wearing for the three years. He overlooked the fact that they were covered in dirt, blood, and shit as was my stick-thin body underneath them. I must have smelt like a small pig, but he did not turn up his nose or turn away from me.

He gently then asked who I was, and I began to tell him as he spoke my own language, though not very well I might add. By the time I had finished telling him everything without sparing any detail tears were running down my cheeks and his. Now it was his turn to tell me his tale.

'So', he began. 'My name's Maloney. I have been avoiding capture since I decided that the Red Army was not where I wanted to be, me being a bit of a Mercenary. Basically, I got hacked off at home, stole a cow and a sheep, and almost ended up in prison. So, knowing the English Army wouldn't have me I hopped onto a Merchant Ship, jumped out at France, did a bit of fighting and then joined the Red Army.

I've been avoiding them as best I can as I skipped out on them. I had a 'minor' fracas with one of the Officers, and here I am now. So, tell me, young man, what gives with the suitcase?'

Taking a deep breath I opened it slowly. I didn't expect any surprises. The suitcase hadn't left my side until I had put the Ark inside it whilst still in Mengele's office, and yet it did contain a surprise that could have been seen as a miracle or a warning. The Ark to my relief was still intact. What made me gasp in both horror and panic was the wording therein.

Written in some kind of red paint on the inside were two words, 'REMEMBER POLAND', and then underneath were the initials of my mother.

Recoiling in horror I swiftly shuffled back. I most certainly had not expected that. This must originally have been Mother's suitcase. When I found it in Mengele's office, I in my haste didn't look inside the lid. Then I started to question myself about her and her association with the Nazis. Was she forced to leave it there, had she left hastily with her paramour, or was she dead? Had she left it deliberately hoping that I would find it?

All these thoughts were buzzing around in my head, and I passed out through sheer exhaustion or possibly fear. I didn't feel strong arms lifting me gently, nor the soothing murmurs of my newfound friend.

I woke up in complete darkness and for a moment I couldn't figure out where I was. Sweet-smelling hay lay softly beneath me, and a horse blanket which felt like the softest wool covered me. Trying to adjust to the dark I spied my suitcase now firmly closed by my side. A few feet away Maloney sat legs outstretched as though he didn't have a care in the world.

'You awake yourself are you now, just to let you know I haven't kidnapped you or your precious suitcase. I haven't touched anything inside I swear to Holy God', he said crossing himself fervently.

I yawned a little and stretched a lot. My default setting for when I didn't feel like talking.

'I thought you were taking gibberish earlier, but I can see you are telling the truth. The only thing now is to get you and your suitcase somewhere safe, and I know just the place.

By now I was so bone-weary that I just nodded mutely and fell straight back asleep. I woke as the new day's light crept in through a hole in the roof. Struggling to get up I managed a half sit- half-prone position propping myself up on one skinny elbow. The suitcase lay at my feet, apparently unopened. I had no reason not to trust Maloney, and yet...

Peering into the shadows of the stables where the sun had not yet reached, I couldn't spot the Irish man Maybe he had gone to fetch someone from the Authorities – unlikely as he sounded as though he was on the run himself. Why would he carry me, comfort me, and help me if he was going to turn me in?

Panic rising through my chest I started to think that I was on my lonesome again when in the distance I heard a cheery whistling. Hope against

against hope I prayed that it was Maloney returning, and to my relief about five minutes later he popped his head around the barn door. In his arms, he carried a bundle. Curiosity got the better of me and I managed to stand up, wavering a bit as I still hadn't got the complete use of my stiff legs. A sudden thump almost knocked me off my feet. Whatever was contained in the bundle landed a few inches shy of me.

'Thought you could do with new threads', laughed Maloney. 'So, I took myself off on a little expedition whilst you were snoring.'

Grinning back at him I rummaged through the bundle. Knowing that I couldn't be too choosey, and discarding my POW attire I pulled on a pair of trousers that were too long, a shirt that was too large, and a jumper that had seen better days, but then anything was better than a telling outfit.

Maloney had also procured an apple, something I hadn't seen apart from in a shop window. He then almost magically produced a flick-blade knife and neatly and precisely cut it into slices and offered me one. Eating it greedily he withheld the rest. Hoping that he would let me have more I glared at him.

'Too much too soon and you'll be sick young sir, and we don't want that, do we? I'll tell you what we'll make tracks, and we can eat as we walk', he explained.

Slightly peeved at him I snatched up the suitcase and followed in his wake. We must have walked for two or so hours when I realised, I desperately needed a pee. I suppose I'd got to talk to him, so I coughed loudly a couple of times until he turned to me with a 'What?'

I whispered that I needed to relieve myself, and good-naturedly he found me a tree which I could stand behind and do my business. After that we walked side by side, chatting occasionally. I had only one thing on my mind, and that was revenge against the Five.

I don't know how long we walked for, but Maloney always found me somewhere to rest my head at night, and most days he managed to scavenge food of some sort, and usually water. I know that it was gradually getting lighter every day, and the sun was giving out more rays, and casting longer shadows until one day we spied an encampment, a dozen or so tents with the biggest one bearing a Red Cross emblem on top.

Grabbing me by my free hand Maloney whispered in my ear. A few minutes late we strolled casually towards the tents until we came upon the biggest one, the one with the Red Cross. A tall rangy woman with long dark hair stepped out drying her hands on a towel. Maloney tightened the grip on my hand. Maybe he thought that I would either bolt or tell her everything.

The woman started to walk towards us eyeing us up cautiously. We must have been a sight. Me in my stolen clothes that were too big for me, and Maloney in a mismatched uniform (though he had managed to steal a pair of army boots from somewhere). Drawing closer I could see her outstretched arms like a beacon of hope or an Angel. All was going to be good until she opened her mouth and spoke in a strange language. Only it wasn't that strange, it was German but not the dialect that I had heard the SS talking.

I was about to fall to my knees in surrender when Maloney tightened his grasp on me even more. He gave a mock salute to the woman and answered back in the same vein. Now I was confused. So, who the hell was Maloney? He spoke Polish and this other German-like language.

Now the two of them were engaged in a conversation of sorts, and the woman was obviously warming to Maloney. Pointing in my direction he said something about me that made her come over and give me a gentle hug.

It then struck me that Maloney could quite easily turn in the charm when he needed to. He smiled again at the woman who took us to the big tent. Trying to extract the suitcase from my hand was difficult as I clung to it for dear life. After another short exchange with Maloney, she gave up and we were both shown two cot-like beds with actual sheets and blankets on them, and pillows as well. Thinking I had died and gone to heaven I was out for the count in about ten seconds. I was rudely awoken by a shake on my shoulder.

Glancing up I saw a ruddy-faced man in a white coat with a six o'clock shadow and tired bloodshot eyes staring down at me. Gently and softly, he asked me in Polish what my name was. I was so used to using my stolen name that I almost let it slip out. Instead, I told him my full name.

With the uttermost care the white-coated and began an examination of me tutting and shaking his legs at my shrivelled body that was still covered in hundreds of bruises and infected scars. He called and I think that it was a nurse who came over and did his bidding washing and cleaning me from head to toe, and then dressing the worst of my infected cuts.

I guess Maloney was getting the same treatment, but I was too tired to care slipping in and out of sleep waking only when the nurse did her rounds. Gently she introduced me to small amounts of food; a small amount of bread soaked in milk, and then as I grew stronger, she started sneaking me a cooked egg. After three weeks it was finally time to face the music.

One rainy morning one of the doctors came in. Brow furrowed he strode over to me and un-looped the stethoscope that had managed to tangle around his neck. Listening to my chest, and then shaking his head briefly he pulled one of the nurses aside and had a quiet conversation with her. The next thing I knew a new doctor turned up, and again a hurried conflab took pace out of my hearing.

The new doctor approached my bed and spoke to me in hushed tones.

'Hello, we have just been discussing your health and recovery young man, I hear you have been doing well. However, we are a little concerned about your chest, and fear that you may have Tuberculosis.'

At this, I began to cry. I could not believe that after everything I had gone through under the SS's regime, the time I spent with Maloney was for nothing when there might be a chance that I would die from TB. Seeing my distress, he laid a hand on my harm, and patting it gently said,

'However, there is a chance of recovery, but we will have to send you away to a clinic in Switzerland.'

Looking around I spotted Maloney hovering nearby trying to be as unobtrusive as possible. He grinned sheepishly in my direction. At that, I began sobbing even more until snot ran down my face. Taking a large white handkerchief from his trouser pocket the Polish doctor handed it to me. When I had blown my snotty nose, I handed it back, but he wouldn't take it. Not surprising really as it was covered in my germ-ridden mucus.

Looking a little pleased with himself the Doctor nodded in Maloney's direction.

'Your brother will be accompanying you though. As you are still young, and as you must take medicine every day, I can't let you go by yourself. We can't spare a nurse to go with you, so we are entrusting your care to him'.

By now I had almost stopped crying. Things couldn't have turned out better. That was it then, Switzerland it was.

For the next six months, I underwent treatment at a clinic in Switzerland. The journey there by train and then car had been exhausting, and yet Maloney was by my side all the time making sure I took my medication or carrying me and the suitcase from platform to platform when we had to change trains.

I am almost certain that there was nothing altruistic about his actions. Even in Switzerland, he was by my side and when he wasn't he had been scavenging for puzzles or picture books, and then books with words which he taught me to read.

Then suddenly it was time for me to go home. The only trouble was I had no home and no parents. That's when Maloney decided we should settle in England, and as luck would have it was where I would get my revenge on the Five.

CHAPTER 7

WE'LL MEET AGAIN

By the time Maloney and I reached France the war was truly over. There was still devastation everywhere, but the French seemed less oppressed and went about their day-to-day business with jour de vie. I had finally persuaded Maloney to leave the Dark-haired waitress with tumbling curls who served in a small café not far from the ferry terminal. He seemed to be enchanted with her and to my chagrin spent more time with her than he did with me.

By now he was going around telling everyone I was a rich orphan and that he was my butler. To give him his due he did look out for me. Arriving back at the café where he had left me earlier, he was waving something in the air.

'Tickets', he shouted, 'Tickets for the Ferry to England'.

Now I knew that tickets to England were in short supply, but for all I cared Maloney could have sold himself to the devil and it wouldn't have bothered me. Gathering up our meagre belongings I happily trotted next to him down towards the Ferry Port. Gasping I caught sight of our ship.

I have travelled a lot since I left Poland but believe me this was the loveliest sight I had seen or so I thought. Boarding the Ferry which was an old Merchant Navy vessel we found ourselves a couple of deckchairs on the Port side. Maloney had managed to acquire a snazzy pair of sunglasses for himself. He laughed when I told him that they didn't quite fit the butler image.

Suitcase safely stowed under Maloney's wooden deckchair where he was gently snoring, I decided to explore a bit of the ship. I had discarded the too-long clothes a long time ago and was kitted out in some of Switzerland's finest attire.

I had covered most of the deck and the café. I couldn't manage the steps down as I still had problems with one of my legs which the five had kicked and beaten over time. No doubt they had broken it as well at some point. Nevertheless, I was determined to make the most of the experience.

Strolling down the Starboard side I heard a group of men talking in my native language. Heads bowed closely together they were obviously discussing something but did not want to be overheard. Curiosity got the better of me, so I walked nonchalantly towards them, hands in my pocket. One of them must have heard me approach, although I don't know how over the noise of the ship's engines.

Not wishing to be caught eavesdropping I quickly turned back the way I came. Just as I made my escape, I heard a voice that still gave me nightmares calling out the name that I had used in Auschwitz. The blood drained from my face, and I stood rooted to the spot. There were only six people who knew my name, one was Maloney, and the rest were the Five.

Spinning me around I was face to face with Stefan the leader of the Five. An evil grin spread across his face. I'd forgotten what a bastard he could be with his yellow teeth protruding like a wolf. He had the same Lupin-like expression as well. Lips pulled back in a permanent snarl, yellow-green eyes with an elliptic-like shape. Licking his lips savouring the moment almost like he could taste blood already he stepped menacingly in front of me blocking out the sunlight, blocking my path.

My whole world seemed to tilt on an axis. When I had escaped from the camp, I never thought that my actions would have consequences. How had the Five survived? Like old times they were hanging back waiting for his word. Raising his left arm, he grabbed me by the throat. Mind still whirling I tried to think how they had managed to survive, not only that but why were they looking so well fed and well clothed; most refuges I had seen were wearing ill-fitting clothes with patches and holes.

'So, you thought you could get away from us', he hissed. 'Surprised to see us ', he went on knowing full well that at that point he was choking the life out of me.

'You're wondering how by some odd coincidence we ended up on the same boat at the same time. Let's just say we've been following your 'career' with your multi-language friend. Not hard to track down when you've still got friends in high places though'.

The noise in my ears was like the sounds that had emitted from the Gas Chamber, shrieking and begging for mercy. It was like a thousand dead Jews. I'd almost blacked out when Stefan released my neck. Rubbing it I thought he'd changed his mind, but he hadn't.

'Let me tell you a story', he began. 'The day before you first went into Mengele's office the Five of us had been in a secret meeting with him. Someone very close to him had let slip that you knew the secrets of the Ark. Mengele let you think you the Ark had burnt me, but it hadn't it was a cigarette burn that he gave me.'

Gaping I wondered how I could have been duped so easily. How could it be that I had healed the burn? As if reading my mind Stefan stepped even closer to me grinding his pelvis against me.

'Chalk', he said. 'Simple as that. I had a piece of chalk hidden in my other hand, and I swiftly transferred it to the other when you were performing your little miracle. I disguised it rather well I thought although I must say that there not be much light in the stable stall helped. After that, it was easy to pretend to be sick in front of the SS guards. They had been tipped off that something was happening that day, and they were to let you be escorted to Mengele's office instead of me.

When the Russians stumbled across Auschwitz plans were already afoot to sneak us out of the camp, which happened only hours after you left. We were put in the back of a lorry and given false papers. We were the Lost Boys just like in the fairy tale Peter Pan. Dropped off you had a few hours start, but with help from 'friends' we managed to track you all the way to Switzerland...'

I could not believe this. Mengele's evil tentacles spread everywhere. So, who could I trust? Could I trust Maloney or was all that a set-up as well? If it was it meant that I had spent the last year sharing my every secret with him. I began to doubt him. I mean how could an Irish man know so many languages, and had I taken what he told me at face value?

I was pondering on this, and how he had suddenly managed to procure tickets across the channel when everyone knew that they were in short supply. The other thing that made me feel sick to the stomach was that I had told him with candour what the Ark contained, and from whence it had come.

Stefan began to stare at me more closely now, and I swear he grew a few inches in front of me. He always looked mean, but now he looked mean and menacing. Realising that Maloney might not be on my side I began to sweat and tremble. Was it my good or bad luck that I had left the suitcase containing the Ark with Maloney? There was a fifty per cent chance that he was on my side, but even then, I did not like the odds one little bit.

Towering over me Stefan spoke the words that I hoped I would never hear again.

'I noticed that you had the suitcase with the Ark inside it with you when you boarded the ship. I do hope for your sake that you haven't lost it. Either way, it's going to be fun, and I doubt that you'll get off this ship alive.

Now I may have been of a shorter stature than Stefan, but one thing I did know was how to fight. I don't mean fisticuffs or anything like that I meant I had learnt along the way how to look after myself, and whatever side Maloney was on he taught me to fight dirty. Balancing on the ball of my left leg I swiftly brought my right knee up and connected it to Stefan's balls.

Howling with pain Stefan's attention wasn't clutching me for a few seconds which gave me enough time to duck out of the way, and so with my knee hurting like hell I legged it as swiftly as I could, the only thought in my mind was to find Maloney and the suitcase. In hot pursuit the Five charged after me but were hampered by the number of people on deck. Being small I managed to duck and dive between them, trying to retrace my steps to the relative (I hoped) safety of the Port side of the ship.

I wasn't as fit as I thought I was. My side was aching, and I was puffing like an old steamtrain. Behind me, I could hear shouts of, 'Let me through'. Summoning every ounce of my energy and running now on empty I spied what I thought was the pillar where Maloney and the suitcase were, but to my dismay neither were there. I could have cried in frustration had not I felt a heavy hand on my shoulder, and a yank and pull on my arm. My feet disappeared from underneath me, and I found myself walking in thin air.

With a hand clamped over my mouth to silence me, I struggled, but to no avail. The person who had nabbed me off the deck was so much stronger than me, and there was only one person I knew like that – Maloney. Deeper and deeper into the bowels of the ship he carried me and my suitcase through a door marked 'No entry', and I found myself in a room of what I could only imagine was something to do with the Ship's engine.

Gently placing me on the ground, hands released me and then spun me around. I came face to face with Maloney and the blessed sight of the suitcase. Pointing to the door and then to his mouth Maloney indicated that I shouldn't speak. Even if I could, he wouldn't have heard a thing as the thumping from the Ship's engines was very loud, and we would have had to shout to be heard. So, for the rest of the journey, we sat in silence, me with my head resting against Maloney's back, and for once I felt safe.

After a while, the sounds of the engines began to recede a little, until eventually they just idled. I surmised that we had reached the coast of England. Now the next stage of the game would begin, and we had to outwit the Five who were still searching for me somewhere. I suppose I trusted Maloney for now. At least he hadn't thrown me overboard and legged it with the suitcase.

'Right ', he said. 'Time to mingle. There will be so many poor souls leaving the boat, so we'll hide in plain sight. If I were a betting man, there would be a tide of people all glad to be in Blighty, so stick with me.'

Cautiously he opened the door and stuck his head around it for a second or two, then he nodded at me, gave me the thumbs up, and grabbed the suitcase in one hand and me by the other. Of course, he was right as there were hordes of people even at this level fighting their way off the ship. We climbed up through decks until we reached the top. By now the number of people had swelled and we didn't see the Five again until forty years later when it was on my terms.

Maloney and I joined the snaking line at immigration. I kept looking over my shoulder for Stefan and his gang but got reprimanded by Maloney. He didn't want us drawing untoward attention to ourselves.

Finally, we were at the front of the queue. A weary man of about thirty with round spectacles and a bald thinning head glanced at us.

'Papers' he snapped. Maloney turned on his full Irish charm and leant towards the man. A quick exchange of words which I didn't understand, and then we were off again. Arriving at Dover's train station we procured tickets to London. Sauntering like we didn't have a care in the world we made our way to the right platform which had a roof of shattered glass over it.

Maloney kept surreptitiously scouting the platform with dark hooded eyes. Nothing was untoward so we slipped into a 3rd class carriage, I guess it was because Maloney didn't have much money, or he hoped that the Five wouldn't find us there.

The carriage was heaving, and we couldn't find a seat, so Maloney plonked the suitcase down in the carriage vestibule. And we leant back with it between our feet. The railway system had suffered heavy damage in some areas due to the Luftwaffe bombing, and it was some time before we arrived in London our destination.

CHAPTER 8

THE CAMP-STEFAN'S STORY

I was born in 1928 in Chelm in South-eastern Poland. My father was a chemist, and my mother was a stay-at-home housewife who looked after me and my three brothers. As early as October 1939 the city was occupied by German Forces. Chelm's population was around 33,000 and 15,000 of these were Jewish. In some ways, we were lucky as we were non-Jews.

Life was hard, but my father managed to keep his business, and I carried on at school where I was supposed to leave at fourteen but in the end, I didn't. Although I was one of four boys at home, I was very solitary and always had my head in a book. Before the War, even at Nine my teachers at school thought I was university material because I was smart, and I had one great passion in life and that was Rocks.

I may have gone in a different direction had this not been the case. When the war started my parents became fully paid-up members of the Nazi Party. Initially, I couldn't have cared less but then I began to see maybe they were right.

It started with my father calling the Jews dirty bastards under his breath, then in 1942 when most of them had been rounded up and sent to internment camps only the very sick and mentally frail from the Jewish community were left behind. He then began to turn them away every time one of them designed to enter his shop. He was in his own way getting rid of the Jews by cutting off their access to medicines.

The only Teacher remaining at my school now was a Mr Bltnez. He was exempt from joining the Forces as he had been gassed during the First World War and was exempt due to his bad chest. Often you would see him in my father's chemist's shop buying whatever he could for a cough or a cold. He was not a good man and frequently I would end up teaching the younger kids at school, so my own education became a bit haphazard.

I knew my mother's family had come from a Military background but I did not know the full extent of it. I had spent the day grubbing around with rocks and soil whist the children at school were forgotten by me. When I returned one evening in early 1942 covered in dirt and grime I was surprised to see an official-looking car outside our house.

My mother had obviously told my brothers to stay away as they were nowhere to be seen. It was uncannily quiet without their constant bickering. The table had been set with our finest China, and my father who must have closed the shop for the afternoon was standing legs akimbo hands tucked into his second-best suit trouser pockets, chest swelling proudly.

Showing me into the kitchen to wash my dirty hands I got the impression that everyone was watching me including the two SS officers that I had seen in our living room. I returned and glanced at them all one by one expectantly. I'd caught them muttering something about a secret mission, so my interest was piqued.

My mother was about to speak when one of the SS officers saluted Hitler and then asked me a strange question.

'Do you love the Fuhrer', he asked rather brusquely.

'Yes Sir', I replied without hesitation.

'In that case', he continued, 'you will embark on a top-secret mission for him and him alone. Even your parents may not know what it is. You will endure hardship like nothing you have experienced before.

Excitement was coursing through my veins. This was every young man's dream – to serve the Fuhrer. I began to feel giddy with excitement. Up until now, my parents had largely ignored me. I hoped that this would make them proud of me. Little did they and I know that I would never see them again.

'Do I need to pack?' I asked in a strangled voice. 'If I'm going away surely, I'll need a few things', I trailed off beginning to feel a little foolish. My father raised his bushy eyebrows and my mother cast her eyes down to the floor where she seemed to have found a sudden interest in the pattern of the rug beneath her feet.

'No need to pack,' snapped back the SS Officer who had spoken before. 'Say goodbye to your parents. Where you're going you won't need much in the way of clothes.

Gulping I nodded silently and began to follow the two SS Officers out of the room. Glancing around I caught my father with his hands on my mother's shoulders. They had never in my seventeen years touched each other let alone like this so what the hell was going on? The memory of them standing there, my mother's lips quivering ever so slightly, my father's chin raised would be etched in my memory forever.

Outside I followed the two SS officers into their official car. They both sat there grimly not taking or smiling, but I caught their eyes darting around, connecting with each other briefly as though they were communicating in some way, then darting off in a different direction.

Those two pairs of eyes reminded me of a lazy summer's day when I had watched a blue and green dragonfly darting around then briefly settling on a leaf or a stone before darting off again. The trouble was a bird swooped down, grabbed it where it had come to rest, then swooped down and gobbled it up. Maybe that was a sign.

The journey to where we were going was arduous. Caught between the two SS officers I couldn't see out of the car windows. Stuck in the middle unable to move my legs being particularly long were beginning to cramp.

Finally, we began slowing down coming to some iron gates which I could see because they were so large and sinister-looking. We didn't have to stop, just waved through as though it was an ordinary day. Then the gates to hell clanged behind me. I was at The Auschwitz concentration camp located on the outskirts of Oświęcim in German-occupied Poland. It was originally established in 1940 and later referred to as "Auschwitz I" or "Main Camp."

Stumbling out of the car I silently followed the two SS officers into a dilapidated block. The air was filled with choking smoke which came from a large chimney in the distance. Naturally, I had heard about this sort of thing, but I kept telling myself it was for the greater good of the Third Reich. One of the SS Officers knocked on a door. After a brief' "come", I was propelled inside by the Officer and came face to face with one of the greatest men ever known, Josef Mengele.

Remembering the words that had passed in my home I gave s Hitler Salute. Mengele looked pleased at that and beckoned me close. In front of him on his desk on which he rested his hands was an object that I had never seen the likes of before. Trying not to stare at it nor reach out to touch it I clasped my hands jointly behind my back, fists clenched so that my fingernails dug into the palms.

CHAPTER 9

PUT TO WORK

It seemed an age before Mengele spoke. He obviously had me here for a reason, but at that time I couldn't guess. Gesturing to the object on his desk which was ark-like in its appearance he asked me to open it. It wasn't easy, and it seemed as though the thing did not want me to unfasten it.

With a gentle, "tsk", the great man himself opened it. Peering inside I saw that it contained an ancient-looking scroll. Rapidly closing it he wrapped it in a cloth.

'That', he said is your mission. 'You do not speak to anyone about it, you do not breathe a word outside this room. If fail to do so you will be sent to the Gas Chamber, do you understand?'

I could only squeak out a 'Yes Sir' before he continued.

'We are rounding up the best of the youth who have a certain knowledge. Yours is that of Geology. I understand that you know all about the earth's crust etc. What you need to help me ascertain is if this is authentic or not. You will have the help of four others who will be arriving shortly.

Holding his hand up so that I wouldn't interrupt his flow of words I listened to him with both fascination and horror. The blood drained from my face, and I became quite nauseous.

Seeing the change in my countenance he went on more quietly now so that I had to strain to hear him. He laid out a plan to me so dastardly, so evil, so frightening that the Fuhrer himself would be impressed.

The premise of the plan was that I and four others would be placed in a stall in a horseblock in Camp II which was known as the Death Camp. To all intents and purposes, we were meant to be treated like the damn Jews. Head shaved pyjama-like clothes, terrible sanitary conditions, and little food or water.

Each day we would be marched the two miles to Mengele's office and carry out his bidding. Anything we needed whilst we were there, we could have any chemical, paper to write our findings on and the free run at women. If I or my fellow stall mates performed well then, we would be allowed 'access' to Mengele's whore herself.

When the Germans won the war, they undoubtedly would be heaped with praise and given the highest honour that Hitler could bestow on us including the Iron Cross. We would get to see our parents again, and they would be showered with gifts and riches.

I mean what seventeen-year-old boy wouldn't want this? I was also the de facto head of the bunk. It would be hard, yes, but I didn't see why Germany should not win the war before the year was out. Also, on the plus side, I would be in charge so to speak.

Getting my head shaved once I reached Camp II was not an easy thing. I may have been the bookish type, but I certainly thought that I was good-looking until then. I rubbed my hand over the top of my shaved head and all I could feel was my skull with its bones sticking through the translucent skin.

I kept on telling myself that it was for the greater good, and even until a few days ago I was still at school, now the probability of annihilation of the Jews was in my hand. Once Mengele had proved that the Ark's contents contained the Torah handed to Moses himself, he then had the Jew's very being, everything that they foolishly believed in was in his keeping and that would finish them off for good.

The shaving of my head was followed by a cold shower alongside a few dozen who had been sent to the camp. After that, we were given our hideous clothing. Now I could begin to blend in. The men in my stable block took me at face value, and to them, I was just another Jew who had the misfortune to be there.

For the first few days, I kept myself to myself. No one in that situation would want to swap life stories. If they did, I could regale with the snippets of information that I had picked up from my father's shop. On the fourth day, I was getting bored, and then the others arrived.

Petroniusz was the first. He told me that he was fifteen and that his interests were serving the Fuhrer and Marine Life. After that came Nelek. At first, I couldn't understand why he was there. He didn't seem to have any scientific knowledge but turned out that he was a gymnastics champion and as strong as an ox, and he could swim for two miles underwater without coming up for air.

Cezer was into his Chemistry and had won some sort of medal for it in his region of Poland. Finally, there was Fredryke who loved numbers. You only had to give him one number and he could turn it into anything related to the universe. I later discovered that he was to count the number of letters words, and lines in the Torah as they had to be a specific number. So, there we were. We were the Five.

Each day we would be escorted to Mengele's office where we worked on the pieces of the scroll to test its ink's authenticity. In ancient times, the ink used for writing a Torah scroll would have been obtained by boiling oils, tar and wax, and collecting the vapours. Afterwards, that mixture would be combined with tree sap and honey, and then dried out and stored. Before its use, it would be mixed with gall-nut juice. A Torah scroll may only be written on parchment from the skin of a kosher animal, and this was another of the Five's tasks.

You may wonder how I knew all about what a Torah should be composed of. Truthfully II had help from one of the SS Officers who wasn't quite what he seemed. I wasn't going to tell on him though as he arranged for me to have more food than the others. In prison food was currency.

If we had a successful day then we were allowed a little pleasure, if not then back to the stable stalls to sleep and then get woken up to repeat the whole thing. After ten days of this, I had the audacity to mention to Mengele that it would help if we had someone who knew the Torah well to come and assist us.

Now it was Mengele's turn for the blood to drain from his face. I was certain I was destined for the Gas Chamber, probably sealing the fate of the other four as well. Mengele started to pace around his office deep in thought. It was then that he came up with an excellent plan. Outlining it to us Five I began to feel the blood in my veins pumping, and I got fired up again by the project.

Sometimes we do things to please people, sometimes we do things because our parents doctorate us with their beliefs. I was, when I asked for a Torah expert, I was following both. I wanted to please Mengele, and I loved what my parents had drilled into me. All Jews were dirty. I had not thought of the consequences. What we did outside Mengele's office was of little consequence.

The things that we did from then on, I am not ashamed of. Having given my life to serve the Third Reich I'd be damned if we could not have a little fun along the way, and fun we had. As I had been one of five children who was largely ignored, I was relishing in the fact that I was going to be in. charge. Up until now, I had only read about worldly things in books that I stole from my father's bookcase. Now I could put into practice everything that I had read, and boy was I going to have some fun.

CHAPTER 10

THE BOY

The Boy arrived a few days later. From the outset, I made sure he'd know who was boss and I was determined to break him. Not so much that he wasn't useful to us, just enough to keep him in line. Eventually, he would come around to our way of thinking. Eventually one way or another he would come around to our way of thinking, and when he did (which according to Mengele would not be long), we would discover the secrets of the Ark.

Meanwhile, we carried on going to Mengele's office every day. We were usually left under the watchful eye of two SS Officers. Mengele carried on with his experiments with twins. So, it was up to us to present something every day. Sometimes he left his mistress with us. A definite perk of the job.

Of course, part of our mission was to get the boy working with us. A couple of years passed, and we continued with our abuse of him. He would not break no matter what we did to him. For a Jew, he was very resilient. Straight from the off, I realised that he was using a false name. It was his mannerisms that gave him away. Eventually, he caved in. The plan was coming to fruition, and I kept a small stub of chalk hidden away should I ever need it. The day happened when the idiot claimed to be the next Messiah. Stupid fool. Everyone knew that Hitler was the next Messiah. Hitler believed that people could be separated into a hierarchy of different races, where some races were superior, and others were inferior. Hitler believed the German race to be the superior race and called the German race 'Aryan'.

Hitler and the Nazis considered Jews to be an inferior race of people, who set out to weaken other races and take over the world. He believed that Jews were particularly destructive to the German 'Aryan' race and did not have any place in Nazi Germany.

Hitler also wanted to rid Germany of the disabled, homosexuals, Roma and Sinti, and other minorities that did not fit into his idea of an Aryan race. The Nazis labelled these groups 'a-social'. Of course, it never entered our heads that none of us with our physical misgivings would be part of that group. We were either tall or fat or short or near-sighted. And of course, we were all Polish.

When the Boy caved in and 'healed' my burn I was delighted. It was worth a burn or two from a cigarette. This is where the chalk came in handy and had been passed from under my 'pillow' from one to the other so that I could cover up the burn. The Boy seemed happy for the first time in ages.

The next day I feigned an illness, which was not so uncommon in a camp like ours. Many prisoners suffered from tuberculosis, ague (malaria), meningitis, pemphigus, dysentery, and Durchfall, a disorder of the digestive system caused by improper and inadequate food. In camp conditions, all these illnesses were highly acute. A characteristic camp illness was starvation sickness.

I clutched my belly when the SS guards came in to escort us. Mengele's office the next day. I noticed that it was always the same two men who collected us. They must have been in on the plot too or how else would they accept an 'unknown' to take my pace?

The Boy hadn't been working with us long when the rumours started. I heard whispered conversations that I shouldn't have. On one such occasion, Mengele shooed us out of his office and told us to wait outside, and not to try to escape on pain of death. The two SS officers who usually guarded us remained inside. This got my senses twitching. Telling the boys to keep a look out I leaned against the door, but I only heard snatched phrases which I tried to piece together myself.

A week later Mengele had the Five in his office, but not the Boy. This time we had to leave him in the stable stalls. At this point, we weren't talking to him anyway because he started a nasty little rumour about two of us being involved in an experiment with Fraternal Twins for Mengele.

Mengele told us that the Red Army was approaching, and the camp inmates had to be taken to somewhere safe. He told us that as he had so much confidence in us we should keep our heads down. We were told to stay at the Camp and keep an eye on the Boy, who would naturally try to escape. He tasked us with following the Boy at a discrete distance and claiming back from him anything that he took. I presume he meant the Ark. Mengele told us that we would meet up both with him and all the artefacts that he had acquired once Germany had trounced the Red Army. Naturally, I believed him.

One morning just after daybreak I noticed that the boy had gone. Since the Germans had fled, we were at a loss as to what to do, but I remember our final task and that was to keep an eye on the boy. At first, I thought that he was just hiding, but after getting the other four to help me search I started to panic. He had escaped.

Knowing that the Boy was too weak to get very far I suspected that he had collapsed before reaching a main road so we ran as fast as we could to try and catch him. As luck would have it, we spotted an old man driving a horse and cart. Assuming that he was Polish I waved for him to stop, and I made a fuss of his horse. Five minutes later we sat in the back of the cart. Explaining that we had lost our 'friend' and could the old man let us stay on the cart until we could spot the boy.

Finally, I could see him in the distance limping along, so jumping down from the cart we ran hell for leather. Just as we were within 30 meters of him a column of Red Army soldiers came marching along the road, so we hid behind a large bush. Emerging from it to our dismay the Boy has disappeared.

Five minutes later his head popped up above a ditch, but I saw that he had a 'Protector' of some sort with him, which made it doubly hard for us to keep tabs on him. There was no way in hell that we could take on this man, so we had to be sneaky and track them. What's more, I saw that the Boy carried a suitcase. It was obvious to me what was inside it.

It was good that there were five of us and only two of them which meant that when they slept two of us could, and the other three stayed on guard. This carried on until we reached the Red Cross Camp. We had the choice of either splitting up or biding our time, so we stuck together hanging around most days, but from a distance. Eventually, the weather got warmer, and the Boy and his protector left the auspicious of the Red Cross. We had these six or so months to recuperate ourselves. This gave us time to steal food and money. It also gave us time to plot our next move.

It should have been on Train to Switzerland that we got hold of the Boy. There were still a few people in the village near the Red Cross camp in Austria who kept their allegiance to the Third Reich, so as lost 'Boys' we managed to move amongst them until eventually they didn't really notice us. We found out about the Train, and what time they were expected to travel, but the boy and his protector must have caught an earlier one as we watched the station for a few days without sight of them. I decided we must jump on a train ourselves and follow. Luckily, I had heard where he was heading for.

Arriving in Switzerland we gave out the impression that we were five refugees who had banded together because we had lost our families. Taking pity on us, and although Switzerland was neutral, we were allowed to stay. The trouble was that the Boy was in a sanatorium. Switzerland was an eye open. Petroniusz used to often say that the Edelweiss was like a carpet of snow on the ground. I never had him down as a dreamer. Easily fooled yes, but a dreamer no.

Being the eldest of the Five people paid more respect to me. I managed to get a job on a farm. Luckily for me, the Farmer's daughter was a cleaner at the Sanatorium. It was through chatting with her that I found out about the Boy's proposed move to France, and then to England. It took all my willpower to talk to her and pretend that I was interested in her. Some would call her homely and buxom. I would call her ugly and fat, but I had to play the game.

The date was fixed. All we had to go was across to France and from there the Ferry to England. Once on the ferry, we would pounce. We knew that the Boy would have his protector with him and that we would have to watch and wait. Having enough money to tip off one of the crew members was not a problem. Apart from relieving the farmer's daughter of her virginity I also relieved her of her poor pa's life savings as she was so eager to keep me happy.

Once on board, we chatted amongst ourselves. Luck was on our side. We knew that as soon as the Boy heard his native language, he would be curious. At first, I thought that I had him, but with a quick glance, I saw that he did not have the suitcase with him. He thought that by kicking me I would let him go free. A chase ensued, but to our disappointment, he disappeared into thin air. I am sure we would catch up with him at the docks, but again he managed to evaporate into thin air. We just had to bide our time. We would find him one day.

CHAPTER 11

ONWARDS

Tie Five heard from those who remained true to the Fuhrer that their Leader had escaped from Berlin. He was supposed to have committed suicide in his hidden bunker. It was not widely known that within this bunker was a secret door that led to another secret bunker, which then connected to a series of tunnels that ran under the U-Bahn where the Further and a few others climbed out, and then left Berlin behind via train to plan the Fourth Reich.

The Five waited for a signal from Hitler to join him. Hitler, it was claimed, had been seen in Ireland dressed as a woman; in Egypt where he had converted to Islam; in a coffee house in Amsterdam; on a train travelling from New Orleans; in a Washington, DC, restaurant; and in Charlottesville, Virginia.

Despite these claims, The Five didn't hear from him anymore. They prepared themselves by getting jobs in Geology, Marine Biology, Swimming, Chemistry and Mathematics waiting for the Ark to fall into their hands again. They spent many hours trying to find the Ark, but it was safely tucked away in a house in Chelsea guarded by Mahony. There was no way in. The Five just had to bide their time.

When the Boy finally settled with Mahoney in England it was in the Midlands a long way from the sea. Hopefully, no one from their past would find them there. Mahoney and the Boy spent many years roaming the countryside and began to know it well. They got acquainted with the undulating hills, dales and peaks of Derbyshire, the way people from Nottingham called our 'Ey up me duck', The influx of people bringing a vivid kaleidoscopic of turbans and Saris to Leicester made from silk the likes of which was never encountered in Poland.

Mahoney and the Boy scoped out the areas. They both understood that they must seek revenge, The International Criminal Court held at The Hauge would one day catch up with some of the perpetrators of War Crimes. As for Josef Mengele, his health has been steadily declining since 1972. He suffered a stroke in 1976, experienced high blood pressure, and developed an ear infection. Mengele suffered another stroke while swimming and drowned in the coastal resort of Bertioga.

After nearly forty years the Five who had made the Boys life a misery had all been tracked down. The Boy was now very rich and living in Chelsea with Mahoney as his manservant. He knew exactly what needed doing and planned in detail where and how. All the Five pieces of the Scroll of Moses had been touched by such evil so should never come into physical contact with anyone again. Although it should have been to be returned to Egypt where its five books came from when it had been handed to Moses, The Boy could not take the risk of the rise of a Fourth Reich. Who knew what hellish things would be released if they. The world could not face another war.

After the Boy had exacted revenge on the Five, he would leave pieces of the scroll where they lay, never to be found, never to be disturbed. The site of the power station where the otters once ran riot was closed and in its place, a nature reserve was established so that all could enjoy it, no further incidents since 1985 have been reported yet.

As for the last Torah manuscript, it was discovered by a schoolboy, by now a man. The Boy needed to find it before he passed away and bury it somewhere that it could not be found. He needed to seek redemption and there was only one way, and that was to break cover after all this time. Strange things had been happening that could not be ignored.

On Friday 4th November 2022 at 12.24 pm, a fire broke out at Montsorrel Quarry. Then a Leicester man, Luke Branston died in the early hours of June 21st, 2017, after becoming trapped there. He was standing on a conveyor that had not been effectively isolated - through cutting the power - before the repair work started. The conveyor was then inadvertently switched on, fatally crushing the 26-year-old.

The lockkeeper's cottage at Foxton Lock was never used again. On the 15th of January 2015, a man who fell into the water at the locks on a Sunday died a few days later in Kettering Hospital.

Spondon's British Celanese factory is still standing but it is better for the local community since the Clean Air Act of 1993. However, the baby girl whom Charles never got to meet was born with a port wine mark on her face. After being teased mercilessly at school about it she committed suicide aged just thirteen.

Stefen was now calling himself Doctor Steven Langton. He quietly anglicised his first name, the Langton he stole from a man buried in a graveyard who just happened to have been a doctor. Not one person questioned what sort of a doctor. When asked to present his qualifications to any Human Resources Department he simply claimed that his diplomas and degrees were lost in the war, and he would get copied if he could. You must remember that this was pre-internet days so nobody could prove or disprove this. Finally, he found a post at Loughborough University, not a million miles from where the Boy had first settled. Knowing Stefan, he would soon get bored, so it was easy enough to post an exciting opportunity for a Geologist in the Newspaper.

Petroniusz changed his name to Peter and became a Lecturer at Nottingham University. He was no more qualified than someone in their first semester. He knew all about pond life having shared a hut with the others at the camp! Again, he blagged his way through life and jobs.

Nelek was now known as Neil. Although he had been a Gymnast when he was younger, he had no ambition and always ended up in dead-end jobs like the one as swimming instructor cum janitor at a council-run swimming bath. Poor deluded fool who thought he could make money from someone who claimed they could not swim. Being avaricious Neil could not resist the idea of getting his hands on extra cash.

He thought that he was the best swimmer in the whole of the Midlands and was not surprised when he was asked by someone to teach him how to swim. He did not personally know that at Foxton Locks all the locks rise to seventy-five feet, and neither did not realise that ultimately, they would be his undoing.

Cezar did not need to prove much either to get his job. It was simply a question of changing his name to Chris and getting a mundane job that involved propylene and its isopropyl alcohol and acetone to produce Nylon. His attention to detail which he used in Germany made him a good choice for someone mixing the exact amount of chemicals. Many people who worked there developed and died from mesothelioma, an asbestos-related illness.

As for Fredryke, he was more honourable and trained as a teacher, married an English woman named Muriel, and worked hard until he was made head of the department. Of all of them, he was the one who wasn't killed as in the end either fate or God had spared him, for he had shown kindness in the darkest of days. His life would have ended had it not been for a van driver running a red light on a road that he did not know. Was it fate that the van driver decided to drive through a red light on the wrong side of the road, or was it something else?

CHAPTER 12

MOTHERS AND SONS

Rosanne was born in Bonn where her father taught medicine at the university. He was always proclaiming that the students there had no interest in the subject. Until one day he started to gush forth about a student who had studied Philosophy at Munich and had come to Bonn to study medicine. He had high hopes for him as this young man was about to sit his medical preliminary examination.

On the day that her father brought this handsome young man to dinner, Rosanne knew that she was in love. Of course, he didn't try and flirt with her at first. He was upright and proud and spent most of the evening discussing things with my father that she could not understand. All she knew was that he had raw, animal magnetism.

Rosanne left home suddenly in a hurry, not caring what she left behind. Her parents would be in shock if they knew that she had one or two dalliances with members of the S. S, and by 1938 she had sought Mengele out again in a battalion where he was medical officer. By now she had a two-year-old son and had married a Jewish husband out of necessity. She was ordered wed and to carry on procreating.

She cried when Mengele left Germany for Poland in 1943 to take up a new position. She was left behind in Poland with a weak-willed husband. Of course, there were promises that the boy's father would return for him one day. She knew this was true because as well, being Jewish, her husband also has a secret, which would have repercussions for years to come.

Rosanne's husband always thought that she was better than him, and although he didn't definitively know that she held the same beliefs as he did, he could tell from her dark hair, and dark eyes that she had

Jewish blood. He had only been seeing her for a few months when she told him she was pregnant. This surprised him greatly as he had succumbed to mumps when he was ten, so there was no way the child was his. She was very pervasive though, and although she apparently had no father to ask permission of, he married her within a week, and they settled down in a flat above his Chemist shop. Little did he know that his life and that of the unborn child were in danger. So far, he had managed to keep his job as a Banker.

It happened very suddenly on a bitterly cold night in December 1941. His wife was apparently tending to the elderly, which to his knowledge she had never done before. His son was asleep tucked up in bed with a picture book that a grateful client had given to him. The banging on the door, followed by the sound of wood splintering sent shivers down his spine. He hurried over to where he kept the Ark. It was important that he kept its contents from falling into the hands of the Germans, as its contents were thousands of years old, and had to be protected at all costs.

The cost was indeed high. The Banker was taken to a concentration camp where he was gassed, and the Ark fell into the possession of the Nazis. When his wife came home, she found a frightened son, and no husband, plus a gap where the Ark used to be. Instead of crying for her lost husband, she simply sat down and waited for her reward. A place at Mengele's side for her, and a place for her son in the gas chamber.

What she didn't know was that her son was wise beyond his years. When he came into her life again, she was heavily pregnant and nearly miscarried when she saw her son standing before her emancipated, cowed and beaten in Mengele's office.

As Mengele was looking for his 'team' of boys, his first thought was the other research students that he had been with at university. Instantly dismissing this as foolish as they would all be in their late twenties or early thirties by now, and no longer pliable he looked towards the boys of men he could trust, men like his personal SS Officers, men who had shown their true colours during occupation, men who supported Hitler.

The Mothers were all proud of their sons., It did not matter one iota if they were not physically perfect. They were wanted for their knowledge. He Mothers believed that their sons would return proudly after the war. None of the Five ever saw their parents again. They always claimed that they were orphans after the war so everyone felt sorry for them. It was convenient for them if ever the conversation arose, and gave them a reason never to talk about their pasts.

The first of the 'Boys' Had excelled in all subjects at school and had a particular interest in Geology. That aside It could have been one of his bastards. There were enough of them. The boy would be in his teens by now. A natural leader if ever there was one. A little coercion and the youth would be working for him.

The rest of them had done well in school – boys who had excelled in Biology, Chemistry, and Mathematics. There was one that he needed though. The boy was a champion swimmer. Arriving under the cover of darkness they were all soon part of the camp, as working inmates. They were all told that they would have their freedom when Germany won the war which was imminent.

It wouldn't do to show them preferential treatment, but they had other 'privileges', and he knew the odd SS officer who slipped them a crafty 'smoke'. They all had been told that what they were doing was for the greater good. They had been told that when Germany had won the war they would be reunited with their families. This never happened, they were left abandoned after the Death March of 1945. The only thing that had been arranged was a lift to coincide with the Boy leaving.

Hitler's tentacles spread far and wide. It may have been a lorry that was passing through, it may have been an old man and his horse and cart. No one really knew the truth, but evil was at work the day that the Five followed and hunted the Boy.

PART 4 – THE TRUTHS

EXTRACT FROM THE DIARY - AUTHOR UNKNOWN.

Of course, everyone had their own version of events, their own truths. By now I was confused by the whole thing. Maybe some of them were lying, and maybe some of them were not, but who?

CHAPTER 1

JOHN O'HOULIHAN TRUTH ABOUT EUROSTAR

On my Mother's Life, I swear that I will tell the truth. Should I have to stand up in a court of law then everyone will believe my truth. What reason have I got to lie, what's done is done and it had nothing to do with me, honestly.

I must give thanks to my wife Sam. After all my indiscretions with my little gambling habit, she of course now controlled the purse strings. Having said that, she is a very avaricious bitch. When I told her that I had the opportunity to visit the Sorbonne in Paris to meet an eminent Doctor of languages with the possibility of a tenure there for myself, she jumped at the chance. On the day before Eurostar, I was so drunk and wished that I could stay in France forever. I had been used to freedom for the past three days. The first day I arrived here, I may have imbibed a little of the vino. The next day I met Alexandre at a café on the left bank, and we drank more wine and a lot of whisky for some reason.

That night I find myself in a room with maybe 60 or 70 people jammed in. They were mainly students. Socialists like me. My dear old dad would turn in his grave if he had one, but the bastard UDR shot him to pieces, then kicked his head in for no good reason. His body was never found. I mean he was only meant to blow up a pub full of protestant drinkers. He was an IRA man through and through.

Seeing what had happened to him turned me away from the IRA, but I still have a friend or two in their midst.

The speaker tonight is rallying the troops so that a major bombing campaign can be planned to blow up the Paris Underground system. Now because of my contacts, plus my ill-spent youth, they are interested in my knowledge of explosives.

They have agreed with me that it will be a quid per quo exchange (or should that be Euros?)

My knowledge was traded for their planning knowledge. I have a group of dissident students at Oxford, and we are planning to blow up Eurostar. Everyone is happy for once, the English and the French. My bit for entente cordial.

The apple cart was completely upset when a young woman approached me. She was so like a girl I knew briefly. She was going to tell me something I'm sure, but then an old friend showed up and the girl disappeared. Such a shame, I would have loved to have got to know her better. After all, Sam was not an exciting person in the bedroom, and a little dalliance on my part would have been good for my morale.

Now it's the day of Eurostar. As I said before in my defence, I had way too much to drink last night and am obviously suffering. I have drunk enough French Coffee to sink a battleship but am still feeling rough.

Carrying my rucksack, I gingerly slide into a seat at the coffee bar in the Gare de Norde. I nearly didn't make the train; the bloody French Taxi Driver took the most tortuous route around Paris. When I got to the station, I noticed two things. Firstly, there was a bunch of rowdies hurray Henrys, secondly a beautiful dark-haired woman in a red coat, expensive-looking shoes, and a handbag strode purposefully towards Eurostar check-in.

Throwing a handful of Euros at the ill-mannered, garlic-smelling taxi driver, who grinned toothlessly at me, I jumped out, almost forgetting my rucksack in my haste to keep tabs on the dark-haired beauty. Now

I'm not one to know fashion brands by name, but my wife seems to have a penchant for Prada boots. I mean how many pairs of black Prada boots does one woman need?

The woman with the expensive clobber could be my way into funding my little surprise, so I followed her, just staying close enough to keep her in sight. Good, she was heading for the coffee place. I could do it with another cup or six.

Nabbing one of the tables next to the stunning beauty, only a French Woman could dress like that, she was studiously trying to avoid. For a minute I was caught up in my own musings. Glancing up, I noticed she had left already. Across the bridge, and onto the concourse, people were scattered hither and thither, searching frantically for their coach numbers. All around the crowd were chattering in a polyglot of different languages. The noise and my poor head were also made much worse by the tannoid announcement in both French and English. I caught sight of a red coat heading towards the 1st class coaches. Of course, she would be travelling first class.

Not long after Eurostar pulled out of the Gare de Norde, I started to get annoyed at the woman sitting next to me who was yattering away on the 'phone. Deciding I'd had enough, I swallowed more painkillers having shielded the plans and schematics for blowing up Eurostar from prying eyes.

Finding the delicious brunette in the buffet car, I suddenly decide; nothing ventured, nothing gained, so I try to engage her in conversation. Giving Myself a good talking too, and as Ms Red-Coat is amused by my poor attempt to speak, I try and wangle her address out of her by innocuously asking where she lived.

Unfortunately, she seems a little reticent about where she lives. With the classic brush-off having-to-return-to my seat excuse, I grumpily return to mine, and to the whining old bat in the seat next to me. After that, I did try and get some sleep. I was rudely awoken by the woman next to me shrieking and yelling and pointing at what appeared to be smoke.

All around me is a mangled mettle, the lighting has failed, and the emergency lighting hasn't kicked in. Covering my face with the sleeve of my jacket I grabbed hold of the arm of the woman next to me. Much as I had hated her on sight, this wasn't the time for my prejudices to surface.

Pulling her towards the exit door between the carriages, I was faced with a barrage of metal, could that possibly be an arm? Beyond the pile of twisted metal, two men were throwing punches at each other. Putting my fingers in his mouth, I whistled loudly enough to stop them.

I then said as gently, but as firmly as I could,

'We are going to get you over the metal my dear, but I'm going to need you to help.'

The loud woman is now quiet. She visibly paled when I suggested it. Shaking her head reluctantly, she cast a mournful eye over her purchases now scattered to the four winds. Grabbing her under one arm, I heaved her up onto the pile of metal as best I could.

The two gents, up until now had been apparently fighting, reached over as far as they could to grab her on the other side. With a little heaving of her rather ample posterior, between us, we managed to get her to the other side, where she managed to stagger a little.

Next thing a couple of strong men had forced open the outer doors and had stuck their heads around it. Seeing the large lady, who after her efforts was laying supine on the floor, they reached in, and with a knowingly nod to each other, hoicked her up, and bundled her off the train.

I didn't expect to see her again, but I caught a glimpse of her being picked up by a chauffeur-driven Bentley, which looked a bit innocuous outside Golders Green Police Station.

I must admit I was a bit sparse with the truth. When I tried to kiss Laura Marchant's hand at the buffet car on Eurostar, I failed to mention that I slipped the expensive watch from her wrist, and then into my rucksack on my way back to my seat. It must have fallen out during the debacle. I have no idea where it ended up. DI White did not mention a watch when we had our chat. He mentioned other things, which got me thinking, Is he telling the whole truth?

CHAPTER 2

GLEN COOPER'S TRUTH

I am a retired officer of HM armed forces, and I vowed to tell the truth, so here is what happened.

The day before Eurostar we had finally made it as high as we could on the Eifel Tower. After queuing with two rebellious pre-teens, and what with Claire having to keep slipping off to the ladies every hour, we finally managed to clamber out of the lift on the 2nd floor. By taking said lift after queuing for what seemed to me hours. It meant that I would not reach the 2nd stage huffing and puffing after

climbing some 600 stairs. The twins would have liked to do so, and no doubt Claire would have done too. She'd taken up running about 3 years ago and could probably do 15-20K without breaking out in a sweat.

Many years ago, when were here before, we did climb all 600 steps, but since the operation on my left knee, I walk with a pronounced limp. You must understand that Paris was a very different place back then. All the little cafes and hangouts where the Mademoiselle and I used to meet up are probably no longer there. Shame, I would really have liked to show the twins what the real Paris is like, but we ended up eating in McDonalds on the Champs Elysees. Coming out of the ladies there Clare did look a little sick.

Originally, I was going to use some of my pension on a Bateaux ride down the Seine. Given the look that I got from Claire maybe the idea of lashing out 75 Euros each was a bit much. That and the fact that she had got a dicky tummy after eating a burger. I guess going off to the loo every hour was part and parcel of eating at a fast-food outlet. I of course only had a cup of rather disgusting tea. I'd kept a banana and a chocolate bar in the pocket of my Mac just in case of emergencies. This proved in time to be rather prudent of me.

At the top of the tower, the twins were zooming around like a tornado. The nice thing about the French is that they just shrug knowingly. Not like Tesco's where everyone is quick to call you out.

After showing the twins the Louvre (boring), took the vernacular up to Sacre Coeur (slightly less boring), had a brief look at the ongoing work regarding Notre Dame (the Twins don't watch much TV, and anyway it got burned down a few years ago), and Claire insisting on us parading around the Science Museum – which infract the twins liked as some of the exhibits were interactive. The only thing that worried me was that they were fascinated by the guillotine, whereby you put a couple of Euros in a slot, and Madam Guillotine did her work.

The pinnacle of the trip was the Eifel Tower. The twins both loved it and thoroughly enjoyed riding in the yellow lift with the glass sides. Dashing from corner to corner at the top, they seemed in awe of the view of Paris before us. The only fly in the ointment is that Claire kept on looking at her 'phone.

Thinking about it, she had been a little distant for the past 18 months. She would occasionally forget things like the shopping or the dry cleaning. When I expressed my concerns, she waved me away with a flap of her hand. I was beginning to think she had Dementia. Her Father had suffered from this, and I hoped she wasn't going to follow in her footsteps.

Before we made a start on the Tower, she whispered that she had to go to the loo pronto. I thought that as we were at the sight of a major tourist attraction, she would find one quickly. In the end, it took about fifteen minutes until she came back red-faced and sweaty.

Just as we were leaving our house a couple of days ago, she had slipped on the ring that her father the General used to wear. Gold and

Engraved with his initials, with a tiny Nightingale, etched on the inner rim, it was one more thing that made me think she was losing her mind.

Giggling like an errant schoolgirl when she pushed it on, she put her finger to her lips. Not normally demonstrative she slipped her hand around my waist and pulled me towards her so that her lips were close to my ear. Thinking she was going to whisper sweet nothings to me, I was surprised when she uttered the words,

'If anything happens, tell the Police that you put the ring on that morning'.

Bemused I looked into her eyes as she pulled back. Then again, we all had our secrets, didn't we?

Even I had a secret, a little something that no one else knew about. Let's just say I am able to get away from Claire and the grandkids from time to time. I have a small bolthole in the 4th Arrondissement, but she doesn't need to know about it, does she?

On the day of Eurostar, we had finally managed to herd the twins reluctantly back to the Gare de Norde. They had insisted on riding the Metro there and kept shouting out how cool it would be if someone decided to set off a bomb underground. Claire frowned a little at that, but she didn't chastise them. I was lost in thought - Maybe, just Maybe I could listen to the Test Match or something more interesting on my pocket-sized radio on the way back home.

The train was running exactly 7 minutes and 8 seconds late. Being a military man (retired), I have a thing about precise times. It's my Achilles heel. Many years ago, Claire and I were fortunate enough to get our hands on a pair of his and her Swiss Watches. Being Swiss they had an excellent time. The twins thundered over the bridge and ran down the platform looking for our carriage. I would have loved to have travelled 1st Class. Claire didn't know about my little cache of money that I received for a job I did. She insisted that it was too expensive, hence we were travelling in 2nd class.

During the journey, after several trips to the loo, once complaining she had to walk all the up to one near the 1st class carriages, Claire settled down a bit. She kept pulling her 'phone out. It was one of those new ones, which I found quite surprising. She was always moaning about the cost of things and was abhorrent at the idea that any of our brood should have a modern type of mobile.

I seemed to remember that she was one of the old-style flip phones. Mind you if she had the beginnings of Dementia, she had probably forgotten she had already got one. Nevertheless, she still allowed the twins to run riot. They were causing mayhem by running up and down the aisle. I was listening to an old-fashioned Dictaphone, trying to make sense of it all. If anyone asked, I was listening to the England Versus Jamaica test match. I knew they were playing that day as my old pal Chris was going to bat first for Jamacia. He would let me know the outcome of the match, wouldn't he?

I couldn't risk a sneaky peek at my iPad at home to glean the results. One of the Grandkids had bought it for me for Christmas last year. Claire thought I hadn't mastered it yet, but little did she know.

Re-winding the tape, and trying to understand it for the umpteenth time, I had those small in-ear headphones in. My eyes shut so that I could concentrate. Yesterday, under the premise of having a small snifter in the bar, I had managed to slip out of the hotel for about ¾ of an hour. Long enough to meet my French Contact in a small side-street café. Yes, there was one of them left if you knew where to look, and if you knew Paris like I did.

We were almost at St Pancras station, our destination. I'm not pedantic by any means, but by the time we added in the 7 minutes and 8 Seconds, plus the 3 minutes and 20 seconds for our unscheduled stop at Ebbsfleet, I calculated that we had 5 minutes before we arrived.

I felt a change in the atmosphere. Seemed to be darker than normal, maybe it was the run-in to the station, but I don't remember it being this dark last time.

I felt a tugging off my knee. One of the twins was crying out that there was smoke everywhere. It was pitch black with smoke billowing everywhere. At this point, I knew it was an emergency and I managed to prise a door open with my Swiss Army Knife, almost breaking the blade in the process. I wanted to be on the King's Honour's list for my brave efforts, then no one would suspect a man with an OBE. I managed to shove the twins towards a couple of men, who had just helped a lady climb over the rubble. Luckily the Emergency Services were at hand rapidly, so making sure that the grandkids were handed over safely I turned to find Claire, but she had disappeared.

After 'phoning St Thomas's later that evening, it wasn't a surprise to me that Claire hadn't turned up there. I hadn't been contacted by the police at this stage, so she wasn't dead as far as I knew. Of course, I was used to her going off at odd times. I mean it was the dementia, wasn't it? Or was there part of her past she lied about?

CHAPTER 3

MARY PICKLES's TRUTH

My husband is a respected Judge you know, so I should think I know the difference between a lie and the truth, so help me God this is the Truth.

After everything that had gone on with my disgraced husband (more of that later) and the fact that the tabloids including the fascist Times as I like to call one of them reported it, I felt that I should be the woman scorned, and decided to take myself off to Paris for a little trip for a couple of days.

My friends were all aghast that George could have done such a terrible thing but let's just say that he had a little help from Moi. You see he always had a roving eye, and after 40 years of marriage, I was beginning to feel like a 2nd class citizen in his eyes. I knew I had to do something about it, and if he divorced me, he wouldn't get his hands on the family fortune.

In his older brother's will, he stood to inherit the lot, including an auspicious pile close to Arundel in Sussex. As for myself, I wasn't that bothered as I has my own money which I'd worked damned hard for that was neatly tucked away in a nice little Swiss Bank Account. I had a girl in Greenwich who occasionally did a little bit of work for me. For a small fee, it could have been to feed her habit (I don't know) I could have all my correspondence sent to her address to a small obscure estate within a bigger grander estate. The Cator estate – the place suited my needs. Also, I hated going and doing the dirty work myself, but I guess beggars can't be choosers,

I had spent the 1st day in Paris wandering around the shops. I went in and out of all the good ones, aimlessly wandering about in. case I was being followed by the press. I visited Gallery Lafayette, and after spending a small fortune there went to see Madame Brouzet's tiny boutique. We conversed in fluent French (one of my many hidden talents), and the naughty girl sold me a delicious pink suit and a blue evening dree. I did notice a rather striking young woman in there, who was buying the most delightfully expensive Red Coat.

Its price tag was 12,000 Euros give or take a cent, but to her credit, she slapped down a Black Amex without saying a word or blinking her beautiful blue eyes. Now personally I would move heaven and earth to get a Black One. The trouble is you must pay a hefty fee of £3,400 per year. As I don't spend 25K a month on my Platinum, I am not on Amex's Radar for a Black Card, but I would be if I had my way.

Once I had paid for my purchases, I was allowed to slip into the back of the shop, where the most exquisite grey velvet chairs were, slip off my shoes, and talk to my French Contact who was waiting for me.

That night in my hotel room in the 8th district I settled back in my bath that had a wonderful view of the Eifel Tower and indulged in some A La Mere de Famille Chocolates that I bought earlier.

The next day, I knew that I had an errand to do. After a leisurely breakfast, I made my way to the Black Cat Café, which was a nice little amble from my hotel. On the way, I stopped at a souvenir shop that only had a few browsers looking around. There were two rowdy kids inside who seemed to want everything in the shop. An Elderly couple just smiled indulgently at them, and let them continue to wreak havoc. Finally, I chose a tiny little Eifel Tower. I would give it to George as a reminder of today, and what I had done.

I eventually wended my way wound the streets for a couple of hundred yards until I found the right place. It's on the same street as Le Chat Noire, which is kind of convenient for me as my fake Louboutins were killing me. It was convenient enough for me at my age.

The Moulin Rouge was only a handful of doors away, but I meandered there in case was being followed. Knowing it would be closed until an hour before showtime I slipped inside via the side entrance. You must understand I had no intention of harming anyone apart from George, and I had sent him on an errand or two.

The first was to visit my elderly mother in her nursing home in Hove. They couldn't stand the sight of each other, so I got a little pleasure in sending him there. The second was to meet me at Ebbsfleet off Eurostar the next day. What the old fool didn't know was that I wasn't getting off there. I was travelling all the way to St. Pancras, where I had a business of my own to take care of.

Anyway, I digress. The reason I was visiting the Moulin Rouge was to see the daughter of an old friend of mine, who just so happened to work there. She had done me a massive favour, so I needed to pay her in cash or some other form of payment for her services.

I had had enough of George, so I set him up deliberately with my dancer friend. The scandal that ensued was just what I wanted and would give me grounds for a divorce. I tipped off my contacts in Fleet Street and the French Newspapers. The scandal spread like wildfire, and to my glee, George's picture was plastered all over the tabloids. It also made a column in the Times, and it sent the Daily Mail into a frenzy, as they were on a witch hunt with Parliament about the appointment of Judges in the UK.

I paid the dancer off. People think you are well off working where she did, but truth be told it's very expensive to live in Paris. My dancer friend has an apartment in the 4th Arrondissement – Ile St Louis. She's coming on in leaps and bounds with her English and finds that the retired English Major who lives on the floor below her some of the time has been a great help to her.

On the day of Eurostar checked into Eurostar at the Gare de Nord about 40 minutes before it was originally due to leave. It was running late though Apparently, there had been a small 'technical' issue with the toilets in 1st Class. Crisis averted I boarded the train as soon as I could. I mean good heavens I needed all the space I could get for my copious amounts of shopping. After settling down in my aisle seat, I hoped that no one would sit next to me. I hate sharing a seat with people, especially with men who always do that man-spread thing which is so undignified.

Just as the train was about to pull out, a man in a tweed jacket carrying only a rucksack came zigzagging down the carriage. He looked harassed, red-faced, and very drunk. I hope to God he wasn't going to sit next to me. Unfortunately, he did, shoving his rucksack under the seat. The smelt of stale sweat, whiskey, and something else permeated through his clothes. I think the something else was cordite. I should know as Daddy served in the Ordnance Corps during the war. He would come home reeking of the stuff, and this would give Mumsy one of her migraines.

Not wanting to engage in any sort of conversation I pulled out my 'phone (Gold Case, Monogrammed) and spoke to my best friend Eve, who I had known since we were both 15 and had known since we had both been sent away to boarding School in Switzerland. There was a rumour that the school had housed refugees after the war, but despite searching for clues Eve and I, both being of a curious nature didn't find a trace of them. What's more, they were supposed to have been boys, I mean actual boys of around our age. I wonder what happened to them.

I tried to have a conversation with Eve, but she's got Parkinson's Disease now, and can't really sit down for long for a nice long natter.

When I'd finished chatting slid my 'phone back into my handbag. Luckily for me, the inebriate man had sloped off to I don't know where. This gave quick chance to dash to the loo in the 1st class section. I mean, after all, I deserved it.

The man next to me came back, sweat on his upper lip. I did hope that he wasn't going to be sick all over me, I had someone I had to meet later that afternoon, and it wouldn't be right if I turned up covered in sick; I mean good heavens I'm not that type of Person, and I do have standards you know.

I was flicking through this month's copy of Vogue when suddenly the train came to a juddering halt, and all the lights went out. There was a loud explosion from somewhere in front of me, the carriages ran into each other and some off the rails. All that was left was a crumpled, smoking, twisted bit of metal. Men were fighting with each other, and I sat rooted to the spot. I had to find my bloody 'phone before anyone else did. I didn't want Aryne going through my call log, least of all the police.

The drunk next to me was trying to grab my arm. I was trying to resist. I think he thought I was frightened, but I was trying to find my 'phone.

It had slipped between the seats, so after pocketing it swiftly, I hoped that it wasn't damaged. I was then manhandled over a pile of twisted metal. Honestly, I could have done it myself as I have often found myself in similar situations.

I must admit I did crumple to the floor after all the effort, but personally, I blame the extra-strong G&T I had before I got on the train. I'd had it at a little bar I know not far from the station. It's funny because people have the impression that it's grimy and dirty around Gare de Norde.

If you go back a couple of streets, you enter a world of magic. A lovely little picture-perfect square with an adorable fountain tinkling away in the middle. Somewhere to smell both heliotrope and lavender. Like angle kisses to your nose with the lavender attracted the Bee population, so one could sit outside a café drinking Coffee (or Gin) whilst the burbling of the fountain, and the buzzing of the Bees drowned out the sound of the Parisienne traffic.

Wishing I were back there I glanced out of the carriage door window and saw to my surprise Paul, who was one of the lovely firemen that I have known for years. He grinned crookedly at me, sent a knowing look to his crewmate, and helped me out through the window.

I hadn't realised that the fire brigade would arrive so quickly. Too quick for my liking. I had banked on them arriving a little later, after all, I had things to sort out. Now Paul wouldn't rat on me, would he? If he stuck to my truth.

CHAPTER 4

GORDON MOSS's TRUTH

Good grief, I am a KC for heaven's sake. I would always tell the truth.

I had slipped away to Paris for two days without telling my wife where I was going. She was still tousled-haired from where she'd slept on it, and the bed was invitingly warm even though I could smell her musky sweat which smelt to me like nectar. I murmured a half excuse in her ear that I had a big case on, but it was in Berkshire, so I would probably crash at Andy's for a couple of days.

She knew that Andy lived in Windsor, and was used to me zigzagging across the country, especially as was now a KC. Also, since I have been forced into changing jobs to jobs due to some stupid bitch and her boyfriend complaining about sexual harassment. My new position meant I had to work ball-breaking hours. Good job I had the junior lawyers to assist me in oh so many ways.

I went to Paris to visit an old Lawyer pal of mine, who had snagged a fantastic job at a French Law firm. Nice work if you can get it. He was lucky in as much as he spoke French, plus his boyfriend was something in French Politics, so although we had officially left Europe, his Boyfriend had a way of cutting through red tape, so the lucky so-and-so had managed to sneak into France under the radar, and now had a nice EU passport, saying that he had been born in Nantes, and he had a couple of years shaved off his real age too.

I was just going out there to test the waters and was taking him for a nice long lunch. It was going to be somewhere he had chosen. By now, and I'm not sure if it's the boyfriend's influence or the fact that he earned about ¾ million Euros a year, but I knew that the place he chose would be very expensive, and I would be picking up the tab.

Added to that my delightful sibling and her long-standing boyfriend had unknowingly booked a break in Paris, so I felt duty-bound to ask them; it would also mean that I had someone in my corner as well as my sister always speaking her mind. In the end, there were four of us. Credit where credits due though my big sis did cough up for her and her boyfriend's meal, which is just as well as she ordered suckling pig, which I refuse to pay for due to my religious beliefs.

After a long lunch, with my sister trying to jolly everyone around the table along since the conversation was stilted, I asked my lawyer friend what the matter was. His reply was less than satisfactory, and wittered on about how keeping secrets was not a good idea. Quite frankly I was glad when he disappeared to take a 'phone call -probably from his boyfriend, as they always seemed to be in cahoots with each other. After a reasonably good start, the gathering sort of petered out. As if by mutual consent the bill was paid, and I was left by myself. To be honest I expected more from my friend. Judging by his countenance when he came back from his 'phone call I suspected that he had other things on his mind, and it wasn't work.

The next day, the day that I was due home on Eurostar I took myself to a nice Bistro and rather overindulged as things hadn't gone quite as planned. There was no offer of a job in France, no chance to catch up with my sister by herself, and all I was left with was a heavy credit card bill that I would have to explain to my wife.

Feeling rather disillusioned by the whole experience, I made it to the Garde de Norde with plenty of time to spare. I almost bumped into a lady carrying a copious amount of shopping. A Polite 'I'm Sorry' (though I have no idea what I was sorry for), and I was on my way, straight through check-in (no lines for first class thank goodness), a quick stop at Parfumiers to get my wife some Channel perfume by way of an apology for the forthcoming credit-card bill, and then as soon as the train was ready, I swiftly loped over the bridge so that I could board the train and find my seat.

To be perfectly honest I did feel queasy, and I just wanted to crawl into my allotted space. A little overindulgent maybe over the last few days.

Groaning inwardly, I plonked myself down. A lovely young lady in a Red Coat sat near to me, and I couldn't help but stare at her beautiful eyes. She quickly turned away from me. Maybe she thought I was giving her the glad eye. Nothing could be further from my mind. I wanted desperately to telephone Fenix. She/They were most definitely interesting. A new kind of friendship for me.

I had forged this friendship if you could call it that over the last couple of months. Apart from getting them to do all my legwork (that's what pupil lawyers are for isn't it?) I needed a run-down of the current situation, plus I thought I would try a little dalliance with them. Like I said before, ring the changes.

Pulling out my mobile, I dialled the number. Nope, the number is not available. Bugger I must have dialled the wrong number. Ok Gordon, try again. Maybe not as I was feeling a little krank (ill) at this point. I tried again but all I got was some stupid women saying in French that it was not possible to connect my call. Didn't the bloody French know who I was?

After what seemed a tedious couple of hours, with the additional stop at Ebbsfleet though the Lord only knows why because as far as I could see only one person got off there, we were on the run up to St Pancras.

I would say that I can't remember much after that. Vaguely aware of smoke, heat, and hunky fireman, I came to the back of an ambulance with a foul-tasting oxygen mask over my face. Panicking slightly in case I had lost my 'phone – as a KC I couldn't let anyone get hold of it, least of all the Police, I tried to rip off the oxygen mask, but it seemed to stick to my face like an Octopus's Tentacles. I was gently and firmly pushed back down by a member of the ambulance crew.

After a check-over at St Thomas's hospital, with me reassuring the medical staff that I was OK to go home (although I had got the biggest headache) I was relieved when my possessions were handed back to me in one of those awful-looking hospital bags. At least my 'phone was in there, but my ring from my aunt was missing. I hated the thing and was glad that it had gone. It was white gold with my initials Monogrammed on it.

Having retrieved my 'phone from the plastic hospital bag my first call was to Fenix. They wouldn't tell the Police anything, would they?

CHAPTER 5

SUSAN PROCTOR's TRUTH

I don't always tell the truth. Since getting involved try to avoid the absolute truth. See I'm so used to lying now that I'm not sure. As far as I can remember this is what happened.

I had come to Paris with Frank with such high hopes. I didn't realise that there would be two other couples, but at the time I didn't realise that he always had to travel with an entourage. His sycophants surrounded him all the time, and there was a newish guy called Marlon or something like that. This Marlon always had cash to splash. He told me it was money from a trust fund, but I'm not sure I believe him.

At first, it was great. We all checked into the prestigious George Cinque Hotel just off The Champs-Elysees. I expect that the fact that the hotel was built in 1928 and was art-deco was wasted on all our little group. What interested him was it was that it was the only hotel in Europe that had three Michelin Starred Restaurants. In my opinion, I would have preferred McDonald's which we had passed here on the way in the cab. Lots of happy smiling families, and grandparents taking the grandkids there for a treat. My nose pressed to the window in the Uber that Frank and I had taken, leaving the other two couples to find their own way to the hotel (a bit rude in my opinion) I swear I recognised one of the older couples with a pair of kids in toe going in there, and briefly wished I could join them.

We partied hard the first day of out, drinking the mini-bars, and most of the main bars were dry! After all, it was all going on Frank's father's bill. I mean why have a well-known member of parliament as a father if not to foot the bill? I was a bit miffed though as his family owned a lot of the property in the 4th arrondissement. Apparently, quite a few of the houses and apartments that they owned there were leased out to other people who paid a hefty premium for the privilege.

As we were so rowdy we got chucked out of the hotel. We only broke a few things, and I chucked up on an expensive-looking Persian rug. Personally, I have seen better rigs at Home Bargains. Who wants a poncy rug anyway? It must have been a few hundred years old and was starting to fade.

The next day, the day before Eurostar, Frank told me that we'd been invited to a party on the left bank somewhere. He was a little vague when I think it was Marlon who pressed him for the address. Quite frankly Marlon was beginning to sound like my idiot sister Jane, who had just been promoted to CID. We don't talk much now as it seems she is more interested in her career. I'm not really bothered anyway. She is only my stepsister.

The party on the left bank was a bit full on, and Frank was so stoned that he picked a fight with Marlon. It was over a silly little thing as Marlon said he only drank coke, not took it, and before long they were exchanging blows. I had to intervene to keep them apart, and that's when Frank's signet ring caught me in the mouth. After that things went a little flat and although we were all still drinking no one had the energy to do anything.

The next morning the day of Eurostar we all stayed sleeping at the Party House. It was probably about midday when I woke up. The rest of the partygoers apart from our group had. All buggered off leaving the house in a terrible state. I always ended up skivvying for Frank, but I decided that I wasn't going to do it anymore.

Having made the decision that it wasn't my job to run around everyone I thought that I should wake the others or else we'd miss our train. I was casting an eye over our motley group when I realised that Marlon was missing. I really liked him. Don't get me wrong, I loved Frank and truthfully, I would never cheat on him.

Then I heard a whistle, and Marlon appeared to compete with coffee and delicious-looking French Pastries for everyone. The smell of good French coffee and pastries must have woken the rest of them up. The offerings from Marlon were devoured at an alarming rate. Only Frank grumbled. As he was the last to wake up the best pastries had gone.

Realising that we didn't have a cat in hell's chance of making our Eurostar reservations Frank went on to the airlines to see if he could get us tickets to Heathrow, which meant us flying out of Charles de Gaulle. After half an hour he chucked his phone down in frustration when it began to ring.

In the end, Frank's dad coughed up for us to travel home first class via Eurostar. Personally, I'm a bit nervous about the train because anything could happen on it, couldn't it?

After two taxis and lots of baggage with the 'packages' distributed between mine and Franks, we eventually made it to the Gare de Norde. We were lucky in as much as the train was running late. Most of our group were hung over or just coming down from the high that the drugs had caused. Frank was getting twitchy and wouldn't settle. I couldn't even get him to drink a cup of coffee. When I suggested water instead, he nearly bit my head off.

It looked like we weren't the only ones who had hangovers. An older guy, a professor type who was all tweed jackets and cravats started morosely into a half-empty coffee cup. I only noticed him because he looked worse than us. Poor old soul, too much of the sauce last night obviously. When Eurostar boarding was announced Frank grabbed me roughly by the arm and shoved me into our first-class seats. The others followed behind lamely.

I knew what Frank wanted me to do when we got back to London, distribute drugs. The truth was I was getting a little scared at what I was doing, and I could only think of one way out, to call my grandmother. We didn't exactly see eye to eye, but I knew she was still worried about me. My old 'phone wasn't up to much these days, but I could hear my grandmother's voice in my ear telling me that a new one was a waste of money, something I didn't seem to have much of.

Snaking my hand into Frank's pocket I was met with a resounding slap, and my hand was gripped tightly. He hissed in my ear, but as I turned away, I saw a look of utter hatred and contempt on his face. Sighing I knew I had to get out. The only thing I could do for a few moments of respite was go to the loo. Frank looked at me quizzingly when I got up. I whispered, "Lavatory," in his ear. He grimaced slightly. I knew he was worse than royalty when it came to using public facilities even though it was on a train. Sliding past, I made my way there just as a young woman in a red coat was coming out. Diving in I sat for a few minutes when there was a rap on the door. Knowing it could be someone desperate I flushed and then washed my hands. Sliding open the toilet door I came face to face with my grandmother of all people.

After a quick exchange of words, I returned to my seat feeling slightly better. Maybe five minutes after that, it happened, and after that, nothing was ever the same again. It was the last time that I saw Frank. After that, he disappeared. I knew that he had a gaffe somewhere in North London, but he never told me where it was. So, there was I, stuck with some of his gear, and I didn't have a fricking clue about what to do with it.

The explosion on Eurostar shook me up. I admit that I was scared. Yet with no Frank around I somehow felt a lot lighter. Did I bother to see if he was taken to one of the Major Hospitals? Truthfully, no.

CHAPTER 6

THE TRUTH ACCORDING TO THE PAIS CONNECTION

My old granddaddy was, let us say 'active' after the Second World War. I was the grandson of a girl who had an affair with Major Glen Cooper. She was a penniless singer and dancer at one of the nightclubs he frequented in Les Pigalle. This was in the early fifties when everyone thought that the Soviets would be the next big power player. My dear grandaddy was sent to France purportedly to collect vital information about the Russians. Only he wasn't. He was working for the side that would mean the Great One should return. He was working to reinstate the Fuhrer, and where better to start than Paris?

He did however set my grandmother up in an apartment in the 4th Arrondissement. When she died, she naturally passed it to me, but the old Buffoon (my grandfather), visits from time to time. He still likes to keep fingers in pies and was here a not-long ago discussing Oxford of all places. Occasionally he would drop in unannounced. He always made his presence known though by cheekily whistling at the apartment upstairs where a young lady who danced at the Moulin Rouge lived. I knew he visited her occasionally for what or why I do not know.

A few weeks after mentioning Oxford he was back in Paris again, this time with his wife and a couple of brats in tow. He obviously had no desire to introduce us and quite rightly so. I was tied up with a few other things. You see I am quite a chip off the old block, and I like to keep fingers in pies too, that's how I knew he was in Paris.

Did I not mention that I have the ear of the French Prime Minister, and a few other Ministers too, so it's not difficult to get things done?

I'm known in some quarters as Mr Fix-It. I knew a lot about people's business because I made it my business. The stories I could tell, like the two male lawyers who were having an affair, or an English Judge's wife who frequented the Moulin Rouge carrying a vast amount of cash.

I met Mr Houlihan at a café on the Left Bank. To me, it sounded a bit cliched, but he wanted to hook up with me there. When I met him, he was drunk. I'd heard on the grapevine that he likes to gamble as well. We chatted over whiskey and wine. He eventually, after much pre-amble told me that he was here at the request of a more senior professor in his department who, like Mr Houlihan was a socialist through and through. They were getting rather tired of the H2 scheme which was tearing up the countryside.

I managed to obtain for him an invite to a little meeting of like-minded people where the speaker's purpose was to rally the troops so that a major bombing campaign could be planned to blow up the Paris Underground system and Eurostar at the same time.

Now although Glen Cooper is my grandfather, it was Claire Cooper who met me a stone's throw from the Eiffel Tower. Trying to be covert was not difficult as there were so many people milling around. She had heard about me from her Yoga Instructor apparently. For an old bird, she did look fit. I texted her where to meet. She had spun me a story about wanting a knife for protection. It wasn't my problem what she did with it. Anything worked well for me, a knife for five thousand Euros, no questions asked, plus I had something on her now.

The Judge's wife, well she wanted to meet me on the same day at a small boutique just off the Boulevard Huaassmann. I had an arrangement with its owner to use one of the tiny rooms at the back to meet with people. Our meeting was swift, and more cash was in my pocket in exchange for yet another knife. I set off back home content that it was a good day.

It was a busy day. I had a call with a Lawyer. I won't reveal his name though. I had helped him get a passport stating that he was born in Nantes. He was just checking in with me about two things. Firstly, he wanted to find out everything I could about Gordon Moss as he was considering offering him a partnership and secondly, that would the package be on board. Had I known what was going to happen I would never have got involved.

The package contained photos and details of one inspector White. The lawyer was sure that there was a corrupt policeman in the Met and suspected White. At every turn White had outwitted him, hence the lawyer moving hastily to Paris when things got a bit heavy in London. Said lawyer and White met a few times in the courtroom, and because of White's apparent 'evidence' cases had been dismissed. The lawyer had caught wind of something, and being tenacious wouldn't let things lie.

In due course, White sussed that the powers that be might have something on him. Cue the heavies making the layer's life impossible. Now I had more concrete evidence. I wasn't to know that the lawyer's special friend would be caught up in a Eurostar explosion, nor that he would be questioned by DI White as well as the Anti-Terrorist Branch. I'm still trying to work out why White was involved at all with Interviews. You see the information I had unearthed on White was a major game changer. I have proof that he isn't who he says he is. If anyone wants to know the truth about the lawyer, I will tell them that it was to discuss a T.V. deal, to get the lawyer more publicity.

CHAPTER 7

THE TRUTH ABOUT THE DRUG DEAL ACCORDING TO TWO RELIABLE WITNESSES

Frank decided that it was time to get away. He soon realised early in the relationship that his girlfriend whom he only used to courier drugs was pliable as hell but too clingy. He'd managed to get his hands on some good stuff in Paris and had been in touch with one of his clients who would be willing to pay over the odds as the stuff was as pure as the driven snow.

The only problem was he had caught Susan sneaking her hand into his pocket, and had he admitted to himself acted badly. He didn't want her dealing with the drugs he had just bought from a very nice Frenchman. Knowing her she would be flogging it at a cut price outside the cinema complex at Greenwich Peninsular. He desperately needed to get home pronto to his crib in Edmonton, hence he blagged some dosh from his dad to get Eurostar tickets instead of the plane. The only problem was he needed a bloody miracle to get rid of Susan Proctor.

The opportunity presented itself in the weirdest circumstances. When the explosion happened on Eurostar, he may have given everyone the impression that he was a drug-raddled idiot, but he had over time built up a tolerance to drugs, so he had a clearer head than most of his cohorts. He had the perfect opportunity to slip away unnoticed leaving Susan and the police thinking that he was dead or injured badly. After all, you don't go to boarding school for six years without learning the art of meeting your mates in the local and skipping lessons unnoticed.

All the tube lines at Kings Cross were suspended, so he called for an Uber from the Euston Road which took him directly to his flat in Edmonton. What he hadn't told his dad he had paid for the flat outright from his ill-gotten gains. Agreed it was a shithole, nothing like the gracious flat that his dad paid the rent on in Pimlico. He couldn't exactly deal drugs from there. He also didn't tell his dad that he had shares in Uber, which was quite useful at times.

Sighing with relief that he had made it in time for the deal to be done he raced up the five flights of stairs as the lift was out yet again. Trying to hold his breath because of the smell of stale piss that always seemed to linger he made it to his front door and unlocked it with a bunch of five keys. He had the mortice locks installed just after he moved in. Back then he had been a novice in the drugs game and came back one night to find his flat broken into and the small cache of drugs that he was going to sell missing, as was his 42" television and Xbox.

Wondering if he had time for a shower, he headed to the small windowless bathroom first making sure the five locks were all secure so that no one could get in. Humming to himself he stripped off and stood under the tepid shower head. The trouble with his place was that you could never get hot water. He was mulling over what had happened and thinking that he had a lucky escape when he thought he heard the front door slam.

Wrapping a towel around his waist he turned off the water and headed through to the lounge where he came face-to-face with Mary Pickles. Thinking that the old bird had taken a wrong turn somewhere he flashed a dazzling smile at her and began to tell her that he had a meeting soon. It would be easy enough to chuck her out he thought. She was only about five feet three, plus a few extra inches due to the spikey high heels she wore. Frank almost burst out laughing though as she wore a Tyvek suit, hairnet, and long polyurethane gloves.

Before he could open his mouth, she kneed him in the groin. Not giving him the chance to retaliate, she punched the bridge of his nose so that he heard it crack and a tsunami of blood poured out of it. Kicking him hard again with a high kick that landed mid spine he fell to the floor in agony clutching his broken nose. Taking off one of her high heels she pressed the side of the heel, and a small but lethal-looking knife sprang out. Frank began to whimper as she knelt beside him and with her unshod foot standing on his right hand.

'I wanted a little chat with you', she said as though she was inviting him to tea. 'Let me introduce myself properly young man.

You may know me as Mrs Pickles. True, that's my name now, but I was called something else before that. Just wondering if you had ever heard of the Richardson Gang, otherwise known as the Torture Gang'?

Frank was in no position to reply. Nodding his head so that he gurgled at her through a trough of blood that had run his face filling his mouth.

'A little history lesson for you then Sonny', she added. 'My dad was running one of the worst feared gangs in South London in the nineteen-sixties Now the police and politicians want the public to think that it was all cleared up, but it was all a whitewash and the Richardson's still flourished. I took over the business. I run it now. In fact, you could call me the Duchess of the South, but one thing that upsets me is that you are trying to take over the North which has always been run by a very good friend of mine.'

Beneath one stiletto-heeled foot which she held to Frank's throat, Mary Pickles heard him gurgle even more satisfactorily. He wasn't dead yet, which made the next part even more fun. Another flick and a small knife came out of her shoe heel. Sitting astride him and ripping open his shirt, she began carving the Richardson name on his chest.

Outside coming from a few floors down she heard a sudden noise, so retrieving the knife she slipped silently out of Frank's Flat. Hearing the click-clack of heels, not dissimilar to the sound of hers she started to walk swiftly past the other flats. The sound of footsteps got closer, so trying the door of another flat as it was well known in this area that the safety of possessions was not the number one priority in that part of town, she was relieved when one opened. A mountain of shit had collected behind the door, so she could only push it open a tiny bit and slide through the gap that she had engineered. Pulling the door she breathed a small sigh of relief. The last thing she wanted to do was to be caught.

Moments later the other heel-wearing person arrived at Frank's door. Finding it unnervingly slightly ajar they felt as though something in the air didn't smell quite right. Beneath their feet was a body that lay supine pumping out blood. It looked like someone had already beaten them to it. Things couldn't have worked out better. A drug deal gone wrong maybe.

Bending down they noticed the beginning of a carving in Frank's chest. Sighing they took out their knife, caved a little bit more in Fank's flesh, pulled out the knife, and walked out of Frank's flat.

As soon as Mary Pickles heard footsteps receding towards the exit, she stuck her head out of the door only to catch a glimpse of the person leaving. Trying hard not to exclaim out loud she shook her head.

Well, well, well, she said to herself. Now what was Claire Copper doing at Frank's flat? Now that's what you called an interesting day.

CHAPTER 8

THE DANCER's TRUTH

Call me Claudette, call me Fifi, call me any name that you want. My stage name is Lulu de Marrison my real name is Michelle Martin. I'm twenty-seven years old. I am a Dancer by trade. Occasionally my bones would ache, and my limbs stiffen up when I performed. I knew that I was getting a little too old for the dancing lark and decided after a particularly exhausting routine it was time I gave up performing and earned some serious money. I was lucky enough to live in a nice apartment in the 4th arrondissement. It belonged to my maternal grandmother. I loved her dearly. On the other hand, I had never met my maternal grandfather. However, there was a nice enough old bloke who visited the apartment below from time to time. I would often dream that he was my grandfather.

I longed for a father figure as my own had never been around. It was just me, my mother, and my grandmother. When I was thirteen my mother caught pneumonia. After she succumbed to it, I only had my grandmother to cling to. She encouraged me to become a dancer, as she kept on pointing out it was in my DNA generations ago.

When I first considered giving up dancing it seemed that fortune was on my side. Firstly, I had an email from Mrs Mary Pickles who was an old friend of my grandmother She and my grandmother both go back a long way and used to sing in the same club. Mrs Pickles told me that she was having trouble on the home front. I must admit that the initial email from her took me by surprise. She was very upfront about what she wanted, no pussyfooting around for her. She wanted revenge on her errant husband; wanted all his wrongdoings exposed. The fact that he was a well-known Judge in England made it even more delightful as I had always despised the establishment, even that of another country.

Having a dancer contact in England made life a little bit easier for me. She arranged with her boss at a little-known club called Oddfelllows or something like that. I was to perform there for one night as an exotic dancer.

One of Oddfellow's clientele was a certain Judge Pickles who had a predilection for exotic dancers, and when at the nightclub always booked a private room for a private dance. I would surprise him in more ways than one. After finishing my dance with him I would sit on his knee. Being scantily clad I would take a great picture taken by a famous sleazy reporter from the Sun newspaper who I would tip off. Next thing you know we were splashed all over the national and international news.

On one of her many shopping trips, I met up with Mary Pickles at my place of work which was The Moulin Rouge. She paid me handsomely for drugs, things that she couldn't post! Drugs were not my thing, but I would deal in them without compunction to make extra cash. I had run out of those bad boys as most of my caches were to someone who was going to have a party on the Left Bank. Mary's payment in drugs was a godsend as it not only meant that I could get my hands on cash but also, and here is my second piece of luck was that I could pay off the man who was hassling me for money. A man known as the French Connection.

Let me explain about the French Connection. I paid him so that I could be in the know about certain things. Only the other night I had attended a meeting of dissidents that he had alerted me to. Mary Pickle's drugs, or the sale of them would mean I could pay the little creep off. The truth is he had the voice of a sexy Frenchman, that one might expect, but the looks and habits of a slimy Toad. The French connection let me know the date, time, and place of a little husting. He also let me know who would be attending. There was one man I wanted to check out. That person is John O'Houlihan.

I had lived with my grandmother up until her demise. She passed after six months of illness that ravaged her. She was still coming to terms with the loss of her only child even though it had been more than ten years. Some things you just don't get over.

I had taken time off work to look after her. In February, when I was too busy partying and gallivanting, I hardly noticed her skin change to a sickly yellow. She could no longer cook her wonderful rabbit stews for me. After another six weeks had passed, one day when I returned from the butchers after trying to find a rabbit so that I could recreate her famous stew I returned to find she had fallen out of bed. Helping her back in I could feel the lightness of her body, her bones protruding through her skin. She must have weighed all of thirty-two kilograms.

With much effort, she held out her mottled ice-cold hands. She never seemed able to get them warm. Pulling me towards her she whispered the words, 'I know who your father was, he was a student at Oxford University. He came here to Paris as a young man to practise his linguistic skills. His name is John O'Houlihan.'

I had already seen too many people die. Some say that there is a death rattle in their throat when they pass. In my grandma's case, her breathing became shallower and shallower until she just slipped away. Always standing up straight and proud she was now an empty shell. Her blue eyes seemed to have turned black, and a little blood trickled from her nose. Flinging myself on top of her I cried until my eyes were red raw. Then I slid off the bed, and knelt, saying a silent prayer with her cherished rosary. I told her that I loved her, and then I called an ambulance. An autopsy later revealed that she died from stage 4 pancreatic cancer. She must have known that she was ill a while back, but never let her façade slip.

After the funeral I was angry. I was also hellbent on revenge. There was one person in my sight. John O'Houlihan. There was only one man who could help me track him down and that was the French Connection. As much as loathed the obnoxious little git I knew that for a price he would be able to help me in my quest. Three days after contacting him I arrived home to an empty apartment. Pushed under my door was a note with a date, time and location. It was coincidental that the French Connection lived in the apartment.

I pulled up the collar on my long military-style coat even though it was warm outside. I didn't want anyone to recognise me. I had forsaken my usual high heels for a pair of long black suede kitten-heeled boots. I had to look good to meet JH, but not so obvious as I wanted to mill around hoping that no one would notice me. Usually, I am all glamour. My natural long red hair which I tied in a high ponytail when I was dancing was now rammed under a black crushed velvet Beatles Cap with the brim pulled firmly down. The fact that I was wearing my mother's old coat must have signified something. Maybe he would spot me and recognise it.

Normally I am ok with crowds. After a cursory search of my handbag by security, I was allowed to enter the room that the French Connection had mentioned in his note. I had left it so that I was late enough to give people enough time to form little cliques.

The French like nothing better than a cigarette and a glass of wine. Both of those were in spades as I entered the smoke-filled room. Someone had managed to bring in a few bottles of cheap red plonk into the building. I was offered both by a crowd of young men who thought that they might be able to charm me with their disarming smiles. They'd be lucky. As the English would put it, I bat for the other side.

The gathering of what appeared to be seventy or so like-minded people sent me into a tailspin. Although I had a place and time, I had no idea what my father looked like. I couldn't breathe. Many of the people there seemed to be of the student generation with ripped jeans, looking gaunt and hollow as only students who burn the candle from both ends can. A dozen or so had donned military-type fatigues as if ready for a fight. I even saw a couple of T-shirts with the image of Che Guevara emblazoned on the front.

Before the meeting began, I circled the room. Bumping into a gaggle of students I began to make my excuses when a man in an Irish accent said, 'No need to apologise my dear'.

There in front of me, towering over my 1.8 Meters (just over 5' 10") height was a man who was tall and good-looking in a rugged sort of way. Around his temples, there was a sprinkling of grey in his tightly curled hair. A bevvy of young twenty-something beauties plus a few young men were hanging on his every word. One of the girls was also hanging onto his arm. He looked confident and comfortable. Unlike me, he seemed to fit right in. Most people were wearing trainers or short ankle boots, and I spotted at least twelve pairs of Doc Martins.

I could see that the man himself, who was the centre of attention didn't wear the uniform of a student, but rather a tweed jacket with leather patches, Cavalier twill trousers and a silk cravat casually knotted over his open-necked shirt, which gave him a rakish air.

I could see why my mother had fallen for him. Rapidly switching back to French, he took my hand in his and kissed it. Before I could snatch it back, he uttered the words I had longed to hear but dreaded them at the same time.

'I once knew a girl who was the spitting image of you. I loved her dearly, but one day she went away never to return. It broke my heart. I had never seen such a beautiful girl as her. And now I seem to have found the answer to my prayers in you'.

Had I heard him correctly? According to my grandmother, he had returned to Oxford never to see her again. He didn't know that she was pregnant. If what he said was true, that my mother had gone away never to be seen again. I could only remember a time when I had lived with my mother and grandmother. I could no longer ask my grandmother if my mother had gone away to have me. Had she simply left, and my father had returned looking for me? I had to know the truth.

Before I could ask John, a middle-aged man tapped him on the shoulder. With a thunderous look on his face at being interrupted. I cursed every Saint that I knew. John dropped my hand and turned his body away from me. Seeing the person in front of him he held out both arms and enveloped them in a bear hug.

'Dinesh bloody Patel, what the devil are you doing here?'.

John was obviously busy with this newcomer who by now had steered him away from the masses and into a corner. When I saw him again, he was knocking back wine whilst the man he had called Dinesh was sipping an orange juice. Deciding that this was not the time or place for a confrontation I pushed my way through the crowds and exited the room as quickly as I could with a feeling of both relief and disappointment. I had found my father. Would I ever see him again?

CHAPTER 9

DINESH PATELS TRUTH FROM 1985-2024

Nish and I were more like brothers than cousins. We had grown up together and scavenged for food together. As boys, we could both usually be found atop of rubbish tips hunting for plastic bottles. When we sold them by weight so that we could get a few. Rupees. That was our contribution to the family's income. We all lived together in one room mine and Nish's families. His dad and my dad were brothers. Nanaji Lived with us as well for a while.

My cousin Nish eventually decided that he had had enough of poverty and moved as quickly as he could to England where another extended family member lived. I could scarcely read or write but was one of the few in our family that could. One day he wrote to mummyji. As the brains of the family O res it to her elaborating its contents quite a bit. I led her to believe that Nish would look after me, that there were many jobs, opportunities, and houses over there, and that everyone had a car.

As it turned out I had to escape to England in the end. Had had violated a young girl of only twelve from the next village. I wished that I had never clapped eyes on her. She was sitting with her legs tucked under her, hands primly folded in her lap at the showing of a pirated copy of a film that was on at her village.

After the film had finished, she turned towards me and smiled at me. Was it love at first sight? Probably not. I felt like I had a thousand butterflies in my stomach. I had led a sheltered life up until now. Obviously, I knew all about the birds and the bees from living in a single room with my extended family, but this was a new sensation for me.

I don't know why I did what I did. It was just that I had the opportunity, the girl was available, and it was dark. Looking back, I must have had many excuses. During the 1980s in our culture, we didn't have the forethought to ask if it was ok to 'be' with someone... Only it wasn't.

The punishment had I been caught for what I had done to a young girl was death by stoning back then. I would have also been lashed by a long-handled whip with twelve leather cruel thongs a few hundred times had I managed to survive the stoning. The Police in India are not like the Police in the UK. They are violent and corrupt. I could well have been killed by one of them in a prison cell.

I had hidden out in a rank smelling small disused house and zigzagged across the countryside until I reached Mumbi. Not only did I rape. A twelve-year-old girl, but I also stole money and her brother's passport from her house which was far grander than our hovel. Shoving a handful of Rupees into a 'phone I rang Nish. This took a lot of my money as calls to the UK were expensive. Luckily it was a Friday, and all the family over there were at the Mosque apart from Nish who was excused by the Imam as he was working long shifts to provide for our family there.

Nish told me to come over, and we would invent a reason for leaving India. I had not told Nish the whole truth just lied and said I was in a bit of trouble and that I needed a new start. Nish told me that I would love England which was warm and sunny. He lied. When I arrived at Heathrow after a twelve-hour flight, I was tired and weary. England wasn't all it was cracked up to be. It was pissing down with rain, and bleddy cold.

I was pulled to one side. Suspicious buggers at border control. Couldn't they see that I was just a young man wanting to better himself? India had been part of the British Empire. Yet they tried everything in the book to stop me from entering the country. After four hours, many terse 'phone calls, three people interviewing me, and a short call to my cousin I was allowed in on a student's visa. Nish told the powers that be that I was enrolled on an accountancy course at Leicester Polytechnic. He convinced them that I had been accepted on the course, but the paperwork was caught up in the UK's marvellous postal system. Nish had to make a lot of promises and do a lot of sucking up, which he hated.

After a few false starts, including how to figure out the railway system and being called a 'darkie' and a 'wog' a few times I found my way to the correct train. This was in the days before the luxury of the Heathrow Express. How Generation Z would have worked it out I don't know. Couldn't use bleddy Google Maps, could they?

Arriving at St Pancras station it reminded me of a Great Old Lady, its façade formidable, its inside more faded. A bit like the British Empire I thought. Getting a train to Leicester was a nightmare. I didn't speak much English at the time. Eventually, the woman behind me in the ticket queue tapped me on the shoulder with an umbrella (rude) and offered to buy my ticket for me (nice). Once on the train people ignored me. Until Luton I had no one sitting next to me, then a man with a bowler hat gingerly took the seat beside me, then complained all the way to Leicester about the smell of curry.

When I finally got off the train at Leicester, I managed to navigate myself to the front of the station by simply following a thong of people who headed towards London Road. I expected Nish to turn up in at least a Rolls Royce. After three hours I was getting cold and hungry. Surely, he hadn't forgotten me. As a young male Asian lurking at the front of a railway station late I must have looked suspicious. Eventually, tiredness overtook me, and I slumped down on the floor and fell asleep.

I was rudely woken up by a torch shining on my face. Opening one bleary eye a face that I thought I recognised swam in front of me. Three frigging hours late it was my cousin Nish. Too tired to be angry with him I got up from the hard cold pavement and followed him through the mean streets of Leicester. After half an hour or so he stopped up short at a shabby front door.

'Welcome to the Khyber Pass my friend', he said fishing a Yale key from inside his jeans pocket. Pushing open the door which groaned in protest, I found myself in the gloom of a small room. Several pairs of eyes stare at me. Had I left one hell hole for another? The smell of curry drifted through the kitchen. A large woman emerged with a plate full of delicious ambrosia.

'Oh, thank goodness to Allah', she exclaimed. 'My stupid nephew forgot you. He was halfway across town with friends from the Mosque. I had to send Amir to find him', she said gesturing to a boy of five or six.

I hadn't met Amir before; he must have been a later addition to the family. At least I was safe here with Aunty Lakshmi. She and her husband (my dad's other brother) had moved to Leicester. Many of Lakshmi's family seemed to live in the house too. Including me, this small, dank house now held nine people. This was almost as bad as home. At least, I hoped, they had more rooms.

As Uncle Ravindra was a night watchman at some hosiery factory that Nish worked in, I didn't get a chance to see him when I arrived. He seemed to sleep on the couch during the day, which meant that I could sleep on it at night, unless you included Amir who thought that I was a novelty and would often sneak on the couch with me, instead of his small bed made of a cardboard box containing a ratty old blanket which had placed by the stove every night for Anmir to keep him warm. I think he had designs on the sofa and would silently size it up at every opportunely.

The next day I was up at the crack of dawn so that I could vacate the sofa. Also, with so many people in the

House (I forgot to mention their twins as well aged about thirteen) It was always a scrum for the bathroom. Everyone moaned at Amir behind his back because he always took ages and always left a smell. Still, compared to India an inside bathroom must have been a luxury for everyone. Even though this one had a door almost off its hinges and a cracked toilet seat. I once asked Nish if he would ask the landlord if it could be repaired, but he laughed half-heartedly and said, 'What a jumped-up piece of scum like me'. And there you have it. We were all jumped up pieces of scum.

I found it hard at first. Nish got me a job at the same hosiery factory as him. The constant clatter of the machines gave me a headache. I longed to be back in India. I had no social life, as Nish was always with his 'friends from the mosque'. So, one evening after I had been in Leicester for about three weeks, I followed him. Not to the Mosque, but to my surprise a public house where inside six or seven Muslim men were sipping pints of Bitter. I was horrified. Everything that the Quran said about intoxicants was being annoyed. I was going to call him out when I felt a hand on my shoulder, and a pint glass thrust into my hand.

'Good to see you little Coz', rang out a voice that belonged to Nish. 'I wondered when you were going to find out my well-kept secret'.

That was it. After one swallow I was hooked on booze. I was also hooked on Nish's little group. We were a pack of angry young men. Often living in squalor. Sometimes there were fifteen or so people living in a two-bedroom condemned house. For us work was no better. We were passed over for promotion; even I had been passed over from a junior floor-walker's job. Nish, who had an accounting degree from New Delhi University could not get an office job.

It was during one of the meetings of the Mosque Mob, that Nish mooted the idea of us blowing up Leicester Market to make our mark so that we would be noticed. After observing the marketplace for two months he noticed that no one was there at night. We hadn't intended to harm anyone. That wasn't our way. We weren't terrorists.

Jamshed had managed to steal some of the things we needed to make a bomb from the chemist where he worked doling out prescriptions every day. He was fortunate enough to have secured a role at a job just off Belvedere Road where lots of coloured people used to live. The rest of the stuff Nish got from various B&Qs in the Leicester area, never the same one, and always paying cash. The plan was for it to happen on a Friday night so that the market and its takings would be affected the next day, Saturday, which was always a busy day for traders and buyers.

Just before I left with Nish for the bus to take us into the centre of Leicester, I received a disturbing phone call at the Shop on the corner from my father who must have walked miles to call me. The Police had turned up at our house looking for me. In one way I was fortunate as there was no Treaty Extradition with the UK until 1992.

On the upstairs deck of the bus that took Nish and me into the City, I started crying wasn't unusual for us 'darkies' to go on the top deck. This was the norm in the 1980s when people made no bones about not sitting next to us, moving seats, or complaining about the smell of curry that always lingered on our clothes, or when we spoke.

Nish leaned against me and gave me a gentle hug. He thought that I was worried about what we were about to undertake. Hugging him back I stuck a knife used for cutting yarn that I had stolen from work straight through his heart. He died instantly and without a sound. As there was only a handful of hardened smokers on the top deck apart from us no one saw me do it. I had already got Amir to steal Nish's passport pretending it was a joke that I was playing on Nish. When the bus arrived at my stop I got off and walked away as Dinesh (Nish) Patel. After all, as someone once commented 'You lot all look the same'. I dumped my passport in a rubbish bin.

Seemingly all went to plan for a while until I was running from the market. One of the stall holders was there for a reason I do not know. The force from the blast threw her backwards, and as she fell, she cracked her head on the concrete. By now the rest of the gang must have scarpered, and in the distance, I could hear sirens, which meant that the emergency services were on their way. Sitting the woman up I applied my clean white handkerchief that Dadaji always insisted I carried as it showed the mark of a true gentleman to her bleeding wound. The poor woman was gasping for breath, and I truly believed that she was having a heart attack and would surely die before me. All I could think of was the long prison sentence I would receive, but far, far worse than that was the further shame I would bring on the family as 'Nish'.

Policemen were now swarming through the market, and I felt a heavy hand on my shoulder. Before I could speak, the woman had recovered a little.

'Oy', she shouted to the young policeman who held my shoulder in a vicelike grip. 'Better leave my staff alone or you'll regret it sonny', she spewed at the 6-foot policeman who was a small errant child. The policeman reluctantly let go of me but insisted that the woman should get her head checked out at the Leicester General Hospital.

'Not on your nelly', she mouthed to his receding back. 'Now come here young'un and tell me why you thought it was a good idea to blow up Leicester's finest including me'".

Stammering I told her of my circumstances, and the loathsome job, and the sleeping on the sofa in shifts. She made me help her to the nearest 'phone box, and the next thing I knew, a taxi whisked us away to a neat two-bedroom bungalow in the middle of nowhere (or so it seemed). From then on, I worked for her, Muriel, on her Market stall, and did other 'Jobs' for her. She taught me how to swear, and taught me East Midlands English as according to her this was the one true surviving dialectic from 924 A.D. She also taught me her craft and introduced me to her husband Frank. Frank was a taciturn man, a maths teacher who had been a POW. He didn't talk much but preferred to read a lot. It was through Muriel that I met My Love. I caught her trying to nick some elastic from Muriel's stall. She was only sixteen or seventeen. I fell in love instantly. I was going to marry her, but fate dictated otherwise.

Five or six years later the girl of my dreams had joined the Police Force, the sort of people I did not want to mix with. Then I heard whisperings that the girl, whose real name was Julia had a nervous breakdown after becoming pregnant by some young no-mark. Eventually, she gave birth to a daughter. Back in the day, people such as social workers were not that bothered about the legality of things, and people could easily slip through the gap which is what Julia's child did. I mean to say she didn't exactly slip through the gap as Julia had turned to her good friend Muriel to look after the baby as she couldn't cope by herself and the dad didn't know owt about the child, and probably didn't want anything to do with it so she turned to her good old mate Muriel, and promptly left the baby with her and then buggered off.

The child who had been named Laura became the darling of Leicester Market, and as she grew older became a great friend of mine.

Then a young Indian girl Marya kept on coming back to Muriel's market stall to buy ribbons, always with her big, useless lump of her sister, Pushpa in tow. They came for one reason and one reason on; to snag a husband for the ugly sister. Although I tried to avoid the daft bint Pushpa, I became closer and closer to her sister.

I had been working for Muriel for a few years now, but behind the scenes and not usually in front of the house. I didn't want any of my extended family coming across me and questioning me as to what had happened to the real Nish. The first job I did for Muriel was part of a minor Indian Royal staying over Market Harborough Way. I also did a job for her in Oxford. You may have heard his name mentioned once or twice; Mortimer or something like that.

Then I flew over to Ireland. I kept on getting strange looks on the plane, but what the hell? I knew that I wanted to settle down and marry Marya, then open a small shop. It was every man's dream wasn't it, and Muriel paid me well. I did her little job for her which involved some chap who had links to the IRA named Tommy O'Houlihan.

I had qualms about that job as it meant that it left Houlihan's child without a father. On my return flight home, I vowed to give it up. I hated having blood on my hands, although I had killed in the past. I also had a gunshot wound to my leg which I could never explain to my wife or her curious family.

From then on, I gave up working for Muriel, married Mayra, bought a shop, and lost a shop. It was quite by chance that I bumped into Robert White, a DI from the Met. He was the copper, who as a young Rookie had collared me at the Market explosion in Leicester. Odd, wasn't it?

I. guessed it was him from the off when he entered my shop in a ski mask and all the other robber-type gear. He had a curious accent that I couldn't quite place. Well-spoken with a very slight German accent.

He never bought Muriel's story, so I owed him big time. He gave me the name of the 'Mark' I was to follow, and report on, along with a lot of cash. Only it turned out that the 'Mark' was Laura Marchant, Julia's daughter and my lifelong friend.

You must really know why we blew up the Market. Yes, it was a protest about us being ignored or despised as a man of colour, but it was that deep down part of our roots were in Egypt. People in the UK in 1985 were the most Christian. Some believed that the bible was true and that the baby in the bushes who later led the Israelites received the Torah to teach the children of Israel.

One of my forefathers lived in Egypt and believed this to be true. So, you see, although the Torah was created for Moses, it should have been passed down to the Egyptians. After all, Moses was originally from there, so it should have been ours, shouldn't it? Ergo we were the true race, and this is why I was protesting. I wanted to be recognised as someone, not just a dirty untouchable.

The final time I left the country was for a meeting in Paris. I may have not been able to cause too much mayhem and destruction on Leicester many years ago, but I had been keeping half an eye out on Tommy O'Houlihan's' kid even though he was only a few years younger than me I still felt that it was my duty to watch out for him. It was easier when John moved to Oxford. I made sure that we met up regularly by way of telling him I used to know his dad but without telling him the reason.

Although he wasn't associated with the IRA John's political leanings despite the Good Friday agreement were 'different'. He was known around Oxford to be a bit of a firebrand. I had other friends in Oxford, and one of them had got John to take a little trip to the Sorbonne. When I knew John was going, I flew over there for one night only and flew back the next day. I intentionally sought John out. It wasn't hard singling him out as he had a thick Irish accent which stood out like the proverbial sore thumb amongst the French in the room.

John appeared to be taking the hand of a beautiful redhead, but any dalliance on his part would have to wait. I had things that I needed to discuss with him urgently, so I pulled him into a corner where we couldn't be overheard.

CHAPTER 10

TWO SIDES OF THE TRUTH

Nina Cohen has her version of the truth. It's true that she was on Eurostar that fateful day. She probably did set off the explosion. Did she regret it? Not for one minute. It was to her mind payback for what had happened earlier on in her home country of Israel.

She probably did it for two reasons. Reason number one as far as she was concerned Laura Marchant was responsible for her brother's death, and number two to get her hands on the Ark so she could return it to her government who she perceived were the rightful owners. On recovering the Ark, she hoped to be reinstated as an agent. Up until eighteen months ago she was a valued member of Mossad. Then she learnt of a bombing in a Kubutz out in the county somewhere. She believed that it was all down to Laura Marchant and thought that it was she who was responsible for killing her brother who had been living in the Kubutz.

Nina used to be a member of the Israeli Central Institution Special Operations and Intelligence. When her brother was killed, she went off the rails just a teeny bit and was admitted to a secure psychiatric unit for six months where she met a girl who had been a top-notch PA.

Whilst in the secure unit she broke into the unit's safe and stole the PA's passport as well as taking her own back. On her release, she took a plane to England on the stolen passport and found herself a job as an agency Temp.

Rosie and she hooked up in a nightclub in Hoxton. It wasn't for romance that they married her, it was the fact that Rosie belonged to the Metropolitan Police. When Nina started to follow Laura Marchant on social media it drove her new wife mad and was occasionally ridiculed by her for trying to emulate Laura. Nina needed to do everything in her power to get right into Laura Marchant's skin, even down to the Red Coat.

Following Laura on social media did have its uses as far as Nina was concerned. The woman shouldn't have given away so many clues and obviously didn't know that Nina was once a member of the Elite Sayeret Matkal who was in Nina's opinion better than the UK's SAS. Of course, Nina had built up my contacts across the world with my various intelligence gathering. One of these contacts was a retired Army Major, Glen Cooper. At the time Nina didn't know that both she and Laura wanted the same thing – the Ark. Ok it didn't matter if the Major was killed or injured, and Nina was certainly not responsible for the disappearance of his wife Clare. It was sheer coincidence that Nina had purchased a Pink Mini for Rosie as a wedding present.

Driving down to Ebbsfleet Nina had felt light-hearted. She was on a mission again. She was free from her stuffy boss who was so rigid in his ways that he would surely snap into two one day. She parked in the car park there in a prominent position that she knew would be captured well on CCYV. She then lugged a heavy rucksack out of the car and bought a ticket to London St Pancras International.

Nina probably had all sorts of contacts in the UK. Let's just say that Eurostar made an unscheduled stop that day. It was easy for Nina to slip in the toilets in first class and hide her bomb, after which she made her way to the back of the train where she knew she would be relatively safe.

Nina's unsuspecting wife picked up her Mini after work. She was miffed that I hadn't got a car park ticket for it, but being a police officer did have some perks.

Nina's cover story was that she was visiting her mum's old friend who lived over that way, and the car park at the station was the safest place for the Mini as it had CCTV. Feigning a migraine was another lie which nicely rounded the whole thing off.

Nina suspected that Ms Marchant would be in first class, but she didn't want her killed, only injured enough so that when she went to visit her in the hospital it was a case of Tell me where the Ark is, or I will inject this untraceable poison into you.

Laura was not injured in the blast though, she walked away unscathed. Nina had to get back to her boss in a hurry before Laura got to Keystone Crescent so that she could carry out her next part of the plan. As his temporary PA, she had access to all the therapist's appointments and knew that the 'One' would be there that afternoon.

A driver was waiting for Nina just outside Kings Cross, so it was a two-minute journey at breakneck speed to get back to the therapist's house and reveal all.

The truth is that Laura was bound by the Official Secrets Act. The only thing that she was able to confirm re that she was being hunted down by an ex-Mossad member. Nina may have thought that she had got the better of Laura by finding out that she was on Eurostar on that day. As an influencer and ticktock magnate Laura herself hat did drop one or two crumbs about her travel plans, but you really think that a member of MI6 would give things away everything to an ex-Mossad member.

Nina had obviously been losing her touch. Not surprising really as she had been out of the game for about eighteen months. She blamed Laura for blowing up the Kubutz and for killing her brother. What she didn't know was that her dear brother had placed himself there a few years ago. The Kubutz was meant to be working towards a common goal, but Mr Cohen had other ideas.

He had first heard rumours a few years ago. He was originally an art dealer and had heard on the arts grapevine that a particular item might be on the market. So, he quit his lucrative job and settled into life at the Kubutz. MI6 had wondered who had started the rumour that a certain item might be for sale. They keep an eye on you and are interested in more than you think. It turned out that it wasn't just Mr. Cohen at the Kubutz that had a secret All of the people were there for one reason or another, and that most definitely was not the idea of sharing and mucking in. Laura had already managed to extract the two innocents from there, two young ladies on a gap year. She convinced them to leave suddenly and told them that their parents were gravely ill (not true) and that the other should leave to support her friend on the long arduous journey back to Austria.

And so, the stage was set for the little fireworks display at the Kubutz. There were several undesirables, who ironically the Israeli government wanted rid of. Laura just lit the blue touch paper and retreated to a safe place in the hills to watch. The Kubutz was decimated. Both the Local and international press were fed disinformation, and a break-off group from Palestine were blamed.

Blowing up the kibbutz tipped Nina Cohen over the edge. She spent the next eighteen months in a secure unit. By chance a nurse there who would do anything for cash intimated that it could be MI6 who was the instigator of the bomb. The woman was a fantasist and watched too many true-life crime dramas. Whatever the reason, Nina Cohen was a woman on a mission.

Nina and Laura had crossed paths a few years ago. Nina thought that Laura was arrogant. Laura didn't like Nina and thought that she was rude. When Nina was subsequently going through her brother's papers, she discovered that he was interested in buying a relic that would restore glory to her country, but more importantly to her.

She surmised that Laura would be interested in it (she was) and was looking for an opportunity to get back at Laura who she was convinced intended to steal the Ark and kill Nina's brother who had put out feelers for the Ark. Nina was on MI6's hot list of people entering the country. MI6 have lots of fingers in lots of pies.

It's interesting to know that Nina was taken on by a temp agency very quickly. Even more surprising was the fact that she was working as a fill-in secretary for a certain therapist whom Laura and MI6 had been keeping tabs on too. Funny thing coincidence isn't it? Everyone has all the pieces of a jigsaw we just have to slot them all together in the right order.

Then something happened that put the kibosh on Laura's efforts. Maybe Nina Cohen was bi, maybe she preferred women or maybe it was part of an elaborate ruse by her. She went and married an actual damn police officer in the Met. MI6 is nothing if not flexible, so there was a regrouping and refocusing exercise. Nina Cohen was now under twenty-four-hour surveillance.

MI6 knew who she visited, knew her connections, and probably even knew when she took a piss. Laura's little trip to Paris was all part of the plan; to flush Nina out. Nina's wife's little pink Mini was followed to Ebbsfleet. Nina Cohen may have thought that she had enough sway to get Eurostar to make an unscheduled stop. Yeah, right as if! It would do that even for the Prime Minister! It was engineered as Laura had direct coms to the driver of the train all throughout its journey.

Everyone at six knew there was going to be an explosion, they knew where and they knew the time. A specialist nerd was consulted as to the effect – the loss of life and limb. The PM and Cobra had a secret meeting. Everyone agreed that things should be allowed to pan out. Laura was to let off a mini explosion to take out comms. Then they had the most ineptitude Met Police Inspector take part in the subsequent enquiry. They banked on him never getting to the bottom of it.

Why let so many people die you might well ask. Why let so many be injured? It wasn't just about the Ark, or a rouge Mossad agent, this was about more, so much more. If you think about it after losing 'H''s bloodhound in the street, why would Laura be careless enough to let Dinesh see her leave the tube station and then hail a cab?

Laura knew exactly where Dinesh was all the time. She wasn't going to let him follow her to find out where she lived. When he 'accidentally' bumped into her near Leicester Square tube station she already knew that he was following her. The distinct smell of Four-Square Cigarettes which are produced in India and would be found in many shops there had followed her around, and the smell she thought she smelt in the Lift at Covent Garden was where he had pushed his back against the side of the lift. You see the trouble with smokers is that their clothes will still linger with the smell of cigarettes for ages, so brushing up against the side of the lift Dinesh had invertedly left a smell against the side.

He was lurking in a dark corner when Laura stormed out of Rules, and no doubt watched her dodge the grey-haired woman following her. When heard the unusual limp, she knew it was him. He had been shot in the leg when he was in Northern Ireland, and although the bullet was removed from his shin, in wet weather, he tended to limp.

When Laura span around to greet him, and that first hug, it wasn't that she had once had a crush on him. She had already heard from my sources that he was in London, so the hug meant Laura could put a tiny tracking device in his coat pocket. Looking at her phone as if looking at the time she was checking that the tracking device was working. The only thing that had bothered Laura about their meeting was how he knew where she was, and what time she would be there.

Laura's brain did a swift analysis of what had happened that night. She mentally ran through the timeline and realised that someone had been feeding Dinesh information about her. She concluded that it was either 'H' himself, or one of his minions. She wondered how her watch had ended up at Golder's Green Nick. It wasn't on her wrist at the time of the blast, she did not lose it down the toilet. It must have been when John had gone to kiss her hand.

When Laura finally got home from meeting Dinesh she struggled out of her dress and slipped into her pyjamas, then opened the tracking device on her 'phone. She could see that he had visited two places, one in Southgate, the other in Edmonton. Both interested her, but it was the address in Edmonton that she was interested in. She knew Southgate well already, as Dinesh had made a stop near one of her favourite Chinese takeaways. She knew the owner well and that he leased out the flat upstairs. He would tell me that anything dodgy was going on there as she always left a generous tip.

As for the Edmonton address, well, she would take a scout round another day. It appeared to be a block of flats she would have to visit to see who went in and out. When she did find out who Dinesh had visited it gave her the shock of her life, and she was even more certain that she should get out of the country. She knew by now that all roads led to Tahiti. It was time to visit her maternal grandmother.

(Extract from the Metro Free Newspaper)

Five days after the bomb that tore up Eurostar, and cost so many people their lives we have exclusive interviews from friends and relatives, that this paper can report were subject to police questioning in a North London Police Station. For security reasons, we cannot reveal the name of the police station, nor the officer in charge of the investigation.

Wesley (surname redacted) is a fast bowler for Jamaica's Cricket Team.

"Look I know what happened. I was supposed to be playing at Lord, the England vs Jamaica Match that day. I'd pulled a muscle in my leg, so couldn't make it. Let's just so I know a man, who knows someone who was key to the investigation. My friend, missed the cricket results as he was on Eurostar man, and he missed the results, so he phoned up asking for them. I swear on my life all this man wanted to know was the results. He was told that England won when it was Jamacia. Don't know if it got him out of hot water".

Fenix (surname redacted) works in law.

"It's true that someone on the train that day works with me. All I can confirm is that they did try and call me over a work thing. They would never do such a terrible thing as blow up a train. I mean we are damn close if you know what I mean. All I know is that they were briefly interviewed and then let go. I'm not in contact with them at this present time.

Eve Jackson is a long-standing friend of one of the passengers.

"No, I don't need my surname redacted, I can confirm that I knew Mary Pickles. We went to finish school in Switzerland together. Of course, this was after the war you know. She and I shared a bedroom, and we knew each other's secrets.

She wouldn't do anything like blowing up Eurostar. I mean her father maybe, but that's a different story. Tell me do you have any connections with the less salubrious newspapers I could certainly tell you things about him that would make your hair curl. Why do you think she was sent to school in Switzerland?"

Leading Firefighter Paul Jackson was one of the first on the scene.

"It was complete carnage. I knew one of the passengers as she was my Godmother. I can't tell you who it was due to confidentiality reasons. I suppose I was lucky in as much as our watch was on exercise somewhere in the vicinity of the explosion, that's how my crew and I managed to get there quickly and not let anyone cast aspersions about out. All I can say is that the lady in question would never set off a bomb. I know her family for goodness' sake, and they have always been very generous in contributing to the Firefighter's benevolent fund".

This reporter can add that there was an eminent professor from Oxford University seen leaving a North London Police Station. A spokesperson from Jesus College Oxford declined to comment.

It has also been reported through an unknown source that this could be in retaliation for an explosion at a Kubutz just north of Elat in Israel where seventeen people were killed.

CHAPTER 11

THE AFTERMATH AS TOLD BY NINA COHEN

'Nina, I'm disappointed in you', said the blonde man. 'I genuinely thought you were a secretary from the agency. Tell me did you really have a bad migraine today?'

Grinning, Nina spoke. 'My true name is Nira. I used my connections for Eurostar to make an unscheduled stop at Ebbsfleet this afternoon. It was easy to plant a bomb in the toilet'.

'So how what about your car, a vintage Pink Mini isn't it?', queried the blonde man.

'Oh, my wife Rosie will pick it up this afternoon after she's finished her shift. It's not her car really. It belonged to her Mum'.

'Can I ask, before any further revelations, said the blonde man. 'What did you come here for Mr Heigham?'

'Please, just call me H,' said the old man. 'I really came here for affirmation that I did the right thing. The things that I told you about that happened nineteen-eighty-five, that was me. The men involved were the boys from the Prisoner of war camp. They were Josef Mangle's little helpers. Each day they went out to do secret things for him. Together they tried to interpret a message for him. A message so powerful it would change the world. A message from God himself to Moses, the Torah.

'And then what, what was your plan once the Ark's contents were scattered to the wind?' asked the blonde man.

'Why send my adoptive granddaughter Birdie to collect and dispose of them? Of course, that isn't her true name, she was christened Laura'.

'And you Nina. What is all your involvement in this?' Asks the blonde man, but now a little puzzled by the odd turn of events.

'Mossad', said Nina succinctly. 'I had to track down Birdie and get rid of her. I knew she would be on Eurostar, our mutual French Connection let me know. Anyway, gents please it's time to leave before Birdie/Laura gets here.'

'One thing before we go,', asked 'H' cautiously, what bloody hell is that smell coming from the basement? I'm sure I recognise it from somewhere?'

'Do you think I'm a fool', laughed Nina, 'you are just trying to buy time until your precious granddaughter gets here aren't you? Well, I have news for you Grandad, she has probably been blown to hell where she deserves to be. So, stop trying to delay this old man and tell me where the bloody Ark is, she said, glancing down at the battered suitcase that he was carrying.

Sighing the old man bent down and slowly opened it. Hardly daring to breathe Nina leaned forward and peered into the ancient valise.

'Oh my god, it's full of old German Marks (currency)!' she exclaimed lunging forward towards the old man and grabbing him by the throat. Wheezing the old man smiled.

'You won't get it that easily young lady', he replied with as much mirth as he could muster.

'So, tell me this one thing old fool where is it?'. Said Nina letting go of his throat.

'I'm sorry to say my dear I don't actually know', the old man replied, 'but I'll tell you this my dear lady, when you find it, it won't be complete. One of the scrolls is missing and has been since nineteen eighty-five. As the therapist so succinctly put it, the five pieces of the scroll were scattered to the wind in eighty-five. With help from Laura, I managed to retrieve all but one. Without it the message from God is incomplete.'

Turning white, Nina shook her head.

'You are lying you bastard', she said between clenched teeth, 'and you,' she said pointing the gun at the therapist, 'you are in cahoots with him aren't you, or why else would you have a secret room underground that you keep disappearing to?'

Holding up his hands in mock surrender the therapist shook his head.

'Oh me,' he said with mock innocence, 'I was after the damn thing as well, so there you have it. This old man here came not for redemption but hoped its location would be revealed in our session. You, my dear, are also keen to find it for reasons unknown. However, as you have the gun, and as I am almost blind, and the old man is frail, I conceded that you have the upper hand.'

'Too true my dear boss. I would say it has been a pleasure working for you, but it has not. You are the rudest most pedantic man I have ever worked for. You want things regimented. Honestly, it could be the Third Reich here,' she said trailing off as she saw the look of thunder on the therapist's face.

Aiming the gun at his head, she prepared to shoot him. With a glimmer in his eye, she whispered,

'Goodbye, you bastard, goodbye.'

'Wait, wait', said the therapist in a strangled voice, 'don't shoot me, I know what happened to the missing scroll. I spent some time counselling a young man many years ago. He was in a lot of distress. At first, I thought it was the loss of his parents at an early age, but after a couple of sessions, I found he was holding back a secret, something that was clearly troubling him.

He had stolen something a long time ago. He felt guilty, and to make matters worse he hadn't told his best friend. This played on his mind. At the end of the day, he admitted that he should have reported the accident involving a white van to the police, but he never did. He took a piece of a scroll out of the van. Does that mean anything to anyone?'

'You mean you have been keeping this as a secret for years Mr. Therapist, and you have not told a fucking soul?' Shouted Nina. 'I want the name of the boy, and I want it now before you all die,' she continued. Glancing down at her watch she realised that she was running out of time. Laura Marchant would be hot on her heels.

'Easy there my dear,' said the therapist,' you are getting quite stressed. The name of the boy was Andrew Bruce.'

'So, where the hell is this Andrew Bruce'? Questioned Nina.

Glancing at his watch, which was the exact make and model of Nina's the therapist sighed softly.

'Hopefully on his way to Heathrow Airport by now. You see his best friend won a fabulous prize in a competition. Marvellous coincidence you think? Of course, he had to take his old Mucker Andrew Bruce with him.

When Mr H here decided to pay me a visit, I knew what he was coming here for, not for redemption, but to find out where the last piece of scroll was. Let us put it this way. I have a great interest in the Scrolls, because as a child as was filled with stories of my heroic father who worked for the greatest man on earth. He undertook the overseeing of five boys. Now isn't it strange how things pan out?' he chuckled to himself.

'That's all well and good,' retorted Nina, 'but we really must get going. As I'm the one with the gun, and you're the ones with the information go figure, and whilst your ailing minds compute this we must get out and get to Heathrow pronto.'

'Why the hurry my dear,' asked the old man, trying to stall for time.

'Because this building is going to explode in three minutes,' said Nina panicking slightly.

'Not only did I plant the Bomb on Eurostar, but I also planted one here you old fools.'

'Well,' said the therapist, 'I wondered why the sudden interest in the work of an old fuddy-duddy piqued your curiosity. Not surprising that you needed this job, and how interesting that you managed to secure it with me isn't it? Now let's do as we are told and get the hell out of here.'

Hurrying out the Therapist sighed. He would never be able to get the prized possession in his shrine. The Ark would have looked grand there in the empty place where a spotlight shone.

Outside Nina pulled the old man along whilst holding the gun to the therapist's back at one end of the crescent but walking away from Kings Cross, which was now absolute mayhem Nina thankfully saw a black cab. Nudging the therapist with the muzzle of the gun, she shoved him in front of the cab, which squealed to a halt.

Not waiting for the driver's verbal protest, she ushered the two men into the cab.

'Heathrow as fast as you can' she snapped at the driver.

Having taken Umbridge at someone virtually hijacking his cab, the driver mentally doubled the price,

'One hundred and ninety quid to you madam', he said as politely as he could. After all, he could not afford to pass up a fare like this. His erstwhile partner Fenix walked all hours as a junior at a renowned Law Firm and was always making up excuses to come home late. Well, it was his turn to get home late.

The thing that had drawn him to Fenix was that he was well, different. They came over as a posh twat who had been to Eaton and then Cambridge and had a stellar lineage that they could trace all the way back to Richard the Third. Fenix would baulk at their friend's lineage if they found out that his great-grandmother was the mistress of Josef Mengele who had born him an illegitimate child, his granddad. As for Mengele himself, it was never proved that it was his great-grandfather after the war.

Advances in DNA analysis later confirmed Mengele's remains in 1992, but the cab driver could not get access to the sealed results. However, one thing that attracted Fenix to him was that he had an identical twin brother.

'I'll make it £500 if you can get me there in less than thirty minutes,' said Nina waving a bunch of twenty- and fifty-pound notes. It was so easy to pick the pocket of the Irishman who she squeezed next to at Ebbsfleet. He was so pissed he wouldn't have noticed it at the time, and when he eventually twigged that money was missing, he would blame it all on the blast.

Nodding in agreement the taxi driver floored it. Weaving in and out of traffic, breaking all speed limits along the Westway he wasn't really arsed if he got a speeding ticket. For lots of the journey, he could use the bus lane.

'Any idea which terminal madam', he said switching the intercom on.

Gripping the old man's arm tighter, and pushing the gun into the Therapists' thigh, she looked at him expectantly.

'Five', he muttered, "Five to LAX'.

'Hear that did you, driver,' said Nina to the cab driver.

'Certainly Madam,' replied the Cab Driver indicating for the exit to Terminal Five. 'No bags, Madam.' inquired mentally rubbing his hands together thinking of all the cash that would be his.

'No bags replied Nina reaching into her handbag and leaning forward as if to pay the taxi driver, whilst calculating if the old man would leg or not if she let go of his arm for a few seconds. Leaning even closer through the small hole in the Perspex glass that separated her from the taxi driver, she pushed her hand through as if to pay as he simultaneously pushed his through from the other end.

Felling a sharp scratch to the palm of his hand a look of horror spread across the taxi driver's face. Slumping over the steering wheel he was dead in ten seconds, by which time Nina and the two men headed towards the Terminal. As it was noisy and bustling inside the terminal, no one heard the loud honking of horns outside.

CHAPTER 12

THE JOURNEY LHR TO LAX

A build-up of cabs and cars was happening right outside Heathrow T5 by now. It took a lone police officer whose job it was to keep people from parking out front five minutes to find the black cab containing one very dead driver. When the autopsy results were returned, they showed that he had died from a heart attack. Not a single trace of poison was found in his body. Although there were plenty of Coke and needle tracks, including an odd one on his hand. The man obviously liked to party, and this could have contributed to his heart attack.

Returning to the swanky flat at London Bridge that they shared with their boyfriend, not only had Fenix been shocked by the news of the bombing but they fainted when a Police Officer knocked on the door and told them the demise of their boyfriend.

Meanwhile, back at the airport, Nina was making a swift phone call. Finishing it quickly, she pushed her way to the front of the BA ticket desk. Slapping down a black Amex she demanded three Business Class seats on the next plane to Los Angeles.

Heading through security, the therapist and the old man wondered how on earth Nina would get her damned weapon through the scanners without setting off a major security alert. Nothing transpired though and they were through in record time.

'I've got to ask', began the old man hesitantly, 'how on earth did you get us through without passports or setting off any alarms?

'There isn't only one H in the world', said Nina succinctly, 'and it's not a question of what you know, but who you know. Especially if they happen to work for MI6'.

All three sat silently through the eleven-hour flight. Declining food, only asking for drinks Nina never let the old man or the Therapist out of her sight. She wouldn't allow them to raise the partitions that could be used to separate their individual pods, but she had managed to secure three adjoining pods across the plane. It was a Catch-22 situation. Nina's funds were rapidly dwindling. If she had bought economy or premium seats, which are usually full or overbooked she wouldn't have been able to keep an eye on the men.

She didn't trust the therapist. He was the loose cannon and had everything to play for. She couldn't wave her gun around without sparking a major incident. The old man was easy to keep under control. She slipped a sleeping draught in his orange juice, which was always served along with champagne in business class. She knew he would not reach for the old suitcase which a crew member had insisted on putting in the overhead locker during take-off.

When the old man woke up five hours later, she escorted him to the toilet, him stumbling a little, so Nina grinned apologetically at the cabin crew. She then insisted that he drank some water which she had also drugged. She certainly wanted him alive at the end of their journey as he was the only one who could validate and read the missing section of the Scroll.

The therapist pretended to be asleep throughout the journey. He was either truly asleep or he was busy plotting his escape. Nina had their arrival all planned out though. She had requested wheelchair assistance for the old man when they landed. The therapist could push it, and Nina would walk directly behind him, holding the gun to his back.

The wheelchair was indeed waiting, and she brushed off any help from the ground crew. This was the tricky part. It didn't worry Nina that they had no ESTAs to enter the United States. Gone were the days when you needed a paper one. As for passports – well another short telephone call at Heathrow would helpfully get them through passport control.

Gone also were the days of fingerprinting and photographing everyone on arrival. Now all they had to do was lazily walk up to Passport Control and see if the phone call had done the trick.

Eleven hours earlier, an ex-president who was favoured by the rednecks of the States and had already been indited was woken from his slumber by his personal mobile ringing. Wearily he reached for it hoping that it wouldn't be one of his ex-wives. A quick exchange of words and a promise from the caller that he would get his fair share of the dibs was all that that was needed to see them waved through passport control by one of his supporters from his last Presidential campaign.

Now Nina had to think quickly. She had no idea where Bruce and Gunn had gone, no money for hotels, and no hope of getting the Ark back. Another call to someone in the FBI got her on the passenger list for all airlines out of LAX. Scanning the passenger lists hurriedly she spotted them; they were heading for Tahiti. Bruce and Gunn had already left on an earlier Air Tahiti flight and were by now halfway to the South Pacific.

Scanning the queue at the Ait Tahiti desk she up the queue and found her target. A portly man who wore an expensive-looking suit, with Louis Vuitton luggage on his side was the perfect choice. Snatching the wheelchair from a surprised therapist she rammed it into the portly gentleman then apologised profusely and squeezed his arm as a comforting gesture. Walking swiftly away with the wheelchair she realised her rooky mistake. She had lost sight of the therapist. Swearing under her breath she quickly scrutinised the terminal. He was nowhere to be seen.

As an ex-Mossad member, she had learnt not to panic under pressure. Instead, she slowly pushed the wheelchair with the old man still sitting in it towards a TSA agent. A swift exchange of words in which the sentence 'I thought I saw a man go into the Gents Restroom with a gun' had the TSA agent running hell for leather towards the Restrooms. Smiling to herself she opened the wallet that she had lifted from the portly man. No credit cards inside but a huge mixture of US Dollars and South Pacific Francs cheered her up even more.

She assumed that the Therapist would be found by the TSA agent, and hopefully detained. That solved one Problem. The next was to get on a flight to Tahiti without a passport. Having travelled the globe on her missions she could get into almost every country without a passport. Tahiti was not on the list. Nina hoped that Tahitian Border Control could easily be bribed. There was a hell of a lot of South Pacific Francs in the wallet.

Having secured two single tickets, she pushed the old man towards the departure gate. This was where things could come unstuck. The gate for departure was modern, and the section where she was seated alongside the wheelchair was relatively quiet. Twenty minutes later it was heaving with passengers who had just disembarked from an Air France plane.

A crowd of people were trying to catch a connecting flight to Tahiti which suited Nina's needs. Gaggles of French-speaking groups were gathered around the boarding gate gesticulating and shouting over each other. The poor harassed check-in staff were trying to get people boarded on the Flight. Using a polite firm voice Nina pushed the wheelchair in front of herself with an 'Exusez-moi, s'ill vous plait' The check-in clerk was too busy to stop her and ask for their passports. Nina just waved the boarding pass under the clerk's nose. The check-in clerk assumed that her colleague had checked passports, and as Nina was pushing a wheelchair with an old man slumped in it, she waved them forward to the plane.

At the end of the plane's bridge, she had to forfeit the wheelchair. This time they were flying Economy Class, which had very little legroom for an eight-hour flight. Nina shoved the old man into a window seat. She tried to grab hold of the walking stick that he insisted on taking everywhere, but he would not let go of it no matter how hard she tried. Eventually, she gave up as she didn't want to attract untoward attention.

There was a need for her gun now. Anyway, she couldn't exactly wave it around in the plane's cabin. The Therapist was long gone, but who would he run to and tell and who would believe him anyway? Sitting next to the old man so that he couldn't move to escape or call for help Nina settled down with a sigh. Looking at HIN now slumbering and snoring gently Nina settled down for the long journey. She hoped that the old git would stay asleep for the whole flight. Purportedly snoozing the old man's snoring increased. Little did Nina know he wasn't asleep, not had he been since they touched down in Los Angeles. He wasn't the only one who had secrets. Before his visit to the Therapist, he had telephoned Laura Marchant telling her where he was going, and what he had planned.

Laura was in Paris when she got the call. When she had finished talking, she knew she had to go home. She had hoped to find out more about the French connection who lived here in a grace and favour flat bought for him by his biological grandfather.

Following the French Connection Paris had been easy. He had supposedly learnt his craft from Mossad but was being a little slapdash about the whole thing considering that she was following him. It may have been that he had twigged what she was doing, and maybe there were one or two red herrings.

She was at the base of the Eiffel Tower when her phone buzzed in her jacket pocket. She had set it to silent so that the French Connection wouldn't hear it. Laura had just spotted him handing over a dangerous knife to an ex-judge's wife. Very interesting indeed. Turning slightly away from her target she answered swiftly in Hebrew thanking God that there weren't many people around her who spoke it.

Laura knew that she had to get back to London quickly. The life of her adopted Grandfather was at stake. The last time she had met him he told her about the need for redemption, but it had to be with a particular therapist who he knew so much about. Laura surmised that this therapist was connected to his past in Poland.

With a little more detective work she discovered the grisly secret of the therapist's Linage.

The Therapist's Father was the son of someone who had been at the death camp at the same time as her grandfather. He in turn was the son of an SS Officer. The apple didn't fall far from the tree, and the therapist was a truly nasty piece of work. Rumour had it that his basement was the recreation of a gas chamber and that he took patients down there to frighten them.

There was no proof that he had murdered anyone yet but reports of a strange smell in the therapist's house set alarm bells ringing.

Laura knew that she, usually the hunter was now being hunted by Nina. Red Herrings and breadcrumbs might be the style of the French Connection, but she was the Master. Laura knew that Nina would have to speed up her plans so an early return to London was an advantage to Laura. The French Connection would have to wait. Hailing a cab Laura spoke rapidly, this time in French. She managed to get a ticket on Eurostar for the next day – the day her adoptive Grandfather was visiting the therapist.

Thinking that she might set up a little distraction of her own Laura spent that evening concocting a small explosive device. It wouldn't cause anyone any harm, just an annoyance.

This was payback for her boss 'H'. She had sussed out what he was up to three months ago. She carried on pretending that everything was normal. Deviating from anything that 'H' expected from her would mean that he had sussed what she was up to. He knew she was in

Paris, and he ordered her to follow up on the French Connection in the knowledge that she was being hunted down by Nina, yet she was following her own agenda which included the French Connection but also knowing that Nina was trying to catch up with and kill her.

On arrival at the Gare de Nord, she encountered an obnoxious drunk who was trying to chat her up. Shaking him off she nearly choked on her coffee when she was at the Trains buffet car. Thinking that not would be good to have an alibi she engaged in a little conversation with him answering his questions with evasion and half-truths i.e., those of her undercover persona.

As expected, the train did make an unexpected stop at Ebbsfleet. Just as it was pulling away from the station her little explosion went off. It meant that the toilet could not be used, and she stuck a sign in French and English on it saying that it was out of order.

Knowing that Nina would have by now tracked which seat and coach number she had booked she made her way to the end of the Train. If Nina pulled off anything it would be the safest place for her. She condemned what 'H' was doing, setting her up at the risk of many people's lives. Standing ready for her escape, she really needed to get to Keystone Crescent in a hurry, so she ran through her plans swiftly. Even so, the explosion took her by surprise. True she had let John Houlihan steal her watch, knowing that it would be found eventually she now had a reason to be interviewed by the police.

In the aftermath of the explosion, Laura's instinct was to save her fellow passengers, but she knew that for some unfortunately it would be too late. She knew that by now all power to the rails would be switched off, so she ran the length of the train jumping over the debris. Panting she managed to get three quatres of the way down when she felt the arms of a burly fireman stop her and bar her way.

'Not going anywhere I'm afraid madam' he said.

Laura had to think quickly. How come the emergency services got there so quickly? Maybe 'H' had grown a conscience and the call to them was instigated by him. Who would ignore a request from MI6?

'I am a doctor, please let me through so that I can help tend those at the front who will have been badly impacted', she said quickly.

Nodding the Fireman let her through. More twisted metal, more bodies. Laura had one purpose.

She needed to get to the therapist's house, and she needed to get there quickly. Pounding the pavements, she stopped to see the therapist and her grandfather being bundled into a cab. Then the unexpected happened. The therapist's house shook and then collapsed taking down the two houses next to it.

Laura stood there blinking. There had been enough devastation already, so she pulled out her burner phone and dialled 999. Briefly explaining what had happened Nina was told to get away from the area as soon as possible. In the background, Laura could hear another dispatcher sobbing softly. The news of Eurostar's devastation was obviously spreading rapidly.

Knowing she didn't stand a chance of catching a Cab anywhere near to where she was Nina walked swiftly to Russell Square. She knew that no underground trains would be running from Kings Cross or Highbury & Islington Stations, but hopefully, she would be able to catch a westbound tube to Heathrow.

Instinct told her that if it were her on the run with an old man and a slightly younger Therapist the object of the exercise would be to get out of the country as soon as possible, and not anywhere too close. Laura knew that Nina had the know-how to get out of the country. The problem was where was she running to?

Exiting the tube at terminal 5 the last terminal on the line Nina thought she had a good chance of catching up with Nina who would be hampered by the Old Man. On her way up the escalator, she heard excited chatter about a hold-up outside the airport, some sort of problems with the set-down and drop-off area apparently. Flashing her ID at all the BA Check-in desks she learnt after about half an hour that Nina and Co. had boarded a plane to Los Angeles. Now Laura knew where Nina was heading. She was going to follow them, but firstly she had to face the music about the bombings and explain to 'H' why she walked away from it.

Two days later she was inside Golders Green police station being interviewed by DI White and his sidekick Sargant who was married to Nina. The police might have been under the impression that they were interviewing her. Laura was an expert in interpreting voice cadence, gestures, and movements. She was interested in what Nina's wife would reveal.

Pausing at the front desk to announce her arrival Laura did a double take when she spotted Dinesh's niece lurking in the background. Surely the young PC should have been having an induction day, but there she was when Laura arrived.

The interview was brief, and as Laura was not under caution so was not recorded. Answering all the questions carefully and succinctly she watched as Sargent Beacker looked all around the room.

Laura surmised that the good sergeant would rather be looking for her wife or was she in cahoots with her. She couldn't ask any questions of her own, but it was obvious that she was in the limelight for the explosion. She had to catch up with 'H' soon and invent some story about why she had set up a little explosion.

Walking away from the police station she walked for a long time. Nina was obviously worried about her wife, and Laura glanced around the police car park and spotted a badly parked Pink Mini. This meant that Nin's wife had collected it from Ebbsfleet and must be wondering where her Wife was.

And then her mobile rang. It was ‘H’ wanting an update and arranging a meeting at rules ASAP.

CHAPTER 13

ROSEDALE BECKER- COHENS FIRST TRUTH

Rosie left the Police Station very late on the night of the bombing of Eurostar. She had to take a cab home which was bloody annoying as she lived with her wife Nina at a hairdresser's salon in Bush Hill Park. It wasn't Rosie's choice of residence. True it was close to work, but the area was rapidly declining and once Covid hit in 2020 one by one shops around where she lived with Nina had begun to close.

When she had first met her Wife, Rosie was in a club in Hoxton dancing the night away after drinking far too many Tequila shots. Someone had grabbed her by the waist from behind and spun her around. Ready to kick the living daylights out of whoever it was she found herself relaxing as a beautiful dark-haired woman was staring into her eyes.

They chatted long into the night at a small café nearby that wasn't in a hurry to close. At 3 a.m. they finally got kicked out of the café. They made it back to the tiny flat in Hoxton next to an all-night petrol station. Two months later they were married and moved to Bush Hill Park. Nina had loved the name of the parade of shops where their new flat was – Queen Annes Place. She thought it sounded rather grand and explained to Rosie that although she was originally from Israel, she was truly a supporter of the royal family.

Rosie arrived back at the flat that she shared with Nina and let out a huge sigh. She was just kicking off her work shoes wondering where Nina was when her mobile rang. It was the British Transport Police telling her that her Pink Mini was found in the car park at Ebbsfleet train station. Going outside and climbing the steps over the footbridge to the other side of Bush Hill Park train station Rosie walked past the shops and eventually onto a main road. A solitary cab was passing, and Rosie Hailed it waving her warrant card in front of her.

After agreeing a reasonable fair to Ebbsfleet, after all Rosie was going there on 'Police Business' she climbed into the back, sighed, closed her eyes and fell asleep. It was going to be a long day tomorrow – Interviews plus a new PC starting. She woke up with a start to find the kindly cab driver shaking her arm. He wouldn't take a penny for the fare as he explained he lived in Gravesend and that this would be his last fare of the. Day.

Collecting her Pink Mini – a wedding gift from Nina, Rosie drove home in a trance. She pulled up in Queen Anne Parade and squeezed her pride and joy into a tiny space. She would be leaving early and by now it was already 2.30 am.

Rosie couldn't sleep and spent the next few hours phoning all the London Hospitals, even the South London ones, but there was no one admitted by the Name of Nina Cohen, nor anyone of her description. By now she was getting worried but telling herself to get her shit together she drove to work, parked badly, and shoulders hunched marched into work.

Interviews didn't take place that day, nor did the new PC make an appearance. HR had got the wrong day, and DI White wanted her to work on a strategy for when they did do the interviews. Still worrying about her wife Rosie painted on a smile and started to look at the evidence so far. Sifting through her notes she was particularly interested in a photograph of a smashed-up Patek Phillipe watch. You didn't get many of those turning up at Golders Green Police Station. Nina had always wanted one and watched some woman on ticktock flashing it around.

Trying to remember who Nina's favourite influencer was logged on to Ticktock, but not being able to find anything she switched to

Instagram using Nina's account, and there it was being displayed by one Laura Marchant. Checking who they were interviewing tomorrow she sent DI White a brief email suggesting that they interview Laura Marchant last. Logging off her work PC Rosie headed home, and for the first time in two days felt a little ray of hope. She would get to the bottom of this and would find Nina safe and sound.

Usually cautious as it went with the job Rosie never questioned why Nina had been in the club in Hoxton when they had first met. She was a little surprised how quickly they got married but all of Nina's paperwork seemed to be in order. Rosie knew that her mother would have liked her to get married preferably to a man in the church that her mother used to attend in Nottingham. Aas her mother was no longer alive even though she felt a tad guilty they had booked their wedding at the Newham registry office.

When it came to witnesses Rosie had thought it romantic of Nina to pull strangers off the street. Truth be told Nina did not know anyone in the UK apart from the woman who ran the small temping agency that Nina worked through. Rosie had a few friends but at Nina's insistence, they kept the wedding small, so small that it was just the two of them celebrating in a dingy back street pub afterwards.

Rosie was so giddily in love and thought that Nina was the love of her life. Nina had even surprised her with a late wedding present of a Pink Mini just like the one her mum used to have. Glowing with happiness Rosie returned to work. She thought that Nina loved her so much because she was always asking about what Rosie did. Trying not to give too much information away – that would have caused Rosie to lose her job she told her of one or two things that were happening and one evening let slip salacious gossip about Judge Pickles.

Rosie still hadn't heard from Nina the next day. She told herself that Nina was a grown woman and therefore there was no point in reporting her as a missing person. Robyn in Tech Support owed her a favour, and Rosie would call in that favour after today's shift. She would get Robyn in Tech Support to ping the last location of Nina's mobile 'phone.

The day seemed long and arduous, not helped by White's short temper nor the witnesses from the bombing who were interviewed. Laura Marchant proved interesting especially as she apparently had a car worth more than the debt of a small country, and a now-defunct Patek Phillipe watch. Rosie was itching to go and see Robyn. After her shift had finished, she ran down to the basement where Robyn had a small office. She called in her favour, and then she wished she hadn't. The last ping of Nina's 'phone was the day of the bombing. Not only that it was from a tower located near to Heathrow airport. Nina was on the run. The question was why?

At this point, Rosie began to panic. Was her wife fleeting the country because she didn't love her anymore or was, she trying to run from what had happened on Eurostar, and if so, what exactly was her involvement? Rosie was morally torn between upholding the law or shielding her wife from the law and not letting her beloved get caught up in all the mayhem, and anyway what if any were Nina's connections to it?

Returning home to an empty flat again Rosie decided that she would analyse all that she knew or didn't know about Nina. The list was thus:

1) Nina was an Israeli National and Rosie had glanced at her papers and right to be in the UK very briefly which led to
2) Were the said papers real or forged?
3) What was a good Jewish girl doing at a nightclub in Hoxton which could be answered by?
4) There was a multicultural Population in Hoxton so Nina could have a reason for being at the Nightclub.
5) Their Romance and Marriage were swift. Was it that Rosie had found her one true love or was it something more sinister?

6) When chatting until 3 in the Morning why did Rosie herself do all the talking? Yes, she was naturally gregarious, but never usually gave her life history to a stranger and
7) Why didn't Nina give much information about herself?
8) How come Nina knew of a café that would be open all night unless she was a local
9) How on earth did Rosie herself end up at the café with Nina? Yes, she had a lot to drink at the Nightclub, but she was used to shots on a night out which was why she woke up with a godawful headache the next day.
10) How come on waking she couldn't remember getting home, and who exactly the hell was the woman in bed with her?
11) If she couldn't remember a thing, then had her drink been spiked by Nina or someone else?
12) Had she told Nina at some point about her mother's Pink Mini? She was sure she hadn't.
13) Why did Nina present her with a Pink Mini days after their wedding?
14) Finally, who the hell was Nina Cohen???

CHAPTER 14

THE DC's TRUTHS

As old by DC Martin Sweet:

I was suddenly and abruptly co-opted into a 'situation' that had arisen. That's how Suzie had sold it to me. I was sort of an in-betweener. Often the butt of people's jokes about my surname I had learned in my line of work to tune it out. Let's just say that this job is like any other i.e. the norm, and when asked to undertake the role of a Detective Constable in the Met I did with my usual gusto. My back story was cast iron. Had anyone wondered about my career, well I was from Lincolnshire. I used this as it was the actual county that I hailed from. Mablethorpe was a lovely family-orientated seaside town, but growing up it wasn't for me, so as soon as I could learned a 'trade' and moved on.

People thought that I was an ordinary country copper, with country copper aspirations, and that suited me fine. My 'transfer' to the Met was supposed because I had at age twenty-eight decided that I wanted to improve my lot. If only my new colleagues knew what I was capable of.

I had a brief telephone conversation with Suzie P, and then there I was at the centre of one of the country's worst explosions since the 2005 Aldgate Bombings. I was ordered to report to a DI White at Golders Green Police Station. I knew from my brief conversation with Suzie P that White was under some sort of covert observation, but that aside I was needed for something else.

White had landed me with investigation Gordon Moss KQ. The man was a bigwig in the North London Jewish Community, he observed the Sabbath, went to Shul Regularly, and often took on cases pro bono.

Yet he did have a darker side to him. Notably, another member of White's new team, Jane Hodges, a trainee Lawyer, now a Police Officer had reported Moss a few years ago for sexual harassment and had left the Law firm that she had been working for. I also found out that Moss batted for both sides and was rather friendly with a well-known T.V. judge.

I only gave DI White the shortest of reports when I reported back to him about Moss. What White didn't know was that due to my various contacts, I knew both Moss and White were on Grindr one of the best Gay dating websites, and both had been rather busy on it a couple of evenings ago. I also tracked down the provenance of the all-important signet ring. It was really a birthday present from Moss's Aunt. However, he was not wearing it on the day of the Eurostar explosion. A tiny detail that I may have forgotten to impart to white. He had given it to Fenix Harper, a pupil in his chambers. Harper was already in a relationship with the cab driver who had found out that Moss had given it to Harper as a token of love. Harper's boyfriend had threatened to top himself one day because of this and apparently had all the connections to lay his hands on certain pharmaceuticals.

Given everything that has been going on the last couple of days I may soon be off to warmer climes in the southern hemisphere. Another contact of mine is currently making their way there, and we should hook - up and exchange notes. Hopefully, we can meet at Moorea Beach Café where there is the best sunset in the world, and you can drink from their extensive champagne menu on the beach at a table with the Ocean lapping around you.

I digress through. Moss went to France for the good food and wine. The truth of the matter is that yes, he did imbibe in both. He will swear that he did nothing more than meet with a fellow Lawyer to discuss the possibility of him moving over there. What a tragic waste of Baloney. What his lawyer friend didn't know was that Moss had planted a small listening device in the restaurant before anyone got there. Unfortunately for Moss, he didn't get much out of the recording as Moss's sister gate-crashed the lunch and she had the loudest of voices. She slurped her oysters noisily and generally took over the conversation. I too have my way of finding shit out. Not that I know a waiter in that restaurant. Great chap who has some sort of cousin who dances at the Moulin Rouge. He has a little side-line in switching labels on wine bottles. Surprising that some folks will pay for a decent bottle of chateau neuf de pap. He does a remarkable trade in the 75 vintages.

According to my waiter friend Moss's colleague left to take a swift phone call. He also happened to overhear the call, it was a tense conversation, though the waiter could not hear what was being said on the other end, but the caller was mightily pissed off, and told the person on the other end that they might as well call everything off now that someone was on to them. I never did find out who that someone was....

As told by DC Imogen Blore:

The truth of the matter is this: I have worked with DI White a few times before now, and then I was abruptly assigned to the Domestic Violence Unit for no reason. I kicked my heels in that damn unit for about six months, and every day that I was there I kept going over and over what I had done to be moved so abruptly. I had worked on murder cases before, and armed robbery cases as well. Nothing was off the table as far as I'm concerned. I'm an ex-army and spent some time fighting the Taliban in Afghanistan. Yes, it was tough sometimes, and yes had to make instant decisions. I left after two tours of duty and six months after leaving I joined the Met as a Detective Constable.

I skipped the Police Constable bit though as I was in ex armed forces, and even though I say so myself very, very bright. After eight months as a DC, I took my sergeant exam and waited. Then a few days ago I got a call from DI White, would I like to work with him again, this time as a Detective Sergeant. I jumped at the chance, but then I heard that White would be using another Sergeant, so my career was on the back burner again. The Chief Super wanted to appear to be politically correct. It's a little like when I collected my MBE from the palace. There were an awful lot of 'friends from the Colonies' on the list. Not that I am complaining. It was like anything else. I had to suck it up.

I reported almost everything to DI White about Major (retired) Glen Andrew Cooper. I had learnt more, but I was holding it back, then I could produce it like a rabbit out of a hat, which would earn me some brownie points, and look like I was wholly invested in the job.

The extra bits I learnt about the Major and his wife were very interesting. Rumour had it that she was suffering from Dementia. He couldn't cope anymore, and for some unfathomable reason, they were at the point of divorce. I mean you stick by someone in sickness and in health, don't you? It was his ring. For some reason, he was trying to cover this up and tried to cloud the issue insisting that it belonged to his wife's father. She had a ring, but it was from an old Jewish lady, and she was going to pass it down the family line through her granddaughter Susan, but she feared that Susan would pawn it so that she could buy drugs.

The Majors wife was not dead, nor MIA, nor was she at a friend in Greenwich. She had simply gone to ground as she had helped to commit a heinous crime, one of murder. Now Claire Cooper had very good reasons for this, and personally, I don't blame her. I think that the correct term for what she had a hand in was 'Rough Justice'.

As for the Major, well he certainly was a different kettle of fish. He owned an apartment in Paris which was worth well over a million Euros by now. His biological grandson known to all and sundry as the French Connection lived there. The Major assumed that his wife knew nothing about it, but his dear father-in-law used to be stationed at Bletchley, so nothing was a secret about the Major, not least to his wife.

The piece that I told white about my contacts clamming up about Bletchley. This is partially true, but I found out that the Major's brother and his father-in-law were also at loggerheads, and though one of them was dead, the other still had influence in Military Circles, and I don't mean that the Port is always passed to the left in the Officer's Mess. I was a Captain myself, so I know all about these age-old traditions. As most fighting men are right-handed passing the port to your left meant that your sword hand was free.

The Major also had another rather large piece of baggage that he carried with him. He was a member of the Nazi party and could not wait for the Fourth Reich. He had been seconded at one point to Garats Hay Barracks, where he learned an awful lot about covertly sending and receiving coded messages. Of course, this was back in the 1980s but I am sure that the old dog remembers it all. After all, how would he get a message about an impending explosion on Eurostar when he was purportedly listening to an England V Jamaica cricket match at Lords when I know personally that Jamaica's opening batsman was out of action with an ankle injury, and the match was scratched at the last minute.

As told by probationer DC Jane Hodge:

I swore my allegiance to the Crown through the oath that I took at my attestation ceremony. This means that I shall tell the truth. I had come across Mary Pickles before when she was being defended by one of the Lawyers at my chambers where I was a Pupil. Before you rush ahead of yourselves it was emphatically not Gordon Moss defending her. It was one of the lesser mortals who was getting her off a shoplifting charge.

Mary Pickles was at it again in Paris. I mean how come she claimed that she had so many shopping bags with her when the explosion happened? I'll tell you, shall I? Full disclosure here. She would sashay into one of the larger stores and scope out how many bags a person (mainly Japanese) had with them. She would then barge into them, and in the confusion between English and Japanese, she would hurry off having swiped at least one of their shopping bags.

She would then make her way to a friend's boutique and in the back open the shopping bags and see what they contained. If it was high-end but size zero stuff, she would flog it to the boutique owner, if not shed take it home, paw through it, and then send it back from whence it came.

Another thing that I must admit to is yes, I was a pupil lawyer at the same chambers as Gordon Moss, but after working more than fifty hours a week for a pittance I wanted out. I could not go crying to the Head of Chambers, so I made up a story about Gordon Moss sexually harassing me. Being a law firm, they had to be seen taking things like that seriously or there might have been a lawsuit against one of their own lawyers, and that would have been embarrassing. The sort of scandal that you would read in the News of the Scum.

The upshot was that Moss moved on, and I moved on to the Police force where my first boss was DI Andy Fletcher. Of course, although he was as old as my father, he liked to brush up against me if you know what I mean. J wasn't averse to this, and it got to the point where we would exchange lingering looks by the coffee machine. Things got a bit out of hand which involved the stationary cupboard, so I moved on, and as luck would have it DI White had an opening.

I played the ingenane with him. Quiet, eyes downcast. I didn't fancy D I White yet but give it time! As you have probably guessed by now Susan Proctor is my half-sister. We have the same mother but a different father. My mother is the daughter of Glen and Claire Cooper which means Claire is my grandmother. She can sort anything or anyone out, including clearing up my sibling's mess. She would stop at nothing, and I mean nothing. I spotted her in a pub just off Islington Road the other day talking to Mary Pickles. Now that's a piece of info I'm going to keep to myself for now.

As told by DC Valentine:

It's true yes, I am a lazy bugger. I have been coasting along through the last few years marking time. I don't want to retire yet; my wife would not want me under her feet right now. I am waiting until I have done my time so that I can retire on a nice big fat pension. There I was whiling away the hours as a Detective Constable in one of the less salubrious parts of North London, which I cannot for legal reasons name. The wife and I live in a nice maisonette which is mortgage-free so that's one less thing to worry about.

About forty years ago a body was found in a garage not far from my place in a lock-up near to the train station. I was a few years in on the job and was an ordinary PC at the time, so I spent most of my time warding off the press and public. As they say, nice work if you can get it. The victim's wife and later his son kept harassing the police. It was a clear case of suicide I tell you. I mean the dude had a bullet hole through his skull, a stressful job on the other side of the river, plus the dead man's Wife was expecting.

The other day I told DI White part of what I did. I didn't put too much effort into it, just asked around a couple of my snouts. Now I personally don't move in the same circles as those using the big posh hotel in Paris, and neither do my snouts. I had never heard of the bloody hotel before and couldn't be arsed to check if Ms Proctor and the Hon Frank had stayed there, let alone been chucked out, but I kind of know Miss Proctor – well CRIMIT did. There it was, a few keystrokes and her stop and search for drugs were there on my computer screen, so I assumed that she had been chucked out of the hotel for a similar misdemeanour, especially as she was hanging around with the Hon. Frank Dwyer who basically was a little prick who always sponged of his father.

I already knew about Dwyer's little crack den. I made my way there a few days ago to see what was happening and if the Hon Frank Dwyer had crawled back to his hellhole. All I could find was that the flat emitted the most godawful smell, so I left rather quickly. I surmised that Dwyer and Co. were chucked out of their hotel. I mean a gut copper feeling means a lot, doesn't it? Susan Procter was dropping off packages on the Cator estate. As far as the drugs squad were concerned, she was small-time and could be delivering Avon parcels for all they or I cared. Funny story one of the Drugs Squad's officers lived there and his mum loved Avon if you get my drift.

So that really is the truth, although I had better really come clean and admit that it might not be the whole truth. You're wondering how I managed to get dragged into the DI White/Eurostar drama. Truth be told I have made a little faux pass. I just happened to get pissed off with the way Frank Dwyer was playing the big I am, and I didn't like him supplying drugs. I mean everyone knew that was Mary Pickles nee Richardson's bosom buddy Eve's patch didn't they, and I wanted the little oik to stay away. So, I may have planted drugs on a certain young lady once upon a time, and my boss's boss at the Met found out, so I was rapidly 'assigned' to DI White's team where I was biding my time and doing bugger all as usual. No chance in hell that I would dig any deeper into Dwyer and Proctor, not if I valued my balls which I did, as it would have ultimately led to Mary Pickles, and I didn't want to fall down that rabbit hole.

Besides, I have another secret. The bullet that a certain Neil (surname redacted) took to his bonce, well the guy was barely five feet five, and the angle of the gunshot wound to his head did not fit with the suicide theory. I kept quiet back then so does that make me a good detective, or a bad detective or just a lazy detective? You decide. I pointed it out to my superior officer at the time. And suddenly I found that I had been promoted to Detective Constable instead of an ordinary PC. No more patrol cars for me. I'm six feet two, and that's how I worked out that Neil could not have killed himself. Wo was my boss at the time. A young Detective Sargant Wiseman suddenly changed his name by deed poll to White. So, you see why I won't do anything for that fucker now.

As told by DC Jock Mackintosh:

I was so eager to be part of the team on the Eurostar case. I knew that the big boys in counter-terrorism would do most of the proper work, but it was grunts like myself who did a lot of the shite work. The chance to have a dig around into someone's life was fascinating to me. I wanted to have a wee dig at least at one of them. I pleaded my case with the Chief Super. I think, but can't be sure that she has a thing for red-haired rodent-like men so there I was, and although DI White thought that he had free rein in choosing his team of investigators my name just happened to land on his desk. Well, my personnel file did, and because I had done a lot of grunt work in the past, I was the ideal candidate to complete DI White's team.

I dug up so much information on John Houlihan that I could have been a reporter for the News of The World newspaper. The thing is though as I watched and listened to the others giving white their findings, I realised that DI White liked the summaries to be short and sweet, so I mentally did a quick synopsis of my notes before White cast his beady eye on me.

Apart from what I outlined to White what I did not go into detail about was the bit of trouble John Houlihan got into when he was a student. He attended Belfast (Ulster) University. Not known to be directly linked with the IRA he did however organise a sit-in. Simply it was about giving Ireland back to the Irish and making Ireland Irish again. He got kicked out, but after making a humble apology to the Dean was allowed back to take his finals.

After that, he moved to Oxford. Having a First-Class degree, Oxford University wants to appear to be diverse. Trying not to get dragged into the political scene he attended many different talks by various eminent professors. One that particularly caught his eye was a visiting Professor of Chemistry from Cambridge University, Clare Mortimer. The talk however turned out to be about explosions and explosives. That's when things seemed to change for John, and he became a pseudo member of the IRA, but couldn't admit to it openly.

John went on to get his M.Sc. then PhD, and finally a tenure as a professor of languages at Oxford. That's where he is now apart from his wee trip to Paris. A quick look wound the Sorbonne at the behest of his wife, and then a meeting of minds shall we say one evening.

I could not find out what he was planning but the devious shite was up to no good I can guarantee that. Like I promised to DI White I will keep digging. Besides I have a score to settle with his whole family. His grandaddy and daddy were full-blown members of the IRA and indoctrinated wee Johnny from an early age.

One day way back the Houlihan's took part in a bombing campaign. The talk was that lads from the Glenrose Penicuik Army Barracks drank at my family pub. Several people were maimed or killed including my parents and wee sister. After that, I threw my lot in with Scotland and moved south to live with an aunt. Eventually, I joined the Metropolitan Pollis, so here I am, and I hope that Mr O' Houlihan rots in hell. Of course, I couldn't tell DI White or the Chief Super why I wanted to join the team, and he's been following the Houlihans for years planning my revenge, but let's say that evidence can be a very, very powerful thing, and I will get the wee bugger. Would I try and frame him? Probably.

CHAPTER 15

THE SENIOR OFFICER'S TRUTHS

This is my second truth, as a Sargent I have found that there is always more than one version of the truth. From now on I will stick with the truth as a promotion to DI is on the cards for me if things go according to plan.

I bet you thought I was the daughter of the girl from Nottingham with the Pink Mini. Well, I'll tell you something man, no production line mini ever came in bright metallic pink. Not even for the King of England. Can't see him driving around in one though, not at his age. No disrespect to him though. The truth is I am Jamaican through and through. My grandparents are from the Windrush generation, my parents were born here: I too so was my brother Winston.

The Pink Mini was a madcap idea. From the first meeting with Nina Cohen, I had her wrapped my little finger. Winston dared me to ask her for a Pink Mini as a wedding gift just so that we could see how far we could push her. She obtained one from some dodgy car dealer in South London and had it resprayed metallic pink for me. God that girl must have loved me, and then she buggers off having committed several severe offences, which as an officer of the law I can't turn a blind eye to.

Now my brother Winston, I know he did a bit of coke occasionally. He used to get it from the Hon. Frank Dwyer which is why I attended the scene when Dwyer was found. It was Winston who found him, called me in a panic, then legged it from the scene so I had to be one of the first there just in case they found something at the scene which would incriminate him. Thankfully they didn't, but they did find the butt of the brand of an Indian imported cigarette. Careless of someone wasn't it? Almost as though they wanted to be caught.

I was already a sergeant at Golders Green police station. I had been posted there three years ago so that the Met could prove that it wasn't institutionally racist, and to fill their quota of coloured officers. DI White hated me from the start because I was better at my job than he was at his.

I let him take all the kudos for the big cases. One day he would get his comeuppance, and it could not come some enough as far as I was concerned.

I led him down the garden path as far as Laura Marchant was concerned. The Chief Superintendent had tipped me the wink as she was very friendly with Laura Marchant and hinted that her work was so secret that I couldn't reveal it all to White. The Chief Super and I met at a spin class that we both take. Suzie liked to know her officers by name, and she certainly knew me. We got on like a house on fire and used to go for a coffee after the spin class. She mentioned that she wasn't sure about White's agenda. OK, I wasn't her spy per se but having me there as a Sergeant Golders Green would help her out tremendously, and I never could resist a pretty face even though she was the older bird of about Fifty.

And Nina, well Nina marrying her was the result of a drunken bet. I hadn't gone to the Shoreditch club by myself, although I probably gave the impression that I was alone. My brother Winston and his ex-army pals were there as well egging me on from the bar, and betting how long it would be before I jumped into bed with her. I have my principals, but when there are two hundred and fifty quid at stake they easily go out of the window.

At first, it was great, and then for some reason, Nina started to follow all the Instagram and how to do your makeup shit. She became obsessed with one influencer – Laura Marchant. Then the day after Eurostar there was the very same renowned influencer was sitting in an interview room. Ms Marchant didn't have much to say for herself. Unlike a lot of people that I have interviewed, she didn't break out in a cold sweat, nor glance nervously around. She didn't stumble on her words, nor cast her eyes furtively around the room. She was as cool as a cucumber.

After the interview when I was digging around to get any deets on her, I kept on running into wall after damn wall. The woman was so elusive, so ghost-like. Interestingly both DI White and my wife seem to take more interest in her, plus I noticed that the new PC Tahira Sharma was always lurking in the background, or causally wandering around when I was doing a deep dive into Ms Marchant. So why was the woman so interesting, and why were so many people interested in her? Was she really our prime suspect?

Yes, the woman had loads of dosh, and a posh car, but that didn't automatically make her a terrorist. She showed her face thousands of times on Instagram and tick-tock, and apparently lived the life of Riley. Take the Patek Phillipe watch of hers that was found. It retails at about £32,000. Believe me, man, I have seen no rich bombers wearing watches like that. Some with fake Rolexes maybe.

It stuck with me though that she could have been a 'sleeper'. Nothing about her from less than a few years, and then bang she suddenly arrives on

the scene. So, what was her story? I finally had an inkling when I went down to the Lamb and Flag last night. I needed Rum, and I had an urge to drink shit loads right then. I strolled casually into the bar, nodding to one or two people who stared at me because I was coloured. The clientele here were mainly white, male, and over fifty.

Then I heard a woman's cackle, followed by another woman snorting. I strolled over to the bar and did my usual 360-degree look around the room when I spotted her. Laura Marchant as bold as brass sitting with Chief Superintendent Suzie Pitts. They both looked chummy, faces close together. My God, what had I stumbled on?

This is what DI White believes is the Truth is it worth trusting him though?

White, Weisman, Wittman. I go by all those names. My family were originally from Germany My grandfather was an officer in the SS during WW2 stationed at Auschwitz. I went there for a day trip once, just so that I could relive my grandfather's past glories. He wasn't exactly Mengele's right-hand man, but he did escort prisoners – mainly Jews to Mengele's office. Mengele was part of a team of doctors who had to select which people were suitable for work and which had to be gassed right away.

My father told me that his father Mengele liked to collect items of interest for Hitler and had acquired what was supposed to be the original Ark containing the Torah but had somehow after the end of the war had it stolen from his office.

When the attack on Eurostar happened, it was quite by chance that I had to interview some of the survivors. My Chief Superintendent Suzie Pitts wanted me on the case. When all the pertinent evidence had been gathered at Golder's Green Police station, I slipped in another 'burnt out ring' with the Initials 'GM'' under the radar with the help of my new exhibits officer Tahira Sharma. I wanted to confuse things, and I wanted Laura Marchant bought down.

I have a cousin, a therapist working in North London who telephoned me one day in early May. He sounded unusually excited. He had an appointment with someone who was in Auschwitz as a prisoner during the war, and who could lead us to the Torah and the Ark again. He had his information from a friend of ours who was the French Connection.

So, there I was primed and ready. Fortune really was smiling at me, although I didn't realise that it would end in the destruction of a Eurostar Train. Interviewing Laura Marchant was like a dream come true for me. The French Connection had told my cousin the therapist that the person of interest was London-bound, and that she was the adopted granddaughter of the boy from Auschwitz. I didn't question why the Chief Superintendent gave me the job of interviewing several people, but as sure as hell going to nail Laura Marchant.

I admit that I am the author of the extracts from the diary author unknown. I was the young PC who turned up at Leicester Market after the explosion. I cautioned Dinesh Patel. I also attended later that night a stabbing on a bus. We never found out who the victim was, but if we take into consideration the bus times, routes, and Patel's appearance at the market it didn't take a genius to work things out. Besides the bus driver remembered Patel and another man boarding the bus and going upstairs to smoke and one of them had the most disgusting, foul-smelling cigarettes.

So now I had something over Dinesh Patel. Years later I called in the favour by paying Dinesh a visit and offering him vast sums of money to spy on Laura Marchant. The woman was a thorn in my side. She had made me look a complete fool in front of my whole team, and my boss by completely and single-handedly destroying a case I was working on about a murder in a Kibbutz. The person who was murdered was known to the Met as a person of interest because rumour had it that he deliberately started a fire at a prestigious Law Firm in Lincoln's Inn.

As Chief Superintendent was Suzie Pitts bound by law to tell the truth, here is what she said.

Right off from the start, I knew that Karl White was bad through and through so why did I still put up with him? I believe in the adage give 'em enough rope and they'll hang themselves, and that's what I hope will happen to Karl any day now. I joined the Police Force five years after Karl White, and yet I have come so much further than him because I am ambitious, and he most definitely is not. When I joined, I had my career path planned out, and I wanted to be a Chief Superintendent by the time I was fifty. I only just made I made it by fair means or foul.

I started out at the same station as Karl White, and from the off, I knew that there was something not quite right about him. I couldn't put my finger on it, just call it a Copper's instinct. I got to patrol with him, but he gave me all the shitty jobs like looking after kids who had been separated from their parents at our thriving market, and he even had me on the coffee run from the beginning. Now I call in on him as much as I can and make sure that he now makes a coffee for me. The job has its perks, and he does make a decent cup of coffee.

The other person in my game of Truths is I had a friend, a very good friend as it happens. Her name was Julia, and we both were assigned to the same class at senior school. She was all glasses, braces, and nervous struggling to fill in the timetable we were given. She was dyslexic and couldn't understand the double and single-period time slots. I helped her, not because I needed a friend, I already had plenty of those, but as one of four girls I knew how the younger one in my family struggled, also my mother had threatened to tan my backside if she heard any bad reports of me from my new school.

The other reason was that I fancied her because she was so exotic-looking. We were used to different nationalities in Loughborough, but I had never met anyone like her. I caught a glimpse of a hint tattoo on her back in the shape of a tiny Gardenia when we were showering in the communal showers after P.E. I put my hand out to touch the small of her back where it was. Tattoos especially on females were unheard of back then. As soon as I touched it, she turned around. From that day on she always wore a plaster over it.

We bonded over the fact that we had double maths last two periods on a Friday afternoon straight after P.E. and groaned about how we were going to get showered and dressed afterwards to make the Math teacher lessons as we knew already of her ferocious persona. She loved swimming and so did I, and at school swimming lessons were taken at the town's swimming baths whilst the rest of the class were struggling to learn she and I were left pretty much to ourselves, so we practised diving into the deep end, with each dive becoming more daring as we tried to outdo each other.

At fourteen both girls and boys joined up at the same school. Luckily Julie and I were doing the same GCEs so we could both sigh at the good-looking male teachers that we had, or so I thought, but there was one boy in our class that Julie couldn't keep her eyes off. She admitted to me at break that they had been in the same class at junior school, and that she had always liked him even when he teased her about her glasses. Now she was done with her glasses and had lovely straight, white teeth. He obviously didn't recognise her as the mousey girl from junior school as she had now long deep chestnut-coloured hair which she coloured with the shampoo from the hint-of-a-tint range. When he saw her, he did a double take, and then that was that. Loved young dream. I had lost a friend, until the time when she needed me again.

We both left school at eighteen with mediocre 'O' and 'A' level results. Unbeknown to me we both joined the police force at the same time and one day after a night spent tossing and turning over whether I should leave the Police Force or not due to Karl White's nastiness towards me, I walked into see my old friend Julie sitting at my desk with her feet up. She had been transferred to the same station as me. It took us all five minutes to catch up, and there we were firm friends again.

Now when we walked the beat, we could do it together. Occasionally we would swing down Baxter Gate as rumour had it a sex shop was opening there. The local papers had made much of this. To our dismay, it wasn't a sex shop, but a tattoo artists shop. As we were both in uniform it seemed only natural that we went in to check it out.

To Julie's delight from behind the counter, a muscly heavily tattooed man appeared. It was Julie's first love. Once more they were inseparable, but then I met another of Julie's old schoolfriends who happened to be best mates with Mr Tattoo Man as I called him. The four of us often went out together, but Julie and her man were far more serious than me who were only really interested in football.

This went on for seven or eight months, and then one morning I found Julie crying in the lady's toilet at work. Between sobs, she managed to tell me that she was pregnant by Mt Tattoo Man and didn't know what to do. Foolishly I told her to have a word with our Sargent, Karl White. Over the course of the next few weeks, he made life very uncomfortable for Julie. So much so that she left the Police Force. I vowed to get back at Karl White.

Julie went on to have her baby, a girl whom she called Laura. Six months later she had a nervous breakdown as she could not cope with a child and Mr Tattoo Man didn't want anything to do with it. The infant was firstly looked after by an old friend of Julie's' s which I'm sure was not entirely legal. Then at the age of twelve put into care by them, the system had caught up with her and she was moved from pillar to post within the care system. It wasn't my finest hour when I alerted the authorities. Because I was responsible for the child's mother leaving the job she loved I felt duty-bound to keep tabs on the child, and as I rose through the ranks this became easier and easier.

Julie's daughter was very bright and beautiful just like her mother was, and I was so proud when she joined MI6. I only wished that her mother was still around, but she had disappeared off the face of the earth.

Julie's daughter and I used to meet up as often as we could, and we would always have a laugh and a giggle. After the Eurostar incident, she was called into Golders Green Police Station for a chat about what had happened. I could have intervened, but it wasn't my place to do so. Besides, because she was working for MI6, she knew exactly how to keep her cool. The clever girl managed to swerve DI White's questions and observations. He didn't even have a clue that I knew her so well. He had no idea of her background; he didn't find out who her parents were. But I knew the truth. I knew who her mother was, and I knew who her father was. He was Andrew Bruce, who was intertwined in this debacle. Yes, Andrew Bruce was Mr Tattoo Artist.

CHAPTER 16

THE WOMAN WHO LIVED IN THE PARK

A knock on the door early one morning had the woman worried. People never called on her, she always called on them as she was known to be a bit of a recluse, and hated unexpected callers as she was a very private person.

She had deliberately chosen the basement flat of the four-storey converted house because of the stairs that you had to climb down to get to it. Teenage kids who kicked a football around the park, or the druggies that hung out there were far too lazy to climb down them. In the icy weather, they became even more perilous and that suited the woman just fine.

Two people stood on her doorstep. One, an older man of about fifty-five who looked like he had swallowed a wasp, the other a woman who had the most beautiful soulful brown eyes. They introduced themselves as a Detective Inspector and a sergeant. Judith could not be bothered to remember their names. It was of little consequence. Ushering them into her tiny front room she didn't offer them tea or coffee and was relieved when they both declined. She wanted them to go away as soon as possible. She didn't want any bother. Life was too precious and too short. The Sergeant glanced around the room. Her eyes alighted on ten or so books neatly placed on the bookcase that the woman's grandfather had made by hand out of the most exquisite merogony wood.

'You're not that famous author, are you? The sergeant inquired.

'That's me', replied the woman colouring slightly. 'I am indeed Judith Roberts, and yes, I wrote all of those books.'

'Wow my nieces and nephews love your fantasy books, I didn't realise it was you.'

Holding her hands up Judith shrugged modestly. She waited for the Police to continue. She had no wish to engage in conversation with them.

'We were just wondering if you have seen a Mrs Claire Mortimer recently', asked the Inspector.

'I know of her, but I haven't seen her for many years now', replied Judith wondering what her friend had got herself into now.

Glancing around the Inspector realised that this was a very small dwelling, and the only place Claire Mortier might be hiding was in the bedroom.

Picking up on this and following his gaze Judith gestured towards the bedroom door. Guiltily the Inspector poked his head around it, but no Claire Mortimer hiding there.

'I'm told you don't have a telephone'? Began the Sargent. 'Can you tell me why that is.'

'Because of my writing I don't want to be interrupted every five minutes that's why, and I don't have a mobile either. I think that they are so intrusive, don't you', responded Judith swiftly cutting that line of inquiry off.

Deciding that there was no future mileage in questioning Judith Roberts the two detectives apologised to her and took their leave. In the pool car, they agreed that Judith was hiding something. She seemed shifty, but also nervous. Now what was she hiding?

Sighing with relief Judith went to her underwear drew into her bedroom and pulled out an unregistered old-style mobile 'phone. It had one number stored in it, and that was Claire Mortimer's. A brief exchange of words ensued then the 'phone went back in the drawer.

Judith knew her rights, and if the Inspector needed proof of any 'phone he needed cause for a search warrant which he didn't have as that would have needed a judge, and Judith thought that this was an ad-hoc visit. As far as anyone was concerned Judith Roberts was a recluse and that was all that people needed to know. However, Judith Roberts had a past, one she didn't want anyone to find out about.

Judith Robert's Truth was that she was once Julie Sweet. She had joined the police force, had a child, had a nervous breakdown, and then managed to disappear after leaving a note along with baby Laura outside her friend Muriel's house. She reinvented herself as Judith Roberts. She had no official paperwork, no passport, and no bank account in the UK. All the royalties from her books were paid into a bank in the Cayman Islands, and someone slipped over there from time to time to withdraw cash for her. All her bills were paid in cash, or by someone who went to the Cayman Islands for her.

She had decided on the surname Roberts as her one true love was called Andrew Robert Bruce. It would keep him close to her every time she wrote a book. Moreso as they had both worked together on a fantasy book project for their GCE English where Andrew had come up with the idea.

After Andrew, she knew that she didn't need anyone else. However, Andrew's best friend Gary had wormed his way into her heart. A few years later she had another baby, a boy whom she called Martin. When she registered his birth, she used Gary's mother's surname Sweet. And so, the boy grew into a man; Martin Sweet was his name. It was he who as an officer of the law once told her that if she thought anyone was trying to find out her past then she should not lie, she should tell the truth as much as she could without giving away everything.

It was a half-truth that she had not seen Claire Mortimer in many years, not in England anyway. She had however been in Paris on the day of the incident, but her son told her that she would be safer on an early plane as she would encounter fewer people. He told her that passport control officers I at Orley were striking later that day, and it would be chaos when she got there just before they started their strike at noon. They would pay little attention to the passport that she had and would think that it was kosher.

DI White and his DS Chatted as they walked back to the car. What white had forgotten to tell Rosie was that when he had glanced in the bedroom at Judith Robert's house, he had spied a comb hastily discarded on the floor. He had seen its edge just under the dingle ned. Whilst Rosie was jabbering away about books he bent down as if to tie his shoelace and had slipped the thing from under the bed. Judith's hair had reverted to her original dark colour, but the colour of the hairs on the comb was blond. Which was interesting.

Extract from the London Evening Standard

A Detective Inspector in the Metropolitan Police who is based in a North London police station has been suspended as they are suspected of concealing and tampering with evidence for what can only be disclosed at this point is a major ongoing operation. A spokesperson from the Police declined to comment. It is believed that a probationer at the same station was the whistle-blower.

The IOPC is carrying out an independent review. Currently, no other officers have been suspended.

CHAPTER 17

TAHIRA SHARMA's TRUTH

When I was a child, I always looked up to my Uncle Dinesh. I remember that he used to let me 'help' in his shop. He would sit me on a high stool behind the counter and let me take the money from the customers. As I grew older, I assisted him when serving the customers.

By now my parents had moved to London, and I was completing my police training and was a few weeks away from my passing out parade. I had taken a few days leave. On the night that a stranger came to call I was in the back of the shop trying to get to grips with the new computer system that had been installed.

I heard the shop bell ring and was about to go outside to help when something stopped me in my tracks. The atmosphere had changed, and an icy chill blew in through the partly open door. At first, I thought that the shop was being robbed, and then I heard the words that made me pause in fear. After the person had left, Uncle D dived into the back room. By now I had firmly shut the door and was pretending that I was engrossed in the computer system. To be honest I always was a whizz with computers as my mum Pushpa was a computer programmer before her marriage, and my dad was a copywriter for a newspaper.

Uncle Dinesh did not say a word, and I did not let on that I had heard anything. My uncle put his hand on my shoulder and whispered that it was time for me to go home. I was staying with a friend of mine, a girl I had known since High School who was called Joanne Pitts. I knew all the Pitts family, six girls in all. Jo's sister was a big wig in the metropolitan police. Afraid of what would happen I telephoned Jo's sister.

Jo's sister asked me not to reveal what I had heard to anyone, but that she would sort things out. When I had completed my training at Hendon, I was assigned to Golders Green police station. I was told to report to Inspector White. I already had an exemplary record, and to my surprise and delight, I became the exhibits officer on a major case. Truthfully, I did eavesdrop on a couple of meetings that White held. This was off my own bat as I knew that Jo's sister would be grateful for any snippet of information that I could find about the man.

I realised after the first hour as exhibits officer that DI White was tampering with the evidence. A little bit of whizzy work on the computer systems, Martin Sweet let me have the necessary access and I had a case against White. Luckily my dad kept in contact with his old copywriting pals. One of them now worked for the London Evening Standard. A quick word with my dad who called his friend, and then White was suspended.

CHAPTER 18

THE THERAPIST's TRUTH

True he was a therapist and had a small practice in North London which was convenient for both catching Eurostar but more importantly it was close to the pub. He had got his Doctorate at a second-rate university somewhere up north, and for the last thirty-five or so years had been talking to and counselling many boring people with mundane issues.

The first time he met up with Andrew Bruce was by chance. He had a GP friend in Leicestershire to whom he owed a favour. The GP wanted the therapist to have a few sessions with one of his patients, and never knowing when he would need another favour in return he agreed, and a small tow-haired boy, accompanied by his grandmother turned up on his doorstep one day.

Extracting the boy from his grandma was easy as soon as he mentioned the pub around the corner, and it being close to lunchtime she could get a drink. Slipping his hand out of his grandma's the boy reluctantly followed the therapist inside. These were the days before to the chagrin of the neighbours he had a basement added below.

Initially, the boy was reluctant to talk, but just near the end of the session, he admitted that he had a secret. He had stolen something that he hadn't told his best friend about, and this was playing on his mind. After much coaxing on the therapist's part, he could hardly believe his luck when the boy revealed that he had stolen from an upturned van a piece of scroll-like parchment which he could not open as his hands burnt every time he tried and therefore, he thought that this was punishment for stealing it.

The therapist was just about to ask the boy to let him have the piece of scroll as it would be safer with a doctor when the boy's grandmother returned from the pub. Seeing that her grandson was weeping copiously by now, and babbling nonsense the grandmother grabbed his arm and pulled him away vowing never to return. After much searching the therapist gave up on his search for the boy. No one knew for certain where he and his grandmother had gone to. Rumour was that they had fled to the wilds of Scotland, but the boy could not be found.

The therapist made many connections during his lifetime. One of those was a man in Paris who was known as the 'French Connection' after the titular name of a film starring Gene Hackman. The French Connection knew that the therapist was always searching for Andrew Bruce, and telephoned late one evening to say that had found someone who could turn out to be more important than Bruce.

So, a small Jewish man with a pronounced limp booked a session with him for an afternoon in May. The old man had been looking for counselling for a while, and through friends of friends with a little coercion from the French Connection, the old man turned up for his counselling session.

The therapist had always been intrigued by the stories that his father had told about his past. His grandfather had to Brazil and would let the therapist take his school holidays there and encouraged him in his studies. It was by the pool in the heat of the midday sun that the therapist learnt of the death camps and gas chambers of the Second World War. His grandfather impressed on him the need to prepare for the start of the Fourth Reich – a new dawn, Eutopia.

When the therapist had been at his lovely house in the smallest crescent in Europe for fifteen years and was by now not only a therapist but a local government councillor, he managed to get permission for a basement to be dug out under his house.

Not only did he talk about Hitler and the gas chambers to his grandfather, but he picked up the art of interrogation. He also learnt a lot about chemistry, and with chemicals purchased through the dark web, he began to emulate the gas chambers of old, but down in his basement. The entrance to the basement was a door hidden by a sliding bookcase.

Now all he needed were some subjects to try it out on. When the old Jew had made an appointment, he got Nina to block out an entire afternoon in his diary. He didn't mind that for a temp Nina was frequently off with migraines, this served his purpose. He would have time alone with the old man to extract information about The Ark from him.

Since those halcyon days in Brazil, he knew that needed to get his hands on The Ark and its entire content. It would complete his collection of religious artefacts. It would come back to its rightful place, and the old Jew would get his just desserts like he should have done years ago. He would die in a gas chamber.

When the old man arrived, the therapist heard him stumbling around opening doors in every room. Finally, he heard him settle in the least cluttered room. He let him wait there a while, hoping that the old man became more relaxed. The therapist could then sneak in unannounced vis the secret stone staircase that led from the basement to the hallway, with a well-concealed door that looked like an innocuous cupboard in the hallway.

The therapist had learnt all about how to conceal rooms. It had once been described to the therapist how the SS and Gestapo had found secret rooms and hidden apartments in Amsterdam concealed by bookcases and such, the therapist liked the element of surprise as it might wrong-foot the old man. All he needed from him was the whereabouts of the Ark. He would gain the old man's trust, and then take him to the basement.

Of course, he wasn't going to release any gas in there. Not yet anyway. He just wanted the old Jew to be frightened just like in the olden days. The therapist knew that he had to tread carefully though, one false move, one word uttered out of place and that would be it. They had to have an elaborate intricate dance of words first, then, and only then would the therapist swoop in. Interrogation techniques were in his DNA.

At first, as planned by the therapist they danced around each other, with the therapist pretending to be the old man's friend. He told the old man that he could confide in him, and with a little gentle prodding finally for him to mention something about the five. The only thing that concerned the therapist was the speed of response when the old man had killed a fly. He knew then that he had to be even more careful as the old man had almost superhuman powers which meant that he might get away quickly.

He had coaxed the old man out of his armchair. Then unexpectedly came the loudest explosion. The old man was kneeling before him. Slowly the therapist closed his eyes. What the hell was going on? When he opened them, the old man had risen and was pointing a gun directly at him. Hearing a sound in the next room the therapist was extremely grateful. He hoped that Nina had returned.

Just then she burst through the door, whacked me on the head, and kicked the old man down. When I became a little less dazed, I glanced around and found to my astonishment that Nina was pointing the gun at my head. Let's just say she 'convinced' the old man and me to leave my house. I was playing along with her all the time and knew that I could use this to my own advantage. Between the lying cheating bitch and the old man one or the other would surely reveal where the Ark and its contents were.

I let us hustle into a cab, then sat silently listening to the exchange between her and the cab driver. If she was as resourceful as she claimed to be getting in and out of countries was not going to be difficult. As soon as I realised, we were America bound my heart lifted a little.

Our arrival in LA was the perfect opportunity for me. When we were switching planes, and with a cumbersome wheelchair hindering Nina I managed to slip into the Men's restroom. I had no idea that Nina had tipped off security, but the next thing I knew I was being carted away by two burly security men.

Ending up in a police station in downtown LA was not my idea of fun. Nor was the full body search when the police were apparently looking for a gun. It took a lot of convincing on my side to convince the authorities that I was part of an elaborate joke, but when my friend who was an inspector in the Met talked to them I was released immediately with their sincere apologies, a temporary passport, a first-class ticket to Tahiti, and a thousand dollars in cash as long as I promised not to sell my story to the press.

It turned out that some bigwig in the Police in LA was a very good friend of my Met Inspector friend. Sitting in my sumptuous first-class seat bound for Tahiti I almost laughed out loud. Nina may have managed to pinch a poor passenger's Black Amex, but I managed to pinch another one from him. Every cloud has a silver lining, but in my case, it was a Platinum lining.

CHAPTER 19

MALIONEY'S TRUTH

I told him not to go to London, but he would not listen to me. Although I am bedridden now and cannot see any more he usually listens to me but now he wants to confess. Maybe I should be confessing to him. I am bedridden now and cannot see and now the cared for has become the carer. It is he who is looking after me now not the other way around as it used to be.

Ireland was neutral during World War two. I had to flee the county as quickly as I could because I had got involved with Tommy O'Houlihan's gang and I would have ended up in jail. I became a Mercenary, a man for hire. I had no compunction as to whose side I was on. True I didn't agree with the daft bastard Hitler and what he was doing, but hey money is money.

I had a run-in with the Red Army and was getting away from them as quickly as I could. Fair enough. They couldn't afford to pay me, so I liberated part of a uniform and a pistol from them. They were not happy, to say the least.

I was whiling away the time in a ditch waiting for them to march on by when a body fell on top of me and winded me. Some poor kid who had escaped from a prison camp. It turns out the cowardly Germans deserted it and the lad had taken his chances and left. At first, I could not understand why he wanted to protect a tatty old suitcase so much. Having let him think I was the answer to his prayers I took him under my wing and became quite fond of him. He looked up to me as if I could procure almost anything.

After many escapades, we managed to catch a boat to England. I looked after the suitcase for him on deck whilst he walked around like a semi-normal kid. What I hadn't told him was that I had peeked into the suitcase one night whilst he lay in a hospital bed. What I saw inside made me stick with him. I didn't know what I was going to do with it if I could lay my hands on it. It might not have been fair, and yes, he was just a kid, but I saw an opportunity. The trouble was that when I tried to take the contents out of the suitcase, they bloody well burnt my fingers. I concluded that he might be able to pick the contents up without being burnt, so from then on, I stuck with him. I didn't get the opportunity again. He even slept with the damned suitcase next to him.

Early in nineteen-eighty-five, he had a job for me. I had never seen even so much as a sly look in his eye, but that day it made me shudder. His focus slid away from me, and he could not look me in the eye. He informed me in no uncertain terms that he wanted revenge, and so I set out to make it happen for him. It wasn't until he started explaining the plan to me that I realised he was going to bury the suitcases' contents forever. I didn't necessarily agree with him, but I did what I had to do as an atonement for my past sins and believe me there were many.

When I lived with him, he gave me the freedom to come and go as I wanted to. We were not a couple plus he knew I liked to have a finger in every pie. That's how I found myself on the right side of the Berlin wall in August of nineteen-sixty-one. The barbed wire cut my fingers to shreds through, that's all I'm saying. Once a Mercenary always a Mercenary. Did I mention the art collection we had at the Chelsea house? Go and look at the Van Gough painting of Sunflowers in the Van Gough Museum one day, and ask yourself this, is it real?

When I first met up with the Boy, he thought that I was a man of the world. As I had literally fought my way around Europe, I was wind-tanned and muscular. You would have probably put my age in the mid-twenties. Truth be told I was sixteen years of age. I worked mainly for Hitler as there was an unknown collaboration between the Nazis and the IRA during the war. If you think I was after the Ark and its contents for monetary gains, then think on. What price treasure would Hitler pay to lay his hands on?

My heart broke in two when the plan was concocted to get revenge on the Five. I was the one who made sure all the van drivers didn't survive or they could have hunted down what was lost. I knew where they were buried or placed. Even with the flow of the tides, streams, rivers, and canals, I knew that they would find their way back to the Boy. Only they didn't. From that day onwards I lost the use of my legs and became bedridden. My sight started to fade too. Tuberculosis that had been lying dormant in my body for many years started to rear its ugly head. Was it because I had not told the Boy the truth or was it because I had looked into the case and tried to liberate its contents?

I might as well tell all the truth now. The rumour that Hitler escaped through tunnels under Berlin, yep that was me. Funny how things turn out isn't it? If you are wondering where all the German Mark in the suitcase case came from, that was my idea as I had amassed a small fortune during the war.

CHAPTER 20

THE TRUTH OF THOSE INVOLVED IN 1985

The girl at Slab Square has arrived from Jamaica to live with her mum, brothers, and her mum's new boyfriend. The whole family had worked firstly at the John Player factory, and when that closed had moved to working at the Raleigh Bike factory. Naomi herself couldn't get a job although she was a fully qualified secretary. She was told that she was too sassy. She would mooch about the city aimlessly going in and out of clothes shops such as Chelsea Girl or Etam. One day in late April she was sitting watching the pigeons in Slab Square as they squabbled noisily over a discarded sandwich. It was, for a mid-April day surprisingly warm and sunny. Naomi missed the Jamaican sun. Somehow it seemed warmer there than in England where it always seemed to rain. She was convinced that it was a different sun.

With her face now turned up towards its rays she suddenly felt a chill run through her body. The sky appeared to cloud over; the pigeons dispersed like angry housewives. Naomi turned her head, and looming over her was a large vagabond-type figure who promptly plonked himself next to her. This unnerved Naomi. She had never encountered a tamp up until now.

The man next to her started chatting in an Irish accent which Naomi had difficulty in following. The gist of it was that he wanted a favour and was willing to pay her handsomely for it. The amount he offered would be enough for her to leave England's damp shores. It would mean that she could get to Spain, where the weather was hot. She could find work in a bar, and not be judged by her colour.

All she had to do was linger in slab every weekday lunchtime between 12 and 1 if the weather was fine. A week later she contacted the man whose photograph she had been shown. She deliberately dropped her copy of the Nottingham Post, just to prove that she was serious about him and by the following Wednesday the Marine Biologist Lecturer from Nottingham University was smitten with her. So much so that he parted with a large amount of cash so that she could buy a Pink Mini, and by early May she promised him that she would meet him by the University Gates and possibly go away with him for a weekend tryst.

While the man paced up and down waiting impatiently for her, she was at East Midlands Airport catching a plane to Alicante. With his £500 plus the generous amount that Maloney had paid her.

Meanwhile, a Blonde switchboard operator was enjoying a shopping trip to Leicester. On the train home she caught sight of some beautiful blue Irish Eyes, and she was smitten. Trying hard not to stare she glanced away, but something kept pulling her back. Eventually, she put down her evening copy of the Leicester Mercury. By the time she alighted at Loughborough, she had found a way to earn extra cash and all she had to do was write a couple of letters. The first was to the Leicester Mercury posting a position of an onsite hands-on Geologist, and the second, once she had sifted through the replies (if there were any) was to write back to anyone who was local to Loughborough, and then send one back from a 'Mr Smith, offering an interview where the chosen one would be picked up outside Loughborough University but it had to be a specific date in May.

The daytime blonde-haired switchboard operator was always made to feel inferior by her night-time counterpart, possibly because she was younger and prettier, so she did this as a kind of stick-up two-fingers-to-you bitch gesture. The bonus was, aside from being paid handsomely via the charming Irish man that she met on the train.

It was Doctor Lawson who responded to the advert, and she could not stand the misogynous, lecherous man, and when he was finally reported as missing the switchboard operator was sunning herself in Benidorm and had chummed up with a Jamaican girl who was about her own age from Nottingham.

Meanwhile in a pub called Ye Old Trip to Jerusalem at the foot of Nottingham Castle, a visiting Minor Indian Prince was worrying how on earth he could afford the rest of his holiday. He had originally rented a cottage in Market Harborough but had run out of funds as he had partied too hard having had many champagned parties by the pool with new friends. He liked to show off his prowess to the ladies by flexing his muscles and swimming in the heated pool that came with the house.

He was staring morosely into a. a half of bitter and was laying out his last few coins in a row lining them up in value order, mostly 10 and 5 pence pieces with the odd copper thrown in. He suddenly got the feeling he was being stared at and swivelled around rapidly on his low stool. Glancing up he found himself staring into a pair of piercing blue eyes of a dark-haired man with a craggy wind-burnt face who appeared to be ageless.

Pointing to the row of course, and sighing he said to blue eyes in a near-perfect English accent,

'I say old chap, could you spare a bob or two, I seemed to have left my wallet at home.'

The owner of the piercing blue eyes had been studying him covertly from the bar and had already watched the Indian take his wallet out of his inside pocket and rummage around inside. The Irish man had been waiting for such an occasion like this to present itself, and he knew that many tourists came to visit Ye Old Trip to Jerusalem as rumour had it that it was England's oldest surviving pub and was built in 1189 being a pit-stop for Crusading Knights before journeying to Jerusalem to fight in the Crusades. It was also a very good place to lift a purse or wallet, or in this case, find someone who was willing to do some dirty work without conciseness.

'I can do more than lend you some money', he said in a thick Irish accent. In fact, you could do me a favour, and make yourself some money as well.'

He then outlined what he had in mind. He wanted someone who appeared not to speak English to present himself at a certain Swimming Bath and pretend he couldn't swim. Then he had to 'arrange' to meet the swimming instructor-cum- cleaner to teach him how to swim, but it had to be at Foxton Locks on a certain day at a certain time.

The minor Indian Royal was more than happy as he had telephoned the very same swimming pool that day to apply for a job but was given short shrift by the man who answered his call, and who had obviously taken an instant dislike to him when he had mentioned his name. He would well and truly like to shaft the man. It meant that now could now afford to get on a plane. He always fancied running a bar on the Costa Blanca and would soon have the money to do so.

Maloney was searching within a certain radius as he wanted local people to do his bidding. When chatting to the Blonde Telephone Operator he found out that she was born in Long Eaton in a district known locally as China Town. No one really knew the origins of why it was called this, but after a quick scout around and a walk through the town he purchased a local paper – the Long Eaton Advertiser.

In it, under the small ads were a few lines that caught his eye. 'Well-educated chemist seeks a job in his specialist field'.

From a 'phone box on Derby Road, he called the number, and a polite voice answered. Following the directions that he had been given to China Town Maloney was surprised that the address given over the phone was a two up to down end of terrace house. It was surprisingly well-kept.

Maloney had the right connections. He called in several favours to get the Chinaman a job as an operator of mixing chemicals at a nearby factory. There was only one proviso through. Mr Pang had to say that he needed a particular day off for a fictional religious holiday, but it had to be a certain day. With the money he made from doing this, Mr Pang opened a Chinese Takeaway near to where he lived and was very successful.

Harold Robbins the American Author once said Every Man has his price. Bearing this in mind off to the Casino went Maloney. Lo and behold he found a man sobbing in the gent's toilets. He had lost all his money. Maloney went to comfort him. It might not have been the man's lucky night, but it certainly was Maloney's.

The man turned out to be the new Head Teacher at a School about fifteen miles away. After buying the Head Teacher a few drinks he suggested that the man mention to the school governors about starting Matheletes at school as then the governors may forgive his lapse at the gaming tables. He suggested that these should take part before school time and should always be on a certain day of the week. By now three sheets to the wind the poor headmaster was so grateful that he readily agreed, but for a price, hence every man has his price, for some its money.

Feeling lighter the errant headmaster went home with more money than he started with. On arriving at school, the next day, and to his senior maths teacher's chagrin he got the new school governor to introduce the Mathaletes idea, and the rest they say is history.

CHAPTER 21

YAHWEH YIR'EH (THE LORD WILL PROVIDE)

There are often said to be five 'theories' of the truth: The correspondence theory of truth states that the truth or falsity of a statement is determined only by how it relates to the world and whether it accurately describes that world. The coherence theory of truth The main idea behind this theory is that a belief is true if it "coheres" or is consistent with other things a person believes. A pragmatic theory of truth is a theory of truth within the philosophies of pragmatism and pragmaticism. The Redundancy theory infers that truth is a redundant concept; in other words, "truth" is merely a word that is conventional to use in certain contexts but not one that points to anything in reality. The semantic theory of truth is a theory of truth in the philosophy of language which holds that truth is a property of sentences. The following is my Truth.

Firstly, the young woman Nina/Nira had tried to poison me by slipping sleeping draughts or worse into my drinks on the flight to Los Angeles. Earlier I had swatted a fly and trampled on it, so I am telling the truth when I say that I have remarkable reactions and strength considering my age. The stupid cow thought that I had drunk them when I slipped the contents into a small bottle of my own. It's useful to carry these things as you never know when you are going to be caught short. The glaring mistake that she made was not to let us slide the partitions up in our seats. I had turned away as if I were sleeping, and every bit of potion that she thought I was drinking found its way into the empty bottle. Pretending I needed to pee about forty-five minutes before the plane landed, I pretended to wake up with a jolt. I indicated that I needed the toilet pee. Nina could not refuse my request as the cabin crew might have become suspicious. Nina wasn't going to follow me into the toilet, but she stayed outside leaning against the door. Inside

I emptied the bottle contents down the sink, rinsed it well, and then chucked the bottle away.

As for the suitcase, it was safe. One of the cabin crew had promised Nina that it would be returned when we landed. Maybe it was my winning smile, but on landing she handed the case to me not Nina. Going through security could have been a nightmare for me but Nina who was also carrying a weapon got us through in double quick time. No one stopped us.

I did not want any more death or destruction, so I did not take my gun out on the plane. I was going to save it until later. Nina must have thought that she had the upper hand but kept on making mistake after mistake. In her haste to bundle us into a taxi, she forgot the gun that I held. After eighteen months in a psychiatric unit, she was losing her touch. She may have an insider in MI6, but she didn't know that I had one too, that was my adopted granddaughter.

A quick 'phone call to her and she was on her way back from Paris. She knew that I knew who Nina was and was partly the reason why I had booked an appointment in Keystone Crescent. If things had gone to plan, I could have killed two birds with one stone. As it was, I let Nina take me to the airport. I wanted to keep tabs on her.

I needed to convince people that I had the Ark with all the pieces of the scroll back where they belonged. I wanted everyone to believe that the Ark was inside the old, battered suitcase, the one that had my mother's initials inside it. That was not the truth. I just wanted folk to believe it. The Truth was me and my adopted granddaughter were on the path of tracking the last piece scroll down. When we had found it needed the complete scroll to settle into the Ark. Although it had been dissembled by Mengele, I am sure that God will make sure that it is one complete scroll as it should be.

I really wish I had not sought redemption. It was a foolish decision on my part as it was the meeting that led to the explosion. The whole thing was supposed to relate to people finding the Torah given to Moses. It upset me that people were killed or maimed along the way. It should never have happened, and I have so many regrets about it. I was, I admit a little early for my appointment with the therapist. The French Connection had not sent the wrong man. I had arrived in London via Poland, then Brussels.

I had taken the tortuous route through Eastern, then into Western Europe, on into Belgium, then a Eurostar to London. Poland was the true reason for my journey. Three days ago, before my planned meeting with the therapist, I had arrived under an assumed name at Krakow airport. Memories came flooding back as I walked along the street where I had lived as a boy. Grim blocks of post-war apartments now stood surrounding where my father used to have his bank many years since, surprisingly the bank and our flat above stood looking like a lost orphan amongst the giant blocks towering over it. The front door to the bank hung off its hinges, and a slowly crept in. Going through to the back, then up the broken wooden stairs to my old family dwelling was almost surreal. The last time I used them was when I went shopping for my mother, never thinking that it would be eighty-two years before I returned.

The wooden stairs must have been riddled with woodworms or rotting away with the dampness that was permutated throughout the building. There was a sharp ‘crack’, and my leg was suddenly dangling through a large hole. I had strength on my side though and you must know that looks can be deceptive. I managed to hoist myself up, but both my leg and foot were now bruised and swollen. Panting I reached what used to be our living room which was devoid of all furniture. A torn velvet curtain lay cast aside on the floor which was covered in layers of grime and dust.

In the corner

The only thing that remained of my childhood propped up the furthest corner of my old abode, and under the sloping part of the eves of the roof was an object shrouded in an old opera cloak. Through much use on it, it now had a raven-like iridescent sheen to it, and inside a moth-eaten silk red lining. Snatching it aside I decided there and then that I would use it so I could conceal the weapon that I had purchased earlier from someone who lived in the underbelly of a well-known Polish City.

Sighing deeply, I wondered what my maternal grandfather would think of me now. He had worn the cloak so many times when he visited the opera. He had fallen in love with a well-known opera singer Claire Dux. He never married her though, and she went on to become one of the renowned female opera singers that emerged from Poland.

Hidden underneath the old opera cloak was an old wooden chair that was made of an ancient wood, possibly cypress. What interested me was that one arm of the chair was long and out of place. Maybe it was a little like the myth of the sword in the stone that my father had once talked about. He told me once that it was my destiny, and until now I had not understood what he meant.

So many people may have tried to separate the arm from the chair, and then given up. Bending over the chair I tugged at the arm, and it easily came off. The fact that I used it as a walking aid from then on was irrelevant. Some people may have assumed incorrectly that my leg was damaged in the concentration camp. It wasn't. I had simply put my leg through a rotten stair.

As for Mengele and Hitler himself, well I had the last laugh. I had something that would see me through whatever was to come. You see the chair arm was not simply too long by chance. It was the very staff that Moses was carrying when he parted the Red Sea enabling the Israelites to become free from their oppression. Or was it just another legend? As I hobbled back downstairs, I did not notice that the tip of the chair arm/stick had turned gold which had then cast a small, shining hallo around its base. That is the gospel truth.

EPILOGUE

Claire Cooper sighed and pulled back the curtains of her cottage. It was snowing hard, but she hoped fervently that the others could make it for Christmas.

The Lockkeeper cottage where no one wanted to live after a double death at the locks over forty years ago was an ideal place for Claire. Nobody bothered her, she was an enigma. One by one her 'gang 'arrived, some by foot, some by taxi. They all came to the lockkeeper's abandoned cottage as it was an ideal place to meet.

The first to arrive was Jack Cooper. Still sprightly and upright at his age. He had been second in command at hut 42. Following on from him came a cab, containing two elderly women. Gittel Moss with diamond rings on her fingers along with Loise Blore, Jenny Blore's grandma. You could almost hear Gittel say to Louise, 'My dear, let's save some money and share a cab', as only an old Jewish lady could.

What Gittel had told Louise in the cab was that her nephew Gordon had lost a signet ring that she had given him for his 21st Birthday in the explosion, and he was bereft. She had it made for his birthday in the likeness of the one she had acquired many years ago only Gordons was cast in white gold. It was fortunate that the jeweller who made the first one had a son who followed in his father's footsteps and was able to make an identical one which she was giving as a present to Gordan for Christmas. She was sure he would be delighted with it.

Marching forcefully through the snow was Ken Mackintosh, the great-uncle of Jock Mackintosh. Finally, Mary Pickles who wasn't a drugs baron after all but had used that persona to help kill the poisonous Frank Dyer with a little help from Claire herself. There was one person missing though. Their dear French compatriot who had died a few years earlier of pancreatic cancer, Eloise Duval; is gone but not forgotten and she lived on through her dancer granddaughter Michelle.

Closing the curtains too tightly Claire let out a sigh, but then she tugged them open rapidly almost ripping their material. A figure of a woman's head bowed inwards from the snow with a younger man helping her along. It was here dear friend Judith along with Judith's son Martin. The gathering was complete. General Mortimer's gang was complete. All those who issued with a signet ring with the letters GM were together. It was a binding thing like the pact that they had undertaken.

No one at Bletchley messed with you if you had a ring with the letters GM emblazed on it. Their work was top secret, with one task and one task only. To retrieve the Ark from Mengele's clutches. Only known to them was this; that the blind woman whose thirteen-year-old daughter had read out the dreaded word Auschwitz to her was hiding a month-old baby wrapped in a shawl. The blind woman was immediately taken to the gas chamber.

The daughter protected her baby sister in the death camp, and with the help of other women kept her a secret. That baby was Claire, adopted after liberation by General Mortimer, which is why she wore his GM ring with pride.

<u>THE END</u>

www.ingramcontent.com/pod-product-compliance
Lightning Source LLC
Chambersburg PA
CBHW051140030726
47504CB00004B/964

* 9 7 9 8 8 9 3 9 7 3 2 9 7 *